DIVINE VENGEANCE

"For what does the blood ask?"

"It cries to Heaven for vengeance; perchance it demands to be washed away with other blood."

"I understand," he said, "and it shall be done, Prophetess."

"By what?" Ayesha asked.

"By this!"

Seizing the dripping veil, he rubbed that which stained it upon his lips and brow. "I swear by the blood of Isis, or of her Priestess, that I will neither rest nor stay till I bring the Persian King to his doom..."

But lines between love and vengeance could often tangle—and sometimes the victor was the greatest loser of all ...

Also by H. Rider Haggard
Published by Ballantine Books:

PEOPLE OF THE MIST

WHEN THE WORLD SHOOK

THE WORLD'S DESIRE (with Andrew Lang)

Wisdom's Daughter

*The Life and Love Story of
She-Who-Must-be-Obeyed*

H. RIDER HAGGARD

A Del Rey Book

BALLANTINE BOOKS • NEW YORK

A Del Rey Book
Published by Ballantine Books

ISBN 0-345-27428-8

Manufactured in the United States of America

First Ballantine Books Edition: June 1978

Cover art by Michael Herring

In bygone years the books "She" and "Ayesha" were dedicated to ANDREW LANG. Now, when he is dead, this, the last romance that will be written concerning "*She-Who-Must-Be-Obeyed*," is offered as a tribute to his beloved and honoured memory.

Ditchingham, 1922.

EDITOR'S NOTE

WHAT was the greatest fault of Ayesha, *She-Who-Must-Be-Obeyed?* Surely a vanity so colossal that, to take one out of many examples, it persuaded her that her mother died after looking upon her, fearing lest, should she live, she might give birth to another child who was less fair.

At least, as her story shows, it was vanity, rather than love of the beauteous Greek, Kallikrates, that stained the hands of She with his innocent blood and, amongst other ills, brought her upon the fearful curse of deathlessness while still inhabiting a sphere where Death is lord of all. Had not Amenartas taunted her with the waning of her imperial beauty, eaten of the tooth of Time, never would she have disobeyed the command of her master, the Prophet Noot, and entered that Fire of Immortality which she was set to guard.

Thus it seems that by denial she would have escaped the net of many woes in which, perchance, she is still entangled and of Ayesha, Daughter of Wisdom yet Folly's Slave, there would have been no tale to tell and, from her parable of the eternal war of flesh and spirit there would have been no lesson to be learned. But Vanity—or was it Fate?—led her down another road.

THE EDITOR.

CONTENTS

INTRODUCTORY

The manuscript of which the contents are printed here was discovered among the effects of the late L. Horace Holly, though not until some years after his death. It was in an envelope on which had been scribbled a direction that it should be forwarded to the present editor "at the appointed time," words that at first he did not understand. However, in due course it arrived without any accompanying note of explanation, so that to this hour he does not know by whom it was sent or where from, since the only postmark on the packet was London, W., and the address was typewritten.

When opened the package proved to contain two thick notebooks, bound in parchment, or rather scraped goat or sheepskin, and very roughly as though by an unskilled hand, perhaps in order to preserve them if exposed to hard usage or weather. The paper of these books is extremely thin and tough so that each of them contains a great number of sheets. It is not of European make, and its appearance suggests that it was manufactured in the East, perhaps in China.

There could be no doubt as to who had owned these notebooks, because on one of them, the first, written in red ink upon the parchment cover in block letters, appears the name of Mr. Holly himself. Also on its first pages are various memoranda of travel evidently made by him and no one else. After these follow sheet upon sheet of apparently indecipherable shorthand mixed up with tiny Arabic characters. This shorthand proved to belong to no known system, and although every effort was made to decipher it, for over two years it remained unread.

At length, when all attempts had been abandoned, almost by chance, it was shown to a great Oriental scholar, a friend of the Editor, who glanced at it and took it to bed with him. Next morning at breakfast he announced calmly that he had discovered the key and could read the stuff as easily as though it were a newspaper leader. It seemed that the writing was an ancient form of contracted Arabic, mixed in places with the Demotic of the Egyptians—a shorthand Arabic and a shorthand Demotic, difficult at first, but once the key was found easily decipherable by some six or eight living men, of whom, as it chanced, the learned scholar into whose hands it had thus fallen accidentally was one.

So it came about that with toil and cost and time, at length those two closely written volumes were transcribed in full and translated. For the rest, they speak for themselves. Let the reader judge of them.

There is but one thing to add. Although it is recorded in notebooks that had been his property, clearly this manuscript was NOT written by Mr. Holly. For reasons which she explains it was written with the hand of SHE herself, during the period of her second incarnation when at last Leo found her in the mountains of Thibet, as is described in the book called "Ayesha."

CHAPTER I

~

The Halls of Heaven

To THE learned man, ugly of form and face but sound at heart, Holly by name, a citizen of a northern land whom at times I think that once I knew as Noot the Holy, that philosopher who was my master in a past which seems far to him and is forgot, but to me is but as yesterday, to this Holly, I say, I, who on earth am named Ayesha, daughter of Yarab the Arab chief, but who have many other titles here and elsewhere, have told certain stories of my past days and the part I played in them. Also I have told the same or other stories to my lord Kallikrates, the Greek, now named Leo Vincey, aforetimes a warrior after the habit of his race and his forefathers, who for religious reasons became a priest of Isis, the great goddess of Egypt and, once I believed, my mother in the spirit. Also I have told these or different tales to one Allan, a wandering hunter of beasts and a fighting man of good blood who visited me at Kôr, though of this I said nothing to Holly or to my lord Kallikrates, now known as Leo or the Lion, because as to this Allan I held it wiser to be silent.

All these stories do not agree together, since often I spoke them as parables, or in order to tell to each that which he would wish to hear, or to hide my mind for my own purposes.

Yet in every one of them lay hid something of the truth, a grain of gold in the ore of fable that might be found by him who had the skill and strength to seek.

Now my spirit moves me to interpret these parables and set down what I am and whence I came and certain of the things that I have seen and done, or at the least

1

such of them as I am permitted to reveal by those mightier than I of whom I am the servant, as they in their turn are the servants of others yet mightier than themselves.

Here in these Asian caves I sit, the Hesea of the Mountain, the last priestess of the worship of Mother Isis upon earth, as aforetime I sat amid the ruins of Kôr in Libya.

At Kôr for two thousand years I watched and waited till at length reborn, Kallikrates, whom unwittingly I slew in a rage of jealousy, came back to me where I had slain him. There, because of the curse that is on me and him, I lost him again, for in this very place, too, I was slain most horribly, slain by an excess of life wherewith I thought to make myself more beautiful even than I was and in striving to overfill the vase, shattered it to the vilest dust. Thus once more Fate made a mock of me; once more I lost Kallikrates whom it is my doom to desire in the flesh and to raise up in the spirit through time untold.

My soul passed out and on and here for a little while it found a home masked in the withered shape of an ancient priestess of my worship.

As was foredoomed my lord came back to me and saw the shining soul within that hideous shape and claimed it with a kiss, as I think the bravest deed and the most faithful that was ever done by man. In the magic of that kiss as also was foredoomed, my beauty grew again before his eyes, so that once more I stand a glory upon earth. Now we are plighted, now, if all goes well, within a year we shall be wed, aye, within one short year after I have borne him back to Kôr and unsealed the hidden Fire of Life and plunged him in its essence, giving to him my own gift of undying days.

And yet and yet—who knows the end? He presses me sore, and the starved woman part of me is passionate and weak and I may yield, and if his lips touch mine, who can say but that the fire within me will destroy him, the unfortified, and bring all my plans to dust and nothingness? I am great, set far above mortals, yet I play against forces I cannot see, that are greater than I, and it may please them to snatch the cup from my lips, and once more to overthrow me; for even though the blood of gods runs in him, as it runs in all of us, who can stand against their master, Doom, and its decrees? Therefore I, named Wisdom's Daughter, named Child of Isis, to-night am as full of fears as any mortal maid craving her lover beneath the moon and not knowing but that war, or chance, or the vile breath of sickness may have borne him away into that gulf where all things must be lost—until they are found again.

From month to month Leo, my lord, hunts upon the mountain after the fashion of men, and I, Ayesha, brood within the caves after the fashion of women. Yes, I who am half a goddess still brood within the caves after the fashion of women who wait and watch. Holly, the instructed, who loves me, as all men must do, bides here with me in the caves and we talk together of ancient things whereof the world has lost count, for he is a learned man skilled in the tongues of Greece and Rome, and one who thinks and, perchance, remembers.

But yesterday he said to me that I who seemed to know the past and to whom doors were opened that cannot be entered by human feet, should write down what I know and have experienced, that in time to come the world may be the wiser.

This the fancy has taken me to do, though whether I shall persevere to the end, I cannot say. He has given me that wherein I can write. 'Tis not the old papyrus, but it will serve, and I have pens of reed and can make ink of various colours, who in the bygone days was no mean scribe. Also I sleep but little, whose body, filled like a cup with life, needs small rest, and the long hours of the night pass wearily for me who lie and brood upon what has been and is to come, searching the darkness of the future with aching, fearful soul. Moreover, I am able to write in characters which, with all his learning, Holly cannot read, I who am not minded that he should know my thoughts and deeds and betray them to my lord whom they might cause to think the worse of me.

Why, then, should I write at all? For this reason: in certain matters I have foreknowledge and my spirit tells me that in a day to come, at the time appointed, some will guess the secret of my script and render it into tongues that all may read, so that when, soon or late, upon the circle of my eternal path, I pass hence to whence I came, and, like to the Fire-God in the caves of Kôr am hid awhile, this record will remain my monument. Ah! there peeps out the mortal in me, for see! like any common man or woman I would not be forgot even among the passing dwellers in a petty world.

Now to my task.

I have a vision of what chanced to my soul before it descended to dwell on earth, and with it I will begin. Maybe it is but a parable not to be strictly rendered, a token and a symbol rather than a truth. Yet of this I am sure that in it there is something of the truth, since otherwise why through the long centuries did it return to me again and yet again? Mayhap Greece and Egypt had no gods save those they fashioned for themselves. Holly tells me, as did the Wanderer, Allan, who also had some smattering of knowledge, that Zeus and Aphrodite and Osiris and Horus and Ammon are now dethroned with all their company and lie in the dust like the shattered columns of their temples, the mock of men who talk of them as the fables of the early world, so that of all the divinities that I knew, He of the Jews, although changed of character and countenance, alone is worshipped and remains.

Doubtless it is so, yet while man lives, always there is God, though his shapes be many. Always there is the eternal Good, as in a dream the holy Noot named the ultimate Divine, and behold! it is called Ammon or otherwise. Always there is Evil and behold! it is called Set or Baal, or Moloch, or otherwise. Always the stained soul of man seeks redemption, and he who saves is called Osiris or otherwise. Always Nature endures and she is called Isis or otherwise. Always the great world that will not die strains and pulses to new life, and the Life-bringer is called Aphrodite or otherwise.

And so on continually. Where man is, again I say, there was and is and will be God, or Good—the Spirit named by many names.

I go to my window-place in this cave-chamber and look out upon the stars shining countless in the frosty sky and lo! there I see God clad in one of the most glorious of His garments. I look at the moth flitting round my lamp or resting on the wall and, by the magic that is in it, summoning its mate from far, and lo! there I see God in another of His humbler garments. For God is in all things and everywhere, and from the great suns down, to Him who sent them forth and to Whom they return again, all that hath life must bow.

This is the vision wherein I read a parable of eternal truths.

I, Ayesha, daughter of Yarab, not yet of the flesh, but above and beyond the flesh inhabited the halls of that great goddess of the earth, a minister of That which rules all the earth (Nature's self as now I know), who in Egypt was named Isis, Mother of Mysteries. *Child,* she named me, and *Messenger;* and in that dream or parable, as a child was I to her, for I drank of the cup of her wisdom and something of her greatness was in my soul.

The goddess sat brooding in her sanctuary where Spirits came and went bearing tidings from all lands or emptying at her feet the cups of offered prayer. About her fell her robes, blue as the sky, and over the robes hung down her hair dusky as the night, and beneath her bent brows shone her eyes like stars of the night. In her hand was the rod of power and the footstool at her feet was shaped like the round world. There, canopied with light, she sat upon an ebon seat and brooded while round her beat music like sea waves upon the shore, such music as is not known upon the earth.

I appeared. I stood before her, I abased myself, I bowed till my forehead lay upon the ground and my hair swept the dust of the ground. She touched me with her sceptre, bidding me arise.

"Speak, Child," she said. "What message dost thou

bring from the shores of Nile? How goes my worship in the temples of Isis and are my servants faithful to my law?"

Then I made answer.

"O Mother divine, I have accomplished my embassy. Unseen, a spirit, I have wandered through the Land of Egypt. I have visited thy temples, I have hearkened to the councils of thy priests, I have watched thy worshippers and read their hearts. This is my report. Thy holy temples are empty; thy priests neglect thine altars; save a remnant who remain faithful, thy worshippers bow themselves before the shrines of another goddess."

"How is this goddess named, O Child of my love and wisdom?"

"She is named Aphrodite of the Greeks, a people who have flowed into Egypt, also other folk know her as Ashtoreth and Venus. Her sanctuary of sanctuaries is at Paphos in Cyprus, an island of the sea over against Egypt. She is the Queen of earthly love and love is the ritual of her worship, and she makes a mock of thee, O Mother, and of all the ancient gods, thy brothers and sisters, swearing that thy day and theirs is done and that she has risen from the sea to rule the world, and will rule it to the end. Here and there she reveals herself and conquers by her beauty, making all men to worship her and teaching all women to follow in her steps and beguile as she does, so that thy very priests turn to her and thy priestesses break from their vows and wanton with them."

"All of this I have learned, O Child, and more; yet it was my desire to hear it from thy lips that cannot lie, since in thee dwells my spirit. Hearken now! I am minded to be avenged upon these false Egyptians, and thou shalt be the sword of vengeance wherewith I will smite them, bringing their ancient glory to the dust and for ever setting the yoke of bondage on their necks. Aye, I am so minded and it shall be done, how, I will teach thee afterward. But first, as I have the power to do, I who under the Strength above me am regent of the ball of earth, will summon this Aphrodite to my presence here and now, and bid her speak out her heart to me.

"Hear me, Aphrodite, wherever thou art in earth or heaven. Aphrodite, I bid thee appear."

Then in my vision the Mother rose from her throne. Standing before it, terrible to see, she beckoned with her sceptre, north and south and east and west, uttering the secret words of power. Thrice she beckoned and thrice she spoke the secret words, and waited.

There was a stir at the end of the great hall and a sound of singing. Behold! floating between the long lines of the flame-clad guardians of that hall, attended by her subject gods, her mænads and her maidens, a shape of naked loveliness, came Aphrodite of the Greeks. Veiled in her curling locks and roped about with gleaming pearls for necklace and for girdle, she stood before the throne and bowed to the Majesty it bore, then asked in a laughing voice of music,

"I have heard thy summons, Mother of Mysteries, and I am here. What wouldst thou of me, Isis, Queen of the World? How can the Sea-born whose name is Beauty and whose gift is Love, serve thee, Isis, Queen of the World?

"Thus, thou who art shameless, thou born of the new gods and fashioned from the evil that is in the race of men—by lifting thy spell from off my worshippers. I know thy works. Drunken with desires they flock to thee in troops and for reward thou givest them the wages of their sin. Thou layest waste their homes; thou defilest their maidens, thou turnest men to beasts and makest a mock of them. Thy flowers fade; thy joys fill the mouth with ashes and those who drink of thy cup suck up poison in their souls. Thy fair flesh is a rottenness and thy perfumes are a stench and the incense of thine altars is the reek of hell. Therefore I command thee, go back to whence thou camest and leave the world in peace."

"Whither, then, should I go, Mother?" answered Aphrodite with her silvery laugh, "save into thy bosom, whence indeed I sprang, seeing that thou art Nature's

self and I am thy child. Stern is thy law and sweet, yet
without me thou wouldst have none over whom to rule.
Aye, without me would no child be born and not even a
flower would blow. Without me thou wouldst rule a wilderness with but the wisdom of which thou boastest to
keep thee company. Hearken! We are at war and in
that war I shall be conqueror, for I am eternal and all
life is my slave, because my name is Life. Get thee to
thy heaven, Isis, and rule there with Osiris, Lord of
Death, but leave me the living. Soon their day is done
and they pass beyond my spells into thy dominion.
There treat them as thou wilt and be content, for then I
have no more need of them, nor they of me. Why of a
sudden art thou so wrath with me, whom thou hast
known from the beginning? Is it because I take new
names and set up my altars in thine own Egypt, altars
wreathed with flowers, leaving all desolate thine where
prayers are mumbled from starved hearts and cold
hands make the offering of denial? Come now, Mother
Isis, let us play a game and let Egypt be the stake. Thou
hast the vantage there, seeing that for æons it has bowed
to thy laws and thy yoke has been upon its neck."

"What, then, O Aphrodite, dost thou promise Egypt
to which I and those who rule with me have given greatness, wisdom, and hope beyond the grave?"

"None of these high things, Mother. My gifts are love
and joy; sweet love and joy in which for a little while all
fears are forgot. Small gains thou mayest think, looking
backward to the past and onward to the future, thou
whose eyes are upon eternity. Yet they shall prevail.
Isis, in Egypt thy day is done; there, as elsewhere, thy
sceptre falls."

"If so, Wanton, with it falls Egypt that henceforth
shall be the world's slave. When conqueror after conqueror sets his foot upon her neck, then let her think on
Isis whom she has forsaken, and wailing, fill her soul
with they swine's food. Lo! I depart, leaving my curse
on Egypt. Have thy little day till before the Judgment
seat we settle our account. No more will I listen to thy
falsehoods and thy blasphemies. Till then, Wanton, look
on my majesty no more."

So in that vision
With her, flashing l
guardians that atten
place empty save for
the soul of me, Aye
wondering. The Path
then glided to the v
thereon, laughed agai
echoing from pillar to

"It is an omen," she
henceforth her seat an
ministers, I queen it he

WISDOM'

10

Thus this vision e
have learned that Is
ancient time, is
which is set a
that, as I b
changele

...no vulture cap
or symbols of the moon, whose brow is better graced by
these abundant locks and whose sceptre is a flower
whereof the odours make men mad. Yes, I queen it
here as everywhere, though in this solemn melancholy
fane I lack a subject."

She glanced about her till her glorious, roving eyes
fell upon that spirit which was I.

"Come hither, thou," she said, "and do me homage."

Now in my dream I, that spirit who in the world am
named Ayesha, came and stood before her, saying,

"Nay, I am the child of Isis and to her I bow alone."

"Thinkest thou so?" she answered, smiling and looking me up and down. "Well, I have another mind. It
seems to me that soon thou wilt descend from this sad
realm to the joyous fields of earth, that there thou mayest fulfil a certain purpose, for such is the fate decreed
for thee. Now, I, Aphrodite, add to that fate and lighten
it. Look behind thee, Spirit that shall be woman!"

I turned and looked, there to behold a shape of
beauty that I knew for Man. So beautiful was he that
my breast rose and the life in me stood still. He smiled
at me and I smiled back at him. Then he was gone,
leaving his picture stamped upon my soul.

"This is what I add to that tragic fate of thine, O
Spirit that shall be woman. Take him, the man appointed to thee, who from the beginning was always
thine, and as perchance thou hast done before, in his
kiss forget thy Mother Isis and thy crown of woes."

ds, and though now I, Ayesha,
s, as we knew and named her in the
but a symbol of that eternal holiness
ove all heavens and all earths, I say again
elieve, in its parable is hid something of the
s truth.

CHAPTER II

~

Noot the Prophet Comes to Ozal

SUCH is the vision, such the dream that has haunted me
through the centuries, and brooding over it from age to
age, I, Ayesha, doubt not that in its substance it is true,
though its trappings may be fancy-wrought. At least this
I know, that my spirit is the child of immortal Wisdom,
such as once men believed that Isis held, as my undying
shape is born of the beauty that is fabled Aphrodite's
gift. At least it is certain that even before I dipped me
in the Fire of Life, the most of learning and all human
loveliness were mine. I know also that it was my mission to bring Egypt to the dust, and did I not bring it to
the dust, smiting to its heart through proud Sidon, and
Cyprus, Aphrodite's home? And have I not for these
deeds borne Aphrodite's curse, as, because of Aphrodite's yoke laid upon my helpless neck, I have borne and
bear the curse of Isis, I whose destiny it is thus at once
to be the instrument and sport of rival powers whose
battle-ground is the heart of every one of us.

Alas! were my tale known, the world in its haste
might judge me hardly and think that I, who by burning
its Phœnician props overturned and ancient empire, am
cruel-natured, or that because I sought the love of a
certain man and in my anger slew him when he turned

from me, which in truth I did not desire to do, that I am wanton and ungoverned. Yet these things are not so, seeing that it was Fate, not I, that gave Egypt to the Persian dog (whom in his turn I overthrew) and made of its people slaves, and my flesh, not I, which after I had tasted of the Fire that is Nature's Soul, cursed me with passion and its fruits, perchance because I hated it and would never bow myself to it wholly, I who followed after purity, desiring not man's love but Wisdom's gift and a crown of spiritual gold.

Moreover, I had earthly and righteous warrant to bring about Sidon's fall and through it that of Egypt, seeing that their kings would have put me to utter shame and robbed my father of his life, as shall be told. So, too, I had the warrant of a woman's heart to worship the man I sought and for the death I brought upon him in my jealous madness my soul has paid full measure in remorse and tears. Still, since justice is hard to come by here on the earth, or even in the heaven above, I know that some would judge me harshly and must bear it with the rest. Even Holly, and at times my Lord Leo who once was named Kallikrates, have cherished such thoughts, though their lips dare not utter them, for I read it in their minds which to me are as an open book. Therefore never shall Holly, nor my lord either, look upon this written truth, lest therefrom they might distil some poison of mistrustful doubt, for it is sure that all men stain the whiteness of pure verity to the colour of their twisted minds. Therefore, too, I write it in tongues and symbols that they do not understand, which yet shall be deciphered in their season.

As I taught Holly long ago in the caves of Kôr, and truly, though afterward for some forgotten reason of my own or to give him food for thought, I may perhaps have changed my tale, puzzling him with stories of great Alexander and the rest, by my mortal brith I am an Arabian of the purest and most noble blood, born in Yaman the Happy and in the sweet city of Ozal. My father was named Yarab after the great ancestor of our race, and I, his only child, was named Ayesha after my highborn mother. Of her, whom I never knew, for she was gathered to the bosom of whatever god she worshipped but one moon from my birth, this is said.

At first she would not look on me, being angered because I was not a son, but at length at my father's pleading she was prevailed upon to command that I should be brought to her. When she saw how fair a babe Heaven had given her, such a babe as had not been known or told of among our people, she was amazed and put up a prayer that she might die. This, those who knew her declared, she did for two reasons:—first because, foreseeing my greatness, she desired that I alone should hold my father's heart and that of all our tribe, and secondly because she feared lest, should she live, she might bear other children whom she would hate when she compared them to my perfectness.

So it came about as, amongst others, my father told me often, that her prayer was granted and having kissed and blessed me, for a while she entered into rest.

This is the true story of her end, not the other, which those who envied me put about in after days, that owing to certain revelations which came to her at the time of my birth, as to the deeds which I was doomed to do and the loves and hates which I was doomed to earn, my mother thought it better to ask death from her gods rather than to continue in a life which she must live out at my side. This tale, my father often swore to me when I asked him of it, was as false as the changeful pictures which are seen at sunset on the desert, and sometimes at noonday also.

For the rest this beloved father of mine took no other wife while I was yet a child, fearing lest for her own sake, or her children's, she should be jealous and maltreat me, and afterward when I became a maiden, because I would not suffer that another woman should share the rule of his household with me. As I showed to him, he had servants in plenty and these should be enough, to which he bowed his head and answered that without doubt my will was that of God.

Thus it came about that I grew up with my noble father, his adviser and his strength, and through him, or rather with him, ruled all his great tribe, who always worshipped me. Be it admitted that from the first, or at least from the time that I came to womanhood, I brought him trouble as well as blessing, though through no fault of my own, but because of the beauty with which, as in those days I believed, Isis, or Aphrodite, or both of them, had endowed me for their own divine purposes. Very soon this beauty of mine, also my wit and knowledge, were noised abroad through all Arabia, so that princes came from far to court me, and afterward quarrelled and fought, for, being gentle-hearted, I said a kind word to everyone of them and left them to reason out which was the kindest.

This, for the most part, they did with spears and arrows after the fashion of violent and insensate men, so that there was much fighting on my account, which made my father some enemies, because the people of certain of the princes who were killed swore that I had promised myself in marriage to them. This, however, I had never done, who desired to marry no man that I might become a slave, cooped up in a fortress to bear children that I did not desire with some jealous tyrant for their father. Nay, being higher-hearted than any of my time, already I sought to rule the world, and if I must have any lover, to choose one whom I wished, and, when I wished, to have done with him.

But at that time I asked no lover who myself was in love—with wisdom. Knowledge, I saw, was strength, and if I would rule, first I must learn. Therefore I studied deeply, taking for masters all the wisest in Arabia who were proud to teach Ayesha the Beautiful, daughter and heiress of Yarab the great chief who could call ten thousand spears to his standards, all of his own tribe; and ten thousand more sworn to us but not of our blood.

I learned of the stars, a deep learning this that taught my soul its littleness, though it is true that while I studied I wondered, as still I wonder now, in which of them I was destined to rule when my day on earth was done. For always from the beginning I knew that wherever I am, there I must be the first and reign.

Perchance I had learned this aforetime in the halls of

Isis who then to me had seemed so great, though afterward contemplating those stars in the silence of the desert night, I came to understand that even the Universal Mother, as men named her in those far days, was herself but small, one who must fight for sovereignty with Aphrodite and other gods.

Holly has told me much of what the astronomers in these latter years have won of Nature's secrets: of how they number and weigh the stars, and measure to a mile their infinite distance from the earth, and how assuredly that each of them, even the farthest, is a sun as great or greater than our own, round which revolve worlds unseen. He has been astonished also, and affected to disbelieve, when I answered him, that we of Arabia guessed all these things over two thousand years ago, and indeed knew some of them. Yet, so it was.

Thus communing with greatness, my soul grew ever greater.

Moreover, I sought other and deeper lore. There wandered a certain strange man to our town, Ozal, where my father kept his court, if so it may be called, that is when we were not camping with our great herds in the desert, as we did at certain seasons of the year after the rains had caused the wilderness to throw up herbage. This man, named Noot, was always aged and white-haired, ugly to look on, with a curious wrinkled face of the colour of parchment, much such a face as that of Holly will be should he attain to his years. Indeed in this and other ways he was so like to Holly that often I think that in him dwells something of Noot's spirit now returned again to earth, as that of Kallikrates has returned as Leo.

Now this Noot, who came to Egypt none knew whence, for by birth he was not Egyptian, had been the high-priest of Isis and *Kherheb* or Chief Magician in Egypt, one who had much power on earth and still more beyond the earth, since he was in touch with things divine. Moreover, he was an honest magician and told the truth even to kings, as the gods and his wisdom showed it to him, and this was the cause of his downfall, for woe betide those who tell the truth to kings or to any who wield the sceptre of their might. On a certain day Nectanebes, the first of that name, the Pharaoh of Egypt whom others called Nekht-nebf, after a victory he had gained over the Persians, was filled with pride and took counsel with Noot, his Chief Magician, bidding Noot search out the future and tell him of glories to come to Egypt and to the Royal House, after he had been gathered to Osiris, that thereon he might feed his soul.

Noot answered that it was wiser to leave the future to care for itself and to satisfy his heart with the present and its joys and greatness.

Then the Pharaoh grew wrath and bade him fulfil his command.

So Noot bowed and went, and alone in some tomb or sanctuary drew the circles, uttered the words of power, and called upon the gods he served to show him such things as should befall to Egypt and to Pharaoh's House.

The magic sleep fell upon him and in it appeared the Spirit of Truth and spoke to him dreadful words of fate and doom. These she bade him deliver to Pharaoh, but when they were spoken to fly for his life's sake from Egypt and seek out a maiden called Ayesha, the daughter of Yarab, the Sheik of Ozal, and with her take refuge since she was an appointed instrument of Heaven. Moreover, this spirit commanded him to consult the maiden Ayesha in everything and impart to her all his gathered learning and the very secrets of the gods that had been revealed to him, that to any other it would be death to speak.

Now in the morning Noot went into the presence of Pharaoh who rejoiced to see him, and cried,

"Be welcome, *Kherheb*, the first of all magicians, you that men say were born beyond the earth, you in whom lives the spirit of Maat, goddess of Truth. Tell me now what the gods have revealed to you as to the glories they prepare for the ancient land of Egypt, and the House of me the Pharaoh who have made her great again, driving out the dogs of Persians."

"Life! Blood! Strength! O Pharaoh!" answered

Noot, saluting in the ancient form. "I have heard the word of Pharaoh who commanded me against my counsel to make divination and to seek to learn of the future from the gods. Behold! the gods hearkened. Behold! by the mouth of Maat, Lady of Truth, the goddess of the land where I was born, they spoke to me in the silence of the night. Thus they spoke. 'Say to Nectanebes who impiously dares to lift the veil of Time, that because he has fought for Egypt against the Barbarians who worship other gods, it is granted to him to die in his bed which shall chance ere long. Say that after him shall come a usurper whom the Barbarians shall defeat, so that he dies a slave in the land of Persia. Say that after him the son of Pharaoh shall wear the Double Crown and be called by the name of Pharaoh, the last of the true Blood of Egypt who shall ever sit upon its throne. Say that this son of his is accursed because he is in league with evil spirits and has worked apostasy, putting about his neck the chain of Aphrodite of the Greeks and the chains of Baal and of Moloch which never can be broken. Therefore, though he make many false offerings, yet is he accursed and the Barbarians shall overcome him, so that he flees away, nor shall all his magic be a shield to him. Because of him Egypt shall fall and her cities shall be burned and her children slaughtered and her temples desecrated, and never more shall one of her pure and ancient blood hold her sceptre.' Such is the oracle that the gods have commanded me to speak, O Pharaoh."

Now when Nectanebes heard these awful decrees of Fate upon him and upon his son, he trembled and rent his robs. Then rage took him and he reviled Noot the Prophet, calling him a liar and a traitor, and saying that he would make an end of him and his prophecies together. But because they were alone together within a chamber, before he could summon guards to kill him, Noot, helped of Heaven, fled away out of the palace and as darkness was falling, mingled with the throng and could not be found by the soldiers who sought him.

Ere daylight he was far from the city and, disguised, escaped from Egypt, bringing with him only his *Kher-*

heb's staff of power, also the ancient sacred books of spells or words of strength that were hidden in his robes. With these he brought, moreover, a little ancient image of Isis which he made use of in his divinations and prayed before by day and night.

~Thus it came about awhile later, one eve when I, the young maiden Ayesha, stood alone in the desert communing with my soul and drawing wisdom from the stars, that there appeared before me a withered, ancient man who, when he saw me, knelt down and bowed to me. I looked on him and asked,

"Why, aged One, do you kneel to me who am but a mortal?"

"Are you indeed a mortal?" he asked. "Me-thought that I who am the head-priest of Isis saw in you the goddess come to earth, and indeed, Lady, I seem to see the holy blood of Isis coursing in your veins."

"It is true, Priest, that of this goddess whom my mother worshipped I have dreams and memories and that sometimes she seems to speak with me in sleep, yet I tell you that I am but a mortal, the daughter of Yarab the far-famed," I answered to him.

"Then you are that maiden whom I am commanded to seek, she who is named Ayesha. Know, Lady, that great is your destiny, greater than that of any king, and that it is revealed to me that you will become immortal."

"All who believe on the gods trust to find the pearl, Immortality, beneath Death's waters, O Priest."

"Yes, Lady, but the immortality that is foretold for you is different and begins upon the earth, and I confess that I understand it not, though perhaps it may be an immortality of fame."

"Nor I, Priest. But meanwhile, what would you of me?"

"Shelter and food, Lady."

"And what can you offer for these, Priest?"

"Learning, Lady."

"That I think I have already."

"Nay, Lady Ayesha, not such learning as I can give:

the knowledge of the secrets of the gods; spells that will
sway the hearts of kings, magic that will show things
afar and call ghosts from the grave, power that will set
him who wields it upon the pinnacle of worship——"

"Stay!" I broke in. "You are old and ugly! you are
tired, your foot bleeds, you seek protection, and it
seems to me that you need food. How comes it that one
who can command so much lore and power is in want
of such things as these that the humblest peasant does
not lack, and must seek to purchase them with flatter-
ies?"

When he heard these words, of a sudden the aspect
of that old man changed. To me his shrunken body
seemed to swell, his face grew fierce and set, and a
strange light shone in his deep eyes.

"Maiden," he said in another voice, "I perceive that
you are in truth in need of such a teacher as I am. Had
you the inner wisdom, you would not judge by the out-
ward appearance and you would know that ofttimes the
gods bring misfortunes upon those they love in order
that thereby they may work their ends. Beauty is yours,
wit is yours, and a great destiny awaits you, though with
it, as I think, great sorrow. Yet one thing is lacking to
you—humility—and that you must learn beneath the
rods of destiny. But of these matters we will talk afterward. Meanwhile, as you say, I need food and shelter,
which are necessary to all while still they labour in the
flesh. Lead me to your father!"

Without more talk though not without fear, I guided
this strange wanderer to our tents, for at the time we
were camping in the desert, and into the presence of my
father, Yarab, who gave him hospitality after the Arab
fashion, but save for the common words of courtesy,
held no converse with him that night.

On the following morning before we struck our
camp, however, they had much speech together, and at
the end of it I was summoned to the great tent.

"Daughter," said my father, pointing to the wanderer
who was seated cross-legged on a carpet before him
after the fashion of an Egyptian scribe, "I have ques-

tioned this learned man, our guest. I discover from him
that he is the First Magician of Egypt, the head-priest
also of the greatest goddess of that land, she whom your
mother worshipped. At least, he says he was these
things—but now, having quarrelled with Pharaoh, that
he is nothing but a beggar, which is a strange state for a
magician. Also, according to his tale, Pharaoh seeks his
life, as he declares, because of certain prophecies that
he made to him concerning the fate of Egypt and of
Pharaoh's House. It seems that he desires to abide here
with us and to impart his wisdom to you, which wisdom, it is evident, has brought him to an evil case. Now
I ask you, as one gifted with discretion beyond your
years, what answer shall I return to him? If I keep this
Noot here, for that he tells me, in his name, though of
his race and country he will say nothing, perchance
Pharaoh, whose arm is long, will come to seek him and
bring war upon us, and if I send him away, perchance I
turn my back upon a messenger from the gods. What
then shall I do?"

"Ask him, my Father; seeing that one who prophesies
evil to the Pharaoh to his own ruin must be a truthful
man."

Then my father stroked his long beard, being perplexed, and inquired of the wanderer whether he should
keep him or send him away.

Noot replied that he thought that my father would do
well to send him away, but better to keep him. He said
that he had no revelation on the matter, though if it
were wished he would seek one, but he believed that
although his presence might bring trouble, from his dismissal would come yet worse trouble. He added that in
a vision he had been commanded by the goddess Isis to
find out a certain Lady Ayesha and become her instruc-
tor in mysteries that the purposes of Heaven might be
fulfilled, and that it was ill to flout goddesses whose
arms were even longer than those of Pharaoh.

Now for the second time my father who did nothing
great or small without my counsel, asked my judgment
on this matter after I had heard the words of Noot. I
pondered, remembering what the wanderer had prom-

ised to me in the desert, namely, knowledge and the secrets of the gods, also spells that would sway the hearts
of kings, with the gifts of magic and of power. At length
I answered,

"To what end is all this empty talk, my Father? Has
not this stranger eaten of your bread and salt and is it
the custom of our people to drive away from their doors
for no fault those to whom they have given hospitality?"

"True," said my father. "If he were to be sent hence,
it should have been done at once. Abide in my shadow,
Noot, and pray your gods to bring a blessing on me."

So Noot, the priest and prophet, remained with us
and from the first day of his coming, opened out to my
eager eyes all the scrolls of his secret lore. Still it is true
that he brought to my father, not blessing but death, as
shall be told, though this did not come for many moons.

Meanwhile he taught and I learned, for his knowledge flowed into my soul like a river into the desert and
filled its thirsty sand with life. Of all that I learned from
him, because of the oaths I swore, even now it is not
lawful that I should write, but it is true that in those
years of study I grew near to the gods and wrested
many a secret from the clenched hands of Nature.

Moreover, though as yet I did not take the vows, I
became a votary of Isis, as Noot, her high-priest, had
authority to make me, and one of the inner circle. Yes,
I determined even then that I would forswear marriage
and all fleshly joys and make to Isis the offering of my
life, while she through her priest vowed to me in return
such power and wisdom as had scarce been given to any
woman before me.

Thus the time went by till at length fell the blow and
I—for all my wisdom—never heard Aphrodite laughing
behind her veil. Nor indeed did Noot, but then he was
an old man who, as I drew out of him, save those of his
mother, had not once touched a woman's lips. All learning was his, but it seemed that in his search for it there
were some things he had passed by. At least so I believed, or rather half-believed, at this time, but as I
learned afterward, there are matters upon which even

the most holy think it no shame to lie, since in the end Noot confessed to me that in his youth he had been as are other men. Also I think that he heard the laughter of Aphrodite, though I did not. However these things may be, as I was to discover afterward, Mother Isis is a stern mistress to whoever looks the other way.

Also, although Noot told me much, he hid more. Not for many a year was I to learn that he was a citizen of the ancient, ruined land of Kôr and the only one who knew the fearful mystery it hid, which in a far day to come he was commanded to reveal to me, Ayesha, and to no other man or woman. Nor did he tell me that it was the purpose of Heaven that under her other shape and name of Truth I should again establish the worship of Isis in that land and once more make of it a queen of the world. Yet these things were so and therefore was he sent to me and for no other reason. Therefore was he commanded to reveal the doom of Egypt to Nectanebes, that this Pharaoh in his wrath might drive him, a wanderer, to our tents at Ozal there to dwell for years and instruct me, the chosen, in all things that I must learn, so that when at last the appointed hour dawned, I might be fitted for my mighty task.

But all this while Aphrodite laughed on behind her veil!

CHAPTER III

The Battle and the Flight

IN THE end trouble came upon us thus. As I have said already, my beauty was the talk of men throughout Arabia, and of women also, who were jealous of it, since those who travelled in caravans bore its fame from tribe to tribe and those who sailed upon the sea took up

the report and carried it to distant shores. But now to
this tale was added another, namely that the wearer of
so much loveliness was also a vessel into which the gods
had poured all their wisdom, so that there were few
marvels which she could not work and little or nothing
that she did not know. It was added, truly enough, that
the channel through which this wisdom flowed into her
heart was a certain Noot who aforetime had been *Kherheb* in Egypt and high-priest of Isis.

Presently this tale, carried by the mariners, came to
the ears of the Pharaoh Nectanebes in his city of Sais,
who knew well enough that Noot was the prophet whom
he had driven from the land and whom by now he desired to have back again, for his inspired counsel's sake.

The end of it was that the Pharaoh sent an embassy
to my father, Yarab, demanding that I should be given
to him or to his son, the young Nectanebes, I know not
which, in marriage, and that Noot should return to
Egypt as my guardian, and there be reinstated in all his
offices.

My father answered, speaking with my voice, that
least of anything did I desire to become one of the
women of Pharaoh, a man already near the grave, or
even of Pharaoh's son, I who was a free-born Arabian,
and that as for Noot, his head felt safer on his shoulders
in Ozal where he was an honoured guest, than it would
at Pharaoh's court.

These words Nectanebes took ill, so ill indeed that,
for this and other reasons of policy, he sent an army to
invade Yaman the Happy, and to capture me and kill
Noot, or drag him away to Egypt in chains. Of all these
plans we had warnings, partly through the priests of Isis
in Egypt who still acknowledged Noot as their head, although another had been raised up in his place and
filled his office, and partly through dreams and revelations that came to him from Heaven. Therefore we
made ready and gathered in great strength to fight
against Pharoah.

At length his hosts came, borne for the most part in
ships of Cyprus and of Sidon whereof at that time the
kings were his allies, or rather vassals.

They landed upon a plain by the seashore and watching from our hills beyond, we suffered them to land. But that night, or rather just before the following dawn when their camp was still unfortified, we poured down upon them from our hills. Great was the fray! for they fought well. I led the horsemen of our tribe in this, my first battle, and by the light of the rising sun charged again and yet again into the heart of the hosts of Pharaoh, having no fear since I knew well that none could harm me.

There was a certain company of Greeks, two thousand of them perhaps, who served Pharaoh, and in the centre of them was his general, which company stood firm when the others fled. Thrice we attacked it with the horsemen and thrice were beaten back. Then my father came to my aid with his picked kinsmen mounted upon camels. Again we charged and this time broke through. Those about Pharaoh's general saw me and strove to make me captive, hoping to carry me back to him, whatever happened to the host. They surrounded me, one caught the bridle of my horse. Him I slew with a javelin, but others snatched at me. Then I cried to Isis and I think that she clothed me in some garment of her majesty, since foes fell away in front of me, calling out—

"This is a goddess, not a woman!"

Yet I was cut off, ringed round by them, for all my companions were slain or driven back.

They pressed in on me to take me living, till I was hedged in with a ring of swords. My father appeared mounted on his swift white dromedary that was called Desert Wind, followed by others. They broke through the ring and there was a fierce fight. My father fell, pierced by the spear of the general of the Egyptians. I saw it and, filled with madness, I charged at that general and drove my javelin through his throat, so that he fell also. Then a cry went up and the host of Pharaoh melted away, flying for the ships. Some gained them, but the most remained dead upon the shore or were taken captive.

Thus ended that battle and such was the answer that

we of Ozal sent to Pharaoh Nectanebes. Therefore it was also that because of the death of my beloved father at their hands I hated Egypt, and not only Egypt but Cyprus and Sidon in whose ships her hosts had been borne to attack us, yes, and swore to be avenged upon them all, which oath I kept to the full.

Now my father being dead, I the daughter of Yarab, became ruler of our tribe in his place with Noot for my counsellor. For certain years I ruled it well. Yet troubles arose—in this fashion. By now the fame of my glory and loveliness had spread through all the earth, so that, even more than before, I was beset with demands for my hand from chiefs and kings who went well-nigh mad when I refused them. In the end, being brothers in their grief because I would have none of them, I whom they called by the names of Hathor and Aphrodite and other goddesses famed for beauty according to their separate worships, they made a great conspiracy together and sent envoys bearing a message. This was the message:—

That unless my people would give me up so that my husband might be chosen from among their number by the casting of lots, they would join their armies together and fall upon us and kill out our tribe so that not one remained to look upon the sun, save myself alone, who should then be the reward of him who could take me.

Now when I heard this I was filled with rage and having caused those messengers to be scourged before me, sent them back to their masters bearing my defiance. But when they were gone, the elders of the tribe came to me and said through their spokesman,

"O Daughter of Yarab, O Ayesha the Wise and Lovely, we adore you as one beyond price. Yet it is true that we love our wives and children and desire to live, not to die. How can we who are but few stand against so many kings? We pray you, therefore, Ayesha, to choose one of them to be your husband, for then because of jealousy doubtless they will destroy each other and we, your servants, shall be left in peace. Or if you will not marry, then we pray you to hide your beauty elsewhere for a while, so that the kings do not come to seek it here."

I hearkened and was angry because of the cowardice of this people who set their own welfare above my will and refused to fight with those who threatened me. Still, being politic, I hid my mind and said that I would consider and give them an answer on the third day. Then I took counsel of Noot and together we made divinations and prayed to the gods, but most of all to Isis.

The end of it was that before the dawn on the second day a small caravan of five camels might have been seen, had there been any to watch, leaving the city of Ozal and heading for the sea.

On the first of those camels sat an old merchant. On the second his wife or his daughter, or his woman, heavily veiled. On the three others was his merchandise. Woven carpets it seemed to be, though if opened, those carpets would have proved to be filled with a very great treasure in gold and pearls and sapphires and other gems, which for generations had been gathered together by my father, Yarab, and those who went before him out of the profits of their trade and of their flocks and herds, and hid away against the time of need.

That merchant was Noot the priest and prophet, and that woman was I—Ayesha. That treasure was mine and the camels were led by certain men who had served my father and now served me, being sworn to me by secret oaths that might not be broken.

We gained the sea and took ship to Egypt in a vessel that I had caused to be prepared. Yes, before we were missed the coast of Arabia was behind us, since I had given it out that I had gone to a secret place to consider of my answer to the elders of the people. As I heard afterward, when it was known that I had turned my back on them, there were woe and lamentations in every household of the tribe. Understanding what they had lost the men among them beat their breasts and wept, though it is said that some of the women rejoiced, because I outshone them all and they were jealous of me.

Afterward the kings and chiefs of whom I have spoken descended upon them to seek me, whereupon my people swore that I had been changed into a goddess and gone up into heaven. Some believed this, declaring that they had always held me to be more than mortal, but others of a coarser, common mind declared that I had been hidden away; and falling on the tribe, dispersed it, seizing many and selling them into slavery.

Thus then did the children of Yarab pay the price of their treachery to me, though I have heard that afterward once more they became a people under the rule of some baseborn grandson of my father, and worshipped me as a guardian goddess from generation to generation, having come to believe that I was not a woman, but a spirit whom the gods sent to dwell with them for a while.

So Noot and I came safely to Naukratis, a Grecian city upon the Canopic mouth of the Nile, and there abode disguised as a merchant and his daughter trading in precious stones and other costly wares, and thus adding to my wealth, though of this there was little need, since already it was great.

It was here that for the first time I went veiled in the Eastern fashion, in order to hide my beauty from the eyes of men.

Under cover of this trade I and Noot lived for two years or more while I studied the lore and language of the Egyptians, learning to read their picture-writing which the Greeks called heiroglyphs, and mastering their history. Also I perfected myself in the Grecian tongue and read the works of their great writers as well as those of the Romans. Moreover, I learned other things, since at the beginning of the second year Necta-nebes, the Pharaoh who had sought me in marriage, being now dead, and Egypt for a while in the hands of the usurper Zehir, who some say was his son born of a concubine, we travelled up the Nile disguised and came to the ancient city of Thebes. This we did slowly, stopping at every great town, where we received the hospitality of the head priests of the various gods, Ammon, Ptah, and the rest, since to these priests Noot by secret signs revealed himself. Indeed the news of our coming was passed on before us so that always we found some waiting to welcome us who, once within the temple walls, were treated like the greatest, although we were garbed as humble travellers. All of these priests we found full of rage, both because the gods of the Greeks, and even of the Persians and Sidonians, were being set above their own, and still more for the reason that their revenues were seized and used to pay Grecian mercenaries, so that they who had been very rich were now poor and the gods lacked their offerings, nor could their holy temples be repaired.

Of all these things I took note whose heart was set upon one thing only,—to bring about the fall of the Egyptians and their allies that had slain my father whom I loved, as indeed I was fated to do. Therefore by a word here and a word there I blew the anger that smouldered in them to flame, hinting of rebellion and the setting up of a new dynasty in Egypt, of which at that time I thought to be the first, a priestess-queen, Isis-come-to-Earth. Of this plan I hinted also through the mouth of Noot, nor was it ill received, since already those priests to whom he had told my history and the revelations that had come to him concerning me, looked on me as something more than a woman. Could a mortal maid, they asked, have so much beauty and so much learning; was I not in truth a goddess clothed in woman's flesh?

Only on the road I purposed to tread there was this stumbling block, that each of those high-priests desired that he himself, or at least one who worshipped *his* god, were it Ammon or Osiris or Ptah, or Khonsu, should be the Pharaoh of that new dynasty. For they were jealous each of the other and could not agree together, as is common among rival priests.

We passed on to Thebes where I saw the wonders of the mighty temples which stood there reared by a hundred kings, which Holly tells me now are but ruins, though the great hall of columns among which I used to wander still stands in part. Also I crossed the Nile and visited the tombs of the Pharaohs.

Standing beneath the moon in that desolate Valley of Dead Kings, for the first time, I think I came to know all the littleness of Life and of the vanities of earth. Life, I saw, was but a dream; its ambitions and its joys were naught but dust. Those kings and those queens, some of them had been very great in their day; the people worshipped them as gods and when they stretched out their sceptres, the world trembled. And now what were they? But names, if so much as a name remained of them.

I saw a great queen whose tomb some while before had been broken into by robbers, Persians or Greeks I was told. They had unrolled her mummy and stripped her of her royal ornaments and there she lay, she in whom had centred all the world's pomp, a little black and withered thing, grinning at us from the dust, like a dead ape, a sight so strange and unhuman that the priest who guided us, a coarse fellow, broke into laughter. I remembered that laugh and afterward paid him back for it, though he never knew whence his misfortune came.

I, Ayesha, have many sins to my count and at that time was full of faults, as perchance still I am to-day. Thus I was proud of my beauty and my genius which were given to me above any other woman; passionate and revengeful, too, and led on by ambitions. Yet this I swear by all the gods of all the heavens, that ever in my secret self I have set the spirit above the flesh and desired to attain to another glory than that of earth. From the flesh came my sins, because it was begotten of other flesh and the flesh is sin incarnate. Yet my soul sins not, because it comes from that which is sinless and, its tasks accomplished here, laden with knowledge and purified by suffering, to this holy fount at last it shall return again. At the least such are my faith and hope.

So it came about that there in the Valley of Dead Kings I swore myself to the worship of God (since all the gods are one God) and to use the world as a ladder whereby I might climb nearer to His throne.

Thus I swore with old Noot for witness, noting that he shook his wise head and smiled a little at the oath.

For if I forgot Aphrodite and the flesh, he remembered them, or perchance he to whom the Future spoke already guessed something of my fate which it was not lawful that he should tell. Also at that time I knew nothing of that everlasting King of Fire who dwells in majesty beneath the rocks of Kôr, nor of his evil gifts. Least of all did I know that Noot himself was by inheritance and appointment the guardian of the Fire.

From Thebes we passed up Nile to Philæ on the Isle of Elephantine, where Mother Isis had her holy sanctuary, and Nectanebes, the first of that name, he who had sought me as a wife and now was not long dead, had begun to build a temple of surpassing beauty to the goddess, which temple was completed in my time by his son, the second Nectanebes, he with whom I had to do and brought to nothingness.

Here I abode a year making final preparations utterly to vow myself to the goddess. I kept the fasts, I purified my heart, I passed the trials and at length alone I seemed to die and descended into the gulf of death and fled through the Halls of Death pursued by terrors, till I saw, or dreamed I saw, the goddess in her glory and fell swooning at her feet. More I may not say, even now that over two thousand years have passed since that holy hour of fears and victory, save this one thing which indeed has come to pass. When I rose from that swoon certain words were written on my mind, though whether the goddess whom I seemed to see or some spirit spoke them to me I do not know. These were the words:—

"Far to the south in this land of Libya beyond the region of Punt, is an ancient city, whence my worship came ere Egypt had a people. Thither, Daughter of Isis, shalt thou bear it back and there shalt thou blow upon it with thy breath and keep alive the holy spark that at last is doomed to die upon the earth amidst those snows which as yet no southern foot has trod. There, Daughter, in that fallen and deserted land, my prophet Noot shall welcome thee. There shall he guard the Door of Life which of mortal women thou alone shalt pass. There shalt thou stain thy hands with blood, and there in solitude amidst the tombs, with tears from thy re-

pentant eyes, shalt thou wash thy sin away. Yet of the
seed that thou sowest in fire in the womb of the world,
thou shalt reap the harvest upon the mountain tops
amidst the snows."

Such were the words branded upon my memory
when I awoke from the swoon after the night of trial.
Later I repeated them to Noot, my Master, praying him
to read their meaning, which either he could not or
would not do. He said, however, it was true that far to
the south there stood a great city, now a ruin sparsely
peopled, whence came the first forefathers of the Egyptians thousands of years before the pyramids were built.
He said also that he knew the road to that city by sea
and by land, though how he knew it he would not tell.
Nor would he interpret the rest of those dream words.
Yet, when I harassed him with questions he said carelessly, as one who hazards a guess, that perchance the
goddess meant that it would be my lot after its fall or
corruption in Egypt, to bear back her worship to this its
earlier home and there establish a great nation of her
servants. As to the "Door of Life" that I alone could
pass, of which he was named the Guardian, and the
"northern snows," he declared that he knew not what
was meant by them, but doubtless these things would be
made clear in their season.

So he spoke somewhat lightly, like one who humours
a frightened child, as though he would make me think
that I had but dreamed a dream. This indeed I came to
believe, as is the fashion of mankind concerning things
that they cannot see or handle, however real those
things may appear in the hour of their experience. For
these in the end always we write down as dreams, such
as haunt us by the thousand in our sleep.

Yet now that two thousand years have gone by, I
know that this dream was true. For is there not a city
called Kôr and was I not there doomed to find the Door
of Life whereof Noot was guardian? And did I not sin
there and from generation to generation wash the shed
blood from off my hands with tears of bitterest repentance, and afterward expiate that sin in loss and shame
and agony? And lastly do I not reap that harvest of

tears upon the mountain tops amidst the northern snows whither the spirit bore me, still holding in those hands the embers of the worship of that regnant Good who to us of the ancient world was known as the Universal Mother to whom I swore myself in Philæ's temples?

But enough of these things now; let them be spoken of in their season.

CHAPTER IV

❧

The Kiss of Fate

THERE came a man to Philæ. Watching from a pylon top whither I had gone to pray alone, I saw him land upon the island and from far off noted that he was a godlike man, clad in armour such as the Grecians used, over which was thrown a common cloak, hooded as though to disguise him; one who had the air of a warrior. At a distance from the temple gate he halted and looked upward as though something drew his glance to me standing high above him upon the pylon top. I could not see his face because of the shadow thrown by the great walls behind which the sun was sinking, but doubtless he could see me well enough, whose shape was outlined against the veil of golden light that must have touched me with its glory, though, as that light was behind me, my face also would be hidden from him. At least he stood a little while as though amazed, staring upward steadily, then bowed his head and passed into the temple, followed by men bearing burdens.

Some pilgrim to the shrine, I thought to myself, then turned my mind to other matters, remembering that with men I had no more to do. Thus for the first time here in the body, all unknowing, I looked upon Kallikrates and he looked on me, but often afterward I have

thought that there was a veiled lesson or a parable in
the fashion of this meeting.

For did I not stand far above him, clothed in the
glory of heaven's gold, and did he not stand far beneath
in the gloom of the shadows that lay upon the lowly
earth, so that between us there was space unclimbable?
And has it not been ever thus throughout the centuries,
for am I not still upon the pylon top clad in the splendour of the spirit, and is he not still far beneath me
wrapped with the shadows of the flesh? And since as
yet the secret of the pylon stair is hidden from him,
must I not descent to earth if we would meet, leaving
the light and my pride of place that I may walk humbly
with him in the shadow? And is it not often so between
those that love, that one is set far above the other,
though still this rope of love draws them together,
uplifting the one, or dragging down the other?

The man passed into the temple and that night I
heard he was a Grecian captain of high blood, one who
though young had seen much service in the wars and
done great deeds, Kallikrates by name, who had come
to seek the counsel of the goddess, bringing precious
gifts of gold and Eastern silks, the spoil of battles in
which he had fought.

I asked why such an one sought the wisdom of Isis,
and was told that it was because his heart was troubled.
It seemed that he had been dwelling at Pharaoh's court
as a captain of the Grecian guard, and that there he had
quarrelled with and slain one who was as a brother to
him, if indeed he were not his very brother. This ill
deed, it was said, preyed upon his soul and drove him
into the arms of Mother Isis, seeking for pardon and
that comfort which he could not find at the hand of any
of the gods of the Greeks.

Again I asked idly enough why this Kallikrates had
killed his familiar friend or his brother, whichever it
might be. The answer was—because of some highly
placed maiden whom both of them loved, so that they
fought from jealousy, after the fashion of men. For this
reason the life of Kallikrates was held to be forfeit according to the stern military law of the Grecian soldiers,

and he must fly. Also the deed had tarnished that great
lady's name; also his heart was broken with remorse
and hither he came to pray Isis to mend it of her mercy,
he who had forsaken the world.

The tale moved me a little, but again I cast it from
my mind, for are not such things common among men?
Always the story is the same: two men and a woman, or
two women and a man, and bloodshed and remorse and
memories which will not die and the cry for pardon that
is so hard to find.

Yes, I cast it from my mind, saying lightly—oh!
those evil-omened words—that doubtless his own blood
in a day to come would pay for that which he had split.

For a while, some months indeed, this Grecian Kallikrates vanished from my sight and even from my
thoughts, save when, from time to time, I heard of him
as studying the Mysteries among the priests, having, it
was said, determined to renounce the world and be
sworn to the service of the goddess. Noot told me that
he was very earnest in this design and made great progress in the faith, which pleased the priests who desired
above all things to convert those that served Grecian
gods with whom the deities of Egypt, and above all Isis,
were at war. Therefore they hastened his preparation so
that as soon as might be he should be bound to the
Heavenly Queen by bonds that could not be loosed.

At length his fasts and instruction were completed;
his trials had been passed and the hour came when he
must make his last confession to the goddess and swear
the awful oaths to her very self.

Now since Isis did not descend to earth to stand face
to face with every neophyte, it was needful in this great
ceremony that one filled with her spirit should take her
place and as may be guessed, that one was I, Ayesha the
Arab. To speak truth, in all Egypt, because of my
beauty, my learning, and the grace that was given to
me, there was none so fitting to wear her mantle as myself. Indeed afterward this was acknowledged when,
with a single voice, the Colleges of her servants
throughout the land, men and women together, pro-

moted me to be her high-priestess, and gave me, who aforetime among them was known by the title of Wisdom's Daughter, the new name of *Isis-come-to-earth,* or in shorter words, *The Isis.* For my own name of Ayesha I kept hid lest it should be discovered that I was that chieftainess, the child of Yarab, who had defeated the army of Nectanebes.

Therefore at a certain hour of the night, draped in the holy robes, wearing on my brow the vulture cap and the bent symbol of the moon, holding in my hand the *sistrum* and the cross of Life, I was conducted to the pillared sanctuary and seated alone upon the throne of blackest marble, with the round symbol of the world for my footstool.

Thus, having learned my part and the ancient hallowed words that I must say, I sat awhile wondering in my heart whether Isis herself could be more glorious or more fair. So indeed did the priests and priestesses who saw me thus arrayed and bent the knee to me as though I were the very goddess, which in truth many of the humbler among them half believed.

Thus I sat in the moonlight that flowed from the unroofed hall beyond, while the carven gods watched me with their quiet eyes.

At length I heard the sound of footsteps whereon there came a priestess and flung over me the white veil of innocence sewn with golden stars that until the appointed moment must hide Isis from her worshipper. The priestess withdrew and, wrapped in the dark, hooded robe that signified the stained flesh about to be cast away, which hid all of him so that his face could not be seen, came that tall neophyte led by two priests who held his right hand and his left. I noted those hands because they were so white against the blackness of the robe, and even by the moonlight saw that they were beautiful, long and thin and shapely, though the palm of one, the right, was somewhat broadened as though by long handling of the tools of war.

The priests led him to the entrance of the shrine and in hushed whispers bade him kneel upon a footstool and make his sacrifice and confession to the goddess as he had been taught to do. Then they departed leaving us alone.

There followed silence which at length I broke, whispering,

"Who is this that comes to visit the Mother in her earthly shrine and what is his prayer to the Queen of Heaven and Earth?"

Though I spoke so gently and so low, perhaps because of their very sweetness, my words seemed to frighten him, or perhaps he believed that he stood in the very presence of the goddess; at least he answered in a voice that trembled,

"O holy Queen adored, in the world I was named Kallikrates the comely. But the priests, O Queen, have given me a new name, and it is, *Lover-of-Isis.*"

"And what have you to say to Isis, O Lover-of-Isis?"

"O Queen eternal, I have to tell my sins and ask her pardon for them, I who have passed the Trials and am accepted by her servants. If it is granted, then to her I must make the oath, binding myself eternally to love and serve her, her and no other in heaven or on earth."

"Set out those sins, O Lover-of-Isis, that my Majesty may judge of them, whether they can be forgiven or are beyond forgiveness," I answered in the words of the appointed ritual.

Then he began and told a tale that made me redden behind my veil, for all of it had to do with women, and never before had I learned what wantons those Greeks could be. Also he told of men whom he had slain in war, one of them in the battle against my tribe, in which strangely enough it seemed he had fought as a lad, for this man was a great warrior. Of these killings, however, I took no account, because they had been of those who were the enemies of himself or of his cause.

In stern silence I listened, noting that save for these matters of light love and fightings, the man seemed innocent enough, for in his story there was naught of baseness or of betrayal. Moreover, it seemed that he was one in whom the spirit had striven against the flesh, and who, however much his feet were tangled in the poisonous snares of earth, from time to time had set his eyes on Heaven.

At length he paused and I asked of him,

"Is the black count finished? Tell now the truth and dare to hold nothing back from the goddess who notes all."

"Nay, O Queen," he answered, "the worst is yet to come. I came to Egypt as a captain of the Grecian guard that watches the House of Pharaoh at Sais. With me came another man, my half-brother, for our father was the same, with whom I was brought up and loved as never I loved any other man, and who loved me. He was a glorious warrior, though some held that I was more handsome in my person, Tisisthenes by name, that in my Grecian tongue in which I speak means the Avenger. Thus was he called because my father, whose first-born he was, desired that he might grow up to work vengeance upon the Persians who slew his father named like myself, Kallikrates, the most beauteous Spartan that was ever born. Foully they slew him before the battle of Platæa, whilst he was aiding the great Pausanius to make sacrifice to the gods. This Tisisthenes my brother I killed with my own hand."

"For what cause did you kill him?"

"There was a royal maiden at that court, one fairer than any woman has been, is, or will be—ask not her name, O Mother, though doubtless it is known to you already. This lady both of us saw at the same time and by the decree of Aphrodite both of us loved. As it chanced it was I who won her favour, not my brother. We were spied upon; the tale was told; trouble fell upon that royal maiden who, when she should be old enough, was sworn in marriage to a distant king. To save her name she made denial, as she must do. She swore there was naught between her and me, and to prove it turned her face from me and toward my brother. I came upon them together in a garden. She had plucked a flower which she gave to him and he kissed the hand that held the flower. She saw me and fled away. I, maddened with jealousy, smote my beloved brother in the face and forced him to fight with me. We fought. He guarded himself but ill, as though he cared nothing of the end of that fray. I cut him down. He lay before me dying, but ere he died, he spoke:

" 'This is a very evil business,' he said. 'Know, Kallikrates, my most beloved brother, that what you saw in the garden between that royal maid and myself was but a plot to save you both, since thereby I purposed to take on to my own head the weight of your transgression against the law of this land, because she prayed it and it was my wish. This I have done, and for this reason I suffered you to slay me, though during that fight twice I could have pierced you, because you were blinded with rage and forgot your swordsmanship. Now it will be said that you found me pursuing this royal maiden and rightly slew me according to your duty and that it was I who loved her and not you, as has been commonly reported. Yet in truth I love her well and am glad to die because it was to you that her heart turned and not to me; also because thereby I saved both her and you. Yet, Kallikrates, my brother, the gods give me wisdom and foresight in this the hour of my death, and I say that you will do well to have done with this lady and all women, and to seek rest in the bosom of the gods, since, if you do not, great trouble will come upon you, and through this same curse of jealousy such a death as mine shall be yours also. Now let us who are the victims of Fate kiss each other on the brow as we used to do when we were children, playing together in the happy fields of Greece, from whom death was yet a long way off, forgiving each other all and hoping that we may meet once more in the region of the Shades.'

"So we embraced, and my brother Tisisthenes gave up his spirit in my arms and looking on him I wished that I were dead in his place. Then as I turned to go the soldiers of our company found me and seeing that I had slain my brother, would have brought me to trial, not because we had fought together, but because he was my superior in rank and therefore I who, being under his command, drew sword on him, by the law of the Greeks, must die. Yet before I could be put upon my trial, some of those who loved me and guessed the truth of the business thrust me out of our camp disguised, with all the treasure that I had won in war, bidding me hide myself awhile till the matter was forgotten. O Queen, I did not desire to go; nay, I desired to stay and to pay the price of my sin. But they would not have it so. I think indeed that there were others behind, great ones of Egypt, moving in this matter; at least I was thrust forth, all being made easy for me, and all eyes growing blind."

Again he paused, and I, Ayesha, clothed as the goddess, asked,

"And what did you then, you who could slay your brother for the sake of woman?"

"Then, Divine One, I fled up Nile where, because of the trouble that was in the land, Pharaoh's arm could not reach me, nor the arm of the commander of the Greeks. Tarrying not and without speech with that high maiden who was the cause of my sin, I fled up Nile."

"Why did you fly up Nile and not back to your own people, O most sinful man?"

"Because my heart is broken, Queen, and I desired to seek the mercy of Isis whose law I had learned already and to become her priest. I knew that those who bow themselves to her may look no more on woman, but thenceforth must live virgin to the death, and it was my will to look no more on woman, since woman had stained my hands with a brother's blood, and therefore I hated her."

Now I, Ayesha, asked,

"What gods did you worship before your heart was turned to Isis, Queen of Heaven?"

"I worshipped the gods of Greece and first among them Aphrodite, Lady of Love."

"Who has paid you well for your service, making of you a murderer of one of your own blood who, before she blinded your eyes, was more to you than any on the earth. Do you then renounce this wanton Aphrodite?"

"Aye, Queen, I renounce her for ever. Never more will I offer at her altars or look on woman in the way of love. If I may have pardon for my sins, here and now I vow myself to Isis as her faithful priest and servant.

Here and now I blot the name of Aphrodite from my heart; yea, I reject her gifts and tread down all her memories beneath my aspiring feet that at last shall bear my soul to peace."

Thus the man spoke in a quivering and earnest voice, and was silent. Yes, deep silence reigned in that holy place, whilst I, Ayesha, although it is true that as a woman I misdoubted me of such rash oaths, as the minister of the goddess, prepared myself to grant pardon to this seeker in the hallowed, immemorial words, and to open to his troubled heart the doors of purity and rest eternal.

Then suddenly in that silence clearly I heard the sound of silvern laughter, soft, sweet laughter that seemed to come from the skies above and though it was so low to fill the shrine and all the hall beyond. I looked about me but could see naught. It would seem, too, that the Greek heard also, for he turned his head and looked behind him, then once more let it fall upon his hands.

Whence came that sound? Could it be that she of Paphos———? Nay, it was impossible, and not thus would I be turned from my office, I who was clothed with the robe and for that hour wielded the might of Isis.

"Hearken, O man, in the world named Kallikrates," I said. "On behalf of Isis, the All-Mother, goddess of virtue and of wisdom, speaking with her voice, hearing with her ears, and filled with her soul, I wash you clean of all your sins and accept you as her priest, promising to you light burdens on the earth and beyond the earth great rewards for ever. First swear the oath that may not be broken, and then draw near that I may kiss you on the brow, accepting you as the slave and lover of Isis, from this day until the moon, her heavenly throne, shall crumble into nothingness."

Having spoken thus, letting the words fall one by one, slowly as the tears of the penitent fell upon the ground, I uttered the oath, the form of which even now I must not write.

It was a dreadful oath covering all things, and binding him who took it to Isis alone, an oath that if it were forgot wrought upon the traitor the age-long doom of death in this world and woe in the worlds to come, till by slow steps, with pierced heart and bleeding feet, the holy height from which he had fallen should be climbed again.

At length it was finished and he said faintly,

"I swear! With fear and trembling still I swear!"

Then I beckoned to him with the *sistrum* of which the little shaken bells made a faint compelling music that already he had learned to follow, and he came and kneeled before me. There I laid the Cross of Life upon his head and gave him blessing, laid it upon his lips and gave him wisdom, laid it upon his heart and gave him existence for thousands upon thousands of years. All these things I did in the name and with the strength of Isis the Mother.

Came the last rite, the greeting of the Mother to her child new-born in spirit, the rite of the Kiss of welcome. At that moment supreme a light fell on me from above: perchance it came from Heaven, perchance it was an art of the watching priests; I do not know. At least it fell upon me illumining my glittering robes and jewelled headdress with a soft splendour in the darkness of that shrine. At that moment, too, at a touch my veil fell down, so that the moonlight struck full upon my face making it mystical and lovely in the frame of my flowing hair.

The priest new-ordained lifted his bent head that I might consecrate his brow with the Kiss of welcome, and his hood fell back. The moonlight shone on his face also, his beautiful face like to that of a sculptured Grecian god, shapely, fine-featured, large-eyed, and crowned with little golden curls—for as yet he was unshorn; yes, a face more beautiful than that which I had seen on any man, set above a warrior's tall and sinewy form.

By Isis! I knew this face; it was that which had haunted me from childhood, that which often I had seen in a dream of halls beyond the earth, that of a man who in this dream had been sworn to me to complete my womanhood. Oh! I could not doubt, it was the same,

the very same, and looking on it, the curse of Aphrodite
fell upon me and for the first time I knew the madness
of our mortal flesh. Yea, my being was rent and shattered like a cedar beneath the lightning stroke; I was
smitten through and through. I, the priestess of Isis,
proud and pure, was as lost as my village maid within
her lover's arms.

The man, too! He saw me and his aspect changed;
the holy fervour went out of his eyes and into them entered something more human, something more fateful.
It was as though he, too, remembered—I know not
what.

With a mighty effort of the will, aware that the eyes
of the goddess and perchance of her priests also were
upon me, I conquered myself and with beating heart
and heaving breast bent down to touch his brow with
the Kiss of ceremony. Yet, I know not how—I know
not if the fault were his or mine or perchance of both of
us—it was his *lips* I touched, not his brow, just touched
them and no more.

It was nothing, or at any rate but a little thing, in one
instant come and gone, and yet to me it was all. For in
that touch I broke my holy vows, and he, new-sworn to
the worship of the goddess, broke his, yes, in the very
act of sacrifice. What drove us to it? I do not know, but
once again I thought I heard that low, triumphant
laughter, and it came into my mind that we were the
sport of an indomitable power greater than ourselves
and all the oaths that mortals swear to gods or men.

I waved my sceptre. The new-made priest arose,
bowed and withdrew, I wondering of whom he was the
priest—of Isis or of Aphrodite. The singing of a distant
choir broke out upon the silence, the heirophants came
and led him away to be of their company till his death:
the ceremony was ended. My attendants, arrayed as the
goddesses Hathor and Nut, conducted me from the
shrine. I was unrobed of my sacred panoplies and once
more from a goddess became a woman, and as a
woman I sought my couch and wept and wept.

For had I not at the first temptation in my heart broken the law and betrayed the trust of her who, as then I believed, is and was and shall be; her whose veil no mortal man had lifted, the Mother of the sun and all its stars?

CHAPTER V

~

The Summons

NONE knew my fault. Yet I knew, and what is known to one soul is known to all souls, since one is all and all are one. Moreover, it was known to That which begets souls, That from which they come and to which they return again, again to come, as Plato, the great philosopher, who died before my day, has taught us in his writings. Also it was known to that accursed priest who was the cause and partner of my crime. I was overcome; I was eaten up with shame, I who thought myself purer than the mountain snows; as indeed I was and, in the flesh, to this hour have remained.

Soon I could no longer bear my torment. To Noot I went, Noot the high-priest, my counsellor and master, and in a secret place kneeling on my knees, there I told him all.

He hearkened with a little smile upon his withered face, then answered,

"Daughter, in your honesty you do but reveal that which I knew—how I knew it matters not. And now take comfort, since the blame is not altogether yours; or even that of this new-made priest, whose foot was caught in the same snare. You worship Isis, as I do, but what is Isis whom we portray on earth as a woman glorious above all women? Is she not Nature's self, the universal Mother, the Supreme in whom all gods and goddesses have a part? She wars on Aphrodite, it is true, yet does not that mean that in verity she wars upon herself? And are we not as Isis is, not one but many poured into a single mould, for do we not all war upon ourselves? Believe me, Daughter, the human heart is a great battleground where the higher and the lower parts of us fight with spiritual spears and arrows, till one side or the other wins victory and hoists the banner of good or evil, of Isis or of Set. Only out of struggle comes perfectness; that which has never struggled is a dead creature from whom little may be hoped. The ore must be melted in the fire and lo! the most of it is dross, refuse to be thrown away. Had it never known the fire, there could be no pure gold to adorn the brows of Heaven, nor even copper and iron to shape the swords of men. Rejoice, then, that you have felt the hurt of fire."

"Master," I answered, "Lord of Wisdom to whom alone Ayesha bows the knee, your words are true and comfortable, yet bethink you, and if it is permitted, interpret me this riddle. I dreamed a dream of the time before my earthly days—you know it well for I have told it to you. I dreamed of a place in Heaven and of two goddesses matched against each other and of a command that was laid upon me to bring woe upon those who had deserted the one and turned to the other. Now if they were parts of a single whole, why should this command be laid upon me?"

"Daughter, in your dream you were ordained to be a Sword of Vengeance, not because the Egyptians turned from one part of the holy Unity to another part of that Unity, but because they have become corrupt and faithless, worshipping no gods save themselves and following after that which is low, not that which is high. Such is my answer, yet of the truth or the falsehood of that dream I say nothing. Perchance it was but a dream."

"Perchance, Master. Yet in that dream, true or false, I saw a face, and lo! a few nights gone I, draped as Isis in the shrine, I saw that face again and knew it; knew also that with it my fate is intertwined. What of this?"

"Daugher, who are we that we should read the mysteries of Fate, we who know not whence we come nor whither we go, nor what we have been, nor why we are? It may be that you have some mission toward the spirit that is clothed in the flesh of yonder man. It may be that you are destined to uplift that spirit, and in so doing yourself to be trodden down. If so, I say that in the end you shall rise again and bear him upward with you."

He paused, and I knelt silent, pondering the prophecy, for such I knew it well to be. Then again he spoke, "You heard a laughter in the shrine, yet there was no laughter save that of the evil in your own heart, mocking and triumphant. Such laughter mayhap you will often hear, but while you can hear it and repent, be not dismayed. When the ears of the soul grow deaf then utter loss is near; while they are open, hope remains. Those who still strive can never wholly fall. Fate rules us every one, yet within the circle of that Fate power is given to us to work out our redemption. I have finished. Ask me no more."

"What punishment, Master?" I asked.

"Daughter, this. For a while look no more upon that man. I say for a while, since with you I hold that his destiny and yours are intertwined. I have a command for you: that presently you accompany me hence to lands beyond the seas. Now, go rest, and in rest find forgetfulness."

So I went, wondering yet comforted, though I knew well that Noot the Holy had not told me all, no, nor yet the half of what he knew. For often those to whom the gods give vision are forbid to speak it, lest, as in the old Hebrew parable, men should eat of the tree of knowledge and grow like to them. Or perchance they cannot speak it, since it comes to them in a tongue which may not be rendered in the words that the passer-by would understand. So indeed it is with me to-day.

Thus it came about that soon I and my master, Noot, left Philæ and as before travelled the Nile disguised. Never since then have my eyes looked upon that island and its holy fane which Holly, who has visited it, tells me is now a ruin with stark, Hathor-headed columns standing here and there amongst the tumbled stones. He says, moreover, that his people who rule the land to-day

purpose to sink it beneath the Nile that the lands below
may be enriched and multiplied. Herein I see an alle-
gory; the temples of Isis are drowned and the learning
they held is lost in order that more food may grow to
feed the common and the ignorant. Yet to what end,
seeing that if there is more food, more men will come to
eat it, all of them common and ignorant, while Isis and
her wisdom are swallowed in the slime. Thus has it ever
been in Egypt, and doubtless elsewhere, for such is Nature's law. Food breeds multitudes and where carrion is,
there are flies, while in the deserts both are lacking. Yet
I think that the deserts and the few that wander on
them beneath the sun and stars are nearer far to God.

Once more disguised as merchants, I and Noot, my
master, took ship and visited far lands to see their state
and gather wisdom. We visited Rome, then breaking her
shackles and rising to her greatness. They were a great
people, those Romans that Noot out of his foresight told
me would one day rule the world. Or perhaps it was I
who told Noot, judging them by their qualities; I am not
sure. At least I loved them not, because of their rude
natures, their lack of arts and their love of power and
gain. Therefore when I had studied their language and
their politics I passed on.

We came to Greece and tarried there awhile, studying philosophies and other things. The Greeks I did
love, because they were beautiful and called forth
beauty from all they touched. Also they were brave who
defied the Persian might and had they but stood together, might have queened it on the earth. But they
would not, for ever State tore out the throat of State, so
that in the end all were undone and overwhelmed by a
multitude of commoner folk who held Greece before
them, for such was their destiny. Moreover, they worshipped gods made like themselves, with all the faults of
men grown greater and more vile, and told fables concerning them fit to please children, which I thought
strange in a people that could produce such philosophers and poets. Yet those gods had come down to
them from their fathers, and it is hard to shake off the

yoke of gods until some greater god appears and breaks
it with the hammer of war.

Here in Greece it was that I posed to its most famous
sculptor for a statute of Aphrodite, or rather it was a
mould of perfect Womanhood that I posed, desiring
that this sculptor, who pleased me, should have one
flawless model to copy in his future work, for which he
blessed me, naming that statue "Beauty's Self." Yet
when I visited him a while afterward I found that he
had changed this name to Aphrodite.

I was angered who did not desire that my loveliness
should be accredited to mine enemy and that of Isis
whom I served, and asked him why this had been done.

He answered, humbly enough, because of a dream in
which the Paphian had appeared to him and threatened
him with blindness unless he gave her own name to so
divine a face and form. Moreover, being in the thrall of
superstition he prayed me, even with tears, that thus it
might remain, since otherwise he must break that statue
and as he thought, be blinded as well. So out of pity I
let him have his way and even gave him my hand to kiss
in token of forgiveness.

Thus it comes about that Aphrodite unashamed
throughout the ages has taken the tribute of a million
eyes, clothed in a borrowed loveliness. So be it, since
what she had stolen is but a fraction of the truth. No
sculptor, however great, can mould the perfect out of
frozen stone.

From Greece, still disguised as a merchant and his
daughter, we wandered to Jerusalem, feigning to trade
in pearls and gems, since there I would study the religion of the Jews whereof I had heard so much. The
"City of Peace" it was called among the Egyptians of
old times, or so they interpreted its name, but never
found I one in which there was less of peace. Fierce-
faced were those Jews and quarrelsome; revengeful too
and ever waging war, public and private, upon one another. A peculiar people, as they name themselves, full
of hate, particularly of the stranger within their gates.
To trade with them was scarcely possible, because he
who sold them wares was always left the loser, though

for this I who sought their philosophy, not their gold, cared nothing.

So I turned myself to the study of their faith, and found that God, as they interpreted Him, was well-nigh as fierce as were his worshippers. Yet this I will say, that He was one God, not many, and a true God also, since otherwise how could his prophets have written so gloriously concerning Him? Moreover, it was their belief that He would come to earth and lead them to the conquest of the world. This, Holly tells me, has chanced though not in the shape they hoped, since the King who came would have led them but to the conquest of the evil that is in the hearts of men and to the knowledge of a life to be, in which they had small faith. Therefore they persecuted and slew Him as a malefactor after their cruel fashion, and what is now accepted by millions, so says Holly, they still reject.

I preached to them, for my heart burned in me at the sight of their sacrifices. Yes, I preached to them against the shedding of blood, telling them of a higher philosophy of gentleness and mercy. For a while they listened, then took up stones and stoned me, so that had I and Noot not been protected by Heaven, we should have been slain. After this affront I turned my back upon Jerusalem and its hook-nosed, fierce-eyed people, and went to Cyprus where I debated with the lewd priests of Aphrodite at Paphos. Thence I got me back to Egypt whence I had been absent many years.

At Naukratis priests of Isis who knew of our coming, how I cannot tell, perchance Noot had told them by messenger, or in a dream as he could do, met us and conducted us up the Nile to the temple of Isis at Memphis. Here we were received in state in the great hall of the temple and lo! at the head of those who welcomed us was the Greek Kallikrates, now by his holiness and zeal risen high in the service of the goddess.

When I saw him, beauteous as of old, my heart stood still and the blood rushed to my brow.

Yet I gave no sigh, treating him as a stranger on whom my eyes had never fallen until that hour. He for his part stared at me with a puzzled air, then shook his

head as one does who sees a face that he believes he has
met in dream and yet is doubtful. For be it remembered, this man had looked on me but once, when
robed as Isis I received him into the company of her
priests at Philæ, and then but for a moment in the light
of the moon. Perchance he still thought that it was the
goddess herself whom he saw thus and not a mortal. At
the least he did not know that I, the beauteous prophetess who came to Memphis after wandering through the
world, was the same as she who had sat upon the throne
of Isis at Philæ and whom by chance he had kissed
upon the lips. Mayhap even he did not remember the
kiss, or if he remembered, set it down as part of the
ceremonial. Thus, if I knew him but too well, to him I
was a stranger.

I bethought me of flight, knowing in my heart that to
me this man was as the fabled sword that hung above
the head of Damocles, though what harm I had to fear
from him, I did not know.

Again I sought the counsel of Noot who smiled and
answered,

"Have I not told you, Daughter, that perils must be
faced since those from which we flee will be swift to
overtake us? If Destiny has brought you and this man
together, be certain that it is for its own purposes.
Surely you have learned your lesson and steeled your
soul against all fleshly vanities."

"Yes, my Father," I answered proudly, "I have
learned my lesson and steeled my soul. Moreover, your
thought is my thought, nor will I turn my back on any
man. Here I bide, defying woman's weakness and all
the wiles of evil gods."

"Well spoken," answered Noot, and blessed me in
the ancient words. Yet as he did so I noted that he
sighed and shook his head.

For many a moon, I know not how many who, having all time at my command, seem to have lost its petty
count, I remained there in the temple at Memphis of
which soon I became the prophetess and the head of the
priestesses. Ere long the fame of my divinations spread

far and wide, so that from all the land those who sought wisdom or knowledge of the future would come to consult me, bringing great gifts to the goddess, though not one gem or piece of gold did Noot or I keep for ourselves, who indeed had no need of such common dross.

So I sat in a carven chair in the sanctuary, my diviner's bowl at my side, and uttered dark sayings like to those of the famous oracles of the Greeks at Delphi, many of which fulfilled themselves. For in truth, I think that there was a spirit in me—whether it came from the Heavens or elsewhere I do not know—which enabled me to read much that was passing upon the earth and even sometimes that which had not yet happened upon the earth. So the renown of the Lady Isis spread till I became a power in the land. Moreover, thus I learned many things, for those who consult an oracle, like those who seek the help of a physician, lay bare their souls, keeping no secret back.

Now at this time Egypt and all the countries round seethed with war like a pot boiling on the flames. For years Egypt had beaten off the attacks of the Persians, but now the Pharaoh Nectanebes, the second of that name who then sat upon the throne, the last native king who reigned upon the Nile, was threatened by Artaxerxes, that one of this accursed race who was named Ochus. This Persian Ochus had gathered a mighty force to subdue Egypt, hundreds of thousands of men, tens of thousands of horsemen, hundreds of triremes and of transport ships.

The last act of the tragedy had begun of which the end was to be the crushing of Egypt who never more should know a Pharaoh of her own blood and choosing. Of all these things I learned through those who came to consult the oracle of Isis, and much did I talk of them with Noot.

Now of myself during these long years of quiet and preparation for great events, I will say that ever my spirit grew in purity and strength. I put the things of earth behind me, I grew nearer to the Divine, and in the night time I communed with my soul which seemed to have become a part of that which is above the world.

The Greek, Kallikrates, I saw continually, but no word passed between us save such as had to do with matters of our faith and of the worship of Isis in whose service he now stood high. Never did we interchange a touch or a look of love. He was apart from me and I from him. And yet always in my heart I feared this man, this beautiful man, the warrior who had become a priest, for some prescience told me that he would bring disaster on my head, or I should bring it upon his, I knew not which.

So there we sat in the sanctuary, Noot the wise and aged, who yet never seemed to change, Kallikrates the priest, and I, and alone or together gave counsel to kings and captains, or uttered oracles. Clear seemed our sky and free from trouble, yet on the far horizon in my spirit I discerned the tempest clouds arising, the terrible clouds in which the lightnings played like the swords of Destiny that in a day to come were doomed to overwhelm and pierce us through.

Nectanebes the second, the Pharaoh, came to his palace at Memphis to gather troops from Upper Egypt and made great offerings to the gods, seeking their favour in the coming war. Now I saw him for the first time, a gray-haired, fat, heavy-jowled man, bald-headed, large-nosed, with great eyes like to those of an ox. Such was Nectanebes, the magician, the consorter with familiar spirits, named the Destroyer, a title which the gods who hated him must have given him in irony since himself he was doomed to be destroyed. But one good thing can I say of this Nectanebes, that he was a lover of the arts and raised glorious buildings to the gods. Learning that I, the high-priestess, had dwelt at Philæ, he came to consult me as to the beautiful temple with the Hathor-headed columns which he built there and through my counsel it was made perfect, for I drew its plans, or at least those of its adornments. Holly tells me that even as a ruin, although so small, there is no lovelier building in all Egypt.

Now this Pharaoh thought me a Greek and did not know that I was Arab and the daughter of him of Ozal in Yamen, whom his father, the first Nectanebes, had brought to his death because once long ago I had been refused as a wife to himself or to this son of his who now had succeeded him. Of these things doubtless he remembered little or nothing, since that was one of the smallest of Egypt's wars. But I, I remembered and swore that in payment for my father's blood I would bring his accursed House to ruin. Always also I received him veiled since I did not desire that he should look upon my beauty and inquire concerning my history; therefore, as a prophetess had a right to do, I received the Pharaoh veiled.

Often he came to visit me because he had learned that I was a mistress of Magic and he who practised magic much hoped that I would teach him secrets he did not know, and show him how to lay spells upon his enemies. This indeed I did, but the secrets that I taught him were evil and the spells were spears that when he threw them would fall back upon his head.

So the scene was set, and at length came the summons to begin the play with the watching world for audience.

A writing sealed with Pharaoh's seal was brought to the temple of Isis, commanding Noot the high-priest, and me, Ayesha, who now was named *Oracle-of-Isis,* and the Greek Kallikrates, Chief of the Ceremonies, whose office it was to assist me in my divinations, to attend the court of Pharaoh and there declare to him the future of the war as it should be revealed to us by the great goddess whom we served. At first we refused to go, whereupon there came another message which said that if we continued to refuse, we should be brought. The Pharaoh wished to offer no affront to Isis, the messenger declared, but the matter was urgent, as great things hung upon the revelations which we alone could make, and some of the kings and generals who were gathered in the temple as allies of Nectanebes, being the worshippers of other gods, could not set foot in the holy shrine of Isis.

Then, there being no help for it, we answered that we would come that very night at the rising of the moon.

Hastily consulting together we planned the words of

an oracle, double-edged words that yet prophesied good
to Nectanebes and encouraged him to war; for thus we
believed we should most quickly bring about his downfall.

Yet as those words were never spoken I will not write
them down.

CHAPTER VI

✣

The Divination

Accompanied by the priests and priestesses of Isis clad
in their robes and chanting the holy songs, I was borne
veiled to the palace of the Pharaoh in a litter, with its
curtains drawn. On my right hand walked Noot the
high-priest, white-bearded, venerable; and on my left
the Greek Kallikrates, Master of the Rites.

Thus we came to the palace of which the outer courts
were filled with Grecian soldiers of the guard, some of
whom in past years Kallikrates had once commanded,
although as a shaven priest of Isis, disguised in his white
robes, they knew him no more. These men stared at us,
ready to mock and yet afraid, as did Phœnicians, Sidonians, men of Cyprus, and others who were gathered
in the courts as though awaiting some great event.

In an outer hall a captain of the guard bade our escort of priests and priestesses to await our return, but
we three, that is I, Ayesha, Noot, and Kallikrates, were
summoned to the small banqueting chamber where
Nectanebes with a few of the most highly placed of his
guests sat at their feast. Among these were the King of
Sidon, two more kings from Cyprus, three Grecian generals, some great nobles of Egypt, and others. Also certain royal ladies were present, and among them one
who instantly drew my eyes to her. She was younger
than I—perchance there may have been ten years be-

tween us, tall, slender, and lovely in her dark fashion, with a strong, quiet face and large brooding eyes, soft as a deer's and rather blue than black in colour.

Suddenly as we entered I, who note all, saw these eyes grow frightened like to those of one who sees some spirit returned from the halls of Death; saw also the rich-hued face turn pale, then grow red again as the blood flowed back; saw the breast heave beneath the jewelled robes, so sharply that a flower fell from them, and the lips of coral part as though to utter some remembered name.

Wondering what had thus disturbed this beauteous royalty since I, being veiled, it could not have been the vision of myself, I glanced round and perceived that Kallikrates, who was on my left, but a little behind me, had become pale as a dead man and stood like one frozen into stone.

"Who is that royal woman?" I whispered to Noot through my veil, for royal I knew her to be by the Uræus circlet she wore upon her raven hair.

"Pharaoh's daughter, Amenartas," he whispered back, "whom the Greeks call *The Maiden* because she will take no man in marriage."

Then I remembered a certain confession that once I had heard sitting on the throne of the goddess Isis at Philæ, of how the penitent had loved a girl of the royal House of Egypt, and for her sake killed his own dear brother; remembered also that this penitent was none other than the priest Kallikrates. Now I understood all, and though Kallikrates was naught to me save a fellow servant of the goddess, I hated that Amenartas and became aware that between her and me there was war unending, though how and why I knew not.

Next I looked at a man clad in kingly robes who sat on Pharaoh's right. He was a large man of about five and forty years of age with dark, handsome face and shifting eyes; one with a jovial aspect which yet I felt to be but a mask covering a heart full of evil schemes. From his purple robe sewn with pearls and the style of his attire and headdress I guessed that this must be Tenes the Phœnician, King of the city of Sidon that was

reported the wealthiest in the world, which city, having
revolted, had joined Egypt in its war against the Persians. Instantly I weighed that man in the balance of my
mind and wrote him down as an ambitious rogue who
was also a coward and, as I judged from the many
charms he wore, full of superstition.

The others I had no time to study for at once the
Pharaoh began to speak.

"Greeting, Prophetess," he said, rising from his chair
and bowing to us, or rather to me, "Greeting, High-
priest of Isis, Queen of Heaven, Mistress of the World;
greeting also, Priest, Master of the Rites of Isis. Pharaoh thanks you all for thus promptly answering to his
summons, since this night Egypt needs your wisdom
more perchance than ever before in all the ages of its
history."

"Be pleased, O Pharaoh, to set out what you desire
of us, the servants of the eternal goddess," said Noot.

"This, High-priest: that you should declare the future
to us. Hearken! As you know, the great war has begun.
The mighty Tenes here, King of Sidon, my ally, by the
help of the Greeks I sent him, has defeated the Persians
and against these Cyprus also is in revolt. But now Artaxerxes Ochus has seized the throne of Persia, having
murdered all who stood between it and him, with the
help of Bagoas the eunuch, his counsellor and general.
He has raised a countless host and is pouring down
upon Sidon and upon Egypt. Therefore we would learn
how the war shall go and to what gods we must sacrifice
to secure the victory."

"O Pharaoh," answered Noot, "in bygone years when
your father sat upon the throne and I was the *Kherheb*,
yes, the first magician of Egypt, he asked me such questions as these, and having prayed to my goddess, I answered him in the words that she commanded. None
heard those words save your father himself, for he and I
were alone together. Yet there was that in them which
made him wroth so that he sought to kill me, and to
save my life I fled out of Egypt, going whither the goddess led me. Afterward I was called back to Egypt
where once more I am high-priest of Isis though the of-

fice of *Kherheb* is filled by another. How know I, Pharaoh, if I obey you as I obeyed your father, and again the goddess should utter prophecies which are not pleasing to the ears of kings, that once more my life may not be sought in payment?"

"I swear, High-priest," answered Nectanebes eagerly, "that whatever may be revealed by the goddess, you shall take no harm. I swear it by the name and throne of the holy Isis, to whom I will make great gifts, and all this company are witnesses of the oath. If it be broken, may the curse of Isis and of all the gods of Egypt fall upon the head of me and mine. Draw nigh now that I may touch you with my sceptre, thereby forgiving all that you have said or shall say against me or my House, and restoring to you your office of *Kherheb* of Egypt, whereof my father, who to-day is gathered in Osiris, robbed you."

So Noot drew near and Pharaoh touched him with his sceptre, a cedar wand surmounted with a little golden image of Horus, which he always carried because of his throne-name which signified *"Horus-of-Gold."* Moreover, he re-created him *Kherheb* and in token of it set upon his shoulders the gold chain from his own neck, and swore to him his place and power for life and the gift of an alabaster coffin wherein to lie after life was done. This sarcophagus, however, Noot refused, saying darkly that it was fated that he should sleep his last sleep far away from Egypt. Then he, Noot, drew back and as he went I saw Pharaoh's daughter rise and whisper awhile in her father's ear. He listened and nodded. Then he said,

"Come hither, priest who is named 'Lover-of-Isis' and Master of her rites, the royal Lady of Egypt says to me that in begone days when she was scarce a woman, she thinks that before you were a pirest, you held some command amongst the Greeks of my guard, as from your stature and bearing I can well believe. She says also that if her memory serves her, you slew some man in a quarrel and for this reason fled away and sought refuge with Isis. If such things happened I have forgotten them, nor do I ask concerning them. Let them lie.

Yet, lest you should be afraid that old tales may be told against you or vengeance wrought upon you, come hither also and receive pardon for the past, and protection and advancement for the future and with these a gift from Pharoah."

Now I marvelled at this lady's foresight and cunning which showed her how to take advantage of Pharaoh's mood and safeguard one who once had loved her, all of which told me that she must be a wise woman as well as beauteous. Also it told me that the worship of this man had been pleasing to her. Then Kallikrates drew near and was touched with the sceptre. Moreover, Pharaoh spoke to him in like words that he had spoken to Noot, pardoning him all and promising him much. Moreover, in token of his favour he gave him a gold cup of Grecian workmanship having two handles, that was chased about with the story of the loves of Aphrodite and Adonis, and boardered with a wreath of those anemones which were fabled to have sprung from his blood. This glorious, flower-like cup from which the guests, when we entered, were pledging themselves in wine of Cyprus, Pharaoh lifted from the board and sent to Kallikrates, a great gift which made it clear to me how deeply he desired to propitiate the goddess in the persons of her servants.

Lastly the private scribe was commanded to write down these decrees that he had spoken, which he did forthwith, sealing them with Pharaoh's seal and giving one copy to Noot whilst keeping the other to be filed among the records.

Thus Noot and Kallikrates were protected from all things, but to me, the Prophetess, nothing was said, as I thought for two reasons, first because I was known to Pharaoh, who as I have told, had often consulted me upon matters of magic, and secondly because as the "voice of the goddess" I was holy and above reward or punishment at the hands of man. Thus I thought, with how much truth shall be seen.

The gifts were received, the papyrus had been hidden away in the robe of Noot, and there was silence in the chamber. To me, Ayesha, this heavy silence was full of omen. My soul, made keen and fine with ceaseless contemplation of things that are above the earth, in that silence seemed to hear the breath of the watching gods of Egypt. To me it was as though they had gathered there to listen to the fate of this their ancient home on earth. Yes, I felt them about me; or at the least I felt a spirit stirring.

The company at the table drank no more wine and ceased from speech. They sat still staring in front of them and notwithstanding the glitter of the ornaments that proclaimed their royalty or rule, to me they were as dead men in a tomb. Only the Princess of Egypt, Amenartas, seemed to be alive and outside the circle of this doom, for I noted that her splendid eyes sought the face, the perfect, carven face of the priest Kallikrates and that though he stood with folded arms and gazed fixed upon the ground, he knew it, for now and again covertly he glanced back at her.

At length one of those guests could bear no more, and spoke. He was a close-lipped, war-worn Grecian general who afterward I learned was named Kleinios of Cos, the commander of Pharaoh's mercenary forces.

"By Zeus!" he cried, "are we men or are we stones, or are we shades in Hades? Let these diviners divine and have done, for I would get me to my wine again."

"Aye," broke in Tenes, King of Sidon. "Bid them divine, Pharaoh, since we have much to agree upon ere I sail at dawn."

Then all the company cried, *"Divine! Divine!"* save Amenartas only, who searched the face of Kallikrates with her eyes, as though she would learn what lay behind its cold and priestly mask.

"So be it," said Noot, "but first I pray Pharaoh to bid all mean men depart."

Pharaoh waved his sceptre and the butlers and attendants bowed and went. Then Noot motioned to Kallikrates, who thereon shook the *sistrum* that he bore and, in his rich, low voice, uttered a chant to the goddess, that which was used to summon her presence.

He ended his chant and Noot began to pray.

"Hear me, thy prophet, O thou who wast and art and

shalt be, thou in whose bosom is locked all the wisdom of heaven and earth," he prayed. "These kings and great ones desire knowledge, declare it unto them according to thy will. They desire truth—let them learn the truth in such fashion as thou shalt decree."

Then he was silent. None spoke, yet it seemed that a command came to the three of us, for suddenly Noot looked at the priest Kallikrates, a very strange look. Next the priest Kallikrates, rising from his knees, laid down the *sistrum* and taking the beautiful cup that Pharaoh had given him, went to the table and washed it with pure water from a silver ewer, then filled it to the brim from the ewer and brought it to me, Ayesha. Now I knew that I was commanded to gaze into that cup and to say what things I saw.

So I set it on the ground in front of me and kneeling, threw my veil over it and gazed into the water in the shallow golden cup.

For a little while I saw nothing, till presently a face formed in the water, the face of the royal lady, Amenartas, which stared up at me out of the cup. Yes, it stared hard and seemed to threaten me, for in its eyes were hate and vengeance. Then another face came and covered it, the face of Kallikrates the priest, and in its eyes were trouble and desire.

Now I knew that the goddess Isis, or perchance another, she of the Greeks, spoke to me of matters that had to do with myself and not with the fate of Egypt. In my heart I prayed to the Queen of Heaven to rid me of these visions, though to give me others I did not pray her, since it was my design to speak certain politic words which we had prepared.

Yet other visions came unsought, for some spirit possessed me, a spirit of truth and destiny. They were many and all of them terrible. I saw battlefields; I saw men fall in thousands, I saw cities in flames. I saw that false-eyed king, Tenes, dead. I saw the General, Kleinios of Cos, also dead, lying on a heap of Grecian slain. I saw the Pharaoh Nectanebes flying up Nile upon a boat—I knew it was up Nile because the current rippled against the prow of his ship, I saw him seized by black

savages and throttled with a rope till his tongue hung
out and the great round eyes started from his head. I
saw the temples of Egypt burning and a fierce-faced,
drunken king hacking at the statues of the gods with a
Persian sword and butchering the priests upon the altar.
Then I saw no more but a voice called in my ears,

"Death to Egypt! Death and desolation! Death to
her king, death to her priests, death to her gods! Finished, finished, all is finished!"

I cast the bowl from me. It overset but lo! there
flowed from it not water but blood, or dark-hued wine,
staining the white marble of the pavement. I stared at
it! All stared at this god-sent horror!

"A trick!" cried the Princess Amenartas. "She has
coloured the water behind the shelter of her veil."

The others too, especially the Greeks, took up the
cry, echoing,

"A trick, a brazen trick!"

Only I noted that Pharaoh was silent, Pharaoh who
knew that Ayesha, named *Isis-come-to-Earth,* did not
deal in tricks; Pharaoh who himself practised magic and
had seen such omens sent by Set. Lo! Pharaoh looked
afraid and spoke no word, only glared with his great
eyes at the stain upon the marble.

"What answer did the goddess give to your prayer,
Prophetess," asked Amenartas, sneering at me.

"This answer, royal Lady of Egypt," and I pointed to
the marble, "the answer of blood."

"Blood! Whose blood? That of the Persians?"

"Nay, Lady, that of many who sit at this feast and
who ere long shall sit at the table of Osiris, and of thousands who cling to them. Yet be comforted, Lady, not
your blood. I think that you have much mischief to
work ere you sit also at the table of Osiris, or mayhap
at that of Set," I added, giving thrust for thrust.

"Declare then their names, Seeress."

"Nay, I declare them not. Go, seek them for yourself,
Lady, or let Pharaoh your father seek, for is he not a
magician? though what god gives him vision I do not
know. You name me cheat, or rather you name the god-

dess cheat. Therefore the goddess is dumb and her prophetess is dumb."

"Aye, I name you cheat," she cried, who in her heart was mad with fear, "and cheat you are. Now let this temple hag who hides her hideousness behind a silken screen unveil that we may see her as she is, and let her be searched and the vase of dye be taken from her bosom or her robes."

"Aye, let her be searched," shouted the guests who were also afraid.

"No need to search, high lords," I said in a quavering voice, as though I too were overcome with fear. "I will obey the Princess. I will unveil, yet I beseech you all, make not a mock of me when you see me as I am. Once I was perchance as fair as that royal Lady who commands, but years of abstinence and the sleepless search for wisdom mar the features and wither the frame. Moreover, time touches the locks, such of them as remain to me, since these too grow thin with age. Yet I will unveil and the vase of precious dye shall be the prize of him who first can snatch it from my bosom or my robe."

"Aye," said one of them, it was the king Tenes, "and in payment for her trick we will make her drink what remains of it to give colour to her poor old carcase."

"Aye," I answered, "and I will drink what remains of it for I think the stuff is harmless. Oh! be not angry because a poor conjurer plays her tricks."

Now Noot stared at me as though he were about to speak. Then his face changed like to that of a man who of a sudden receives a command that others cannot hear. He let fall his eyes, remaining silent, and I, watching, knew that it was the will of the goddess, or at least Noot's will, that I should unveil.

I glanced at the priest Kallikrates but he stood still, looking like Apollo's self frozen into stone.

During this play I had loosened the fastenings of my veil and hood and now of a sudden I cast them from me, revealing myself clad as Isis, that is in little save a transparent, clinging robe fastened about my middle. On my breast, hanging from a chain of pearls, were her holy symbols carved in gems and gold, and on my head her vulture cap beneath which my tresses hung almost to my feet, having the golden feathers of the cap adorned with sapphires and with rubies and the uræus rising from it fashioned of glittering diamonds.

Aye, I unveiled and stood before them, my arms folded upon the jewelled girdle beneath my breast.

"Behold! Kings and Lords," I said, "the temple hag stands before you in such poor shape as it has pleased the gods to fashion her. Now let him who can see it, come, take the vase that hides this unveiled trickster's dye."

For a moment there was silence while those brutal men devoured my white loveliness with their eyes, taking count of every beauty of my perfect face and form. Amenartas stared at me and her ruddy cheeks went pale; yes, even the coral faded from her rich lips. Then from between those lips there burst these words:

"This is not a woman! This is the very goddess. Beware of her, ye men, for she is terrible."

"Nay, nay," I answered humbly, "I am but a poor mortal, not even royal like to yourself, Lady—but a poor mortal with some wits and wisdom, though perchance Isis for a while to your sight has touched me with her splendour. Come, take the vase ere I veil myself again."

Then those men went mad, all save Pharaoh, who sat brooding.

"Goddess or woman," they cried, "give her to us who henceforward can never look upon the beauty of another."

King Tenes rose, his coarse face afire and his shifting eyes fixed upon me greedily.

"By Baal and by Ashtoreth!" he cried, "goddess or woman, never have I seen such an one as this prophetess of Isis. Hearken, Pharaoh, before the feast we disputed together concerning a great sum of gold and in the end it was confessed by you that it was due to me in aid of my costs of war although, so you said, it could not be found in Egypt save by raiding the rich treasury of Isis. Perchance the goddess learned of this design of yours and by the way of answer sent us an evil oracle. I know not, but this I do know, that she sent you also a means to pay the debt without cost to yourself or the robbing of her sacred treasury. Give me this fair priestess to comfort me with her wisdom and otherwise"—here the company laughed coarsely—"and I will talk no more of the matter of that gold."

Pharaoh listened without raising his head, then looked on me with rolling eyes and answered:

"Which would anger the goddess most, King Tenes—to lose her gold or her prophetess?"

"The former as I think, Pharaoh, seeing that gold is scarce, and prophetesses—true or false—are many. Give her to me, I say."

"I cannot for my oath's sake, King Tenes."

"You swore an oath to yonder high-priest and to yonder man, who looks like a Grecian god clad in a priest's robe and is called Master-of-the-Rites, but to this lady you swore none."

"I swore the oath to Isis, King Tenes, and if I break it doubtless she will be avenged upon me. Go your way; the gold shall follow you to the last ounce, but the prophetess is not mine to give."

Now Tenes stared at me again and I, who hated him with all my soul, gave him back his stare with interest, though this did but seem to inflame him the more. Then he turned on Pharaoh furiously and answered in a cold voice,

"Hear me, Pharaoh. It is but a small matter, yet my mind is set upon this woman who knows the heart of the gods and can pour their wisdom into my ears. Therefore make your choice:

"In Sidon there are two factions of almost equal strength. One of them says 'Make an alliance with Egypt and fight the Persian Ochus whom already you have defeated once.' The other says 'Make an alliance with Ochus and as reward in a day to come sit on Pharaoh's throne!' I have taken the first counsel as you know. Yet it is not too late to change that counsel for a second which perchance would prove the wiser, if there be aught in yonder divination," and he pointed to the blood-stain upon the marble floor. Then he went on:

"Moreover, I have my captains about me at this board and those that serve me wait without with all my fleet, and therefore should it be changed I need not fear to tell you so and to your face. So I say to you that if you will not please me in this small matter, presently my ambassadors go forth to Susa with a message for the ear of Ochus to which it would rejoice you to listen, seeing that without the strong aid of Sidon and her fleets Egypt cannot conquer in this war."

Thus Tenes spoke and laid his hand upon the pommel of his short Phœnician sword.

Now the face of Pharaoh, bearded thus in his own city and at his own board, grew red with rage and I saw that he was about to answer this outland king, defying him as many of the great monarchs who filled his throne before him would have done. But ere he could speak his royal daughter Amenartas whispered in his ear and although I could not hear her words, I read their purport in her face. They were—"Tenes speaks truth. Without Sidon you cannot stand against the Persians and Egypt is lost. Let the woman go. Isis, understanding, will forgive, who otherwise must see the Persian Holy Fire burning on her altars."

Pharaoh heard and the anger written in his eyes was changed to trouble. Rolling them in his fashion he looked on Noot and said to him as one who asks a question,

"I swore an oath to you, *Kherheb,* and to yonder priest, but to the prophetess I swore no oath and perchance Egypt's fate hangs upon this business."

The old high-priest paused awhile like a man who awaits a message. If so, it seemed to come, for presently he answered in a quiet voice,

"Pharaoh is right; Egypt's fate hangs upon this business; also Pharaoh's fate; also that of King Tenes and many others. The only fate which is not touched, whether it be finished in this way or in that, is the fate of yonder seeress who is named *Isis-come-to-Earth,* since the goddess will protect her own. Settle the matter as you will, Pharaoh. Only settle it swiftly, because under our rule it is time that I and my company who wait without should return to the temple to make our nightly prayer and offerings to the goddess, the Queen of all the earth, the Queen of Pharaoh and of Egypt; the Queen of the King of Sidon, and in the end the Queen also of Artaxerxes Ochus, the Persian, as one day surely he shall learn."

Thus spoke Noot unconcernedly and hearing him, I laughed, for now I was sure that I had nothing to fear from Tenes or from any other man upon the earth. Therefore I laughed, which that company thought strange in one who was about to be borne away a slave, and bade Kallikrates give me my veil and hood, also the cloak that I had thrown off when I entered the banqueting hall.

He obeyed, and while he was assisting me to cover up my beauty in the folds of that veil, I noted that alone among all the men here present, this beauty did not seem to stir him at all. Had he been clothing a marble or an ivory image of the goddess, as every day it was his duty to do at sunrise, anointing it with perfumes and garlanding it with flowers, he could not have been less moved. Or perhaps so truly had the priest in him overcome the man that he had learned to cloak all the feelings of a man. Or perhaps it was because that royal Amenartas watched his every movement with her eyes. I know not, but this I do know, that his calm angered me and it came into my mind that were I not the head-priestess of Isis and sworn to her, there should be a different tale to tell. Yes, even in that moment of destiny this came into my mind, which shows that in my soul I had not forgotten the meeting of our lips in yonder shrine at Philæ. At least I have often thought so since, I, who have had much time for thought.

"Priestess, you are mine," cried King Tenes in triumph. "Make ready to sail with me for Sidon within an hour."

"Do you think that I am yours, King Tenes?" I asked in a musing voice as I fastened the folds of my veil and arranged the hood. "If so, I hold otherwise. I hold that I, Ayesha, a free-born lady of the ancient Arab blood, am not the slave of any Phœnician who for a little while chances to be a king, but of her who is the Queen of kings, Isis the Mother. Nay, Tenes, I am more, I am Isis herself, *Isis-come-to-Earth*. It seems that go with you I must, since such is the will of the goddess, but, Phœnician, take heed. Should you dare to befoul me even with a touch, I tell you that I have strength at my command and that ere long Sidon shall lack a king and Set shall gain a subject. For your own sake therefore and for that of Sidon, think again and let me be!"

Now the great jaws of Tenes fell and he stared at me open-mouthed.

"Yet you shall go with me," he muttered thickly, "and for the rest Ashtoreth rules in Sidon, not Isis, for know that there are two Queens of Heaven."

"Aye, Tenes, a false queen and a true, and let the false beware of the true."

Then I turned to Nectanebes and said,

"Is it still your command, O Pharaoh, that I accompany this ally of yours to Sidon? Bethink you ere you answer, since much hangs upon your words."

"Yea, Priestess, it must be so. I have spoken and my decree is recorded. The fate of Egypt is more than that of any priestess and doubtless King Tenes will treat you well. If not, you say that you have strength to defend yourself against him."

Now as I answered, I laughed lightly and the sound of my laughter was like the tinkle of falling silver.

"So be it, Pharaoh. To me it is nothing; indeed I would see Sidon, the glorious city, while she still is Sidon, home of merchants, mistress of the seas. Still ere I go, shall I tell you something, Pharaoh, of what was shewn to me in yonder bowl before its water was turned to blood—by dye from that vase which none of you has found? If I remember right, for as you who practise magic, know, Pharaoh, such visions fade quickly like dreams at dawn—I say that if I remember right, it had to do with the fate of a great king. Have you ever seen a king, O Pharaoh, when in place of the chain of royalty a collar of rope is set about his throat and drawn hard till the tongue is thrust from the royal mouth and the royal eyes start from their sockets? Nay? Then shall I draw his picture? Perchance in days to come you would know it again?"

"Witch, accursed witch!" shouted Pharaoh. "Take her, Tenes, and begone, though sooner would I nurture a viper in my bosom," and rising from the board, he turned and fled away.

Again I laughed as I answered,

"I must go, but it seems that Pharaoh has gone first. Royal Amenartas, watch the good god, your father, for I think that he is too superstitious and that which men believe fulfils itself upon them."

Then I went to Noot and spoke with him—few words for already the guards were advancing upon me.

"Fear nothing, Daughter," he said, "you are safe."

"I know that I am safe, Master, yet be ready to come to my aid when I call; as my spirit tells me that call I shall."

He bent his head and the guards came up. As I went I glanced at the priest Kallikrates, who taking no note of me or of my fate, still stood staring at the royal Amenartas like a statue cut in stone, while she stared back at him.

CHAPTER VII

✇

The Quelling of the Storm

THEY set me on board a great ship, on the prow of which were images of certain gods of the Phœnicians, called by the Greeks *Pataeci,* not unlike to that which the Egyptians worshipped by the name of Bes, before which images burned fire. There was a royal cabin in that ship which was given to me, and with it splendid robes and furnishings of gold for my table.

At dawn we cast off from the quay of the white-walled city while thousands of the worshippers of Isis who learned that I was being taken from them, stood upon the quay and wailed, crying that the *Mouth-of-Isis* was sent away to slavery and that where her "Mouth" went, there the goddess would follow, leaving vengeance to fall upon their heads. For that the head-priestess of Isis should be given into the hands of barbarians and their foreign gods was such a crime as had not been known in Egypt.

Therefore they wailed, prophesying evil, and I stood upon the stern alone in my white robes, veiled, and hearkened to them, for none dared to come near to me. Yes, I hearkened and blessed them with my hands, whereat they knelt and wailed the more.

When at last we had passed down the Nile and were out upon the great sea, sailing swiftly for Sidon over quiet waters, I, Ayesha, having taken counsel of the goddess and of my woman's craft, sent for King Tenes, who was also on board the ship, and received him in his own cabin that had been given up to me.

For my heart was black with rage against him, and against Nectanebes, Pharaoh of Egypt, who had betrayed me, and in my heart I swore that I would destroy them both. Yes, there I, the captive, sat and received the captor king in his own cabin, purposing his doom, though how this was to be accomplished as yet I did not know.

"O King," I said, "I, your slave who, when not a slave, was high-priestess of Isis in Egypt and her seeress, into whose breast the goddess poured her wisdom and her secrets, as indeed still she does, would speak with you, and since I could not come to you among so many men, have prayed your Majesty to come to me. What would you do with me, King Tenes, since it has pleased you to force Pharaoh to give me into your keeping? Is it an oracle that you desire concerning your fate or that of your country in the war? If so, I will——"

"Nay, Priestess," he broke in hurriedly, "of your oracles I and others have had enough. They are bitter bread for daily food. Keep them, I pray you, to nurture your own soul."

"What would you of me then, King Tenes, that you have been at such pains to steal me away from Egypt, even threatening Pharaoh to break your solemn pact with him if he did not give me into your hands, me, the snared bird, who by chance was left out of his oath to the high-priest and Isis's officer, the Greek."

"Lady Ayesha," blurted out Tenes, "that I have learned to be by birth, daughter of Yarab, once ruler of Ozal, upon whom, with the Egyptians, I made war in the past and brought to his death, because of *you*, Lady, tell me, you who are wise, what would any man of you who had beheld your beauty as I saw it some nights gone?"

"Man, being man, that is, a ravening beast fashioned like a god in shape but not in soul, would make me his prey, Tenes. Such at least was the desire of the first Nectanebes whom you aided with the ships of Sidon to destroy my father, and of many since his time."

"Good. Well, I who am a man and something more, being not a god indeed, but a great king, would make you my prey, as you say, for to tell truth, having once looked on you I seek no other woman in the whole world."

Now I threw back my veil and studied him with my eyes.

"So you would take me for your queen, Tenes? Indeed I guessed as much. But what would your other queen, for doubtless you have one, say to this, O King?"

"My queen!" he said in an astonished voice, "my queen?"

"Surely, Tenes, you would scarcely dare to proffer less than queenship to such a one as I?"

"May be not. Well, let us say that I would make you my queen, since in Sidon it is not difficult to be rid of others of whom one may be weary; that is, it is not difficult to a king who also is high-priest of Baal and of Ashtoreth. Yes, yes, I am sure that I would make you my queen. I will offer it to you in writing if you desire."

"Aye, I do desire it, King, and that there may be no faults or traps in it, I myself will draw up the writing for you to sign. Only I doubt much whether I shall accept the offer if it is made."

"Why not, Lady? Is it a small thing to be Queen of Sidon?"

"For Ayesha, daughter of Yarab, high-priestess and prophetess of Isis, the wisest and most beauteous woman in the world, one who has never turned to look on man, it is a very small thing indeed, King Tenes. It is so small a thing that I will not deign to accept that proffered crown of yours, unless——"

"Unless what, Lady?"

"Unless it is made larger, King, so large and wide that she who wears it holds rule over all the earth."

"By Baal, Ashtoreth, and Moloch, all three of them, what mean you, Woman?"

"What I say, Man. I mean that when you are monarch, not of Sidon only, but of Egypt, Cyprus, Persia, and all the East, then perchance I will marry you, unless my fancy changes, as it may do, but certainly not before."

"Surely you are mad," he gasped. "How can I gather all these diadems upon a single brow? It is impossible."

"Aye, for you it is impossible, King Tenes, but for me it is possible. I can gather them and set them on your brow and on my own, I who have within me all the wisdom of the earth and much of the strength of Heaven. Understand that if I desire it and you follow my counsel, I can crown you emperor of the world, no less, but the question is, do I desire it and will you follow my counsel?"

"Lady, I swear that you are mad, unless in truth you are a goddess as they say in Egypt."

"Perchance I am somewhat of a goddess, and being so, marvel whether for any reward that can be given I shall debase myself by taking such a one as you to husband, King Tenes. Now, first, look on me well and answer whether you do indeed desire me and are ready to win me through toil and danger, or whether you will let me be. For know, Tenes, that though I seem to be your captive, you cannot snare me or do me violence. Lay but a finger on me against my will, and it shall be your death, since I have those to aid me whom you cannot see. Now look—and answer."

He looked, devouring me with his greedy eyes, then said,

"Of a truth I desire you more than anything on the earth, and since I may not do so otherwise, for I perceive that you are too strong for me, will take you at your own price. Yea, even if I must wait for years, still I will take you. Now tell me, most beauteous and most wise, what I must do, and swear to me that when I am king of all things you will wed me."

"Aye, Tenes, I swear that when you are king of all things I will wed you," I answered gently, laughing in my heart as I remembered that the first and last of all things, the greatest of all things, is—Death. "Hearken. You shall bring me to Sidon, not as a captive but as a strange goddess who has come to aid you and your people, and with honour shall you receive me in Sidon, causing your priests and priestesses to offer me worship and incense."

"And if so, what then?"

"Then, when I have studied your people and your preparations for war, we will take counsel together and I will show you how you may prevail. Tell me, Tenes, do you love Pharaoh Nectanebes?"

"Nay, Lady, I hate him who asks too much and gives too little, as I hated his father before him. Still we sleep in the same bed and prop up the same wall, and if one of us ceases to support the wall, the Persians will push it down on both."

"I understand. Yet even so it comes into my mind that perchance you would have been safer had you been pushing at the wall with the Persian Ochus and not holding it up with the Egyptian Nectanebes."

He glanced at me with his shifting eyes and answered,

"I have had that thought, as you know well, but having rebelled against Ochus, defeated his satraps, and slain thousands of his soldiers, or rather those of his father, if I climb the wall I might find spears waiting for me on the farther side. Lady, it is too late."

"Yes, King Tenes, perhaps it is too late; I will consider of the matter in your interest and my own. But first send me papyrus and writing tools that I may set down our pact. When you have approved and signed it, then I will consider of this and other matters and not before. For the while, farewell.

He rose and went unwillingly enough and when I was alone in the cabin I laughed in my heart. This fish had been easy to hook, but he was a large fish and strong, and I must beware lest he pull me into the deep sea where both might drown together. Moreover, the man was hateful to me, more so even than that ox-eyed, heavy-jowled Pharaoh, and his presence seemed to poison the air I breathed. Yet if I entered into this pact with him doubtless I must breathe it often, which vexed me who shrank from men and their desires, and above all from this man. Yet he had done me wrong and insult; he had helped the Egyptians to make war upon my people and he had taken me as a slave, me, Ayesha, thinking to make of me his woman, and cost what it might, I would pay him back as I would pay back Nectanebes who sold me.

The papyrus was brought to me by a slave and on it I wrote such a contract as I think was never signed by a king before. It was brief and ran thus:—

"Ayesha, daughter of Yarab, high-priestess of Isis, prophetess of Isis, known in Heaven and among her servants as *Isis-come-to-Earth,* and *Child of Wisdom,* to Tenes, King of Sidon.

"When you, Tenes, are king not only of Sidon but of Egypt, Cyprus, Persia, and the East, as I can make you, if you obey me in all things, then I, Ayesha, vow myself to you as your sole wife and queen. But if, ere this dignity is mine and yours, you dare even to touch my robe, then in the name of Isis and speaking with the voice of Isis, I, Ayesha, vow to you shame and death in the world and after it all the torments of hell and the jaws of the Devourer that await the judgment of Thoth on perjured souls beyond the Sun.

"Accepted and sealed by Ayesha, daughter of Yarab and by Tenes, King of Sidon."

Having copied this writing, I sent it to Tenes by the slave that he might study it. Awhile later he asked audience of me, and entering, said in a thick voice that only a madman would set his seal to such words.

I looked at him and answered that it was nothing to me whether he sealed or did not seal them; indeed that considering all, I should be better pleased if he let the bargain be.

He stared at me and rage took hold of him who was inflamed with wine.

"Who are you," he said, "that dare to talk thus to Tenes the King? You are but a woman clad in the robes of a priestess who pretend to powers you have not. Why should I not take you and have done?"

Now I mocked him, answering,

"Because I think you love to sit upon a throne better than to lie in a grave, Tenes, even, in a king's coffin. Still, as you desire to know more particularly, I will put your question to the goddess, who is not far from me even on this ship, and to-morrow when the sun is up I will pass on her words to you—that is, if you live to look upon to-morrow's sun, King Tenes," I added, staring him in the eyes.

These words seemed to sober him, for he turned pale and left the cabin, making a sign to avert the evil eye, but as I noted, taking the writing with him. Yet me he left perplexed and afraid, for my heart was not so bold as my mouth!

Now that night, whether by chance or by the will of Heaven, a great tempest sprang up suddenly. The captain of the trireme, a Greek or a half-Greek of Naukratis, Philo by name, whom now upon this ship I met for the first time, came himself to warn me, and to make sure that all was fast in my cabin. He was a quick-brained man, very active in his body and pleasant-faced, with a brown, pointed beard, who had seen some five and thirty years upon the earth. I had made inquiries concerning him from a certain slave who attended me, and was told that although he pretended to timidity, this Philo was in truth a great warrior and one of the best handlers of a bow upon the mouths of Nile, since that which he aimed at he always hit, even if it were a fowl in flight. Moreover, he was a very good seaman and, it was said, faithful to those he served and a worshipper of the gods.

"If so," I answered to that old slave, "how comes it that this Philo, instead of a humble captain, is not the first general or admiral among the Greeks, as a man of such quality should be?"

"Because, divine Lady, of certain faults," answered the slave, "such faults as have made of me what I am instead of the Count of a Nome upon the Nile as I should have been. This Philo has always thought more of the welfare of others than of his own, which is a very evil weakness; also he has loved women too much, which is a worse."

"Vile sins indeed," I said, "more particularly the second. The wise always think of themselves first, and the holy never love more than one woman, and her not too much, which perhaps is why the wise and the holy are so hateful and so dull. Bring this Philo to me; he is one whom I should wish to know."

In the end Philo came, though whether because my message had reached him, or because of the advancing storm, I am not certain. At least he came, and as he bowed before me, made a certain secret sign whereby I knew that he was a worshipper of Isis and one of high degree, though not of the highest, since when I tried him with that sign he could not answer. Still his rank in our great company was enough, and thenceforward we spoke to each other under the seal of the goddess, or as our phrase went in those days "within the shadow of her wings," as brother and sister might, or rather as mother and son.

That is, we did this after I had proved him further and brought to his mind the fate of those who betray the goddess and her ministers upon earth.

This Philo told me in a few words, that although the trireme was Egyptian and named *Hapi* after the god of Nile, for this voyage she was under charter to Tenes and for the most part manned with Sidonians, also with low fellows from Cyprus and the coast-ports. These like the Phœnician guards of Tenes, of whom there were fifty on the vessel, worshipped other gods than those of Egypt, that is, such of them as worshipped any gods at all.

Many of these men, Philo said warningly, murmured because a priestess of Isis was on board their ship, which they thought would anger the Phœnician gods of whom the images had been set upon the prow, as might lawfully be done when a vessel was hired by Tyre or Sidon.

I answered laughing that as he and I knew, Isis could hold her own against Baal, Astarte, and all their company. Then, changing my mien, I asked him suddenly what he meant.

"Only this, Holy one," he answered: "That if by chance the ship came into danger—and I like not the signs of the sky and the moaning of the black north wind with rocks not two leagues away upon our lee, then I say if this ship came into danger, as might chance this very night, for here gales grow suddenly—well, Holy one, you might be in danger also. In such cases, Holy one, sometimes the Phœnicians demand a sacrifice to the *Cabiri,* the great gods of the sea whom we do not worship."

"Is it so?" I answered coldly. "Then tell them that those who demand sacrifices often furnish the victims. Have no fear, my brother-in-the-goddess. But if trouble comes, call to me to help you."

Then I stretched out to him the *sistrum* that was part of my ornaments of office in which I had been brought aboard that ship, and he kissed it with his lips and went about his business.

Scarce had he gone when the black north wind began to blow. It blew fearfully, rising hour by hour and even minute by minute, till the gale was terrible. The rowers could no longer row, for the great seas broke their oars, of which the handles struck them, hurling them backward from the benches, and the sail they tried to hoist upon the mast was torn away and went flapping down the wind like a wounded gull. Thus continually the *Hapi* was driven in toward the coast of Syria where, still some miles away, the moonlight when it broke out between the clouds showed the white surf of breakers foaming on the iron rocks of Carmel.

Toward midnight the tall mast snapped in two like a rotten stick and went overboard, carrying with it certain men and crushing others. Then terror took hold of all the company upon this ship, so that they began to cry aloud who believed that black death was on them.

Now one shouted,

"We are bewitched! At this season there should be no such gale, it is against nature."

Another answered,

"Little wonder that we are bewitched who carry with us a sorceress of Egypt, one who hates our gods, wherefore they are angry."

This they said because they had heard the tale of the water turned to blood, also of the oracles I was wont to utter in the temples at Memphis. For in that city dwelt many Phœnicians who were great talkers and lovers of strange tales, though now, Holly tells me all their race is silent for ever and the only tales they hear are those of Gehenna.

Then arose another shout from many throats,

"Sacrifice the witch to the gods of the Sea. Throw her into the sea that they may take her and we may live to look upon to-morrow's sun!"

Next there was a rush toward the afterpart of the trireme where I was in the cabin. In the waist of the ship appeared the captain, Philo, as I saw watching from between the curtains, and with him a number of the crew who were Egyptians and faithful to him, perhaps six in all, not more. In his hands Philo held a bow, and a drawn short-sword was thrust through his belt.

He shouted to the mob of madmen to stand back, but they would not, and led by one of the guards of Tenes, crept forward. Philo knelt, resting his back against a water-cask, waiting till the ship steadied herself a little on the crest of a wave. Then he drew the bow and shot.

Very well and straight did he shoot, for the arrow pierced that leader of the guard of Tenes from breast to back, so that he fell down dead. Seeing this, the others grew afraid and stayed where they were, clinging to the bulwarks of the ship or whatever they could grasp with their hands.

Tenes appeared among them. They shouted to him and he shouted back to them, but what they said I could not hear because of the howling of the wind.

Philo crept into the cabin and his face was very heavy.

"Holy one," he said, "make ready to join Isis in the heavens. Fearing for his own life, that dog of a Sidonian king has consented to your sacrifice and I am come to die with you."

"The goddess thanks you, O great-hearted man, and I, her servant, thank you also," I said, smiling at him. "Yet have no fear, since my spirit tells me that neither I nor you shall die this night. Help me now and let us go forth and talk with these hissing snakes of Sidon."

"But what will you say to them, Holy one?"

"The goddess will teach me what to say," I answered, who in truth did not know what I should say. All I knew was that some spirit moved me to go forth and to talk with them.

So we went, I leaning upon Philo as it was hard to stand upon my feet, and came to the stump of the broken mast in the midst of the hollow ship, all the mob of the crew drawing back before me. Here with one arm I clung to the mast, and beckoned to them with the other in which I held the *sistrum* of our worship. They drew near, Tenes among them, his face covered by a cloak.

"Hearken!" I cried. "I learn that you would offer me, the Prophetess of Isis, as a sacrifice to your gods. Fools! Is not Isis greater than your gods? O Queen of Heaven! send a sign to show that thou art greater than these foreign gods!"

So I spoke and stared upward at the moon, for the wind had torn away my veil, and waited.

A great billow came and struck the forepart of the ship, burying it deep in green water. As she rose I saw two dark forms fly from her high-tossed prow and a voice cried,

"The guardian images have gone and the sacred fire is quenched!"

"Aye," I answered, "they are gone where you shall go, every one of you, if you dare to touch me. Know that I do not fear for my own life which cannot be taken from me, but for your lives I fear, and for Sidon, which presently shall lack a king—if you dare to touch me. Be silent now and though you deserve it not, I will pray Isis to save you."

Then gaping on me standing there like one inspired, as indeed I think I was, they were struck to silence and through the roaring gale and flying foam I prayed to Heaven to preserve that ship and those she bore from the grinding rocks on which the surf beat not a mile away.

A marvel happened, whether because the tempest had grown weary of its raging, or because That which hears the prayers of men had accepted my prayer for its own purposes, to this hour I know not. At least the marvel happened, for although the sea still beat and rushed, wave following wave, like white-maned, countless charging steeds, of a sudden the gale died down and there was calm between sky and sea.

"It has pleased the great goddess to hearken to me and to save your lives, yes, even the lives of you who would have murdered her priestess," I said in a quiet voice. "Now get you to your oars and row as never you rowed before, if you would hold the ship off yonder rocks."

They gasped. They stared with open mouths! One said,

"*Thou* art the goddess; *thou* art the very goddess! Pardon us, pardon us, thy slaves, O Queen of Heaven!"

Then they rushed to their oars and with toil and danger drew the *Hapi* past the promontory of Carmel where the water boiled upon the rocks, and out into the deep sea beyond.

"What did I say to you, Philo?" I said, as he led me
back to the cabin.

He made no answer, only lifting the hem of my garment, he pressed it to his brow.

CHAPTER VIII

~

The King of Sidon

NEXT morning the sun came up in a sky of perfect blue
and the *Hapi,* driven forward by the oars, since her
mast was gone, passed northward over a quiet sea. Not
a league away upon our right, gleaming like gold, were
the roofs of the glorious city of Tyre, set like a queen
upon her island throne, Tyre that as yet did not dream
of evil days when her marble palaces should melt in
flame and her merchant princes and citizens lie butchered by the thousand in her streets; Tyre the wanton,
the beauteous, the wealthy, who sucked riches from all
the lands.

Seeing our shattered state, a boat manned by red-
capped seamen came out from the Egyptian harbour to
learn if we needed help. But Philo shouted back to its
officer that, save for the loss of a mast and some men,
we had taken no harm in the gale and hoped ere night
to be safe in Sidon.

So the boat returned and we rowed on.

By midday we caught sight of the towers of Sidon
and within three more hours, the sea being calm, had
dropped anchor in the southern harbour.

Now after we left Tyre Tenes the King came to visit
me in my cabin. At the sight of him my gorge rose for I
remembered that this dog of a Sidonian had consented
to the demand of the sailors that I should be hurled into

the deep as a sacrifice to his gods. Yet I restrained my soul and received him smiling and unveiled.

"Hail, King Tenes," I said, "Isis has been very merciful to you in answer to my prayer; for know that never again did I think to look upon you living."

"You are great, Lady," he answered, staring at me with frightened yet devouring eyes. "I think that you are as great as that Isis whom you serve, if indeed you are not that Isis come to earth, as they name you in Egypt. Isis I know not who worship Ashtoreth, she who is also styled Tanith and Baaltis, and like your Isis, is an acknowledged Queen of Heaven, but you I know, and your power, for did you not cause the terrible tempest to cease last night and save us all from death upon the rocks of Carmel?"

"Aye, I did this, Tenes, having strength given to me, whence it matters not. It is strange to think, is it not?"—here I bent forward and stared him in the eyes—"that on board this ship there are men so cowardly and so evil that they took counsel to cast me to the deep as a sacrifice to their gods, and that had they done so, though me, had they known it, they could not harm, they themselves, every one of them, would have been that sacrifice."

Now he writhed and turned colour beneath my glance, but answered,

"Is it so, Lady? Name me those men and they shall be slain."

"Aye, King Tenes, without doubt they shall be slain, every one of them, since Isis does not forget a threat of murder against her priestess. Yet I name them not. Where is the need when already those names are written on the tablets of Heaven? Let them be till Fate finds them, since I would not have you in your rage stain your hands with their vile blood. But what would you with me, King?"

"You know well," he answered thickly. "I worship you. I am mad with love of you. When I saw you standing by the broken mast and making prayer, even then upon the edge of doom, my heart melted for you. I say that there is a raging fire in my breast that only you can quench," and he made as though he would fall upon his knees before me.

I motioned to him to remain seated, and answered,

"I remember, King, that you spoke in this same fashion before the storm and that, half in jest, I wrote certain terms upon which I would become your queen, namely, when you could give me rule over all the earth. Wisely, perhaps, to these terms you would not set your seal; indeed you asked me why you should not take me to be your toy, and to that question an answer came to you last night when the ship wallowed water-logged and on her lee you saw the billows spouting on the rocks of Carmel. Also the goddess has told me more of what would chance to you should you dare to lift a hand against her priestess. I tell you that it is horrible, so horrible that I spare you, since if you heard it, you would tremble. What need to talk of such a crime when such a judgment would follow hard upon its heels? So have done, Tenes, and learn that it is my pleasure to return to Egypt in this ship."

"Nay, nay!" he cried, "I cannot part with you; sooner would I lose my crown. I tell you that if I lost sight of you and hope of you, I should go mad——"

"Which perchance you may do yet, Tenes," I replied laughing, "if indeed you are not already mad after the fashion of tyrants who for the first time are robbed of that which they desire. You have my commands, so have done. I would speak with Philo the captain as to when he can be ready to sail for Nile."

"Hearken, Lady, hearken!" he said thickly. "I have the writing here. I will sign it in your presence if you swear to abide by it."

"It is so? Well, Tenes, I do not change my word. When you can crown me Queen of Phœnicia, Egypt, Persia, and the rest, as I can show you how to do, then I will take you for husband and reign as your sole wife. But until then never shall you dare so much as to touch me. Now I am weary, who last night slept so ill. Do you wish to seal the writing, for if so it shall be done before a witness whose life and welfare henceforth shall be as sacred to you as my own."

"Aye, aye, I will seal, I will seal," he said.

Then I clapped my hands and the slave who waited without appeared. I bade him summon Philo, the captain of the ship, and to bring wax. Presently Philo came and I told him what was needed of him. More, demanding the papyrus from Tenes, I read it to both of them, Philo listening with a stony stare of amazement. Then the wax was spread upon the papyrus and Tenes sealed it with his seal, which was a cylinder of lapis lazuli having images of gods upon it after the old Babylonian fashion. Also, beneath my own, he wrote his name in Phœnician letters which I could not read. Then Philo as witness wrote his, for being half a Greek, he knew this art, and sealed it with his seal, a scarab cut in cornelian by no mean artist, doubtless a Grecian, which scarab, he said, he had taken many years before from the finger of one whom he killed in battle. When I looked at what it left upon the wax, I laughed, for behold the device was that of a Diana, or perchance of nymph, shooting with an arrow a brute-faced faun that had surprised her at the bath. To my mind the face of that faun or satyr was very like to the face of Tenes, and Philo thought it also for I saw him glance from one to the other, and heard him mutter, "An omen! An omen!" beneath his breath in the Egyptian tongue which Tenes did not understand.

When the roll was signed Tenes would have taken it, but I answered,

"Nay, on that day when its conditions are fulfilled it shall be yours. But till then it is mine."

Still I promised to give him a copy of the writing, and with this he was, or feigned to be, content.

When Philo had gone Tenes asked me how he was to become ruler of the world and thus to win me.

I answered that I would tell him later in Sidon after I had thought and prayed. But one thing he must swear, namely, to listen to no counsels save my own, since otherwise he might lose me and with me all. He did so by his gods, being at that time so bemused that he would have sworn anything if thereby he might keep near to me. Moreover, he told me that it was his purpose to set me in a palace near his own, or perchance in a part of his own, that there he might visit me daily and learn my counsels.

I bowed my head and said, the more often the better, so long as he came for counsel and no more. Then I dismissed him and he went like any slave.

When he had gone once more I summoned Philo and, "under the wings of the goddess," that is, under an oath of secrecy to break which is death, I told him, my brother-in-Isis, the meaning of this play, namely that I would be avenged upon Tenes who had affronted me and the goddess, who also, in his cowardice, had proposed to sacrifice me in the deep, an offering to his false divinities. Moreover, I gave him that copy of the writing which I had made and, his charter being fulfilled, bade him get back to Egypt as soon as might be and deliver it to Noot, the high-priest of Isis, and with it all this story.

There at Memphis I bade him bide, having a great ship, this one or another, ready, manned with brave men, all of them followers of Isis, with whom Noot would furnish him, also with the moneys needful to hire or buy that ship. There he was to wait till my word came. How it would come I did not know as yet. Perchance this would be by messenger, or perchance I should talk with the spirit of Noot, by means at the command of those initiated in the highest mysteries of the goddess. At least when my word came he must sail at once and come to me at Sidon.

These things he swore to do. Moreover, I wrote a letter which afterward I gave to him to deliver to Noot.

We cast anchor in the harbour, hoisting the royal standard of Tenes as best we could on a tall pole at the prow. At once gilded barges, on board of which were generals and priests, put off from the quay, and watching from my cabin, I saw Tenes talk earnestly with these notables who from time to time glanced toward where I was hidden. Then a messenger came to pray me to be pleased to abide on board the ship till preparation had been made to receive me, a matter to which the king departed to attend. So I stayed there and spoke with Philo about many things, learning from him much concerning the Sidonians, their wealth and their strength in war.

Two hours later a barge arrived, the royal barge, I think, for it was glorious with silks and gold and the rowers wore blazoned uniforms. On board this barge was Tenes himself and with him, among others, priests who wore tall caps, also some priestesses. The king came and bowing, led me to a carpeted ladder by which I descended into the barge. As I went down its steps I said with a laugh,

"If some had won their way last night, O King, I should have left this ship in a very different fashion. Well, I forgive them, poor fools and cowards, but whether the goddess whom I serve will forgive them is another matter"—words at which I saw him wince.

Before I went also I stepped aside and again spoke to Philo who stood near the head of the ladder, cap in hand. That speech was short yet sufficient, being of but two words,

"Remember everything."

"To the death! Child of Wisdom," he answered.

"What says the mariner?" asked Tenes suspiciously.

"Naught, O King. That is, he only prays me to intercede with the goddess lest the fate of those who would have harmed me on this ship should overtake him also who is its captain."

Again Tenes winced and again I smiled.

We were rowed ashore, and there upon the quay waited a chariot drawn by milk-white horses in which chariot I was seated, splendidly apparelled men leading the horses. In front of me went the king in another chariot and behind followed an escort of guards.

Thus we proceeded through the glorious streets of Sidon and being moved thereto, I lifted my veil and stood up in the chariot as though I would see these better. Already the fame of my coming had spread abroad, so that those streets and the flat roofs of the houses were crowded with thousands of the people. These, when they saw my beauty, gasped with wonder and cried in their own tongue,

"No woman! No woman! A goddess indeed!"

Yet I thought that I heard others answer,

"Aye, a false goddess sent to Sidon to be her ruin."

True words indeed, though, as I think, inspired by hate and jealousy rather than from on high.

We came to a great and noble square, the Holy Place it was called, round which stood statues of those whom the Sidonians worshipped, Baal, Ashtoreth, and the rest of their dæmons. Moreover, with its back to a temple stood a huge and hideous god of brass, who in front of him, upon great hands which seemed to be discoloured with fire, held a curved tray whereof the inner edge rested on an opening in the belly of the figure. I asked of one who walked by the chariot what was the name of this god. He answered,

"Dagon whom some call Moloch, to whom the first-born are sacrificed by fire. See, the priests are storing the hollow place beneath with wood. Soon, doubtless, there will be a great offering."

Thenceforward I hated this people, for what could one born in Arabia and a servant of Isis, the holy and gentle, think of a race that offered sacrifice of those born of them to a dæmon? Yes, I looked on their faces, keen, handsome, and cruel, and hated them, one and all.

We came to the door of the palace where slaves ran forward, assisting me from the chariot. By it stood Tenes surrounded with glittering nobles and white-robed priests who stared at me doubtfully.

"Be pleased to enter my house, Lady, fearing nothing, for there you shall be well lodged and given of the best that Sidon has to offer," said Tenes.

"I thank you," I answered, bowing and letting fall my veil, "and I doubt it not, for what less than her best could Sidon give to the Daughter of Isis, the Queen of Heaven?"

Yes, thus I answered proudly, I who played a great game and staked all upon a throw.

"Here we have another Queen of Heaven and she is not named Isis," I heard one of the dark-browed priests mutter to a companion, thinking that I did not understand his words.

They led me into a glorious dwelling wherein were chambers more splendid than any that I had seen in my journeys through the Eastern world. Gold and gems were everywhere and on the walls hung priceless trappings dyed with the Tyrian purple of that costly sort to use which is the prerogative of kings. The very carpets on the floors shone like silk and were woven to things of beauty, while the lamps seemed to be hollowed from great gems.

"Who lodges in this place?" I asked of a slave when I was alone.

"Who but the Queen Beltis, divine one," answered the slave, bowing low before me.

"Where then is the Queen Beltis? I see her not."

"Nay, divine one, she visits her father at Jerusalem, whence she should return shortly. Indeed, the King has issued orders that other chambers should be prepared for her against her coming."

"Is it so?" I replied indifferently, but within my heart I wondered what this queen would say when she came to find her palace inhabited by a stranger and a rival.

Then to the sound of sweet music I ate from services of gold and drank out of jewelled cups, and afterward, being weary, who had rested little on that ship and was tempest-tossed, laid me down to sleep in a soft and scented bed guarded by women and by eunuchs.

"Easy enough," thought I to myself, "would it be for these to murder me, one unfriended and alone in a strange land," and because of this for a little felt afraid who at that time was but as other mortals are. On the ship I had feared nothing, for there was Philo, a brother of my faith, and with him some others who could be trusted. But here I was but as a lamb ringed round with wolves. Moreover, besides the wolves there was a lion, the king-brute Tenes, who sought to snare me, and whom I knew for a liar, not to be trusted whatever he might swear.

Yes, for a little while, perhaps for the first time in my life, and certainly for the last, that is, where my body was at stake, I felt somewhat afraid, so much so that I went to a window-place to watch the rising of the moon and to make my prayer to Isis of whom it was the symbol, that she would be pleased to protect me in this city whither by her will I had wandered.

This window looked out upon that flame-lit square which was called the Holy Place. There I noted that thousands of those of Sidon were gathered, some of them staring up at the palace to which it was known I had been taken, pointing and talking. The most of them, however, wandered round the great brazen statue, that hideous, devil-faced thing whereof I have written, and when they could, caught one of the priests by the arm and put questions to him.

Among these, I noticed, were many women, some of whom from their mien seemed to be noble, whose faces were strange to see. Defiant they were, yet in a way proud, as might be the faces of those about to do some great deed. Moreover, many of these women led or carried children, which little ones they showed to the priests who smiled horribly and nodded approval, patting the children on the arm and even kissing them.

One lady, after her son had received such a kiss, wailed aloud and, clasping him to her breast, turned and fled away, whereon the priest cursed her and the other women shouted "Shame!" then strove to cover up the misery that peeped out of their eyes by singing some fierce song in honour of their gods.

Studying this scene, presently the meaning of it came home to me. Those children were doomed to be sacrificed to the brazen Dagon or Moloch whereof I remembered having heard in Jerusalem as a devil to whom the firstborn were passed through the fire. Yes, and these the mothers had brought them there that they might look upon the god and grow accustomed to the sight of him.

Oh! it was horrible, and my heart chilled at the thought of such iniquity. What reward from Heaven, I marvelled, for a people who practised such a faith?

As I marvelled an answer seemed to come to me. The sun had sunk but there were heavy clouds in the

sky above upon which struck its departing rays. Thence
they were reflected on to the city and chiefly upon this
Holy Place, as it was called, and the brazen image that
sat there before the temple. Yes, from those clouds
came red light that filled the air and the city beneath
and the Holy Place, as it were with a mist of blood. It
was as though everything were dyed with blood, and in
the midst, ringed round with torches, glowed Moloch, a
god of blood!

Then I knew that Sidon was doomed to be drowned
in blood; that such was the decree of Heaven and that I,
Ayesha, was the instrument appointed to loose this
spear of death upon her beauteous, sinful breast. I shivered at the thought, I who love not cruelty or to spend
the lives of men, though it was true that I would kill
Tenes. Yet what was I but the lightning in the hands of
Fate, and can the lightning choose where it will strike?
Must it not fall whither it is drawn? To this end had I
been sent to earth, namely that I might bring woe upon
false Egypt and the peoples who clung to her.

Such was the burden of that dream by which my
sleep was haunted, such too the command of Heaven
which again and again Noot the prophet had whispered
in my ear. I must destroy Egypt, or rather her apostate
priests and rulers, and afterward once more build up the
worship of Isis in some far land that should be revealed
to me. Such was my mission, whereof it was decreed
that I should fulfil the first part and because of my sin
leave the rest undone.

Holly the learned tells me that the new faith he follows, to which I will not listen who am weary of reli-
gions and their changeful march toward a changeless
end, writes it down that free will is given to man, that
he is able to choose this path and reject the other; that
he is the master of his own soul which he can guide here
or there as the horseman guides his steed or Philo
steered his ship.

And yet he read to me from the writings of one of the
great apostles of that faith, a certain holy one named
Paulus, words which declared that man is predestined
ere he was born to eternal life or eternal death, to the

glory of the light or the unfathomed dark. To me these doctrines seem to war one upon the other, though for aught I know both may be true, seeing that within the circle of the starry spheres and the vast soul of That which made them, there is room for a multitude of truths whereof the shadows falling upon the gross earth take a thousand shapes of error.

Moreover, I hold that whatever is, is true because it is, and that men do but tangle themselves in seeming differences that are only varying lights darting from the eternal eyes of Truth. On all hearts shine those eyes, but none beholds them as his brother does, for to each they burn as a separate torch of different-coloured flame. Therefore it is that men worship many gods not knowing that these are the same God whose hands hold all things.

Thus I sum up the matter. At least through the millions of the ages and the multitudes of lives man may attain to freedom if his face be set that way of his own desire. Yet in his little hour on the earth, that falsely he believes his all, looking from birth to death and the blackness that bounds them both, he is not free but a part of Strengths that are greater than his own. Have I, Ayesha, been free, I who chose the holy path and fell from it into Nature's gulfs? Did I desire to fall? Did I not desire to climb that steep road to the heights of Heaven and sit enthroned upon the topmost snows of purity and peace? And yet another Might hurled me thence and now it is my fate to climb again; by slow and painful steps to climb eternally.

But of these things I will speak in their season, telling what is the price those pay who seek to overleap the bounds that hem us in and to match their pettiness against divine decrees.

These in the midst of the red light that filled Sidon like a bowl with blood and shone on me and all; on me, the priestess, on the brazen Dagon towering up against me, on fantastic, lamp-lit temples and palaces, on the great place about which they stood and the fierce-faced multitude that wandered on its marble pavements, there in the window-opening I knelt me

down and prayed, lifting my face to the pure heavens
above. To Isis did I pray, as an idolater prays to an
image in a cave, because Isis was my symbol, or rather
to That which is as far above Isis as Isis was above me.
For I prayed to the Soul of that Universe whereof my
eyes could see a part in the arching skies, and of this
Soul what was Isis but as one golden thread in a glittering garment that wraps the majesty of God? And what
then was I and what were those fierce-faced worshippers of Dagon?

Oh! in that hour of dedication, for such I felt it to
be, these truths came home to my heart as never they
had done before. And this was the sum of them, that I
and all I could see and know were but as impalpable
grains of dust, not sufficient to cause the delicately
hung balance wherein the wilfulness of the world is
poised against the decrees of the immortal Law to vary
by a hair's breadth. Still I prayed and because that
which is small yet ever contains that which is smaller,
and the smaller finds a god in the small, as the small
does in the great, from that prayer I won comfort.

My prayer finished I laid me down to rest in the
golden bed of Beltis, the queen into whose place I had
been thrust, bethinking me how many and near were
the dangers by which I was surrounded. That brute king
desired me for a prey and here in his palace I lay in the
hollow of his hand. He had the key to all my doors; the
servants who stood about them were his creatures whom
at a nod he could send to death. I was a stranger in a
strange land, utterly unfriended, for Philo was far off
upon his ship; there was nothing between me and him
save the impalpable veil of fear which I had woven between us by the strength of my spirit. I was a prize to be
taken, unarmoured, without javelin or arrow to protect
me, with nothing, nothing save that veil of fear. If he
chose to break through it, daring my curse and that of
my goddess, he could do so. Then the curse would fall
indeed, but it would be too late to save me, and I the
proud and pure, must pass hence defiled, as pass I
would. Still trusting to the goddess, or rather to the part

of her which dwelt in me, or to That which was above us both, I laid me down and slept.

At midnight I awoke. The light of the moon flowing through the window-places flooded the splendid chamber, catching on the cornices of gold, the polished mirrors and the silver vessels. The door opened and through it wrapped in a dark cloak came Tenes. Though his face was hidden I knew him by his heavy shape and shambling step. He crept toward me like a wolf upon a sleeping lamb. There I lay in the golden bed illumined by the moon, and watched through the web of my outstretched hair, my hand upon the dagger that was buckled to my girdle. He drew near, he bent over me breathing heavily, and his eyes devoured my beauty. Still I feigned sleep and watched him, while my fingers closed upon the handle of the dagger. He unbuckled his cloak, revealing his hook-nosed visage, and a draught of wind seemed to catch it, for it flapped and fell from his shoulders, though I felt no wind. He stooped as though to lift it, and it would seem came face to face with I know not what. Perchance it was the goddess invisible to me. Perchance it was some picture of his own death to come. I cannot say. At least his shifting eyes sank in till they seemed to vanish beneath the hairy brows, and his fat cheeks grew pallid as though the blood were draining from them by a mortal wound. Words came hissing from his thick lips and they were,

"Horrible! Horrible! She is indeed divine, for gods and ghosts protect her! Horrible! Death walks the air!"

Then he reeled from the room dragging the cloak after him, and knowing that I had no more to fear, I returned thanks to the guardian spirits and slept sweetly. The danger that I dreaded had drawn near and passed—to return no more.

CHAPTER IX

✧

Dagon Takes His Sacrifice

THE sun arose on Sidon and drove away the terrors of the dark. I too arose and was led to the bath by slaves. Then those slaves clothed me in the silks of Cyprus, over which I threw a new veil bordered with the purple of Tyre. More, they brought me gifts from the King, priceless jewels, pearls with rubies and sapphires set in gold. Those I laid aside who would not wear his gems. Then, in another chamber, I ate as before of meats delicately served by bowing maidens. Scarce had I finished my meal of fish from the sea and fruit and snow-cooled water drunk from a crystal cup, when a eunuch came saying the King Tenes craved audience of me.

"Let him enter," I answered.

Presently he stood before me, making salutation, and asked me with feigned carelessness whether I had rested well.

"Aye, great King," I answered, "well enough, save for a single, very vivid dream. I dreamed that Set, the god of Evil, rose out of the darkness of hell wearing the shape of a man whose face I could not see, and that this fiend would have seized me and dragged me down into the pit of hell. I was afraid, and while I lay as one in a net, there came to me a vision of the divine Isis who said,

" 'Where is thy faith, Daughter? If I saved thee on the ship, giving thee the lives of all her company, cannot I save thee now and always? Fiends shall not harm thee, nor men; swords shall not pierce thee nor fires burn, and if any would lay hands on thee, on them I give thee power to call down my vengeance and to cast

91

them to the jaws of the Devourer who, awaiting evil-doers, watches ever in the black depth of death.'

"Then in my dreams the Mother whispered into the ears of that fiend shaped like a man, and passing her hand before his eyes, showed him certain visions, though what these were I know not. At the least they caused him to wail aloud with terror, also to my sight to fall as from a precipice and, like some foul vulture pierced by an archer's shaft, go whirling down, down, and down, into gulfs that had no bottom. It was a very evil dream, King Tenes, and yet sweet, because it told me that though I should journey to the ends of the earth, still I shall not pass out of the shelter of the circling arms of Isis."

"Evil indeed, Lady," he said hoarsely, biting his lips to still the quaver in his voice. "Yet it ended well, so what of dreams?"

"Very well, O King—for me. And as for dreams, I, who by gifts and training am skilled in their interpretations, hold that for the most part they are a shadow of the Truth. I know that certainly no harm can come to me in your palace over which one day I must rule, or in your city where I am a guest. Yet doubtless some peril of the spirit did threaten me last night, and by the help of Heaven was brought to nothing."

"Doubtless, doubtless! though of such matters *I* know nothing, who deal with the things of earth, not with those of Heaven. But, Lady, I came to tell you that this day there is a great sacrifice on the Holy Place yonder, and that from these windows you will be able to watch it well. It is to propitiate our gods that they may give us victory in the war against the Persians."

"Is it so, King? But where are the victims? I see no kine, nor sheep, nor doves, such as are offered in Rome and in Jerusalem, or even flowers and fruit such as in Egypt we lay upon our gentler altars."

"Nay, Lady; here we make more costly offerings, tithing our own blood. Yes, here Moloch claims the fruit of our bodies, taking them to his purifying fires so that their innocent breath may rise as a sweet savour to the nostrils of the devouring and protecting gods."

"Do you, perchance, mean children, King?"

"Aye, Lady, children, many children, and among these to-day one of my own, the son of a certain Beltis who is of my household. He is a child of promise, yet I grudge him not to the god if thereby my people may be benefited."

"And does this Beltis not grudge him, King?"

"I know not," he answered sullenly. "She is a woman of the royal House of Israel and is absent on a journey. Therefore I know not, and when she returns the boy will have joined the gods and it will be too late for her to make trouble concerning him, should she be so minded."

Now horror took hold of me, Ayesha, and my soul sickened.

"King Tenes," I said, "bethink you of that mother's heart and, I pray you, spare this child."

"How can I, Lady? Must not the king bear that yoke which is laid upon the necks of his people? If I spare him, would not the mothers of Sidon whose young have passed into the fire spit at me and curse me—aye, and tear me to pieces if they might? Nay, he must die with the rest. The priests have so decreed."

"On your head be it, King," I said and choked in my loathing of him. Then a thought took me, and I cried to those who were gathered about the door of the chamber, captains of the guard, eunuchs, slaves, scribes, and a priest or two,

"Come hither, ye of Sidon, and hearken to the words of her who in Egypt is named *Oracle-of-Isis*."

They came, drawn by wonder, or perchance because my strength compelled them.

"Take note of my words and record them," I said, while they stared on me. "Take note and forget it not, that I, the daughter of Isis, have made prayer to King Tenes of Sidon, that he will spare the life of his son and the son of a lady named Beltis, and that he has refused my prayer. Ye have heard me. It is enough. Go!"

They went, looking at each other, the scribes, as I saw, writing down what I had said upon their tablets. Tenes also stared at me curiously.

"You are an Arab by birth, born of an Egyptian mother, and wholly Egyptian in your faith and mind, though the Arab courage still strikes through these qualities," he said. "Therefore I forgive you who do not understand our customs. Yet, know, Lady, that those of Sidon whom it pleases you to call as witnesses will think you mad."

"Doubtless, Tenes, before all is done, those of Sidon will think many things of me, as you will also. But what will this lady Beltis think?"

"I neither know nor care who weary of Beltis and her moods," he answered, scowling. "Beauteous one, I sent you jewels. Why do you not wear them?"

"The daughter of Isis wears no jewels save those the goddess gives her, King. Yet yours shall go to enrich her shrines when I return to Egypt, and in her name I thank you for them, bounteous King.'

"Aye, when you return to Egypt. But how can you return if you bide here as my wife?"

"If I bide here as your wife, then I shall bide as the Queen of Egypt as is written in our bond, and from time to time the Queen of Egypt must visit her dominions, King, and give thanks to the goddess for her advancement. Do you understand?"

"I understand that you are a very strange woman, so strange that I would I had never set eyes on you and your accursed beauty," he answered in a rage.

"What! So soon?" I said, laughing. "That this should be so in the beginning makes me wonder what you will wish in the end. Why not take your eyes off me and have done, King Tenes?"

"Because I cannot. Because I am bewitched," he answered furiously, and rising left me, while I laughed and laughed.

He departed and I went to the window-place to breathe air free from the poison of his presence. There I saw that the Holy Place beneath was already filled with tens of thousands of the Sidonians. I saw, moreover, that priests were engaged in lighting fire at the foot of the great brazen image of Dagon, which fire seemed to burn within the image, since smoke poured out far above from an opening in his head. Moreover, by degrees the copper plates of which its vast and hideous bulk was built up grew red with heat, so that the upper part of it became one glowing furnace.

White-robed priests, gathered in troops, began to offer prayers and celebrate rites of which I did not know the meaning. They bowed themselves to the image, they gashed their arms with knives and catching the blood that fell from them in shallow shells of the sea, cast it into the fire. Orators made speeches, prophets uttered prophecies. Bands of fair women appeared naked to the middle and having their breasts gilded, who danced wildly before the god.

Then suddenly there was a great silence and from the mouth of some gateway that I could not see, because it lay almost beneath the balconies of the palace, appeared the King Tenes clad in gorgeous, sacerdotal robes, those, I think, of the high-priest of Baal. With him was a woman who led by the hand a little boy who perhaps had seen three summers, dressed in white with a garland of flowers about his neck. Tenes bowed to the glowing image and cried in a loud voice,

"People of Sidon, I the King make sacrifice of my son to Dagon the great god, that Dagon may be propitiated and Sidon may conquer in this war. O Dagon, take my son that his spirit may pass through the flames and be gathered to thy spirit and that thine appetite may feed upon his blood."

At these words a great and joyous shout went up from the tens of thousands of people, and in the midst of the shout Tenes bent down and kissed his son, which was the only kindly, human thing that ever I saw him do. The child, affrighted, clung to his robes, but the woman at his side snatched the boy away and ran with him, struggling, to a priest who stood by the foot of a little iron ladder of which the top rested against the outstretched giant hands of the glowing image.

The priest took the child from the woman, holding him aloft that the multitude might see him and know him for the very son of the king. Oh! never shall I forget the look upon that child's face as he was thus held aloft in the hands of the brutal priest who stood upon the lower rungs of the ladder. He had ceased to scream, but his ruddy cheeks were blanched, his black eyes seemed to start from his head, and his little hands grasped emptily at the air or were lifted up to heaven, which indeed was near to him, as though in supplication for deliverance from the cruelty of man.

The priest climbed the ladder, bearing the child, and I noted a kind of metal covering upon his breast and head, set there to shield him from the heat of the fiery idol.

He reached the platform of the outstretched hands. The child's fingers clung to his garments, but he tore them free and with a cry of triumph let fall the little body into the hollow of the hot hands. Then, to drown the victim's cries, priests standing below began to play upon instruments of music, as they played, singing some hymn to the god. I saw the little arms tossed aloft above the edge of the hollow of the brazen hands. Then I saw those arms lift themselves, feebly for the last time, and that poor, tortured, innocent babe rolled slowly into the red abyss beneath, while the savage multitude screamed its delight to heaven.

This royal sacrifice was accomplished, yet it was but the first of many, for woman after woman brought her child, or sometimes it was a man who brought it, and babe after babe was thrown upon the red-hot hands and rolled thence into the flames beneath. All the while the priests played upon their instruments and sang their songs while the shameless priestesses, and others, those with the gilded breasts, danced lewdly, tossing up their white arms, and the thousands of the people of Sidon, filled with the lust of blood, roared aloud in their drunken joy, and the poor mothers, now that the deed was done, crept thence, laughing and crying both together, back to their desolated homes, there to stare at the cots emptied into "the bosom of the god."

At length I could bear no more of this scene of hell, and departing to my sleeping-chamber, caused women to draw curtains over the window-places and having dismissed them, sat myself down and thought.

A great rage filled me, Ayesha, who have never loved children—will a day come when I shall nurse one upon my breast, I wonder, and if so in what star will it be born?—and a mighty hate of those accursed Sidonians. All pity left my heart, even for the young who would grow up to be as were those who begat them. These sharks and tigers loved blood. Good. They should be filled with blood, their own blood. All of them were guilty, all, all were murderers. Hearken to their horrible rejoicings! Old men and maidens, young men and matrons, the toothless crone and the budding girl, the great lords and ladies, the toilers on the deep and the traders of the city, the bond and the free, from the king down to the meanest slave, all of them screamed with hideous rejoicing as babe after babe was swallowed by the glowing gorge of the dæmon they named a god. Therefore, I vowed by Isis that all of them should pay the price of this innocent blood and go down to find their god in hell. Yes, I swore it by the Mother and by my own outraged soul!

The next day Beltis came. The King Tenes was in my outer chamber fawning on me and watching me out of his crafty eyes, as I saw through the veil that I had let fall over my face, and my flesh crept at the sight of him. Trained though I was and wise though I was, who knew well that the hour had not come to strike, scarce could I bear him near me who longed to drive my dagger through his lying throat. Yet I sat still and listened to his flattery and answered him with double-edged and mocking words of which he could not read the meaning. He told me that already the great sacrifice had borne good fruit, since tidings had come of a new victory over the vanguard of the Persians, in which five thousand of the men of Ochus had perished.

I answered that I doubted not it would bear yet better fruit, then asked him how many of his folk dwelt in Sidon.

He answered, some sixty thousand.

"Then, O King," I said, "I who am filled with the spirit of the Mother, make a prophecy to you. I prophesy that in reward of the piety of this people of yours who do not grudge their own children to the gods, the gods will take sixty thousand lives from among the wicked of the earth who worship fire—as I am told these Persians do."

"That is a good saying, Lady," he said, rubbing his fat hands, "though it is true that some might say that we Sidonians also worship fire, or rather Moloch whose belly is filled with flame as we saw yesterday."

Now while we were speaking and this brute bemused was talking thus almost at hazard, for his mind was set on me only, I noted that those who attended him slipped from the place, taking with them the waiting women and closing the carven doors behind them, so that he and I were now alone. Guessing that this was done by order, I knew that I must prepare for some outburst of the man's passion and took counsel with myself. What it was does not matter because of that which followed.

Already he had begun, for the words, "O most beauteous!" had passed his lips when the door burst open and through it came a noble-looking woman. She was tall, dark, and handsome with swift-glancing, tragic eyes, as I knew at once, a Jewess, since I had seen others like her in Jerusalem. She glanced at me as though wondering what my veil hid, and advancing, stood before Tenes. He had not heard her come or seen her, his mind being full of other matters and his back toward the doorway. At the sound of her feet he turned and, coming face to face with her, stepped backward three paces with a frightened face and uttering some Phœnician curse.

"Have you returned so soon, Beltis?" he asked. "What has brought you here before the appointed time?"

"My heart, O Tenes, king and husband. Yonder in Jerusalem a prophet of Jehovah said words to me that caused me to return and swiftly. Tell me, Tenes, where is our son? On my path to this chamber I passed through those where he should be and found him not. All I found was his nurse weeping; aye, so choked with tears that she could not answer my question. Where is our son, Tenes?"

Now he cast his eyes about him like one who finds himself in a snare, and answered thickly,

"Alas! Lady, the gods have taken our son."

She gasped and clasped her hands upon her heart, saying, or rather moaning,

"How did they take him, Husband?"

He looked through the window-place at the hideous brazen image dulled with heat and blackened by smoke; he looked at the lady with the white face and the terrible eyes. Then he strove to speak, but as it seemed, could not, for the mumbled words choked each other in his throat.

"Answer!" she said coldly, but he could not, or would not answer.

Then my spirit moving me, I played a part in this ineffable tragedy. Yes, I, Ayesha, threw back my veil, saying,

"Queen, if it pleases you to listen I will tell you how your son died."

She looked at me wondering, and asked like one who dreams,

"Is this a woman or a goddess, or perchance a spirit? Speak on, woman, or goddess, or spirit."

"Queen," I said, "look through the window-place and tell me what you see."

"I see the image of Dagon, the brazen image towering to the housetops, blackened with fire and staring at me with empty eyes, and beyond it the temple and above it Heaven."

"Queen, yesterday I looked from this window-place and saw that image of Dagon, only then from those empty eyes came flame. Also I saw King Tenes lead out a beauteous, black-eyed boy of three summers or so, which boy he declared to be his son. This boy he gave to a woman, although the child clung wailing to his robe. The woman gave him to a priest. The priest climbed a ladder—look, there it stands—and laid him upon the red-hot hands of the idol whence he rolled amidst the plaudits of the people into a womb of fire, to be perchance reborn in Heaven."

Beltis heard, and as she heard her face seemed to freeze into a mask of ice. Then she stared at Tenes and asked almost in a whisper,

"Are these things so, O dog of a Sidonian, that like a dog can devour your own flesh?"

"The god claimed him," he mumbled, "and like others I must give when the god claims, that victory may crown our arms. Who can deny the god? Rejoice, O mother, that he has been pleased to accept that which was born of you."

So he mumbled on as priests patter to their idols, till at length in that cold silence his voice died away.

Then Beltis the Queen began to hiss a curse at him, such a curse as, save once only, I have never heard come from the lips of woman. In the Name of Jehovah, God of the Jews, she cursed him, calling down woe and desolation upon his head, consigning him to a death in blood and appointing Gehenna, as she named hell, as a resting-place for his soul, where devils fashioned as children should tear him eternally with hooks of flame. Yes, she cursed him living and dead, but always in that low, whispering voice, that inhuman voice which did not seem to come from the throat of woman, such a voice as the gods or spirits use when from time to time they speak to their servants in the inmost sanctuaries.

He cowered before her. Once even he sank to his knees, holding his hands above his head as though to ward off her words of evil omen. Then, as she would not cease, he sprang up, shouting,

"You also shall be a sacrifice, you worshipper of the God of the Jews. Dagon is greater than the God of the Jews. Be you a sacrifice to him, O Sorceress of Israel!"

He drew the sword at his side and shook it. She did not stir, only with her hands she tore upon the robes upon her breast, saying,

"Smite on, dog of a Sidonian, and complete the circle

of your crimes. Where the son went, there let the mother follow!"

Now in madness, or in rage, or in terror, he lifted the sword and was about to do the deed, when I stepped between him and her. Loosing the veil I wore I threw it over her head, and turning, said to Tenes,

"Now, King, touch her who is hid in the veil of Isis if you dare. Of Isis I think you have learned something on a certain ship when the breakers called for you off Carmel, yes, of Isis and her prophetess. Know then that she who could save can also slay, and give you over to such dreams as came to you, Tenes, at midnight by a bed in yonder room. Aye, she can slay, and swiftly. Strike then through the Veil of Isis and learn whether her prophetess speaks truth."

He looked at me; he looked at Beltis standing still and ghostlike beneath the veil. Then he cast down the sword and fled.

When he had gone I went to the door and shot its bolt. I returned, I lifted the veil from about that queen.

"Who and what are you?" she asked, "that can brave Tenes in his palace and save one whom he would slay, though for that I thank you not. So little do I thank you that——" And she stooped to grasp the sword.

Moving swiftly as a swallow flies, I flitted between her and it. Before her fingers could touch it, I had snatched it away who understood her purpose.

"Be seated, Lady, and listen," I said.

She sank into a chair and, resting her head upon her hand, regarded me with a cold and curious look.

"Queen," I went on, "I am one whom Heaven has sent to this land to destroy Tenes and the Sidonians."

"Then I welcome you, Stranger. Speak on."

So briefly I told her all my tale, and in proof of it read to her the writing in which I promised myself to Tenes when he could crown me queen of the world.

"So you desire my place and this man?"

"Aye," I answered, "as much, or as little, as life desires death. Study the conditions. Can he crown me queen of all the earth, and under them until he does so,

can he take me? Do you not understand that I would
lead the fool on to his ruin?"

She nodded her head.

"Then will you not help me?"

"Aye, Lady, but how?"

"I will show you how," and bending forward, I whispered in her ear.

"It is good," she said when I had finished. "By Jehovah my God, and by the blood of my son, with you I
stand or fall, and when all is done take Tenes if you
will."

CHAPTER X

The Vengeance of Beltis

So IT came about that this queen, whose name I learned
was Elisheba among her own people, the Hebrews, Beltis being a title given to her in Sidon, and I dwelt together in the palace of Tenes. Leave me she dared not,
nor would I suffer it who knew that then certainly she
would be murdered, while with me she was safe because
Tenes dared not touch one whom I sheltered, being
afraid of me; one, moreover, over whom I had placed
the veil of Isis. For the rest she was glad to stay with me
whom soon she learned to love, especially after she had
heard how I pleaded for her son's life.

I, too, was glad that she should do so, both because
she was a companion to my loneliness and a protection,
since Tenes could not persecute me with his passion in
her presence, and because she had those who loved her
in Sidon, certain Hebrews through whom we learned
much. Yet we were in a strange case, the queen who
reigned and the queen to whom her place was promised,
dwelling together like sisters, and both sworn to destroy
him who was her husband and who desired to be mine.

For we made a pact together, she swearing by Jeho-

vah and I by Isis, that we would neither rest nor stay till
we saw Tenes dead and his Sidonians with him. Oh! if I
hated him and these, she, the robbed mother, hated
them worse, so deeply indeed that if only she might
come by vengeance she cared nothing for her life. She
was a fierce-natured woman, such as those of the Hebrews often are, and all her heart's love had been given
to this boy, her only child, whom Tenes butchered at
the bidding of the priests and because of his superstitions.

From the beginning this Beltis or Elisheba had hated
the Sidonians and Tenes, to whom she was given in a
marriage of policy by the rulers of Jerusalem because of
her beauty and her royal blood, and now to her they
were but as wild beasts and snakes to be destroyed. Yet
she was clever also and played her part well, feigning
sorrow for the wild words she spoke in the hour of her
agony and with it obedience to the wishes of the King.
She even told him in my presence that when the time
came she would be willing that I should take her crown
and she but a second place, or if it pleased him better,
that she would return to her own people. This, however,
he did not desire, since he feared lest the disgrace of so
great a lady should bring the wrath of Jerusalem upon
him, or even cause the Hebrews to join his enemies.

So well did she play that part, indeed, making it appear that her spirit was crushed and that she was one
from whom there was nothing to fear, that soon Tenes
came to believe that this was so, and in order to please
me he suffered her to dwell on there in peace.

Now I have to tell of the war and of the end of Sidon.
First I should say, however, that before he sailed for
Egypt, after the *Hapi* had been fitted with a new mast
of cedar, I caused Philo to be summoned to the palace
by the help of those Jews who were the friends of Beltis.
He was brought to my presence with two merchants,
disguised as one of their company, and, while Beltis
made pretence to chaffer with them for their costly
goods, I spoke with him apart.

I told him to get him to Memphis as quickly as he
might, and there make all ready as we had agreed,

awaiting my message. How this would reach him, or
Noot, or both of them, I did not know. It might be by
writing, or by messenger who would bear certain to-
kens, or it might be otherwise. At least when it came he
must sail at once, and arriving off the port of Sidon,
every night after the setting of the sun and before its
rising, must light a flare of green fire at his masthead,
causing it to burn for the fourth part of an hour, so that
I might be sure that the ship which signalled was his
and no other. Then in this way or in that I would find
means to come aboard that vessel, and the rest was in
the hands of the gods.

These things he vowed to do and departed safely with
the merchants, nor did Tenes ever learn that Philo had
visited the palace.

Meanwhile Tenes was making mighty preparations
for the war. He dug a triple ditch about Sidon and
heightened its walls. He hired ten thousand Grecian
mercenaries and armed the citizens. By help of the
Greeks he drove the Persian vanguard out of Phœnicia,
and for a while all went well for him and Egypt. At
length came the news that the vast army of Ochus was
rolling down on Sidon, together with three hundred triremes and five hundred transports; such an army as
Phœnicia had never seen.

One morning Tenes came to my chamber and told of
the march of Ochus, Beltis withdrawing herself. He was
in a very evil case, for he trembled and even forgot to
say sweet words or to devour me with his eyes after his
fashion. I asked him why his hand shook and his lips
were pale, he, who as a warrior king, should be rejoicing at the prospect of battle. He answered because of a
dream he had dreamed, in which he seemed to see himself defeated by the Persians and cast down living from
the wall of the city. Then he added these words:

"You, Lady, promised to show me how to conquer
the world. Do so, I pray you, for I say that my heart is
afraid and I know not how I shall stand against Ochus."

Now I laughed at him and answered,

"So at last you come to me for counsel, Tenes, who
for days have been wondering for how long you would

be content to take that of Mentor of Rhodes and of the King of Cyprus. Well, what would you learn?"

"I would learn how I may defeat the Persians, Lady, the Persians who pour upon us like a flood through a broken wall."

"I do not know, Tenes. To me it seems impossible. I think that dream of yours is coming true, Tenes, that is——" And I ceased.

"What, then, must I do, Lady? What is your meaning?"

"I mean that you are mad to fight Ochus."

"But I am fighting Ochus."

"Those who have been enemies may become friends, King Tenes. Have I not told you that you would be safer as the ally of Ochus than as his foe? What is Egypt to you that you should destroy yourself to save Necta-nebes?"

"Egypt may be little, Lady, but Sidon is much. The Sidonians are pledged to this war and the hand of Ochus might be heavy on them."

Again I laughed and answered,

"Which is dearer to a man, his own life or those of others? Fight and die if you will, O King; or make peace and perchance let others die if you will, O King. They say that Ochus is generous and knows how to re-ward those who serve him."

"Do you mean that I should make a pact with him and betray my people?" he asked hoarsely.

"Aye, my words may be so read. Hearken. You have great ambitions. You would win the world—and me. My wisdom tells me that only thus can you win the world—and me. Continue this war, and very soon you will lose me and all that you will command of Earth shall be such small part of it as hides your bones. Now make your choice and trouble me no more, who in truth find little joy in timid hearts that fear to take hold of opportunity. Therefore, follow your counsel or my own, I care not which who would be gone back to Egypt to seek a higher destiny than that of consort to a con-quered slave."

"Whatever I may lose, you I cannot lose," he said

slowly. "Also your mind is mine. This Persian is too strong for me, and on Egypt I cannot lean too hard lest it break beneath me. These Sidonians, also, are rebellious and murmur against me. I think that they would kill me if they dared, who now call me Child-murderer because I gave my son in sacrifice to please the priests."

"Mayhap, King," I answered carelessly, "since mobs are fickle. I repeat that the wise man and he who would be great does not think of others but of himself."

"I will consult with my General, Mentor the Greek, for he is far-sighted," he said, and left me.

"The poison works," I thought to myself as I watched him go. Then I called Beltis and told her all that had passed between her lord and me. She listened and asked,

"Why do you lead Tenes down this road, Ayesha?"

"Because of the pit at the end of it," I answered. "Have not your spies told us that this Ochus is implacable? He will make a pact with Tenes and then he will destroy him. Such at least is the counsel that comes to me from Heaven, which he has angered, as I think."

"Then I pray that Tenes may follow it, Ayesha, so long as it hurls him down to hell, and the Sidonians with him."

As it chanced he did, for it was of a sort that his false heart loved. The rest may be told in few words. Tenes sent his minister, Thessalion, another crafty fellow, to make a treaty with Ochus. These were the terms of this treaty: That he, Tenes, should surrender Sidon and in payment receive the royalty of Egypt after it had been conquered, and of all Phœnicia also, and with it that of Cyprus. Ochus swore these gifts to him and continued his advance. When he reached a certain spot, he halted. Then Tenes, as he had undertaken to do, led out a hundred of the chief citizens of Sidon to a Council of the States of Phœnicia, or so he said.

Howbeit, presently they found themselves in the camp of Ochus who butchered them to the last man, all save Tenes himself, who returned to Sidon with a tale of an ambush from which he had escaped.

Then it was I saw that the end drew near, and in a

ship, which not Tenes, but the captains of the Sidonians sent to Nectanebes at Memphis to pray for more aid, I caused a faithful Jew to sail, one sworn to the service of Beltis, who carried with him hidden in the hollow sole of his sandal a letter addressed to Noot and to Philo, praying that Philo would sail at once and do all those things that had been agreed upon between us. Also night by night I sent out my spirit, or rather my thought, to seek the spirit of Noot, as he had taught me to do, and it seemed to me that answers came from Noot telling me that he read my thought and would do those things which I desired.

The chief men of the Sidonians held a council in the great hall of the palace. Hidden behind curtains in a gallery of the hall, Beltis and I saw and heard all that passed at this council, over which Tenes presided as King. Bitter was the talk of those lords, for doubts were abroad. They thought it very strange that Tenes alone should have escaped from that ambush. Yet like the liar that he was, he cozened them with false tales, showing them also that the gods of the Sidonians had preserved his life, that he in his turn might preserve theirs. Yes, he said this and other things, he the knave and traitor, who already plotted to destroy them all.

At this council the Sidonians took a desperate road. Day by day many were escaping from the city by sea and otherwise. Already nigh a third of the people had gone, and among them some thousands of the best soldiers, so that the captains saw that soon the great city would be left with few to defend her. Therefore they came to this resolve—to burn all their ships so that no more could flee upon them, and to set watches at the gates and round the walls with orders to slay any who might attempt flight by land.

Fearing for his life, Tenes consented to these deeds, swearing that he desired but one thing, to conquer or to die with the citizens of Sidon.

So it came about that soon the darkness was made as light as day by the flames which sprang from over a hundred vessels of war besides a multitude of smaller ships, while the Sidonians, watching them burn from the roofs of their houses, beat their breasts and moaned. For now they knew they were cut off and must conquer or perish.

The ships of Ochus watched the port of Sidon, though somewhat carelessly because it was known to him that its harbours were empty, and the vast army of Ochus rolled down in countless hosts upon its walls.

Hour by hour spies came in with terrible reports, causing the hearts of the Sidonians to melt with fear. For now they understood that all hope of victory was gone and that they were doomed, though as yet they did not know that it was their king who had betrayed them.

Another council was held, at which Beltis and I watched as before, and there it was agreed that the city should throw itself upon the mercy of Ochus. Tenes affected to protest and at last to allow himself to be overruled, as I, to whom he came day by day for guidance, put it into his black heart to do. Heralds were sent to the camp of Ochus, offering to surrender upon honourable terms, and while they were absent bloody sacrifices of children and others were made to Dagon and his company in the Holy Place before the temple, till its pavements ran red with blood. For thus these cruel folk hoped to propitiate Heaven and to win mercy from Ochus.

The heralds returned bearing the word of Ochus. He said that if five hundred of the chief citizens came out unarmed and made submission to him, he would grant their prayer and spare Sidon; but if they did not, that he would pull it stone from stone and slaughter all who lived within its walls. Also one of the Persian ambassadors who accompanied them brought a secret letter for Tenes. This letter Tenes, who by now did nothing without my counsel, read to me.

It was brief. This was its substance:

If he would put Sidon into his hands, Ochus swore to Tenes by his most solemn Persian oaths advancement greater than he had ever dreamed; and to Mentor the Rhodian and the general of the Grecian and Egyptian Mercenaries, he swore a vast sum in gold and one of the first commands in the Persian army. If Tenes would not do this, then Ochus proposed to make peace with Sidon for a while but afterward to destroy it. To Tenes himself, however, he promised death at the hands of the Sidonians themselves, to whom all his treachery should be revealed. Lastly an answer was demanded without delay.

"What shall I say to Ochus, Lady?" asked Tenes of me.

"I know not," I answered. "Honour would seem to demand that you should lay down your life and save Sidon and her citizens, if only for a while. Yet, O King, what is honour? How will honour help you when you have been torn to pieces by the maddened mob upon yonder Holy Place, and your spirit has gone to Baal, or wherever the spirits of those sacrificed to Moloch may go. Will this empty honour give you that great advancement of which the Persian speaks, which doubtless will carry with it the rule of Phœnicia and of Egypt, and perchance also that of the East? For Ochus being mortal, Tenes, once you have brought him to his death, as I can show you how to do, who is fitter than yourself to fill his throne? Lastly, will death with honour bring me whom you desire to your side, King Tenes? I have spoken, now judge," and lifting my veil, I sat and smiled at him.

"It is not safe," he said. "All hangs on Mentor and the Greeks. Unless they join in the plot the Sidonians will fight to the last with their aid, and when they discover my traffic with Ochus they will slay me. And if I fly to Ochus and the Sidonians fight, then mayhap he will slay me as one who has helped him nothing. But if Mentor joins us, then we can open the gates to the Persians and ourselves go out safe to reap our reward."

"There speaks a great man," I said, "one who is foresighted, one not tied by petty scruples; there speaks such a one as I would take to be my lord. Aye, there speaks a man fit to rule the world, to whom the great advancement the Persian promises is but the first rung in the ladder of glorious triumph—that ladder which reaches to the very stars. Already these Sidonians hate you, Tenes. I saw them mutter when you passed among them yesterday; aye, and one laid his hand upon his dagger, but another checked him, having a look in his eyes that seemed to say—'Not yet.' If once they learn the truth, Tenes, perchance soon you also will lie on the altar of sacrifice and be cast living into the fiery jaws of Dagon, where your son went before you, Tenes. Why do you not send for Mentor and search his mind?"

So Mentor was sent for, and meanwhile I gave Tenes my hand to kiss. Yes, I even suffered this that I might fix him the more firmly on my hook.

Mentor came. He was a burly Greek, a great soldier with a keen brain behind his laughing eyes; one who loved gold and wine and women, and for these and high place and generalship was ready to sell his sword to whoever bid the most.

Tenes set out the matter to him very craftily and showed him the writing of Ochus. He listened, then asked,

"And what does this veiled Daughter of Isis think? I remember hearing in Egypt where she was held the first of Oracles and named Child of Wisdom, that her prophecies never fail to fulfill themselves."

"The Daughter of Isis thinks that among the Persians Mentor will grow tall, but that here among the Sidonians he will be felled like a forest tree and go to feed a mighty fire, such a fire as consumed the fleets of Sidon awhile ago."

Thus I answered, and when Mentor heard my words, he laughed and said that he was of the same mind, which without doubt was true, for afterward I learned that already he had been in treaty with Ochus.

So he and Tenes struck hands upon their bargain, the most infamous perhaps that was ever made by men, since it gave to slaughter forty thousand or more who trusted to them.

Thus was signed the doom of an accursed people, that doom which I was destined to bring upon their heads, and thus was Tenes sent down the road to hell. Only Mentor prospered greatly for a while in the service of the Persians, and what was the end of him I do not know. After all, he was but one of many who flit from master to master as advantage leads them. Doubtless long ago the world has forgotten him, his Grecian cunning, his generalship, and his treachery.

The five hundred went out to the Persian camp to plead with Ochus, bearing palm branches in their hands; yea, they went with light hearts, for Tenes had told them that certainly their prayer would be granted and that he knew this from the lips of Ochus himself. Led by the priesthoods of the various gods—oh! how it rejoiced me to see those vile and cruel priests in that company!—they went, but not one of them returned again, for Ochus received them with mockeries and reviling, and to make sport for himself and his soldiers, told them to run back to Sidon. Then he loosed his horsemen on them and slew them with swords and javelins and set their heads on stakes around the walls.

When the Sidonians knew and saw, they went mad with rage and terror. They gathered themselves by thousands in the Holy Place and had it not been for Montor and his Greeks, would have stormed the palace, for now they were sure that Tenes had betrayed them. Indeed Beltis had made the truth of this treachery known through the Hebrews who served her. Also they clamoured that I, Ayesha, should be led forth and sacrificed, saying that it was the presence of a priestess of Isis in the city which had caused their gods to desert them. For a little while I was afraid, who remembered what had chanced upon the ship *Hapi* when Tenes would have suffered me to be thrown to the deep to satisfy the superstitions of the sailors. Therefore thinking it best to be bold, I sent for Tenes and said to him,

"If by evil chance I should be slain, O King, then know that I have it from the goddess whom I serve that you with whose lot mine is intertwined will die within an hour. I, Tenes, am the bright star of your fortunes, and if I set, farewell to them and you."

"I know it," he answered, "as I know that without you I can never rise to be king of the world. Therefore I will defend you to the last; also, beauteous one, I desire you for my wife. Yet," he added, "some might think that this star of your wisdom had hitherto led my feet into dark and evil places," and he looked at me doubtfully.

"Fear nothing," I answered. " 'Tis ever darkest before the dawn and out of evil arises good. Great glory awaits you, Tenes, or rather great glory awaits both of us. History will embalm your name, Tenes." But to myself I thought that it was the Persians who would embalm his body, unless indeed they cast it to the dogs!

Now every evening after sundown it was my custom to walk upon the flat roof of the palace and look out over the ocean which, also for reasons my own, rising early, I did before the dawn. That night while I walked I put up my prayers to Heaven, for though I played so bold a game, its odds seemed to be gathering against me. Doubtless, as it deserved, this hateful Sidon would fall, but when its walls were crashing down, with what should I protect my head? I did not know. Yet it is true that never did I lose faith. Always I knew that I was the instrument of that Strength which directs the fate of men and nations, that what I did was because I was driven and commanded so to do for reasons that were dark to me; moreover, that I was not an instrument to be broken and thrown aside. Nay, however strait the path and however great the perils that beset it, I was sure that I should walk it with safety, because it was fated that I should do so, though whither it would lead me I could not tell in those days when I was but as other women are. Still I put up my prayer to Heaven and scanned the horizon with my eyes.

Lo! far away beyond the lights of the watching triremes of Ochus, so far that it seemed almost set upon the surface of the sea, burned a faint green fire. For the fourth part of an hour it burned, and went out. Then I knew that my words had reached Egypt, whether in the writing or by the swift path of the spirit, and that Noot or Philo had come to save me.

Before the dawn once more I climbed to the roof of the palace, and behold! far away again the green fire burned upon the bosom of the deep, telling me that out yonder the great trireme waited for my coming. Aye, but how was I to come?

Tenes the vile and Mentor the venal played their parts well. They opened the gates of the outmost wall which the Greeks held, and let in the Persians whom these Greeks greeted as brothers, having at times served under them in the past. The Sidonians saw and knew that the dice had fallen against them; knew too that they were loaded dice.

They gathered in the Holy Place and raved for the blood of Tenes who cowered behind a curtain and hearkened to them. Beltis and I, playing our parts, came to comfort him,

"Be brave!" I said gently. "The road to the kingship of the world is steep and difficult. Yet when the peak is gained, how glorious, O Conqueror, will be the prospect spread out before your eyes."

"It is steep and difficult indeed," he muttered, wiping his brow with the fringe of his broidered robe.

Had he but seen the look which Beltis cast upon him, standing behind him with folded arms and humble air, perchance he would have thought it steeper still.

"Let us talk," I said, "for the end draws near. What is your plan? How will you and we, your queens, escape from this city?"

"All is prepared," he answered. "At the King's wharf, to which a covered way runs from the palace, in the house where the royal boats are moored, is my own barge that, being thus secured, escaped burning with the ships. In this barge, which is manned with Greeks to whom a great reward is promised and who wait in the boathouse day and night, we will row from the harbour for a hidden bay three leagues down the coast where we will land and be escorted thence to the encampment of the Great King. Yet perchance it may be wiser that I should be with Mentor to welcome Ochus when he enters to take peaceful possession of the city. If so, Daughter of Isis, you will do well to leave it by yourself, or with the lady Beltis if she wishes to accompany you, and to meet me in the camp of Ochus."

"Perhaps that would be better," I answered, "since it might not be thought seemly that the great King Tenes should slip away to his ally by night. Nay, let him rather march out as a monarch should. Only then we must have authority to act as occasion may direct."

"Aye, Lady, take this ring," and slipping the royal signet from his finger he gave it to me. "It will be obeyed by all who see it; moreover, I will issue certain orders. So long as we meet again at last, we whose fates are intertwined, it matters not by what separate roads we travel."

"It matters not at all, my lord Tenes," I answered as swiftly I hid away the signet.

It was just then, at the hour of sunset, that Mentor entered the chamber. No longer was he gay and light-hearted; indeed his brows were bent and his eyes full of trouble.

"By Zeus!" he said, "a dreadful thing has happened. In their despair these Sidonians of yours, King Tenes, have taken counsel together. They have determined that rather than fall into the hands of Ochus, they will burn the city and with it themselves and their wives and children. Yes, uttering the curse of all the gods upon you, thus they have determined. Look, the fires begin!"

We went to the window-places and gazing from them, saw desperate men rushing to and fro with lighted torches of cedar wood in their hands, while other men drove mobs of screaming women and children into the houses, yes, and into the temples, and shut the doors upon them. Here and there, too, from the roofs of these houses rose wisps of smoke that soon were mingled with flame. East and west and north and south, through the great city of Sidon arose that smoke and flame. Everywhere also mobs of the people whose courage failed them and who did not desire to die thus were rushing toward the gates and into the camp of the Greeks. In this fashion, I believe, that from ten to twenty thousand of the inhabitants of Sidon escaped, though afterward

Ochus the cruel slew many of them and enslaved the rest.

I looked, I saw, and my heart melted within me. Hateful as were these insolent, bloodstained folk, I grieved that I should have had any hand in bringing their reward upon them. After all, they were brave and would have fought to the end, who now made expiation by a great self-sacrifice, which was also brave. Oh! if I could I would have lifted that doom from off them. Then I remembered that it was not I who did these things, but Fate which made of me is instrument; remembered also that only thus could I escape the foul hands of Tenes.

I turned to look upon that traitor. He trembled, and trembling tried to seem brave; he laughed, and in the midst of his laughter burst into tears.

"Behold the fate of those who would have slain their king! Truly the gods are just," he said. "Now let us fly to the great Ochus and receive from him his royal welcome and reward. Truly the gods are just!"

He turned about seeking for Mentor, but Mentor had gone. There remained in that chamber only Beltis the Queen, he, and I, Ayesha. Beltis glided to the door and made it fast. Then she came to Tenes and before he guessed her purpose, snatched the gold-hilted sword from his belt. She stood before him with fierce white face and blazing eyes.

"Truly the gods are just," she repeated in a low and terrible voice. "Fool, do you not know what welcome Ochus will give you yonder and what rewards? Hearken! That false Greek, Mentor, told me of these but now, or pitying my lot, he offered me his love and to take me to safety. After I had refused him, he went his way while you stared from the window-place."

"What words are these, Woman?" gasped Tenes. "Ochus is my ally; Ochus will greet me well who have served him well. Let us be going."

"Ochus will greet you thus, O Tenes; I have it from the mouth of Mentor who has it from Ochus himself. Slowly he will cause you, a king, to be beaten to death with rods, which is the fate the Persians give to slaves and traitors. Then he will stuff your body with spices and tie it to the masthead of his ship, that when presently he sails for Egypt it may be a warning to Nectanebes the Pharaoh whom also you have betrayed."

"It is a lie, it is a lie!" shouted Tenes. "Daughter of Isis, tell this mad woman that it is a lie."

I stood still, answering nothing, and Beltis went on,

"Tenes, Fate is upon you. Will you meet it less bravely than the meanest of the thousands of this people whom you have given to doom? Take my last counsel and leap from yonder window, that you who have lived a coward and a traitor may at least die a man."

He gnashed his teeth, he stared about him. He even went to the window-place and looked out as though he would brave the deed.

"I dare not," he muttered, "I dare not. The gods are just; they will save me who sacrificed my son to them."

Then he knelt down in the window-place and began to pray to Moloch whose brazen image showed redly in the gathering gloom.

"Take your sword, Tenes, if you dare not leap, and make an end," said the cold voice of the fierce-faced Hebrew lady who stood behind him, whilst I, Ayesha, watched all this play as a spirit might that is afar from the affairs of earth, wondering how it would end.

But Tenes only answered,

"Nay, sharp steel is worse than steep air. I would live, not die. The gods are just, the gods are just!"

Then he went on praying to Moloch.

Queen Beltis grasped the handle of the short sword with both her hands and with all her strength drove it down between the broad shoulders of Tenes.

"Aye, dog of a Sidonian," she cried, "the gods are very just, or at the least my God is just, and here— child-slayer—is the justice!"

Tenes screamed aloud, then struggled to his feet and stood striking at the air, the short sword still fixed in his back, a dreadful sight to behold.

"Would you murder me, Jewess?" he babbled, and staggered after her, still beating at the air with his clenched fist.

"Nay," she answered, ever retreating before him, "I would but give you your due, or some of it. Go, garner the rest in Gehenna's deep, O butcher of children and traitor blacker than the world has ever seen. Die, hound! Die, lurking jackal who would have mumbled the bones of greatness left by the full-fed Persian lion. Die, slaughterer of the son that sprang from us, and go meet his spirit in the world below, telling him that Elisheba his mother, a woman of the royal house of Israel, the Queen whom you had rejected, sent you thither. Die, while the city, the great City of the Seas, burns with the fires that your treachery has lighted and the cries of its tortured citizens ring in your ears. Pass with them to Gehenna and there strike your account, having their fire-shrivelled souls for witnesses and Moloch and Baal and Ashtoreth for judges and for company. Die, dog, die! and while your brain darkens, remember to the last that it was Elisheba, the robbed mother, who gave you to drink of the cup of death."

So she reviled, ever flitting before him, while he staggered slowly after her round the great chamber. At length he could no more and fell at my feet, grasping my robe,

"Daughter of Isis," he babbled, "whom I desired and would have made my queen, save me! Is this the great advancement that you swore to me?"

"Aye, mighty Tenes," I answered, "since death is the greatest of all advancements. In death be king of Phœnicia, of Egypt and of the East, since surely there you will stand above all thrones, powers, and dominions. In death all things will be yours, O traitor Tenes, who would have done violence to the daughter of Isis, everything save Ayesha's self, who here bids you farewell, vile Tenes."

Then, wailing and moaning, he died, and thus robbed Ochus of his vengeance upon a tool of which he had no further need.

CHAPTER XI

~

The Escape from Sidon

ALL was over and done. Within that royal chamber was silence, though without the flames roared and the cries of the Sidonians went up to Heaven. I, Ayesha, and Beltis the Queen, faced each other in the gloom and between us lay the body of Tenes, on whose white, distorted face flickered the light of the fires that burned without.

"What now, Queen?" I said.

"Death, I think," she answered in a quiet voice, for all her rage seemed to have left her. "Why cheat his jaws of their richest morsel?"

"I have still work to do, my hour has not yet come, Queen."

"Aye, I forgot. Follow me, Daughter of Isis; Beltis does not forsake those who have served her. Look your last upon this carrion that hoped to call you wife, and follow me."

As we passed from that chamber I glanced through the window and saw that, although darkness now had fallen, the Holy Place beneath was bright as noon with the flames of the burning temple, and that in them the vast graven image of Moloch glowed as it had done upon the day of sacrifice when the child of Beltis was swallowed in its red-hot jaws. There it sat hideous; grinning as though in unholy triumph over this greatest of all sacrifices.

Then suddenly a pinnacle from the temple fell upon it, grinding it to powder. This was the end of Moloch, since, although Sidon, as I have learned, was rebuilt in the after years, never more was sacrifice made to that devil within its walls. This at least I, Ayesha, brought to pass—the end of the worship of Moloch at Sidon.

We passed through my sleeping-chamber, and as we went I seized the cabinet of priceless gems that Tenes from time to time had heaped upon me, since these were sworn to Isis and no goddess loves to be robbed of her offerings. At the back of the chamber was a passage leading to a door by which a lighted lamp had been set in readiness. At this door stood a man whom I knew for one of the Jewish servants sworn to the service of Beltis.

"You are late, royal Lady," he exclaimed. "So late that I was about to flee, for look, the palace burns beneath us," and he pointed to little wreaths of smoke that forced themselves up between the boards of the flooring of the bedchamber that we had passed.

"Late, but not too late," she answered. "The King detained us and has gone another way. You have his orders and here is his ring," and she pointed to the royal signet upon my hand. "Obey it and lead on."

The man held up the lantern and glanced at the ring. Then he bowed and beckoned to us to follow him.

We went down passages, long passages with many turnings, and at length came to another door which he opened with a key. Passing it, we found ourselves in a vaulted place beneath which was water, where floated the royal barge, the same in which I had been rowed to the shore of Sidon. Oarsmen sat waiting within this barge, and guarding it were two Grecian soldiers, who commanded us to halt.

"This boat awaits King Tenes," said one of them "and none else may enter it."

"I am the Queen," answered Beltis.

"With whom I hear the King has quarrelled," broke in the Greek with a sneer. "Queen or no, Lady, you cannot enter that boat without the King, or an order under his signet."

Then I held up my hand, saying,

"Here is the signet itself. Let us pass."

He stared at it by the light of the lamp, then said something to the other Greek and very doubtfully they obeyed. It was certain that these guards standing in that vaulted place did not know what was passing in the city. Moreover, I think it had come into their minds to rob us, or worse. At the least this is sure, that unless we could have killed those two Greeks, without the signet never should we have won to the boat.

We went on twelve paces or so and reached the barge, which was manned with sailors who wore the uniform of the King's bodyguard, men who knew the Queen and saluted her by raising their oars. Beltis motioned first to me and afterward to the Jew who had been our guide from the palace, to enter the barge, then suddenly she said to the steersman who commanded the sailors,

"Go now whither this lady shall direct you, and know that if harm comes to her your lives shall pay the price of it, for she is no woman, but a goddess whom Death obeys."

Now I stared at her and asked,

"Do you not come also, Queen Beltis?"

"Nay," she whispered. "I choose another road to safety. Fear not for me, I will tell you all when we meet again. For a while farewell, Child of Wisdom and my friend. May the gods with whom you commune be your shield upon earth and receive you when you leave the earth, you who strove to save a certain one and cast your mantle over Beltis when a sword that now is set in another's heart was at her own. Give way, sailors," she cried, "and if you would look once more upon the sun, obey."

Then with her own hands she thrust at the stern of the boat, causing it to move into the channel. Next moment Beltis had shrunk back into the darkness and was gone.

Now I would have returned to seek for her, but the Jew at my side called out,

"Give way! Give way and question not the word of the Queen who doubtless has work elsewhere. Be swift; doom is behind you."

For a moment they hesitated, then bent them to their oars while I wondered what might be the meaning of the part that Beltis played. Did she perchance plan

some trap for me? I did not know, but this I knew, that
behind was the burning city, whereas in front lay the
open sea. Whatever its perils I would face the sea, trusting to destiny to be my guide. As for Beltis, doubtless
she took some other road to freedom. Mayhap after all
she would shelter with Mentor, or Ochus had promised
her deliverance in payment for the blood of Tenes.

So I sat silent, and presently the channel took a turn;
the swinging water-gates that hid its mouth were thrust
open with an oar by a man who stood at the barge's
prow, and we passed into the southern harbour.

Yes, out of the darkness we passed into a blaze of
light, and out of the silence into a hideous tumult of
sound. For all around us the city burned furiously and
from it rose one horrible wail of woe.

The rowers saw and understood who until now had
known nothing in the silence of the secret harbour cave.
They hung upon their oars. Then they brought round
the barge's prow seeking to return into the cave, but
could not because those doors had swung to behind
them and, having locked themselves by some device,
could only be opened from within. Nor indeed could I
tell where these were since they seemed to form part of
the harbour wall.

The helmsman looked back and from side to side at
the hell of fire which raged behind and around him. He
looked at the jutting pier upon our right and noted that
already its timbers were ablaze. Then he looked in front
and cried,

"Now I see why the Queen left us! Well, there is but
one chance. Onward to the open sea."

"Aye," I echoed, "onward to the open sea. Here you
must die; there I will lead you to safety. I swear it by
the Queen of Heaven."

"'Tis well to talk," said one, "but how shall we gain
the sea? Look, the Persians are barring the harbour
mouth and slaying those who strive to escape."

It was true. Many of the miserable inhabitants of Sidon had found boats of this sort or of that, or even were
swimming upon logs or barrels. For these the Persians
or those in their pay waited at the mouth of the harbour

and with mocking words and laughter butchered them
as they came. Yes, from their smaller ships they slew
them with spears and arrows or by throwing stones that
drove out the bottoms of the boats.

"Keep in the shadow of the jetty," I said, "where the
wind-driven smoke hangs thick and near which the triremes dare not come because of the rocks whereon it is
built, and row, row fast."

They heard and obeyed. On we went beneath an arching canopy of smoke laced with bursts of flame from
the kindling timbers, till at length we reached the head
of the jetty on which stood a wooden tower where a
light burned at night to be a guide to mariners entering
the harbour. Here we waited a while, clinging to one of
the piers, for although the wind was rising, in this sheltered place the sea remained calm.

Rowing across the head of the jetty was a Persian
trireme, and until she had gone by we dared not attempt
the sea. At length she passed, leisurely, and our chance
came. At a muttered word the oarsmen gave way with
all their strength and we shot clear of the mole into the
open deep. As we did so, I looked back and perceived
behind and above me a sight that after more than two
thousand years still haunts me in my sleep.

Upon the end of this timber-crested mole, as I have
said, there was a wooden tower from which in times of
peace a beacon burned. Now this tower was blazing like
the pierway behind it and no beacon shone there. Only
where it should be stood a woman on whose face the
strong light beat, since the wind swept away the smoke
and revealed her like a statue on a column that rises
above mist. I looked at this shape and this face and saw
that they were those of Beltis the Queen of Sidon. How
she had come there, I do not know, but I think that she
had run along the burning mole before it was too late,
being well acquainted with the path, and had climbed
the stairway of the tower, that from its crest she might
look her last upon Sidon and on life.

There at least she stood, royal-looking, silent, with
her arms crossed upon her breast, while the purple

cloak that marked her rank floated behind her like a banner on the breeze.

She saw the barge that bore us shoot out of the gloom and reek into the deep sea. I know that she saw because she stretched out her arm as though to bless us. Then she turned and lifted her hands toward the burning city as though to curse it. Lastly, once more she folded her arms upon her breast and stood motionless, her white face raised to the heavens.

Thus she remained while one might count an hundred, till suddenly the timbers of the tower, gnawed through by the flames, fell in and she vanished in a roaring gulf of fire.

Such was the end of that great and ill-fated woman, the royal Beltis, Queen of Sidon, whom mayhap in expiation of sin done in another star, the gods gave to the arms of perchance the vilest man that ever lived upon the earth. Greatly she died, a sacrifice, as her son had been a sacrifice, but not before she had wrought a fitting vengeance upon the murderer of her child and the betrayer of his people. Moloch, god of fire, took her as he took them all, but now she was beyond the reach of Moloch, Moloch who was but molten metal, an offering to himself.

In the great flame of the fallen tower the trireme that bore the banner of Ochus saw our boat escaping out to sea and put about to pursue it.

"Row on!" I cried, "row into the darkness," and knowing that their lives hung on the issue, since, as we had already seen, the Persians spared none whom they overtook in the boats but drove the triremes over them, shooting any who swam with arrows, those sailors rowed sturdily. Yet our progress was but slow and that of the three-banked ship behind us fast; moreover, the fires of burning Sidon lit up the sea for miles.

Could we reach the darkness before we were overtaken? We came to its edge with the great trireme not a hundred paces from our stern—so near indeed that the soldiers on board of her began to shoot at us, though in the gathering gloom and because of the rolling platform on which they stood, their shafts went wide. She was right upon us; her hull had vanished in the shadows but the light from the fires still gleamed upon her gilded masthead, while her great oars beat the sea with a sound like thunder.

"Put about," I cried, "or she will sink us."

Very skilfully the steersman obeyed so that we doubled like a hunted hare and the Persian shot past us. Then once more we turned and rowed on into the night. When it wrapped us round, the sailors, exhausted, rested on their oars. Again we heard the thunder of the great slave-manned sweeps, and again the brazen prow of the tall ship, cruel, enormous, hung almost over us. Only by an ell or two did the broad blades of the oars miss us, the eddies that they made causing our little craft to rock dangerously. But this time that huge sea-hound was blinded by the darkness and not seeing us, nor hearing anything, for we sat silent as the grave, she rushed upon her way, and for a time we saw her no more.

All was quiet upon the breast of ocean. Far off burned Sidon like a gigantic beacon fire, but there came to us no whisper of her agony. Yes, all was quiet, save for the sighing of the night wind that, to my strange fancy, seemed like to such a sound as might be made by the rush of ten thousand spirits passing from the cruel earth upward to the peace above. Slowly the wearied oarsmen drove the boat still farther out to sea; then their captain said,

"Whither away, Lady? It is in my mind to change our course and run for the coast northward, where perchance there are no Persians."

"Nay," I answered, "we stay where we are, I search for a ship."

"Mayhap we shall find one," he said with a hoarse laugh, "a ship of the fleet of Ochus."

They began to dispute as to what course they should take.

"Obey me," I said, "or obey me not, as you will. Only then I, who have the counsel of the gods, tell you that save I only, by sunrise to-morrow everyone of you will be dead."

They whispered together, for my words frightened them. At length the captain spoke, saying,

"The great Queen Beltis who is gone told us that this woman is a goddess and that what she commanded, that we must do. Let us remember the words of the great Queen Beltis who is dead and doubtless watches us from the sky."

So this danger passed also, and all that night we floated, keeping the boat's stern to burning Sidon while the most of the oarsmen slept in their places. So weary were they that not even the horror behind them and the loss of their kinsfolk, or even their own fears, could hold them back from sleep.

But I, Ayesha, did not sleep; nay, I watched and thought. If Philo had fled away, or if his ship had been sunk, what then? Then all was finished. Nay, not so, since it could not be that I should die with but half my task accomplished. I was friendless among strange men, yet in my breast there dwelt the greatest of friends, that spirit whose name is Fate. I threw out my soul to my master Noot the Seer, and lo! it seemed to me that his soul answered, saying,

"Fear nothing, Daughter of Isis, for the wings of Isis shadow thee."

It drew near to the dawn; I knew it by the stars which I was wont to watch and by the smell of the air. I rose in my seat and stared into the darkness. Behold! not four furlongs from our prow suddenly there sprang into life a fire of green flame.

"Awake," I cried, "and row on swiftly, for if you would live you must reach the ship upon which yonder fire burns before the breaking of dawn."

They obeyed, wondering, who knew not what this fire might mean. We sped forward, and as the first light gleamed saw almost above us the bulk of the great trireme named *Hapi*.

"Hail her!" I cried, and the captain did so. One appeared by her bulwark rail, holding a lantern. Its light shone upon his face and I saw that it was that of Philo the Greek.

"Ye are saved," I said quietly, "for yonder is the vessel that awaits me."

"Of a truth this is a goddess!" muttered the captain of the barge.

Now Philo saw us in the growing light, and cried to us to come swiftly, pointing to something which he could discover but we could not. We were alongside, eager hands dragged us from the boat. We were aboard, I still carrying the casket of jewels though at the time I did not know I held it fast. Philo bowed the knee to me as to one divine, at which our oarsmen stared. Then he shouted a command and again pointed behind us.

Lo! there, scarce two bowshots away, was the great Persian ship which we had escaped in the gloom of the night.

Our oars struck the water, we leapt forward like an unleashed hound, and after us came the trireme like a lion springing on the hound. Trireme have I called her? Nay, as we saw now, she was a quinquereme, one of the new five-banked ships built by Ochus, a mighty monster. For a little while she hesitated as though wondering whether to attack or let us be. Then as the light strengthened the eyes of her watchmen caught sight of our abandoned boat and by its gilding and emblems knew it for the royal barge of Tenes.

A great shout arose, a shout of

"The King escapes. The King and Queen Beltis escape. After them!"

Then the quinquereme leapt forward in pursuit. Because of her bulk she was slow in gathering speed and we who had the start of her drew away quickly, especially after a shift of wind which seemed to miss the *Holy Fire,* for so Philo, who knew her, said the Persian was named, filled our great sail.

Seeing this and hoping that our danger was past, I went to that same cabin which had been mine when as the captive of Tenes I sailed upon this ship, which seemed to be just as I had left it. This I did without speech to Philo, save a word to commend to his care the Jew and those others who had been my companions upon the barge.

For now that all was over, it seemed to me as though I must rest or die; moreover, I was foul with travel and needed food. This indeed I found ready upon a table which caused me to wonder, though dully, which I did even more when I saw clean woman's garments such as I was accustomed to use spread out upon the cabin couch. So I cleansed and clothed myself and ate a little, drinking some wine, which I did rarely, then lay down upon the couch and for a space, an hour perhaps, slept as though I were dead.

I woke, I knew not why who could have slumbered on for hours, yet feeling as though the most of my weariness had rolled off me. The place was very dim for the curtained door was shut and at first I could see nothing. Presently, however, I became aware that I was not alone in the cabin. For as my eyes grew accustomed to such light as reached it, I discovered the shape of a man, an old, white-bearded man, kneeling at its far end as though in prayer, and wondered whether I dreamed, for what could such a one be doing there? Soon indeed I was sure that I dreamed, since this shape was that of the high-priest Noot, my Master, whom I supposed to be far away in Egypt. Or perchance Noot was dead and this was his spirit that visited me in my sleep. Spirit or dream or man, words came from the lips of that vision spoken in the very voice of Noot; such words as these,

"O Mother Isis, and Thou without a name whom Isis and all the gods serve and obey, I thank ye that ye have been pleased to bring this maiden in safety through her appointed tasks, throwing over her the shield of a strength divine. I thank ye that ye have led her back to me, her father in the spirit, that defilement has not touched her, that fire has not burned her, that water has not drowned her, and that the foeman's spears have not pierced her heart. I pray ye, O Mother Isis and O Thou without a name in the hollow of whose hand lie the world and all that live thereon, that as has been the beginning, so may be the end, and that this chosen woman may return safe to whence she came, there to accomplish those tasks that she was created to fulfil."

Thus that voice prayed on, the holy, well-remembered voice, till at length I brought its supplications to an end, saying,

"Tell me, Noot my father, why do you still fear in this hour of deliverance?"

He rose, he came to me, and drawing aside a curtain on a little window-place, scanned me with kind and gentle eyes. Then he took my outstretched hand, kissed it, and answered,

"Alas! there is still much to fear, O my daughter, but of that you shall learn presently. First tell me the story of what has chanced to you since we parted."

Briefly, omitting much, I told him that tale.

"It is as my spirit showed me," he said when I had finished. "Heaven has not deceived its servant. Your messenger reached us, Daughter, but had he died upon the road it would have mattered little, since long ere he had set foot in Egypt my soul had heard your soul and made all things ready. Yet last night, when Sidon burned, I confess that my faith failed me and this soul of mine shook with fear. Indeed an hour after sunset I thought that your ghost passed me, crying that all was done."

"Perchance it was the ghost of Beltis that passed. But of these things we will talk afterward. I see fear in your eyes. Of what are you afraid?"

"Rise and look through that window-place, Daughter."

I did so and behold! but a little distance away the great quinquereme named the *Holy Fire* sped upon our track, so fast that her five banks of oars lashed the sea to foam.

"Father divine," said a voice without, a voice that I seemed to know, "I have words to say."

"Enter and speak," answered Noot.

The door was opened and the curtain drawn, admitting a rush of sunlight. Lo! there before me stood a warrior clad in such armour as the Greeks wear and, thus attired, the most beautiful and glorious-looking man that ever my eyes beheld.

It was *Kallikrates, Kallikrates himself,* only now in place of the priest's robe his great form was clad in

bronze; in place of a chaplet a helm was on his head
and in place of the *sistrum* his hand gripped a sword
hilt. Yes, it was Kallikrates, he whose lips in past days
had met mine in the holy shrine, but as he had been
before he had vowed himself to Isis because of a certain
crime. For now again he was a man and a captain of
men, not one who with bent brows and humble mien
from hour to hour mutters prayers to an unseen divinity.

Oh! I will tell truth. When I saw him thus I liked
him well. Yes, though for long he had been nothing to
me save a fellow servant of the goddess, once more I
was thrilled with a cup of that same wine which I had
seemed to drink when our lips met far away in Egypt;
once again that fire which I had stamped to ashes beneath my feet sprang to life and scorched my heart.

Mayhap it was his beauty, as great perhaps as that of
any man who ever lived, or mayhap it was the light of
battle that shone in his gray eyes which thus stirred the
woman in me. At least I who had sickened at the sight
of Tenes and all other men, I who had given myself to
higher things and, rejecting the flesh, followed the spirit
only, was stirred like any common maid who finds her
lover at the moonrise. Moreover, Noot, who could read
hearts and above all my heart, noted it for I saw him
smile and heard him sigh.

Perchance Kallikrates also noted something, for the
colour came to his brow—I saw it redden beneath the
plumed helm of bronze, and he dropped those bold and
beautiful eyes. More, he sank upon his knee, saluting
me with the secret sign and saying,

"Pardon, Child of Wisdom, High-priestess of the
Queen of Heaven, that once again, if only for a little
while, I have put on the harness which I used to wear.
It is done to save you, Child of Wisdom. It is done by
command."

"Aye," said Noot, "it is the command of Her we
serve that this priest should lift sword on behalf of Her
and us, her slaves."

I bowed my head, but answered—naught.

CHAPTER XII

The Sea Battle

THE great Persian ship was on us. Strive as we would, we could not escape her. She raced upon our beam not a spear's cast away. I stood upon the high poop of the *Hapi* and saw it all, for the old Arab blood was on fire in me, as it had been when I charged in the battle where my father fell, and I would play no woman's part. Moreover, my spirit told me that I had not escaped from the hands of Tenes and out of the burning hell of Sidon, to die there upon the sea.

Standing thus upon the poop by the side of Philo the cunning captain, I noted this strange thing, that no arrow was shot and no spear thrown from the Persian's decks. She raced alongside of us, that was all. I looked at Philo, a question in my eyes, and he answered the question briefly between his set lips.

"They think the King and Queen are aboard and would take us living. Hark! They shout to us to surrender."

Again I looked at him, wondering what he would do.

He issued an order and presently our speed slackened so that we fell a little behind the Persian. He issued another order and we leapt forward again under a changed helm. Now I saw that he was minded to ram the *Holy Fire*. The Persian saw it also and sheered off. We ran alongside of her, shipping our oars as we came on that side which was nearest to her. But the Persian had no time to ship hers. Our sharp prow caught her fivefold line of sweeps, smashing the most of them as though they were but twigs, and casting the rowers in a broken, tumbled heap within her deep hold.

"That was worthy of Philo," I said, but he, ever a

humble man, as are all masters of their trade, shook his head and answered,

"Nay, Lady, I missed my mark and now we must pay for it. Ah! I thought so."

As he spoke, from sundry places on the *Holy Fire* grapnels flew out which caught in the rails, ropes and rowing benches of the *Hapi*, binding the two ships together.

"They are about to board us," said Philo. "Now, Lady, pray to Mother Isis to give us aid."

Then he blew two blasts upon his whistle. Instantly rose up upon our deck a band of men, nigh a hundred of them, perhaps, clad in armour and captained by the Greek, Kallikrates. Also behind these I saw the crew of the royal barge, armed with such weapons as they could find, and the sailors of the *Hapi*.

The Persians thrust out boards or ladders from one ship to the other, across which their boarders, most of them Greeks, came on in swarms. The fighting began and it was very fierce. Our men cut down many of the foe and drowned others by casting off the boards and ladders, so that those on them fell into the sea. Still a great number of them won on board of us, and oh! fierce was that fray. Always in the thickest of it I saw Kallikrates towering a head above the others, and who now would have dreamed that he was a priest of Isis? For he smote and smote and man after man went down before him, while as his sword rose and fell he shouted out some old Greek battle cry, such as once his fathers used.

On a space of deck ringed round with dead and dying, he came face to face with the captain of the boarders, a great and burly man, also, as I think, a Greek. They fought terribly, whilst others paused to watch that fray which Homer might have sung. Kallikrates was down and my heart stood still. Nay, he was up again but his bronze sword had broken on the foemen's mail.

That foeman had an axe; he swung it up to make an end. Kallikrates, rushing beneath it, seized him in his arms and they wrestled there upon the slippery deck.

The ship lurched; together they staggered to the bulwarks. The foeman loosed one arm and drew a dagger; with it he smote Kallikrates again and again. Kallikrates bent, and with his freed hand seized the man beneath the knee. By a mighty effort he lifted him to the bulwark's edge and there they clung awhile. Then Kallikrates with that same freed hand smote the other on the brow. Thrice he smote and his blows were as those of a hammer falling on an anvil.

The grip of the captain of the boarders loosened and his head hung back. Once more Kallikrates smote and behold! his foe rolled down and was crushed to powder between the swelling sides of the two great ships as they ground one against the other, while the servants of Isis cheered and the sullen Persian hordes gave back.

I caught sight of Philo thrusting his way along the bulwarks. He held an axe in his hand but he was not fighting. Nay, he avoided those who fought. Once indeed he stood still and gave an order, noting, as I had done, that of a sudden the wind had begun to blow. Certain sailors who heard this order ran to the mast and I saw the great sail rising slowly.

Meanwhile Philo slipped along those bulwarks, taking cover beneath them like a jackal beneath a wall. But whenever he came to one of the grapnels he stopped and smote with his axe, severing the rope that held it. Three of them did he sever thus, so that the prows of the vessels swung apart.

Now the great sail was up and filled. The *Hapi* forged ahead, dragging round the stern of the *Holy Fire* by those grapnels that remained. The Persians understood and grew frightened. Those who were still alive upon our decks rushed to the planks and ladders, but few gained them, for Kallikrates and the men of Isis were on their heels. They were cut down; they fell from the sliding planks and ladders, or they leapt into the sea and for the most part drowned there. Very soon not one of them was left upon our deck.

The grapnels were torn away, or the ropes broke. We were free. Yet the Persian was not beaten, for she was full of men of whom those who had been killed were but a tithe.

She, too, hoisted her sail and thrust out fresh sweeps to continue the pursuit. Her captain, standing on her prow, roared out,

"Dogs of Egyptians, I'll hang you yet."

Philo heard and took up his bow. Now we were sweeping across the bow of the *Holy Fire;* mayhap it was a hundred paces away. Philo aimed and shot. So truly did he shoot that his arrow struck the Persian captain beneath his helm and down he went.

His fall seemed to bewilder the crew of the *Holy Fire*. They hung upon their oars shouting at each other, as though they knew not what to do. Then their sail began to rise and I saw that they were putting about.

Philo at my side laughed, a hard little laugh.

"Mother Isis is good to us," he said. "See, the hunter has become the hunted!"

Then he gave orders and we came round so that our great sail taken aback flapped against the mast.

"Down with the sail and row," he shouted, "row as never ye rowed before!"

Those at the sweeps obeyed. Oh! it was splendid to see them bending their broad backs and tugging at the oars till these also bent like bows in the water. Here was no slave work, for they were servants of Isis and free men, every one of them. Philo rushed to the steering gear and with the aid of another man took charge of it himself. We leapt forward like a panther on its prey. The *Holy Fire* saw and strove to escape. Too late, too late! For presently the sharp prow of the *Hapi* crashed into her side with such a shock that all who stood upon the deck were thrown down, I among them. I struggled to my feet again and heard Philo screaming,

"Back water! Back! lest she take us with her."

We backed. Slowly the prow appeared again from where it was buried three paces deep in the foeman's flank.

The *Holy Fire* reeled over; the water rushed in through the gap. Crippled and helpless she wallowed;

aye, she began to sink. From her swarming decks went up a yell of terror and dismay. Still the water rushed in with an ever-gathering flood and still she sank and sank. Men threw up their arms, praying for mercy; men sprang into the sea. Then suddenly the *Holy Fire* reared her glittering prow into the air and stern foremost vanished into the deep. It was finished!

The Persians swam about us, or clung to wreckage, praying to be taken aboard. But we rowed on coming to the wind again. I know not how it is in the world today, but then in time of war there was little mercy. Egypt alone was merciful because age had mellowed her and because of her gentle worship of her gentle gods. But now Egypt was fighting for her life against the Persian. So we rowed on, and those barbarians were abandoned to drown and in the world below seek the warmth of the Fire they worshipped.

Philo left the helm and came to where I stood. I noted that he was white and shaken and called to one to bring him wine. He drank of it thankfully, not forgetting first to pour a libation at my feet, or rather at those of the goddess to whom I was so near.

"Bravely done!" I said. "You understand your trade, Philo."

"Not so ill, Lady, though it might have been better. Had I been at the helm we should have rammed that swarming hulk before the boarding and saved some lives. Well, Set has her now and Ochus lacks his finest ship."

"It might have been far otherwise," I said.

"Aye, Lady. Had I commanded the *Holy Fire* it would have been otherwise, for she had two oars and three men to our one, but her captain was wanting in sea-craft, and when my arrow found him, there was none to take his place. They should have swept us with their boarders, but that tall Greek captain called Kallikrates, who they tell me was once a priest, handled his soldiers well. He is a gallant man and I grieve that we are like to lose him."

"Why?" I asked.

"Oh! because in his fight with a fellow whom he

flung over the bulwarks, he took a knife-thrust in the vitals, which they think will be mortal. See, they are bearing him to my cabin," and he pointed to Kallikrates being carried forward by four men—a sight that stirred my heart.

Then Philo was summoned away, for it seemed that when the *Hapi* rammed, she sprang a leak and the carpenters called Philo to consult with them as to how it might be stopped.

When they had gone I followed after Kallikrates and found him laid in Philo's cabin. They had taken off his armour and the leech, an Egyptian, was cleaning a cut in his thigh whence the blood ran down his ivory skin.

"Is it mortal?" I asked.

"I know not, Lady," answered the leech, "I cannot tell the depth of the thrust. Pray Isis for him, for he has lost much blood."

Now I who was skilled in medicine and in the treatment of wounds which I had learned from a great master in my youth among the Arabs, helped that physician as best I might, staunching the blood flow and stitching up the cut with silk before we bandaged it.

Moreover, taking from my hand a charmed and ancient amulet that gave health and had the power, so it was said, to cause the sick or wounded to recover, I set it on the finger of Kallikrates that it might cure him. This amulet was a ring of brown stone on which were graven certain hieroplyphics that meant *Royal Son of the Sun*. He who gave it to me told me that it had been worn by that greatest of all healers and magicians, Khaemuas, the eldest son of the mighty Rameses. Once only did I see this ring again as shall be told. Then of it I lost sight and knowledge till, after more than two thousand years, I beheld it on the hand of Holly in the caves of Kôr.

As I worked thus the pain of the needle awoke Kallikrates from his swoon. He opened his eyes, looked up and saw me, then muttered in Greek so low that only I who was bending over him heard his words. They were:

"I thank thee, Beloved. I thank thee and the gods who have granted that like my forefathers I should die

no priest, but a soldier and a man. Yea, I thank thee, *O
royal and beautiful Amenartas.*"

Then he swooned again and I left him quickly, having learned that it was of the Egyptian he dreamed, and
doubtless that it was for the sake of this same Egyptian
that he had changed his sacred robe for mail, yes, the
Egyptian Amenartas for whom he had mistaken me,
Ayesha, in the wanderings of his weakness.

Well, why not? What had I to do with him or any
man? Yet of a sudden I grew weary of the world and
almost wished that the *Holy Fire* had rammed the *Hapi*
and not the *Hapi* the *Holy Fire.*

Yonder behind us a thousand men were now at peace
beneath the sea. Being overwrought with all that I had
endured and seen, almost I could have wished that I,
too, was at peace beneath the sea, sleeping for ever, or
perchance to wake again nursed in the holy arms of Isis.

In the cabin sat my master, the prophet Noot, staring
through the open doorway at the infinite blue of heaven
above, as I knew that he had done during all that fearsome fight.

He smiled when he saw me and asked,

"Whence come you, Daughter, and why do your eyes
shine like stars?"

"I come from the sight of the death of men, my Father, and my eyes shine with the light of battle."

"With other lights also, I think, Daughter. O Ayesha,
beauty is yours, wisdom is yours, and you are filled with
spirit like a cup with wine. But what of the cup? What
of the cup? I fear me that those fair feet of yours have
far to travel before they reach their home."

"What is their home, Father?"

"Do you not know it after these many years of learning? Hearken. I will tell you. Your home is God, not
this god or that god called by a hundred names, but the
God beyond the gods. Doubtless you will love and you
will hate, as you have loved and hated. And doubtless
you are destined to draw up what you love and to come
to peace with what you hate. Yet know that above all
mortal loves there is another love in which they must be

both lost and found. God is the end of man, O Ayesha, God or—death. All sin, all stumble on the path, but only those who continue on that path or who, having lost it, with tears and broken hearts seek it again and, like the Sisyphus of fable, thrust before them their frozen load of fleshly error, till at length it melts in the light that shines above; only those, I say, attain to the eternal peace."

So solemnly did he speak, uttering the slow words one by one, and so deep and holy was the lesson that they hid, that I, Ayesha, grew afraid.

"What have you seen and what do you know, my Father?" I asked humbly.

"Daughter, I have seen you yonder in Sidon rejoicing in vengeance for vengeance's sake; aye, glad when the vile hound who would have gripped you, gasped out of his life before your eyes. You did not slay him, Ayesha, but it was your counsel that gave cunning to the thought that planned and strength to the arm that dealt the blow."

"It was so fated, O my father, and otherwise——"

"Yes, it was so fated; yet you should not have rejoiced in the hour of your triumph. Nay, you should have sorrowed as the gods sorrow when they fulfil the decrees of Destiny. Again I have seen you burning with the flame of battle, your heart filled with songs of victory when Philo's skill and the Grecian courage of Kallikrates sent those mad brutes of Persians to their account. And lastly unless I dream—— What did you but now in Philo's cabin, Daughter?"

"I tended a wounded man, my Father, as I have the skill to do. Also I gave him an amulet which it is said has virtue to heal the sick."

"Aye, that was right and kind and the just reward of courage. Did he thank you, Daughter? I thought that in the quiet I heard thanks come from his lips."

"Nay," I answered sullenly, "his mind wandered and he thanked—another woman who was not there."

Again Noot smiled a little, and answered,

"Was it so? Then let her name be. Yet remember that from such wanderings of a mind distraught ofttimes

springs the truth, like water from a shattered rock. Oh!
Daughter, Daughter, if this man forgets his vows, must
you do the same? For him there is excuse who is a soldier—can we doubt it who have looked upon his deeds
to-day? He became a priest for love's sake and the shed
blood which it brought. But for you there is none—at
least none upon the earth," he added hastily. "I pray
you, therefore, let this man be, for if you do not, my gift
of wisdom tells me that you will bring much trouble on
your head and his. Why will you seek after vanity? Is it
because in the pride of your beauty you cannot bear
that another should be preferred before you and that a
fruit which it is not lawful for you to pluck, should fall
into some other woman's lap? I say to you, Daughter,
that this beauty is your curse, because to it you demand
obedience night and day, although of it you should
think nothing, remembering its end. You are too proud,
you are too puffed up. Look upon the stars and learn to
be humble, lest you should be humbled by that which is
stronger."

"I am still a woman, Father, a woman whose mission
it is to love and to bear babes."

"Then learn to love that which is above and let the
babes you bear be those of wisdom and good works. Is
it your part to suckle sinners like any hedge-side troll,
you to whom the heavens stretch out their hands? Is it
for you in whose breast springs the tree of life to root it
up and in its place to sow the seed of a woman's common arts, that by their aid you may snatch her lover
from a rival? Because he sins, if sin he does, should you
cease from being holy? Where is your greatness? Where
are your purity and pride? I pray to you, beloved
daughter of my spirit, swear to me by Heaven which we
serve, that with this man you will have no more to do.
Twice have you sinned—once in the sanctuary yonder
at Philæ when his kiss met yours, and now again not an
hour gone upon this ship, when your heart was torn
with jealous rage because the name of another woman
escaped from lips that you thought were about to shape
your own. Twice have you sinned and twice has the
goddess turned her head and shut her eyes. But if for a

third time you should walk into this pit dug of your own hands, then know that escape will be hard indeed. I tell you"—here his face and his low voice hardened—"I tell you that from age to age shall you strive unceasingly to wash the stain of blood from off those hands and that all your breath shall become a sigh and your every heart-beat shall be an agony. Swear then, swear!"

I looked at his eyes and saw that they were alight and unearthly, yes, that some spirit shining from within caused them to glow like alabaster lamps. I looked at the thin hand which he stretched out toward me and saw that it trembled in his passion.

I looked and was moved to obey. Yet ere I did so I asked,

"Were *you* ever young, my Father? Did *you* ever suffer from this eternal curse which Nature lays on men and women because she would not die? Did *you* ever take the bribe of sweet madness with which she baits her hook? Or, as once I think you told me in bygone years, were you always holy and apart?"

He covered his eyes with those thin hands, then answered,

"I was young. I suffered from that curse. Whatever I may have said to you in the past when you were but a child, I gorged that bait, not once but many times, and I have paid the price. Because I have paid it to my ruin, I pray you whom I love not to empty your heart of its purest virgin gold and fill the void with pain and penitence. Easy is it to fall, Daughter, but hard, very hard to rise again. Will you not swear?"

"Aye," I answered, "I swear by Isis and by your spirit, O Purified."

"You swear," he said, whispering, "but will you keep the oath? I wonder, aye, I wonder greatly, will you keep that oath, O high-hearted woman whose blood runs with so red and strong a stream?"

Then bending forward he kissed me on the brow, and rising left me.

Kallikrates did not die. Under the care of that cunning leech or of something above the leech, Death was cheated of him, since it seemed that the knife-thrust had not reached his vitals, or at least had not pierced them beyond repair. Still he was sick for a long while, for his whole body was drained of blood, so that had he been older, or less vigorous, Osiris would have taken him. Or perchance not in vain had I set upon his finger that scarab-talisman once charmed by Khaemuas. I visited him no more, and thus it was not until we were passing up the Nile and drew near to Memphis that I saw him again. Then, very pale and wasted, yet to my fancy more pleasing than he had been, since now his face had grown spiritual and his eyes were those of one that had looked close into those of Death, he was carried in a bed on to the deck. There I spoke with him, thanking him in the name of our goddess for the great deeds that he had done. He smiled and his white face took a little tinge of red as he answered,

"I fear me, O Mouth-of-Isis, that it was not of the goddess that I thought in that fray, but rather of the joy of battle which *I*, a priest, had never hoped to feel again. Nay, nor was it for the goddess that I smote as best I could, since in the extremities of war the gates of heaven, which are then in truth so near, seem very far away, but rather that after all which you had passed, you, with the rest of us, might not fall into the hands of the heathen fire-worshippers."

Now I smiled back, for the words, if false, were courteous, and replied that doubtless also he, who was still young, desired to go on living.

"Nay," he answered earnestly, "I think that I desire to die rather than to live, and to pass hence as often my forefathers have done, sword in hand and helm on head. Life is no boon to a shaven priest, Lady, one who by his vows is cut off from all its joys."

"What is a man's joy in life?" I asked.

"Look at yourself in a mirror, Lady, and you will learn," he answered, and there was that in his voice which caused me to wonder whether it was possible after all that the wrong name came from his lips in the wanderings of his mind.

For then I did not know that a man may love two

women and at the same time; one with his spirit and the other with his flesh, since through all things runs this war between the spirit and the flesh. The spirit of Kallikrates was always mine, having been given to me from the beginning, but with his flesh it was otherwise, and perchance while he is in the flesh it will so remain.

Before we reached Memphis a signal was made for us to anchor. Then a barge, flying the standard of Pharaoh, came off to us from the shore. On board of it was Nectanebes himself and with him his daughter, the Princess of Egypt, the lady Amenartas; also certain councillors and Grecian captains in his service.

The Pharaoh and the others came aboard to learn tidings of what had chanced at Sidon, and were received by Philo and by Noot. Presently they demanded to be led to me and I met them on the deck outside my cabin, noting that the eyes of Nectanebes were troubled and that his fat cheeks had fallen in.

"So you are returned to us, Oracle-of-Isis," he said in a hesitating voice, scanning my form, for my face he could not see because it was veiled.

"I am returned, O Pharaoh," I answered, bowing before his Majesty. "It has pleased Her whom I serve to deliver me out of the hands of King Tenes of Sidon, to whom Pharaoh offered me as a gift."

"Aye, I remember. It was at that feast when the water in the cup you held turned to blood. Well, if all I hear is true, there has been blood enough out yonder."

"Yes, Pharaoh, the Sidonian seas run red with it. Tenes, Egypt's ally, surrendered the city to Ochus the Persian, thinking to find great advancement, which he won by death, whereon the Sidonians burned themselves in their houses with their wives and children. So it comes about that all Phœnicia is in the hands of Ochus who advances upon Egypt with a mighty host."

"The gods have deserted me!" moaned Nectanebes, waving his arms.

"Aye, Pharaoh," I answered in a cold voice, "for the gods are very jealous and seldom forgive those who forsake them and betray their servants into the hands of enemies that hate them."

He understood and answered in a low, babbling voice,

"Be not angry with me, Oracle-of-Isis, for what else could I do? That Sidonian dog, whom may Set devour eternally, was mad for you. Always I mistrusted him and I was sure that if I refused you to him, he would make his peace with Ochus and bite me in the back, as indeed he threatened at the feast. Also I knew well that Mother Isis would protect you from all harm at his hands, which it seems that she has done."

Now when I heard these words rage filled me and I answered,

"Aye, Pharaoh, Mother Isis has done this and more. Have you heard how your poison worked? Nay? Then I will tell you. Having sacrificed her only son to Dagon, Tenes would have put away Beltis, his queen, to give her place to me. Mad with hate, Beltis led him into the arms of the Persian and afterward when his treachery was accomplished, slew him with her own hand, for I saw the deed. And now, Pharaoh, Sidon has fallen and with it all Phœnicia, and soon, Pharaoh, Egypt will follow Sidon. Aye, I, the Oracle, tell you that because you were pleased to throw the high-priestess of Isis into the arms of Tenes as though she were some singing woman of whom you had wearied, these things have come about. Therefore too soon there will no longer be a Pharaoh in Egypt and the Persian will take the Land of Nile and defile the altars of its gods."

He heard. He trembled. He had naught to say. But there was another who heard also. As I had noted, the Princess Amenartas, when she came on to the ship, went straight to where Kallikrates lay upon a couch beneath an awning on the deck, and there talked with him earnestly. What they said I could not hear for they spoke together beneath their breath. But their faces I could see, and watching them I grew sure that the Greek had made no error of a mind distraught when he spoke this royal lady's name as I tended his wounds. For those faces were the faces of lovers who met after long separation and the passing of great dangers.

Leaving Kallikrates this Amenartas had returned to

her father and stood at his side listening to our talk.
Now she broke in fiercely,

"Surely, Priestess, you were ever a bird of evil omen
croaking of disaster. You fly to Sidon and lo! Sidon
burns, yet you escape with wings unscorched. Now you
flit back to Egypt and again wail of woe like a night owl
of the desert. How is it, O Isis-come-to-Earth, as it
pleases you to call yourself, that you alone escape from
Sidon and return here to curdle the blood of men with
prophecies such as those you uttered at the feast when
by a trick you turned the water into blood? Have you
perchance made friends with Ochus?"

"Ask it of Philo the captain of this ship, Lady," I
answered in a quiet voice. "Or stay. Ask it of yonder
priest which perchance will please you better, the Grecian who in the world was named Kallikrates. Ask them
how I showed friendship to Ochus by so working
through the strength of Isis and their skill and valour
that the Persian's finest ship of war with a multitude of
his sailors and fighting men lies to-day at the bottom of
the deep."

"Perchance because a captain was skilled and a certain priest, or soldier, was brave, that ship is sunk with
all she bore, but not, I think, through you or your prayers, O Oracle. I say to you, Pharaoh, my father, that if I
held your sceptre I would send this *Isis-come-to-Earth*
to seek Isis in Heaven ere she bring more sorrows on us
and Egypt."

"Nay, nay," muttered Nectanebes, rolling his big
eyes, "speak not so madly, Daughter, lest the Mother
should hear and once more smite me. Hearken. Last
night I, who have skill, consulted my spirit, the Dæmon
who obeys me. He came, he spoke. I heard him with my
ears. Yes, he spoke of this prophetess. He said that she
drew near to Memphis on a ship. He said that she was
great, almost a goddess, that she must be cherished, that
to you and me she would be a shelter from the storm,
that in her is the power of One who sits above. O Oracle, O Isis-come-to-Earth, O Wisdom's Daughter, forgive the wild words of this royal child of mine who is

distraught with fear, and know that, to the last, Pharaoh is your friend and your protector."

"As mayhap, if this Dæmon of yours speaks truth, before all is done I shall be the protector of Pharaoh and of the Princess of Egypt whom it pleases to revile me," I replied.

Then bowing to him I turned and sought my cabin.

CHAPTER XIII

✦

The Shame of Pharaoh

WHEN Pharaoh and his daughter had gone, though I did not see them go, I bade farewell to Philo, thanking him much and, in reward for all he had done, calling down on him the blessing of the goddess which he received upon his bended knees. Moreover, when he had risen from them he swore himself to my service, saying that while he lived he would come even from the ends of the earth to do my will. Also he showed me how I might call him by certain secret ways.

So we bade farewell for a while, nor did I let him go empty-handed, since from those jewels that Tenes had heaped upon me, which almost by accident I had preserved in my flight, I took certain of great value and gave them to him as a gift from the goddess. Thus we parted though, as both of us were sure, not for the last time.

So soon as our coming was known the priests and priestesses of Isis flocked to the quay in solemn procession to receive Noot, their high-priest, and me their high-priestess, which they did with sacred ceremony and holy chants. By them we were escorted through the streets of Memphis to the temple of Isis accompanied by many of the crew of the *Hapi* that were of our brotherhood. Among them I missed one.

"Where is the priest Kallikrates?" I asked of Noot.
He smiled and answered,

"I think that he has been taken to the palace of Pharaoh to be nursed until he recovers from his wounds.
Perchance for a while he is minded, or it is decreed that
he should continue to play a warrior's part. Yet fear
not, Daughter; those upon whose brow Isis has laid her
hands, in life or death must return to her at last. They
are hawks upon a string which, though it stretches, cannot be broken."

"Aye," I answered, "in life or death," and asked no
more of this Kallikrates.

In the midst of the rejoicings of the city at our safe
return, we came to the temple and made sacrifice.
There it was that I set the jewels of Tenes, all save those
that I had given to Philo, upon the alabaster statue of
the goddess in her inmost shrine that only I and Noot
might enter, and there too by signs and wonders she
signified to me her acceptance of the offering. For here
while we stood alone before the effigy of the goddess in
that holy place, a trance fell upon Noot and in his
trance he spoke to me with the voice of Isis and out of
her infinite heart. This was the divine message that
came to me through the lips of Noot:

"Daughter, I, thy mother, know of all that thou hast
passed and of all that thou must pass. Though the barbarian come and the gods of Egypt are thrown down
and ruin smites the land and thou seemest to be left
alone, abide thou here till my word bids thee to depart.
By myself and That of which under the name of Isis I
am a minister, I swear that no harm shall befall thee or
that place where thou art, or those of my servants who
remain with thee. Therefore await my commands with
patience, doing such things as I inspire thee to do, that
thou mayest bring the vengeance of the gods upon those
dogs who desecrate their shrines."

Thus spoke Noot in his trance, not knowing what he
had said until I told him afterward. He listened earnestly and bade me obey.

"Even if I be taken from you for a while, as it comes
to me will happen—perchance I learned it in my swoon,

Daughter—and you are left unfriended and alone, still I pray you to obey. If so, think not that I am dead, who do but return to my own place and land, but wait until my message comes. Then obey that also though I know not what it will be."

Thus he spoke solemnly and I bowed my head and hid his words within my heart——

The war began, Egypt's last war for life. Nectanebes the Pharaoh, inspired by his evil Dæmon, thrust aside his captains and declared himself General in Chief of his armies, he who had scarce the wit or the courage to command the guard of a harem. At first that Dæmon served him well, since at Barathra, as the gulfs are named which make the Sirbonian bog, the Persians were trapped and lost many thousands of their men who sank through the sand into the marches and there were drowned or speared. But their numbers were uncountable and the rest came on. Pelusium was besieged and for a while held its own against the giant Nicostratus of Argos, a man as strong as Hercules who, like Hercules, clothed himself in a lion's skin and for a weapon bore a great club. The Grecian captain, Kleinios of Cos, he who had been present at the feast when I was given over to Tenes and whom in my vision at that feast I had seen dead, lying upon a heap of slain, attacked Nicostratus and after a mighty fight was defeated, Kleinios and five thousand men of those who were with him being slain. Thus was my vision fulfilled.

Then his Dæmon departed from Nectanebes taking his heart with him, for of a sudden Pharaoh ceased to be a man and, becoming a coward, fled back to Memphis, leaving his fleet, his cities, and their garrisons to their fate.

Rumour ran fast; it told of the fall of city after city, some stormed, some bribed to surrender; it told that Ochus had sworn to burn Memphis and after it Thebes; also to seize Nectanebes and roast him living upon the altar in the great temple of Ptah here at Memphis, or otherwise to make him fight with the bull Apis after the beast had been driven mad by fiery darts. It told that the

Egyptians, enraged at the desertion of their armies by
Pharaoh, would themselves seize him and give him up to
Ochus as a peace-offering. Crowds gathered and rushed
through the streets of Memphis calling imprecations on
his name, or clustered like bees round the altars of the
gods, praying for help in their despair, yes, round the
neglected altars of the gods of Egypt.

Then of a sudden came Amenartas, flying to the temple of Isis for sanctuary, since it was reported that
Ochus had said that the shrines of Isis he would spare
alone, because she was the Mother of all things and her
throne was in the moon and her husband was Osiris-Ra
who was the Father of fire which he worshipped; also
because a certain priestess of the goddess had done him
great service in the war, words that caused me to wonder.

So this royal princess came and put on the veil of a
novice that it might protect her should Ochus take the
city. But though this veil changed her face and form to
the eyes of men, her heart it did not change.

A little later came Kallikrates from the war in the
Delta where I learned he had done great things, fighting
bravely. Indeed he told me himself that he had fought
the giant Nicostratus in single combat and wounded
him, though the matter was not pressed to an end, since
others rushed up and separated them. He said that he
was a very terrible man and that when that huge club of
his wavered above him, for the first time in his life he
felt afraid. Notwithstanding he ran in beneath the club
and stabbed Nicostratus in the shoulder.

Thus it happened that all being lost in war and his
service at an end, Kallikrates the captain once more became Kallikrates the priest and again put on the robes
of Isis. Therefore in that temple, serving together before
its altars were Amenartas, Princess of Egypt, and Kallikrates, priest of Isis.

Often I, Ayesha, seated in my chair of state as first of
that holy company, save the aged Noot alone, watched
them from beneath my veil while they anointed the
statue of the goddess or joined in the sacred chants and
hymns of praise. As I watched I noted this—that always

they drew near together as though some strength compelled them; that always their glances thrown from the corners of their eyes, met and turned away and met again, and that always, if occasion served, the robe of the one brushed the robe of the other, or the hand of the one touched the hand of the other. These things I noted in silence, wondering what judgment the goddess would call down upon this beauteous pair who dared thus to violate her sanctuary with their earthly passion. Oh! much I wondered, though little did I guess what it would be and by whose hand it was destined to fall upon them.

Lastly came Nectanebes himself, his great eyes full of terror and his fat frame wasted with woe and sleeplessness. He sought audience of me.

"O Prophetess," he said, "all is lost! Ochus Artaxerxes has his foot upon my neck. I fly, seeking shelter beneath the wings of Isis, seeking shelter from you, O Isis-come-to-earth. Help me, daughter divine, for my Dæmon has deserted me, or if he comes at all it is but to jibber and to mock."

"Strange words from Pharaoh," I answered in a voice of scorn, "very strange words from Pharaoh who gave this same prophetess to be the woman of a vile, Baal-serving king; from Pharaoh who has deserted his army, his country, and his gods, and now seeks only to save his treasure and his life."

"Reproach me not," he moaned, "Fate has been too strong for me, as perchance one day it may be too strong for you also. At first all went well. In the bygone years I conquered the Persian; I built temples to the gods. Then of a sudden Fortune hid her face and now—and now!"

"Aye, O fallen Pharaoh," I answered, "and why did Fortune hide her face? I will tell it, to whom it has been revealed. It was because although you built temples to the gods, you were false to the gods. In secret, following the counsel of that Dæmon of yours, you made bloody sacrifice to devils, to Baal, to Ashtoreth, and to Aphrodite of the Greeks. Nay, do not start and deny, for I know all. Lastly, to crown your crimes, you gave

me, the high-prophetess of Isis, to the base, red-handed
Tenes, one who offered his own son to idols. What has
chanced to Tenes who took me, and say, what shall
chance to him who sold me, O Nectanebes no more a
Pharaoh?"

Now I thought that surely he would kill me and cared
not if he did. For my heart was sore—oh! because of
many things my heart was sore. But like a beaten cur he
only cowered at my feet, praying me to pardon him,
praying me to cease from beating him with my tongue,
praying me to counsel him. I listened and pity took hold
of me, who was ever tender-minded though a lover of
justice and a hater of traitors.

"Hearken," I said at last. "If Ochus finds you here,
O fallen Pharaoh, first he will make a mock of you and
then he will torture you to death. I have heard what he
will do. He will bring you to his judgment seat and lay
you bound upon your back and grind his sandals upon
your face. Then he will force you to sacrifice to the fire
that he worships and one by one to spit upon the effigies of the gods of Egypt. Lastly, either he will cause
the holy bull Apis to gore you to death, or he will bind
you upon the altar in the temple of Ptah and there
slowly with torments being you to your end."

Now when Nectanebes heard these things, he wept
and I thought that he would swoon away.

"Hearken," I said again, "I will show you a road
whereby although defeated and disgraced you may yet
win glory that shall be told of from age to age. Summon
the people while there is yet time. Go to the temple of
Ammon, King of the gods of Egypt. Stand before the
shrine of Ammon and make confession of your sins in
the ears of all. Then, there in the sight of all, slay yourself, praying Ammon and all the gods to accept your life
as an offering and to spare Egypt and the people upon
whose head you, the hated of the gods, have brought all
these woes. So can you cause the Persian and the world
to marvel and say that though accursed, still you were
great, and so perchance you shall turn away the wrath of
heaven from apostate Egypt."

A flash of pride shone in his eyes that had been

empty of light and filled with tears. He lifted his head stiffly as though still it felt the weight of the great ear-rings of state, the golden uræus, and the double crown. For a moment he looked as once he had done at Sais reviewing his triumphant army after his first victory over the Persians and drinking in the incense of its shouts, yes, he looked as great Thotmes and the proud Rameses might have done in their day, a Pharaoh, the king of all the world he knew.

"It would be well to die thus," he murmured, "it would be very well, and then, perhaps, the gods I have betrayed would forgive me, the old, old gods to whom thirty dynasties of recorded kings have bowed the knee, and those who went before them for unnumbered gener-ations. Yes, then perhaps that great company of Pha-raohs would not turn their backs on me or spit at me when I join them at the table of Osiris. But, Prophet-ess"—here his face fell in again and his crab-like eyes projected and rolled, while his voice sank to a whisper, "Prophetess, *I dare not.*"

"Why, Nectanebes?"

"Because—oh! because years ago I struck a bargain with a certain Power of the Under-world, a dæmon if you will, at least some spirit of evil that comes I know not whence and dwells I know not where, which became manifest to me. It promised me glory and success if I would sacrifice to it—nay, I will not tell what I sacri-ficed, but once I had a son, yes, like Tenes I had a son——"

Here I, Ayesha, shivered, then motioned to him to speak on.

"This was the bargain, that though to please the peo-ple I might build temples to the gods, by certain means I must defile them in their shrines. Aye, and I did defile them, and when the priest dressed me, the Pharaoh, in the trappings of those gods according to custom, by thought and word and deed I blasphemed them. Yet one divinity remained outside the pact because my Dæmon warned me that she was too strong for him and must not be offended," and he paused.

"Was she perchance named Isis?" I asked.

"Aye, Prophetess, she was named Isis and therefore I never polluted her shrine and therefore to her alone in my heart I offered prayer. So all went well and I gathered great armies and vast wealth, I hired Greeks by thousands to fight for me, I made alliances with many kings and was sure that again I should defeat the Persians and be the master of the world. Then came the evil hour of that accursed feast at which you, the Mouth of Isis, were summoned to prophesy and, moved by some madness, you unveiled your beauty before Tenes, and I, forgetting whose minister you were, gave you to Tenes, thereby outraging Isis in your person."

"Did I not warn you, Nectanebes, and did not the holy Noot warn you?"

"Aye, you warned me, but in my need I took the risk, or I forgot. From that moment all went ill and ruin, like a giant before whom none may stand, has hunted me by night and day."

"Yes, Nectanebes, and Isis is the name of that giant."

"I made error upon error," he went on. "I trusted to Tenes and Tenes betrayed me. My Dæmon counselled me to thrust aside the Grecian generals and take command of the armies, and at first there was victory, then came defeat. It might have been retrieved, but of a sudden my courage failed me. It fell like a temple of which the foundations have been washed out by hidden waters. It crashed down; in a moment its proud pylons, its tall columns, its massive, honourable walls blazoned with the records of glorious deeds, fell to a shapeless heap hidden in the dust of shame. I am undone. I am what you see, a loathsome worm, a wounded worm wriggling in the black slime of despair, I who was Pharaoh."

Again pity touched me, Ayesha, and I answered,

"There still remains the road that I have pointed out. While we live, however black our record, repentance is always possible, since otherwise there would be no hope for man the sinner. Moreover, repentance, if it be true, brings amendment in its train, and this god-born pair struggling upward, hand in hand, over cruel rocks, through swamps and streams, through brakes and briars, blinded with tears and the gross darkness of despair, at length see the sweet shape of Forgiveness shining before them like a holy dawn such as never gleams upon this world. Hearken, therefore, to one who speaks not with her own voice, or out of the foolishness of her own weak flesh, but as she is commanded of a spirit that is within her. Go to the temple of Ammon and there in the presence of the people make confession of your sins and fall, a sacrifice, upon your sword. Self-murder is a sin, but occasions come when to live on is a greater sin, since it is better to die for others than to cherish breath that poisons them."

"To die! There you speak it, Prophetess. I say again that I dare not die. When I die I pass to the Dæmon. This was the pact: that for my life he should give me success and glory and that in return after death, I should surrender him my soul."

"Is it so?" I answered. "Well, the bargain is ancient, as old as the world, I think; one also that every human being in his degree seals or refuses to seal in this way or in that. Still my counsel holds. This Dæmon of yours has broken his oath, for where now are the success and glory, Nectanebes? Therefore he cannot claim the fulfilment of your own."

"Nay, Prophetess," he answered in a wailing voice, "he has *not* broken it. From the first he told me that I must work no harm to Isis the Mother, since the Queen of Heaven was more powerful than all the denizens of hell, and that if once it were spoken, her Word of Strength would pierce and shrivel him like a red-hot sword and cutting his web of spells, would bring his oaths to nothingness and me with them. And now the web is cut, and I the painted insect that it meshed, fall from it to where the hell-born spider sits in his hole. Prophetess, I have seen him with these eyes, I have seen his orbs of fire, I have seen his snout and fangs like to those of a crocodile, I have seen his great hairy arms and the searching talons stretched out to grip me, and I tell you that I dare not die to be cast into the jaws of the Devourer and burn eternally in his belly of flames. Show me how to save my life, so that I may continue to look upon the sun. Oh! because you are a tender woman and charitable, though I have sinned against you, show me how to save my life."

Now hearing this creature plead with me thus, this coward who at the last did not dare go face the indignant gods like a man, saying, as a great soul should, "I have deeply erred, O ye Gods; I repent, pardon me of your nobility, or slay my soul and make an end," my pity left me and its place was filled with scorn and loathing.

"Those who would live when the Persian dogs are on their heels, must fly fast and far, Nectanebes; they must fly like the deer of the desert on whom the hunters close. The road up Nile is empty, Nectanebes; as yet there are no Persians there. As you would not die, take it and live."

"Aye," he said as the thought went home, "why not? I have still a vast treasure; for many years I have hoarded against misfortune, for who can put all his trust in any Dæmon? With it I can buy friends in the south; with it I may found another empire among the Ethiopians or those of Punt. Why should I not fly Prophetess?"

"I know not," I answered, "save that Death is always fast and untiring and in the end wears down the swiftest runner."

This I said darkly for at that moment there came into my mind a vision that once I had seen of a certain servile slave, aforetime a Pharaoh, that same royal slave who grovelled before me; yea, a vision of him throttling in a rope while black men mocked him. Yet of that I said nothing, only added,

"If it should please you to go south, Nectanebes, would it please you also to take with you that royal and beautiful lady, Amenartas your daughter, aforetime Princess of Egypt?"

"Nay," he answered sharply, "since hour by hour she scourges me with her tongue because I am fallen. Let her abide here under the veil of Isis. Yet why do you ask this, Prophetess?"

"Because of Isis. Because, as I think, this lady of the royal blood makes play with a certain priest who is sworn to Isis, and the goddess does not love that her vowed servitors should desert her for the sake of mortal woman."

"What priest?" he asked dully.

"A Greek who is named Kallikrates."

"I know him, Prophetess. A very beauteous man, like to their own Apollo; a brave one too who did good service yonder in the marshes, fighting the giant general whom he wounded. Also I remember that in the past he was a captain of my guard before he became a priest and that there was trouble concerning him, though what trouble I forget, save that Amenartas pleaded for him. Well, if he has offended you, there are still those who do my will. Send for him, and if it pleases you, he shall be killed. I give you his life. Yes, his blood shall flow at your feet. Indeed I will command it at once, since you tell me he has shamed the goddess or angered you, her priestess," and he opened his hands to clap them, summoning the messengers of death.

I saw, I thrust my arm between so that they struck not upon each other, but upon my soft flesh, making no sound.

"Nay," I said, "this warrior-priest is a good servant of the Queen Isis, one, moreover, who fought for me, her prophetess, upon the seas. He shall not die for so small a matter. Yet I pray you, Nectanebes, take with you the royal princess Amenartas, when you fly south with your treasure."

"Aye," he answered wearily, "as it is your desire I'll take her if she will come, though if so there will be small rest for me."

Then he went, bowing to me humbly, and this was my farewell to Nectanebes, the last Pharaoh of Egypt. I watched him go and wondered whether I had done well in forbidding him to kill Kallikrates. It came into my mind that the death of this man would save me much trouble. Why should he not die as others did who had sinned against the goddess? An answer rose within me. It was that he had sinned, not only against the goddess, but also against me—and this by perferring another woman before me.

Was I then so feeble that I could not hold my own against another woman should I choose to do so? Nay. Yet my trouble was that I did not choose.

Now I saw the truth. My rebellious flesh desired that which my spirit rejected. My spirit was far from this man, yet my flesh would have him near. Aye, my flesh said: "Let him be slain rather than another should take him," while my spirit answered, "What has he to do with one whose soul is set upon things above? Let him go his way, and go you yours. Above all, be not stained with his blood."

So I let him go, not knowing that it was written in the books of Fate that I *must* be stained with his blood, steeped in it to the eyes. Aye, I saved him from the sword of Nectanebes and let him go, determining to think of him no more.

Yet as it chanced Fate played me an evil trick in this matter. On the morrow, or the next day, I sat in the gloom of the outer sanctuary praying to the goddess to ease me of my sore heart, for alas! strive as I would to hide it, that heart was sore. There came a white-robed priest, Kallikrates himself, but changed indeed from that glorious Grecian warrior who had beat back the boarders on the *Hapi,* or who had fought in single combat with the giant Nicostratus. For now the little golden curls were shaven from his head and he was pale with the thin diet of the fruits of the earth and pure water which alone might pass the lips of those who were sworn to Isis, enough indeed for me who touched no other food, or such a one as the aged Noot, but not for a great-framed man bred to the trade of arms. Moreover, his face was troubled as though with some struggle of the soul.

He passed me unseen and going to the statue of the goddess, knelt down before it and prayed earnestly, perhaps for help and blessing. Rising at length, once more he passed me and I saw that his gray eyes were full of tears and longed to comfort him. Also I saw that still he carried on his hand that ring talisman which I had set there upon the ship *Hapi,* that it might perchance defend him from the evil influences which desire and compass the death of men.

He went out across the pillared court toward the cloister at its end. From this cloister appeared a woman, the dark and beauteous Amenartas herself. This was easy to see since, I know not why, she had put off the veil of Isis and was gloriously attired in the robes of a princess—scanty enough I thought them, for they left bare much of her loveliness—while on her dark and abundant hair shone a golden circlet from which rose the royal uræus, and on her arms and bosom sparkled jewels and necklaces.

They meet by plan, thought I to myself. But it was not so, for seeing her, Kallikrates started and turned to fly; also he covered his eyes with his hand as though to hide her beauty from him. She lifted her face like one who pleads, yes, and when he would not hearken, caught him by the hand and drew him into the shadow of the cloister.

There they remained a long while, for at this hour the place was deserted by all. At length they appeared again on the edge of the shadow and I saw that her arms were about him and that her head rested on his breast. They separated. She vanished into the shadows and went her way, while he walked to and fro across the court, muttering to himself like a man who knows not what he does.

I came from my place and met him, saying,

"Surely you are troubled, Priest. Can it be that the goddess refuses your prayers? Or is it perchance that you weary of them and would still play the part of a warrior of warriors as you did on the galley *Hapi,* or but the other day yonder in the northern marshes? If so, it is too late, Priest, for Egypt is fallen and all is lost. That is, unless, like Mentor and many of your race, you would sell your sword to Ochus Artaxerxes."

"Aye, Prophetess," he answered, "Egypt is lost which, being a Greek, should not trouble me over much, and I too am lost, I, the driven of an evil fate."

"Speak on if it pleases you. Or be silent if it pleases

you, O Priest. What the prophetess hears, she tells only to the Mother."

Then I turned and went back into the shadow of the shrine where I leaned against a pillar—I remember that on it was sculptured the scene of Thoth weighing hearts before Osiris. Here I waited, wondering whether he would follow me or go his ways.

For a while he stood hesitating, but at length he followed me.

"Prophetess," he said hoarsely, "I speak under the veil of Isis, knowing that such confessions cannot be revealed. Yet it is hard to speak, since the matter has to do with woman, aye, and with yourself, most holy Prophetess."

"In Isis I have no self," I answered.

"Prophetess, in bygone years, as I think you know, I learned to love a royal maiden, one set far above me, and it seems that she loved me. That passion brought a brother's blood upon my hands, as you also know. I fled to the goddess, seeking peace and forgiveness. For in me I think there are two selves, the self of my body and the self of my soul."

"As in most that breathe beneath the sun," I answered, sighing.

"I was bred a soldier, one who came from a race of soldiers, men of high blood and good to look upon, as once I was, though in this garb few would guess it."

"I have seen you wearing war-harness and can guess," I answered, smiling a little.

"That soldier-self, Prophetess, was as are others of the breed. I drank and I revelled, I bowed the knee to Aphrodite, loving women and for an hour being loved. I fought, not without honour. Then seeking advancement, with my brother I entered the service of Pharaoh, and of that story doubtless you know the rest."

I bowed my head and he went on,

"I came to Philæ, I made confession, I took the first vows. At night and alone I was led to the sanctuary, there to see the vision of the goddess. I saw that vision glowing in the darkened shrine, and oh! it was glorious."

Here I started and watched him narrowly, wondering how much he knew or guessed.

"Something took hold of me, Prophetess, for now I beheld her whom all my soul adored, her with whom it would be united. It was as though a memory came to me from afar, a memory and a promise. That Power which took hold of me caused me to bend my head as though to kiss the vision and thereby pledge my soul to the divine. The vision also bent its head and our lips met, and lo! hers were like to those of mortal woman, yet sweeter far."

"The Mother is mistress of all shapes, Priest. Yet think not that she forgets the pledge that thus it pleased her to accept. From that moment you were sworn to her, and doubtless in a day to come, in this form or in that, she will claim you—should you remain true to her, O Priest."

"The years passed," he went on, "and true I remained. Fate brought me here to Memphis and in this temple I saw you, holy Prophetess, and learned to worship you from afar, not with the body, but with the spirit; since to me you were and are what the vulgar call you, *Isis-come-to-Earth,* and the sight of you ever put me in mind, as it does today, of that divine vision whose lips met mine in the shrine at Philæ. Perchance you never knew it, but thus with my spirit I worshipped you."

Now I, Ayesha, remained silent, leaning against the pillar, for weakness took hold of me who felt as though I were about to fall. Yet—and let the vengeful gods write this to my honour—yet I made him no sign that I was she who had played the part of Isis in the sanctuary.

"It is well," I said presently, "and doubtless at the appointed hour the goddess will thank you. But what then is your trouble, Priest? To love a goddess with the spirit is no crime."

"Aye, Prophetess. But what if he who loves the goddess with his spirit and is sworn to her alone for ever in a vow of perpetual chastity, should love a woman with his flesh and thus betray both heaven and his own soul?"

"Then, Priest," I answered, speaking very low, "I fear that he is one whose hope of forgiveness is but small. Yet for those who repent and deny, there is pardon. Only they must deny, they must deny while there is still time."

"Easy to say and hard to do," he answered, "at least for him who has to deal with one that will not be denied; with one who holds his heart in the hollow of her hand and crushes it; with one whose eyes are like starbeacons to which the wanderer must fly; with one whose breath is as roses and whose lips are as honey; with one who can drive the desires of man as a racer drives his chariot; with one to whom oaths also have been sworn, such oaths as the youth swears to the maid in the first madness of the flesh, decreed by those who made it. Goddesses are far away, but woman is near; moreover, among men there is a law which even a prophetess may understand, which says that oaths vowed with the lips may not be broken to benefit the vower's soul."

"These are ancient arguments," I answered; "from age to age they echo from the roofs of the temples of Aphrodite and of Ashtoreth, but Isis knows them not. The flesh is given to mankind that its wearers may learn to scorn and trample it; the spirit is given to mankind that its holders may learn to rise upon its wings. Woe to those who choose the flesh and reject the spirit. Repentance is still possible, and after it comes amendment and after amendment, forgiveness."

He brooded awhile, then said,

"Prophetess, I repent who above all things desire at the end—that end which again and again I have sought in battle wherever it has passed me by—to be united with the goddess, shaped like the divine one whom I saw in the shrine at Philæ. Yes, with her and with no other. But how can I amend who am a lion in a net, a net woven of woman's hair?"

Now I searched him with my eyes and learned that although so sore beset, this man spoke nothing but the truth. Then I answered,

"The wise bird flies the snare which it sees spread in its sight. To-morrow at the dawn Noot the Holy sails north to meet certain ambassadors of the Persians and if he can make terms, to ransom the temples of Isis from the rage of Ochus. Will you go with him, breathing no word of his purpose or of yours? If so, perchance thus at last you shall find that goddess whose lips met yours at Philæ, here—or otherwhere."

He thought awhile, then muttered,

"It is hard, very hard, yet I will go; I who would satisfy my soul and not my flesh."

As he spoke a tall priestess flitted past us, passing from shadow into shadow, but thinking that she was one of those whose duty it was to watch the inner shrine at this hour, I took no note of her. Nor did Kallikrates, lost in his own thoughts, so much as see her.

CHAPTER XIV

∾

The Beguiling of Bagoas

THAT night Noot my master came to bid farewell to me.

"I go north as I have been commanded—as to how the command came, let that be—hoping thereby to preserve the temples of our worship and those who serve in them. I know not if I shall return, or when, and therefore, Daughter of my spirit, it grieves me to part from you in these troublous times. Yet the command said that you must not accompany me but bide here. For your comfort, learn two things: first, that no harm shall come to you, as I have told you before; and secondly, though that hour be far away, even in the flesh we shall meet again. Wait then till my word comes to you."

I bowed my head in obedience and asked whether he was unattended.

"Nay, Daughter," he answered. "I take with me certain of our fellowship, and among them that Greek Kallikrates who has asked leave to accompany me. Being a man of war, as you have seen, he may perchance prove of service upon such a mission. How he learned that I was going I cannot say," he added, looking at me curiously.

"I told him. Ask no more, Master."

"There is little need, I think," he answered, smiling. "It may please you to learn," he added bitterly, "that the traitor who was Pharaoh, flies up Nile to-morrow ere the dawn. Already they lade his ship with the chests of Egypt's treasure, many of them, that should have gone to pay his soldiers and strengthen his allies."

"May the counting of them comfort him in his honourable exile among the Ethiopians! Yet, my Master, I think that he will need to count quickly, unless it pleased the gods to send a false vision to me when I prophesied in the palace yonder, ere this shameless Nectanebes gave the Daughter of Isis to Tenes the Sidonian."

"If so, Ayesha, the gods sent a false vision to me also. How will he face them, I wonder, with the blood of Egypt on his hands, and with what voice will he tell them of their desecrated shrines?"

"I know not, Master, yet it was written that because of her apostasies and sins Egypt must fall. Can the gods, then, be wroth with their own instrument?"

Noot pondered awhile, shaking his head, then answered,

"Go ask that question of the Sphinx who sits yonder in the sand by the pyramids of the ancient kings brooding, as the legend says, over the secrets of earth and heaven. Or," he added slowly, "when your own days are done, Ayesha, ask it of your soul. Perchance then some god will make clear the riddle of the world below, but here on earth it cannot be answered, since he who could read it would know all things and be himself a god. Sin must come, and to sin, sinners are necessary.

But to what sin is necessary, I do not know, unless it be that from it good is born at last. At least the sinner can plead that he is but an arrow on the bow of Destiny and that the arrow must fly where the shooter aims, even though it drinks innocent blood, widows women, and makes children fatherless."

"Mayhap, my Master, it will be answered to this arrow that it fashioned itself to deal out death; that it grew the wood and forged the barb and bound upon its shaft the feathers of desire; which wood, had it chosen otherwise, here or elsewhere might have flourished—a tree bearing fruits—or as seasoned wood, shaped itself to be a staff to lean upon or a rod of justice in the hands of kings."

"You are wise, Ayesha, nor have I instructed you in vain," he replied with a gentle smile. "Yet I repeat, when for the last time you watch the sun sink and your soul prepares to follow it over the edge of the world, then again propound to it this riddle and hear the answer of that invisible Sphinx which broods in the heaven above, on the earth below, and in the breast of every child it bears."

Thus he spoke and waved his hand, making an end of that debate. Nor have I ever forgotten it, or his words, and now when sometimes I feel or hope soon I, even I, the half-immortal, may see the sun sink for the last time, once more, as Noot commanded, I ask this riddle of the Sphinx that broods within my instructed spirit, and wait its answer. For alas and alas! how am I better than Nectanebes? He betrayed the gods. Have I not betrayed the gods who were nearer to me than ever they came to his coarse and gluttonous soul? He shed blood to satisfy his rage and lust. Have I not shed blood and shall I not perchance shed more of it before all is done, when my unconquerable appetites are on me and there is a dear prize that I would win? He fled with the treasures of Egypt to waste them in the desert sand. Have I not fled with the treasures that were given me— with the jewelled crowns of my wisdom, with the golden talents of my heaped-up learning, with the alabaster vessel of my beauty, with the perfumes of my power

and my eloquence—that drilled, ordered, and massed
together, and added to the greatest gift of all, my length
of undying days, might have reformed the world and led
it into peace?

Have I, Ayesha, not fled with all these countless
splendours clasped upon my breast, and buried them in
the wilderness, as did Nectanebes with Egypt's wealth,
before the barbarians slew him? Have I not done these
things because of a great desire and because, robbed of
that desire, the world I should have guided was gall to
my tongue and gravel to my teeth? Yet was I to blame?
Was not that blind man I loved to blame who could not
see with his darkened, fleshly eyes the glory that lay
within his grasp and thus stirred my soul to madness?
Was not the woman to blame also who darkened those
eyes of his by arts the evil gods had given her?

Oh! I know not. Perchance they too can put up a
tale before the Judgment Seat which I shall find it hard
to answer, for they too are as they were made, or as
they made themselves, shaping their own arrows from
the wood of circumstance that grew I know not where.
And now my desire has drawn near to me again; it
gleams, a glittering fruit, upon the Tree of Life, and I
stretch out my hand to pluck it. Yes, I stand on tiptoe
and almost reach it with my finger-tips. Yet what if it
prove a corruption? What if it crumble into dust, rotted
by the great sun of my spirit, withered at the fingering
of my undying hand?

Oh! my lord hunts upon the mountain after the fashion of men, and Atene, once named Amenartas, sits in
her dark beauty in the City of the Plains and, as aforetime, plots my ruin and her fleshly theft. Who knows
the end? But there within my soul broods the Sphinx
smiling its immortal smile and to it soon or late I must
put that question to which Noot, the holy and half divine, could give no answer—or would not if he could.

"What of the royal Princess, Amenartas?" I asked.
"Know, Master, that I grow weary of this woman."

"Aye, Daughter, these temple courts are wide, but

not wide enough for both of you. Take comfort, she sails to-morrow."

"North?" I asked.

"Nay, south with her father, Nectanebes. Or so she tells me, saying that his fortune shall be her own and that together they will reign or fall."

"It is well," I answered.

Then we talked of humble matters that had to do with the shrine of the goddess and of the hiding away of her treasures lest the Persians should take them. When all was finished, Noot rose, blessed me, calling on the Powers above to protect me, and went his ways in the ship *Hapi* which he had purchased to bring it to my aid at Sidon, nor did I guess that for years I should see him no more. Yet I think he knew it well.

Like a mighty river in its flood the Persian hosts poured down on Memphis. As such a torrent sweeps away the village and the humble homestead, drowns the cattle, twists out the palm trees by their roots, covers the corn with slime, floods cities, palaces, and temples, chokes the breath from their inhabitants and strews the kind earth with the corpses of those that tilled it, so did Ochus and his barbarians to Egypt. Rapine and massacre, flames of fire and misery marked their path. Men were butchered by the thousand, the aged and women who were no longer fair were driven into the desert to starve. Yes, it was the sport of those Persians to drive them like game to where there was no water, and then watch them die of thirst beneath the burning sun. Only the young women were spared to be concubines or slaves, and the flower of the children to be put to vile purposes. The cities and the temples were pillaged, their citizens tortured to drag from them the secret of the hiding-places of treasure, the priests were forced to sacrifice to the god of fire and to spit upon their own or die, the priestesses were burned or defiled, or both.

So pitiful was the case of Egypt that although I knew that by her sins and faithlessness she had brought these woes upon herself, I who by my work at Sidon had become one of the appointed ministers of her destruction, my heart wept for her and I prayed the avenging gods to hold their hands. Also I prayed them to give Ochus to drink of his own cup and to make of me the butler who mixed his wine. Nor did I pray in vain.

Thus the red Ochus came at length to Memphis, the white-walled city, the ancient, the holy, and filled its streets with horror, till they were spread thick with dead and one wail of woe went up to heaven. Yet he did not burn the place, perchance because our prayers availed and the gods relented, perchance because he wished to keep it to be the seat of his majesty. Only here as elsewhere he sacked the temples and wrought sacrilege.

From the pylon top of the temple of Isis that overlooked the courts of that of Ptah and the gilded stable of the bull Apis, with my own eyes I saw the Persians, for in this business the Greeks would have no hand, drag out the sacred beast whom they held to be a god of the Egyptians, though in truth he was but the emblem of the god, or rather of the generating power that is in Nature, and butcher it with jeers and mockery. More, their scullions came and cooked the sacred flesh after which, at tables spread in the inner court, Ochus and his captains ate it, forcing the priests of Ptah to "taste of their own god" and to drink of the liquor in which it had been seethed. They were cowards, those priests, or surely they would have found means to mix the broth with poison.

After the feast, when all the revellers were drunk with wine, a great jackass was brought and, the statue of the god having been thrown out of it, was stabled in the sanctuary.

Such were some of the things that were done in Memphis and indeed throughout Egypt, for as Apis was served, so was the holy ram of Mendes. Moreover, other things were done too shameful to record.

Now all this while I sat in the temple of Isis awaiting what might befall. I will not say that I was unafraid, because I was afraid. Yet within me was that proud spirit which forbade me to show my fear. Moreover, within me also burned a certain fire of faith whereof the light was my guide in the darkness of despair. The holy

Noot, my Master, had told me that I and those with me should take no harm, and I would not doubt my Master. Moreover, when I prayed at night, a voice from heaven speaking in my heart seemed to command me to be brave, since there fought for me and mine those whom I could not see.

So there I sat quite alone with none to counsel me and none to help me, giving courage as best I could to those poor priests and priestesses, my fellow servants of the goddess. The worship of the temple went on as before, each morn the statue of the Mother was decked and dressed, the perfumes were poured, the offerings were made, the processions wound round the courts preceded by the singers and the shakers of the *sistrum,* while at night the holy hymns were chanted to the stars.

The Persians came to know of these things and gathered at the gates, amazed.

"Who are these," they asked, "who have no fear?"

But we answered nothing though death stared us in the face.

The matter reached the ears of Ochus and stirred his wonder, so that in the end he came in person to visit the temple. I received him in the great hall, veiled and seated in a chair of state that was set at the foot of a statue of the goddess. With him were sundry of his great lords dressed in silks and perfumed, also the general Mentor whom I had known at Sidon where he played traitor, deserting with his Greeks to the Persians. Further there was present Bagoas the eunuch and first councillor of the King of Kings, who commanded his army also; like all these unfortunates, a fat, shrill-voiced man with a smooth and furtive manner, who waved his long hands to and fro when he spoke.

Now this Bagoas was by birth Egyptian; so I had heard, and my first sight of him confirmed the tale. Yes, without doubt by birth he was an Egyptian of the small-boned, large-eyed, round-headed type that had descended from the ancient blood, as I knew by the statues of many that I have seen taken from the earliest tombs before it became the custom to embalm the dead. I noted this, and at once a thought came to me.

Would an Egyptian desire to see the sanctuary of Isis and her priests desecrated and destroyed? Perchance he did not worship Ptah or Apis, or other of the gods, but all born upon the Nile venerated Mother Isis, the Queen of Heaven, and bowed to her sovereignty. That was a faith which where'er they wandered and upon whatever altars they burned incense, they never could forget, because through a hundred generations it came down to them with their blood. Yet who knew? This Bagoas, it was said, was a cunning fellow steeped in murder, who from his crimes had reaped a rich reward, and such an one, looking only to his day of glory, might forget even Isis and the wrath to come.

Ochus, loose-lipped, cruel-faced, and weary-eyed, wearing a look of pride that yet was full of haunting terrors, such as are ever the companions of murderers who know that in a day unborn surely themselves they will be murdered, stood before me. I, rising from my chair, made obeisance to the King of kings—and had he but known it, cast the curse of Isis at him from beneath my veil.

"What is this?" he asked, speaking in Greek, in the thick voice of one who has drunk well at the feast, and pointing at me with his sceptre. "Is it one of those wrapped bodies that we drag from the tombs, such as we used for the cooking of the god Apis, broiling him with his own worshippers? Nay, for it moves and talks and seems to have the shape of woman. Bagoas, strip that veiled thing naked, that we may see whether it be a woman, and if so, of what favour."

Now when I, Ayesha, heard this, at once all my courage came back to me, as ever it does when peril gets me by the throat. At once I laid my plan, which was short and simple.

If that eunuch so much as advanced to lay a finger on me, I would draw the knife that hung to my girdle, the curved, razor-edged Arab knife that had been my father's, and thrusting him aside, I would spring past him and strike it through the heart of yonder King of kings, sending him to sum up his account with Isis. Then if there were time, I would serve Bagoas in the same way, and afterward, if must be, use the knife upon myself. Better thus than that I should be shamed before these barbarians.

I spoke no word and my face was hid, yet I think that out of my soul sprang something which warned these two of their danger. Or perchance it was my guardian spirit that warned them. At the least Bagoas went down upon his knees and bowed till his forehead touched the ground.

"O King of kings," he said, "I pray thee command not thy slave to do this deed. Yonder lady is the prophetess of Isis, Queen of all gods, Queen of Heaven and Earth, and to touch her with an unhallowed hand is a sacrilege that brings death in this world and in that to come everlasting torment."

Now Ochus laughed brutally, then turned and asked, "What do you say, Mentor, who are a Greek and know no more of the gods of Egypt than I do? Is there any reason why we should not strip this veiled priestess and discover what she is like beneath those wrappings?"

Now Mentor rubbed his brow and answered,

"Since I am asked, O King of kings, one does come into my mind. Do you remember Tenes, King of the Sidonians? He took this same prophetess as a gift from Nectanebes, and also wished to strip her in his fashion. Well, Tenes came to a very bad end, and so did Nectanebes who gave her to him, or is in the way of it. Therefore, O King of kings, were I in your place, I should advise that she remain veiled, who perhaps after all is but an ugly old woman. I have known little of Isis, still she is a goddess with a great name and perchance it is scarcely worth while to risk her wrath to look at the wrinkled flesh of an ugly old woman. One never knows, O King of kings, and I have seen so much of it of late that I come to learn that death, with the curse of Heaven thrown in, is a bad business."

Thus spoke Mentor in his bluff, rambling, soldier talk, that yet was so full of Grecian cunning, and Ochus, appearing suddenly to grow sober, listened to him.

"I seem to remember," Ochus said, "that this same

priestess served me well yonder at Sidon, giving the Phœnician dog, Tenes, counsel that led him down to ruin. So at least the tale runs. Therefore, not because of the Egyptian goddess whom I despise," and he spat on the statue of Isis, an act at which I saw Bagoas shiver, "or for the reasons that you fools give, but because by design or chance, I know not which, she served me well at Sidon, let her continue to wear her veil. I command also that this temple, which is beautiful in its fashion, shall not be burned or harmed, and that those who serve it may continue to dwell there and carry on their mad worship as it pleases them, provided that they stay within its walls and do not attempt to stir up the people by pageantry in the streets. In token thereof, I stretch out my sceptre," and he held the ivory-headed wand he carried toward me.

Bagoas whispered to me that I must touch it, so I thrust my arm between the folds of my veil and did so, though next instant I remembered that it would have been wiser to grasp the wand from beneath the veil.

At once Ochus noted the beauty of that arm and exclaimed with a laugh,

"By the holy fire! yonder hand and wrist are not those of an ugly old woman, such as was spoken of by you slaves, but rather those of one who is still young and fair. Had I seen them but a moment gone, surely she should have been stripped. Indeed——"

"I have touched the sceptre of the Great King," I broke in coldly. "Once the sceptre has been touched the decree of the Great King may not be altered."

"Wise also," said Ochus, "for she knows our Persian laws. Well, she is right. The sceptre has been touched and what has been said cannot be changed. See now, all of you who are ignorant, how good a shield is wisdom. Come, Mentor, let us be going to make sport with those young priestesses of Ammon who, not being wise, but only pretty, await us in the palace. It will be a merry night. Bagoas, bide you here, lest you should be shocked," and he laughed brutally, "also to inquire whether this heavenly harlot called Isis decks herself with jewels, for if so, as to them I swore no oath. Farewell, Priestess. Continue to be wise and to wear a veil, because if the rest of you is as shapely as your hand, who knows but that some night when wine has drowned all promises, I, or others, might cause you to be stripped at last."

Then he turned and went, followed by his foul company. Only Bagoas remained behind as he had been bidden.

When the doors had closed and by the shouts from without the walls I knew that the Persians were gone, I said to Bagoas, who was alone with me in the place,

"Tell me, Egyptian, cradled beneath the wings of Isis, are you not afraid?" and I turned my head, glancing at the vile stain upon the alabaster statue.

"Aye, Prophetess," he answered, "I am afraid, as much afraid as you were but now."

"Fool!" I mocked back at him, "I was not afraid. Ere ever a hand had been laid upon me by you, you would have been dead, and that king whom you serve would have been dead also—ask me not how—and by now your souls would be writhing beneath the hooks of the Tormentors of the Under-world. Have you not heard of the curse of Isis, Eunuch, and do you think that your pomp and power can protect you from her swift sword? Now, *now,* should I but breathe one prayer to her, she can slay you if she wills."

He quaked, he fell upon his knees; yes, this murderer of kings fell upon his knees before me, one veiled woman in a shrine, imploring me to spare him and to protect him from the wrath of Heaven. For in his soul Bagoas was still Egyptian, and the blood of his forefathers who had worshipped Isis for a thousand years still ran strong in him. Moreover, he feared me, the priestess whose fame he knew, as he knew the fate of those who had offended me.

"Forgiveness! Protection! Methinks these must be most dearly bought, Bagoas. Are you one of those who have eaten the flesh of Apis and dragged the virgins of Ammon from their sanctuary? Are you one of those who have stabled an ass in the temple of Ptah, have burned the ancient fanes and have butchered the priests upon their altars?"

"Alas! I am," he said, beating his breast, "but not of my own will. What I did I must do, or die."

"It may be so. Make your own peace with those gods if you can. I have little to do with them who serve the supreme Mother. But for her what atonement?" and again I glanced at the foul stain upon the alabaster of the image.

"That is what I need to be told. What atonement, Prophetess? I will swear that there are no jewels here; that the Mother is decked only with flowers and with perfumes. I will guard this shrine so that never again a Persian sets foot within its walls. I will cause any who offend you, Prophetess, to die secretly and at once. Is it enough?"

"Nay, nor by a hundredth part. You would spare the ceremonial trappings of the Mother, but where is vengeance upon him who defiled her with his spittle? You would protect the priestess, but where is vengeance upon him who would have stripped her stark to be his sport and that of his barbarians? If that is all you have to offer, Bagoas, take the Mother's curse and that of her Oracle, and get you down to hell." Here Bagoas lifted his hand as though to protect his head and began to protest, but without heeding him I went on,

"Hurry not, linger as long as you will upon the road. Deck yourself like a woman with broidered robes, perfume yourself with scents; set chains about your neck and jewels upon your fingers. Pander to the lusts you cannot share and take your pay in gold and provinces. Poison those you hate and from pure children wring out their lives, because these stand between you and the fruit of some new phantasy. Glut yourself with the swine's food of earth, swell yourself out with the marsh-gas of power, and then, Bagoas, die! die! one year, ten years, fifty years hence, and get you down to hell and look upon the awful eyes of the goddess you have shamed, of her whom your forefathers worshipped from the beginning, and wait the coming of her priestess, that with every merciless particular she may lay the count against you from the pavement of the Judgment Hall."

"What, then, shall I do? What shall I do to save my soul? Know, Priestess, that I who am maimed in my body would save my soul, and that all these gauds you count are but gall and ashes to me; for having nought else to gain—being robbed of wives and children I needs must seek them and thus drug the spirit that is within me. Oh! it is something—being what I am, that I should feel the necks of all these great ones writhing beneath my foot. Yes," here his voice dropped to a whisper, "even that of the King of kings himself, who forgets that there were other Kings of kings before him. Tell me—what must I do?"

Secretly I drew the curved knife at my girdle; secretly and unwincing, unseen of him, I gashed my arm—oh! I cut deep, for I can see the mark to-day, though this fair flesh of mine once seemed to perish in the immortal fire, but to re-arise elsewhere. The blood from a severed vein leaped forth and stained my veil, a little mark at first which grew and grew, till it cried of murder. The man's eyes fastened themselves upon the prodigy, for so he thought it; then he asked,

"Blood! *Whose* blood?"

"Perchance that of the wounded goddess. Perchance that of a shamed priestess. What does it matter, Bagoas?"

"Blood," he went on, "for what does the blood ask?"

"Perchance it cries to Heaven for vengeance; perchance it demands to be washed away with other blood, Bagoas. Who am I that I should interpret parables?"

Now he understood, and struggling from his knees, bent forward whispering in my ear. Yes, the priceless jewels that hung from his pointed golden cap jingled against my ear.

"I understand," he said, "and be sure it shall be done. But not yet. It cannot be yet. Still I swear that it shall be done when the hour is ripe. I hate him! I say that I hate him who while he showers gifts upon me with his hands, mocks me with his tongue, and who, when by my wit I win victories for him, jeers at the soldiers who are led by one who is neither man nor woman. Yes, I hate him who, knowing that I am of Egypt and in my heart a worshipper of the gods of Egypt, forces me to desecrate their shrines and to butcher those who serve them. Oh! I swear that it shall be done in its season."

"By what, O Bagoas?"

"By this, Prophetess," and seizing the dripping veil he rubbed that which stained it upon his lips and brow, "I swear by the blood of Isis, or of her Priestess and Oracle in whom Isis is, that I will neither rest nor stay till I bring Ochus Artaxerxes to his doom. Years may go by, but still I will bring him to his doom—at a price."

"What price?" I asked.

"That of absolution, Priestess, which is yours to give."

"Aye, it is mine to give or to withhold. Yet I give it not until Ochus lies dead, and by your hand. Then I call it down from Heaven—not before."

"At least protect me till that hour, O Daughter of the Queen of Heaven."

From the necklace I wore beneath my veil I loosed a certain charm of power, the secret symbol of the Queen herself, worked cunningly in jasper, and known only to the initiate. This I breathed upon and blessed.

"Take it," I said, "and wear it on your heart. It shall protect you from all ills while your heart is true. But if once that heart turns from its purpose; aye! even if it fail to accomplish its purpose, then this holy token shall bring all ills upon you, here and hereafter, Bagoas. For then upon your doomed head shall fall the curse of the goddess that even now hangs suspended over it, as in the Grecian fable the sword of Damocles hangs by its single hair. Take it and be gone, to return no more till you come to tell me that Ochus Artaxerxes treads that same road upon which he has set so many feet."

Bagoas took the talisman and pressed it on his brow, as though it had been the very signet of the King of kings, and hid it away about him. Then he prostrated himself before me, who sat upon a greater throne, that of the Queen of queens, prostrated himself till his forehead touched the ground beneath my feet. Then rising, without another word, Bagoas withdrew himself with humble obeisances till he reached the doors where he vanished from my sight.

When the man had gone I, Ayesha, laughed aloud, I who had played a great game and won it.

Yes, I laughed aloud; then, having purified the statue of the goddess and burnt incense before it, I went upon my knees and returned my humble thanks to that just Heaven of which I was the minister.

CHAPTER XV

❧

The Plot and the Voice

THE weary years went by. Ochus returned to Persia, bearing his spoils with him and leaving one Sabaco, a brutal fellow, to rule Egypt and wring tribute from her.

All this while I, Ayesha, sat alone, quite alone, in the temple of Isis at Memphis whose walls I never left, for the command of Ochus was obeyed and whatever happened to those of other gods, the shrine of Isis was left inviolate. Here, then, surrounded by a dwindling company of priests and priestesses, I remained, as Noot, my Master, had commanded me to do, awaiting a word that never came, and carrying on the ceremonies of the temple in such humble fashion as our poverty allowed.

What did I through all that slow and heavy time? I dreamed, I communed with Heaven above, I studied the ancient lore of Egypt and of other lands, growing ever wiser and as full of knowledge as a new-filled jar with perfume or with wine. Yet of what use was this knowledge to me? As it seemed, of none. Yet it was not so, since my heart fed on it like a bee upon its winter store of honey, and without it I should have died, as the bee

must die. Moreover, now I understood that this space of
waiting was a preparation for those long centuries which
afterward I was doomed to pass in the tombs of Kôr. It
was a training and a discipline of the soul.

Thus forgotten of the world I brooded and endured, I
who had thought to rule the world.

So moon added itself to moon, and, still filled with a
divine patience, I abode within those temple walls till
the appointed hour, which I knew would dawn at last.
Of Nectanebes I heard nothing; he had vanished
away—I doubted not to the doom which I had foreseen.
Of Amenartas, his daughter, I heard nothing, she also
had vanished away, as I supposed with him. Of Kallikrates, the soldier priest, I heard nothing. Doubtless he
was dead and that beauty of his had turned to evil-
odoured dust as my own must do, a thought from which
I shrank.

Much I wondered why this man alone upon the earth
should have stirred my soul and awakened the longings
of my woman's flesh. I knew not, unless it was agreed
that when the gates were passed I should meet him in a
world that lies beyond, if such there were. For from the
beginning I was sure that it had been laid upon me to
lift up his spirit to the level of my own, perchance because in some far-off star or state I had sinned against it
and him and dragged them down.

Indeed is not this the common lot of the great, that
with toil and tears and bitter disappointment they must
strive to draw the spirits of others to that high peak
upon which themselves they stand? And amongst all the
sins of our vile condition, is there one blacker than to
cast back some soul that struggles toward the pure and
good into the seething depths of ill?

Thus in those days I thought of that lost Kallikrates
whose lips alone had touched my own. I thought, too,
with a sad wonderment, how strange it was that I to
whose feet men had crept by scores, I the most beautiful of women and the most learned, had been rejected,
or at the least turned from by this man, the favourer of
another, who although she was fair and bold of heart,

still shone with a smaller light, as does the pale moon when compared with the glory of the sun.

Indeed, now that all was over and done, as I believed, and that nought remained of these fires of folly save a pinch of burnt-out ash, I smiled to myself as I remembered them. Yet to tell truth, I smiled sadly, who here alone at the dear feast of love which, to a woman, means more than all other feasts, had been served with the cups of defeat and shame by the grinning varlet, Destiny. Yet I was well served, for what had I, Wisdom's Daughter, the vowed to eternal glory, to do with such matters of our common flesh?

Oh! I was glad to have done with the gray-eyed Kallikrates, who could wield a sword so manly-well in battle, and yet, when remorse took hold of him, could pray with the best of priests. Now at least once more I was the mistress of my own soul with leisure to shape it to the likeness of the gods and, in those days of holy contemplation, truly its wings beat against their bars, struggling to be free. Would that they had burst them, but Fate had built that cage too strong.

At length news came to me, for Isis still had eyes and ears in Egypt and all that these saw or heard I learned, news that Ochus, grown timid or weary in his Persian palace, had determined once more to drink the waters of the Nile, or perchance to check the accounts of his satrap Sabaco whose sum of tribute had fallen off of late.

So he came with all his Eastern pomp and at last took up his abode in the palace of Memphis within two bowshots of the temple where I dwelt. The people received him with rejoicings; it was pitiful to see them decking themselves and the streets with flowers, spreading branches of palm for him to tread on, and flying banners from the lofty tops of the fire-scorched pylons—slaves welcoming their torturer and tryant and grinning to hide the terror in their hearts. He came, and there was festival throughout the great town as though Osiris had returned to earth, companied by all the lesser gods.

Only in the temple of Isis there was none. No palm leaves decked its stark and ancient walls, no bonfires burned within its courts, and no lanterns hung in its window-places. Not thus would I, Ayesha, bow the knee to Baal or sacrifice to Moloch, though it is true that some of my servants looked askance when I forbade it and asked who would protect us from the wrath of the King of kings because of this neglect of his command.

"The goddess will protect us," I answered, "or if she does not, I will," and sent them to their tasks.

On the second night after the coming of Ochus, Bagoas waited on me and I commanded that he should enter, but alone. So his Eastern rabble of gorgeous servitors was turned back from the gates and he came in unattended, splendid in gold-embroidered silk and jewels. Where he had left me, there I received him, seated veiled in the chair of state before the alabaster statue of the goddess, at the entrance to the outer sanctuary that overlooked the great hall.

"Hail! Bagoas," I said, "how goes it with you? Has that amulet of power which I gave to you protected you from harm?"

"Prophetess," he answered, bowing, "it has protected me. It has lifted me up so that now, save for the King of kings, my master most august," he added with a sneer in every word, "I am now the greatest one in the whole world. I give life, I decree death. I lift up, I cast down; satraps and councillors crawl about my feet; generals beg my favour; gold is showered upon me. Yea, I might build my house of gold. There is nought left for me to desire beneath the sun."

"Except certain things to which, thanks to the cruelty of the King of kings, or those who went before him, you cannot attain? For example, children to inherit all this glory and all this gold, Bagoas, although you live among so many of those who might be mothers."

He heard, and his face, that I noted had grown thinner and more fierce since last I saw him, became like to that of the devil.

"Prophetess," he hissed, "surely you are one who knows how to pour acid into an open wound."

"That thereby it may be cleansed, Bagoas."

"Yet your words are true," he went on, unheeding. "All this splendour, all this wealth and power I would give, and gladly, to be as my fathers were before me, gently bred but humbly owners of a patch of land between Thebes and Philæ. There they sat for a score of generations with their women and their children. But where, thanks to the Persians, are *my* women and *my* children? In the western cliff yonder there is a sepulchre. In the chapel of that sepulchre above the coffins of those who lie beneath is an image of him who dug it. He lived some fourteen hundred years ago in the days of Aahmes, he who won back Egypt from the Hyksos kings, the invaders who held it as the Persians do to-day. For he was one of the captains of the troops of Aahmes who, when he conquered, gave him that patch of land in guerdon for his service."

Here Bagoas paused like to one overwhelmed by unhappy memories, then continued,

"From age to age, Prophetess, it has been the custom for the children of the children of this soldier upon a certain day to make offerings to that statue, wherein, as we hold, dwells the *Ka* of him whose face and form it pictures; to set a golden crown, that of Osiris, upon its head, to wind a golden chain about its neck; to give it food, to give it flowers. Such is the sacred duty, from generation to generation, of the descendants of that captain who served Aahmes and helped to free Egypt from the barbarian foe. Myself I have fulfilled that duty, aye, when Ochus the Destroyer first came to Memphis, I travelled up Nile and placed the crown upon the head and wound the chain about the neck, and offered the flowers and the food. But, Prophetess, of this blood I am the last, for because of my beauty as a child the Persian seized me and made of me a dry tree, so that never again will there be one to make offering in the tomb of my forefather, the captain of Aahmes, or to read the story of his deeds that fourteen hundred years ago, while yet living, he caused to be recorded upon his funeral tablet."

I heard and laughed.

"A common tale," I said, "a very common tale in Egypt to-day, the Egypt of the Persians, as doubtless it was long ago in the Egypt of the Hyksos. But this ancestor of yours was a man who smote, or helped to smite, the Hyksos and lived to write his glorious deeds on stone to be an example to those who came after him. Well, the story is finished, is it not? Indeed I wonder that the glorious Bagoas, slave of the Persian, Bagoas with his pomp and pleasures, thinks fit to waste time upon the tale of a forgotten warrior who in his hour struck for freedom. What are the flowers and the humble scents which for more than a thousand years have been offered to the spirit of that warrior, but now can never be offered again since there are none of his blood left to bring them, compared to the priceless balms, the jewels and the gold, that daily are poured upon the feet of Bagoas, the Chief Eunuch and Counsellor of the King of kings, who, did he know of those holy ones that sleep in the tomb of the race of Bagoas, doubtless would drag them out and cause Bagoas, the last of its blood, to fire them, that he might see a merry blaze? That would be a good sport for the King of kings, to force the great Bagoas to burn his ancestors and on their bones to cook a royal meal, as he forced the priests of Ptah to broil Apis for his feast."

The mighty Bagoas heard and understood me, as I could see well, for at every word he winced like a high-bred steed beneath the whip.

"Cease," he said hoarsely, "cease! I can bear no more. Why do you rub sand into my eyes, Prophetess?"

"To clear away their rheum that they may see the better, Bagoas. But let us be done with the tale of that honourable, long-lost ancestor of yours to whose spirit no more offerings will be made, and tell me of the wonders of the great estate of you in whom runs his blood, the last drops of it, that soon will be sucked up in the sands of Death. Seal that sepulchre, Bagoas, but first set it in another writing, graven on a tablet of emerald or gold, telling how he who hallowed it was by the gods given the glory of being the far forefather of Bagoas,

Chief Eunuch of the King of kings, Ochus, who burned the shrines of that forefather's gods."

"Cease, cease!" he moaned. "The hour is at hand."

"What hour, Bagoas?"

"The hour of vengeance which I swore to Isis."

"Does the Egyptian worshipper of the Persian holy Fire remember his vows to Isis? Be plain, Bagoas."

"Hearken, Prophetess. During all these years I have been seeking opportunity. Now of a sudden I see it to my hand. A thought came to me whilst you talked of the captain of Aahmes to whom no more of his blood can make offerings."

"Speak it, then, Bagoas."

"Prophetess, the King of kings is wrath with you, because alone of all the great places in Memphis, on the temple of Isis no welcoming banners hang to greet him at his royal coming and because no priest or priestess of Isis spread flowers before his conquering feet. So wrath is he that, were it not for his oath, which he fears to break, he would pull this sanctuary stone from stone, slaughter its priests, and give its priestesses to the soldiers."

"Is it so?" I asked indifferently.

"Aye, Prophetess. But by that oath you are saved, for ever I keep it before his mind and warn him of the fate of those who do violence to the Queen of Heaven. Only this morning I did this while he stood staring at these unbannered walls and muttered vengeance."

"And what said he then, Bagoas?"

"He laughed and answered that he would do the goddess not violence, but honour, thus. On the third night from this, the night of full moon, he will make a great feast in the inner court of this temple. At that feast the King of kings and his women will sit upon a platform laid over the coffins of the royalties of Egypt dragged from their sepulchres, so that its kings and queens may be beneath his feet. This platform will be supported by the statues of the gods of Egypt which once they worshipped. In front of it will burn the holy Fire of Persia and that fire will be fed with the mortal remnants of priests and priestesses of those Egyptian gods. Ochus

the king will be clad in the robes of Osiris, and at the
end of the feast from behind her consecrated statue,
that before which we sit, the goddess herself, dressed in
the robes of Isis and wearing the holy emblems upon
her head, will appear veiled, led by priestesses or by
royal Persian women. *You* will be that goddess, Prophetess."

"And then?" I asked.

"Then you will be brought up on to the platform and
there this new Osiris will unveil you, embracing you as
his wife in welcome before all that company. This he
will do to make a mock of you because he believes you
to be an ancient woman who goes veiled to hide her
baldness and her wrinkles, for so the rumour runs
among the Persians."

Now when I, Ayesha, heard these horrible words and
my heart understood the height and depth of the sacrilege which this mad king would dare and all that it
might mean to me, I trembled; yes, the bones seemed to
melt within me so that almost I fell from the throne
whereon I sat. Yet gathering up my strength I asked,

"Is this all, Bagoas?"

"Nay. At that feast, Prophetess, I myself as Vizier
and the head of the world under him, must serve Ochus
as his cup-bearer. While the priests of Osiris and the
priestesses of Isis sing the ancient chants of the awaken-
ing of Osiris from the tomb and of his reunion with Isis
the Wife Divine, it will be my part to hand the jewelled
goblet filled with the holy wine to Osiris-Ochus, King of
Heaven and Earth. From it he will drink the marriage
draught, and having drunk, will pour the dregs of the
goblet upon your feet, or for aught I know will cast
them in your face. Nay, I forgot. First the Persian
women of the royal household will strip the coverings
from you that Osiris may see his long-lost bride and the
company may have sport, jeering at her withered age."

"And if she should prove to remain unwithered, if
even she should chance to be passing fair, what then,
Bagoas?"

"Then perchance, Prophetess, it is in the mind of
Ochus to add Isis to the number of his queens, thinking

thus to gain the favour of the Egyptians, if not of their gods. Oh! Prophetess, you are very wise, as all know, yet once your foot slipped—or rather your hand slipped, when in bygone days you stretched it out to touch the sceptre of the King of kings. Ochus has often spoken of the beauty of that hand and arm, and of how, more than all things, he desired to see the face above them and the form of which they are a part. Perchance, Prophetess, that is why he plans all this mummery."

"And if I refuse to act this play, what then, Bagoas?"

"Then since the command is lawful and designed to honour the goddess, the Great King's oath is at an end. Then the temple of Isis will be sacked and burned like others, then her priests will be murdered unless they make offerings to the holy Fire, and her priestesses be enslaved or find a home in the soldiers' tents or Persian households."

"Bagoas," I said, rising and standing over him, "know that the Curse of Isis hovers about your head. Show me a path out of this trouble or you die—not to-morrow or next year, but at once. How, it matters not, still you die; and for the rest, are the Sidonians the only ones who can fire their temples and perish in them?"

He cringed before me after the fashion of his unhappy kind, then answered,

"I waited for such words, Prophetess, and had I not been prepared against them, never would I have entered these gates alone. Did I not tell you that at this feast I shall be the King's cup-bearer? Now," he went on in a whisper, "I add that his own physician, who is in my pay, will mix the marriage wine, that his life is in the hollow of my hand; that the guards and captains are my servants; that the great lords are sworn to me, and that the hour for which I have waited through long years has come at last. Lady, you are not the only one who desires vengeance upon Ochus."

"Fine words," I said. "But how know I that they will be fulfilled? In Egypt Bagoas is called the King's Liar."

"I swear it by Isis, and if I fail you, may the Devourer take my soul."

"And I, who am her Mouth and Oracle, swear by Isis that if you fail me I will take your blood. Aye, though I die, a thousand will live on to avenge me, and the dagger or the shaft of one of them shall reach your heart at last. Or if they miss their aim then the goddess herself will smite."

"I know it, Prophetess, and I will not fail. After drinking of that cup sleep will fall upon the King of kings; yes, the new Osiris will return to his tomb and sleep sound, but *not in the arms of Isis.*"

Then for a while there was silence between us, till at length I motioned to him to begone.

The night of the feast came and all was prepared. I did not trust Bagoas and therefore I made a plan, a splendid and terrible plan. I determined to offer all those feasters, yes, the King of kings with his women, his generals, his chamberlains, his councillors, and his company, as one vast sacrifice to the outraged gods of Egypt, and with them if need were, myself and my servants, to guide them upon the road to hell.

Beneath that hall of the temple which Ochus had appointed for the feast was a vast vault for the storage of oil and fuel against times of want or tumult. This vault, as it chanced, was full to the roof, since in those troublous days I never knew from moon to moon when the place might be besieged. Also in it was much prepared papyrus with many written rolls that for centuries had been hidden there, great weight of bitumen such as the embalmers use, a stack of coffins prepared by the living to receive their bodies at the end; and lastly hundreds of bundles of dried reeds that served to strew the courts. What more was needed, save to open the air shafts to the hall above that the flames might find full play, and to set in the vault one who could be trusted with a lamp of which the light was hidden, commanded at a certain signal to cast it among the oil-soaked reeds and fly?

As it chanced such an instrument was to my hand, an old, fierce-hearted woman in whom ran loyal blood, that for hard on seventy years had served as priestess of this temple.

That very night I summoned the priests and priestesses who remained and in the sanctuary under the
wings of Isis, I told them all: told them how I purposed
to sweep this human dirt of Persians with the red besom
of destruction out of the company of the living over the
edge of the world into the Avenger's everlasting jaws.

This band of the faithful hearkened and bowed their
cowled heads. Then the first of them, an old priest,
asked,

"Is it decreed that we must eat fire with these swine?
If so, we are ready."

"Nay," I answered, "the secret passage that runs
from the back of the sanctuary of the ruined temple of
Osiris will be unbarred, that passage by which in the old
days the holy effigy of Osiris was brought at the great
festival of the Resurrection to be laid upon the breast of
Isis. By this passage at the first sign of fire, you must
flee, as I will if I may. But if I come not you will know
that the goddess has called me. At the water-steps of the
temple of Osiris boats will be waiting manned by brothers of our faith. In the darkness and the tumult, those
boats will pass down Nile to the secret shrine that is
called *Isis-among-the-Reeds*, where once, the legend
tells, the goddess found the heart of Osiris hidden there
by Typhon, the shrine upon the isle that none dare visit,
no not even the Persians, because it is guarded by the
ghosts of the dead, or by spirits sent from the Under-
world fashioned like flames of fire. Thither fly and
there lie hid until the word of Isis comes to you, as
come it will."

Again they bowed their cowled heads in the gloomy
sanctuary lit by a single lamp. Then the old priest said,

"Great is the dead that we shall do, and worthy.
Surely the song of it shall echo through all the courts of
Heaven and the gods themselves shall crown our brows
with splendour. Yet ere it is decreed, O Prophetess inspired, let us seek a sign from the Queen immortal that
such is her command."

"Aye," I answered, "let us seek a sign."

So there in the half darkness we chanted the mystic
ritual, hand in hand before the goddess we chanted it,

bowing and swaying, weeping and praying, demanding that a sign be given to us who were prepared to die that her splendour might shine forth as a star.

Yet no sign came.

"O Oracle inspired," said the old priest, "it is not enough. Yet in your heart are locked the unutterable Words, the Words of Power, the Words of the Opening of the Mouth Divine, that may not be spoken save at the last extreme. Are not these words known to you, the Oracle inspired?"

"They are known to me," I answered. "From Noot I had them under the Seven Oaths when I was ordained prophetess; yea, under the Seven Curses if those words should be used unworthily, the seven dreadful curses, deer-footed, snake-headed, lion-maned with red fire, that shall hunt the betrayer's soul from star to star, till the black vault of space falls in and buries Time. Kneel now and bow your heads and stop your ears till they be spoken. Then open your ears and hearken."

They knelt in a double row and I, I the Oracle, clothed in the might of my Queen, I dared to draw near to her holy effigy gleaming white above us in the darkness of the shrine. Yes, this I dared, not knowing what would chance. I took the jewelled *sistrum* of my office; I laid it upon the lips of the goddess, I shook it till it chimed before her face, I clasped her feet and kissed them.

Then I rose and into her ear I whispered the dreadful Words of Power, which even now, after so many ages, I dare not so much as shape in the halls of memory. I whispered them and returning to my company of kneeling worshippers, I motioned to them to unstop their ears and folding my arms upon my breast, I waited with downcast eyes.

Presently there was a stir in that sanctuary as of beating wings; a cold air blew upon us; then a voice spoke, the very voice of Noot my Master, Noot, the holy priest of priests. Said the voice:

"Fulfil! It is decreed. Fulfil and fear not!"

"Ye have heard," I said.

"We have heard," they answered.

"Whose voice did ye hear?" I asked.

"The voice of Noot, the holy priest of priests who has gone from us," they answered.

"Is it enough?" I asked.

"It is enough," they answered.

Then I departed rejoicing, who knew by this sign that Noot, who spoke with his human voice, still lived upon the earth, and that through him it had pleased Heaven to utter its decree.

CHAPTER XVI

The Feast of the King of Kings

IT WAS the night of the great feast. All day long artficers by scores had toiled in the court of the temple. Adown its length tables had been set up and by them couches and benches upon which hundreds of the feasters would lie or sit according to their degree. Near to the head of the court a platform had been built, of which the foundation beams were supported by the statues of gods dragged from a score of temples where they had stood in solemn peace for ages. Yes, there were Ptah, Ammon, Osiris, Mut, Khonsu, Hathor, Maat, Thoth, Ra, Horus, and the rest, bearing on their sacred brows and headdresses the eating-table of a heathen horde. But they bore more than this, since around and between them and the platform upon which stood this table were laid the coffins of long-dead kings or queens, and other great ones, torn, it was said, from the pyramids or their surrounding tombs. Dark with the dust of ages there they lay, some of them uncovered, so as to reveal the grim shapes that slept within.

Above these again was placed the wide platform carpeted with purple cloth of Tyre, and on it stood the board and gilded furniture of the feast. Here, too, was a golden throne at the back of which was a peacock fan of jewels, while to its front was set a table fashioned of black wood inlaid with ivory, and around it other smaller thrones and tables. These were the seats of the King of kings and some of his favoured women.

Nor was this all, for in an outer court but within the pylon gates, cooks and scullions had built fires whereon they dressed meats, and butlers set out their store of wines. Never before within the memory of man had so strange and rich a feast been seen in Egypt as that which was now preparing in the courts of Isis, to defile which with the smell of flesh was a sacrilege and the eating of it there an abomination.

When the sun had turned toward the west came Bagoas with other eunuchs and chamberlains, and being admitted to the inner courts, summoned our company and issued his commands as to the ceremonial that we must keep. We hearkened meekly, saying that we were the slaves of the King of kings, we and our goddess together, and in all things would obey his words.

Then they went away, but as he passed me, affecting to stumble, he whispered in my ear,

"Be not afraid, Prophetess. All is well and the end shall be good."

"I am not afraid, Eunuch," I answered, "who know that all is well and that the end will be good."

The night fell; great flares of light set upon stands of bronze were lit adown the hall, and with them countless lamps placed at intervals along the tables. The feasters gathered; they came by scores and hundreds; Persian lords in their rich robes, generals and captains in their armour, merchants of many lands, Egyptian apostates, and I know not who besides, men, all of them, whom it pleased the King of kings to honour. They were marshalled in their appointed places by the stewards and butlers, and there waited in silence, or speaking only in low voices.

From behind the curtains of the outer sanctuary I

and my company watched it all. These were clad in
their festal garments of white, garlanded with flowers.
But I, according to command, wore the glorious robes
of Isis beneath my veil, and on my head the vulture cap
of Isis, the golden Uræus, the earrings and the crescent
of the moon. Moreover, about my bosom were hung the
sacred necklaces and the other jewelled emblems of the
goddess, while in my hands I held the *sistrum* and the
Cross of Life.

Trumpets blew announcing the advent of the King of
kings. Up the long hall he marched, clad in the mummy
wrappings of Osiris, somewhat widened at the feet so
that he might walk in them, wearing on his head the tall
feathered crown and holding in his hands the Crook of
Dominion and the Scourge of Rule. His chamberlains
and great officers led him by a stairway to the platform
that was built above the bodies of ancient kings, where
was set a tiny altar upon which burned the Holy Persian
Fire. There for a while he stood in pride, waving the
scourge with which he flogged the world, while all that
company fell upon their faces and adored him as a god,
after which they lay still as corpses in the grave.

It was strange to see them lying on their faces like
dead men, who indeed soon were to be dead, every one
of them, and adoring this human image, this dressed-up
doll, fashioned in their own likeness, to be the plaything
of the gods and about to be broken by them and cast
upon the rubbish heap of time.

I, Ayesha, watching through the veil and alive with
that spirit which in the hour of great events comes to
such as I am, thought it very strange; so strange that I
could have laughed. For there in this mime, this puppet
king upon the platform, with the tame tiger, Bagoas,
that was about to tear out his throat, crouching at his
feet, I saw the very type of all grandeur that is built of
clay and not of spirit, since assuredly there is one grandeur of the earth and another of the spirit. Whether by
the poison of Bagoas or by the fire of Isis, yonder man
who stood triumphing over the mighty monarchs that
lay coffined beneath his feet, like a wind-filled toad

upon a consecrated altar, was about to die and then
what of his triumph and what of his pomp?

His cup of blood was full, and when the blast of
doom overturned it into the sands of Death, what
tongues would it take, I wondered, in which to urge a
million accusations against his trembling soul? Lastly,
what mocking devil had persuaded him to don the robes
of Osiris, that in them he might do insult to Isis who,
whate'er she may not be, at least under her royal name
of Nature is the mighty vassal of the Most High, forgetting that Osiris is the god of Death and that Isis-Nature
ever avenges herself upon those who violate her laws?
Little wonder then that I who laughed but seldom in
those days did so in my heart, while my eyes took their
fill of the tinselled panoply of this lost madman.

Ochus-Osiris waved his sceptre, and the seeming
dead who lay around him, as they had been drilled to
do by those who planned this play, came to life in a
grim mockery of ghosts called from the grave. They
rose up and each, according to his degree, took his
place at this Table of Osiris brought to earth.

The feast went on; they ate much; they drank more,
till their brains were bemused with wine and scarce
could they stand upon their feet. At length the climax
came; the coping-stone was set upon this black pyramid
of mortal sin against the spirit of Divinity.

Ochus rose, waving the Crook of Dominion.

"Osiris is risen again in Egypt!" he cried. "Let his
wife, the divine Isis, be brought forth that he may drink
with her the cup of marriage and embrace her as her
husband."

Thereon that ribald company shouted,

"Yea, the god Osiris is risen again in Egypt. Bring
out Queen Isis. Bring her out, that we may see her
drink with him and be kissed!"

Guards summoned us. We came forth from the curtained sanctuary, white-robed in simple state. Singing
the ancient hymn of Reunion to the music of harps and
of shaken *sistra,* our company came forth into the great
hall, I at the head of them. We walked into the hall, a
solemn troop at whom the drunken feasters forgot to

mock; indeed some of them bowed their heads as though in awe. We came to the dais that was supported by the statues of the gods of Egypt and platformed with her ancient royalties, and here we halted. Guards led me up a stairway so that I stood upon the platform, facing Ochus-Osiris. He spoke, saying, mockingly,

"Hail! Queen of Heaven. Behold Osiris rearisen on the Nile has found you at last. Unveil, Queen of Heaven, that he may look upon your glory, for as goddesses do not grow old, doubtless you are glorious."

At these words of insult the company broke into coarse laughter. I waited till it had died away, then answered,

"O King wrapped in the robes of a greater king, yea, in the robes of Death, have you not heard that it is very dangerous to draw the veil of Isis, that none, indeed, has drawn it and lived? You think me but a woman, but know that here in the shrine of Isis, aye, here in her holy House which you desecrate with revellings and with the flesh of butchered beasts, I, her Prophetess and Oracle, am the very goddess and clothed with her divinity. I pray you, therefore, think again ere you bid me to draw my veil."

For a moment he seemed to grow afraid, as did that company, for they were silent. Then rage took hold of him who was full of wine and pride.

"What?" he shouted. "Am I, the King of the world to be defied and threatened by an old hag who calls herself a priestess, or a goddess, or both? Woman, once before I listened to your prayer and left you wrapped in that rag, but now when I come both as your king and as your god, why I claim the privilege of the god. Off with that veil or I will bid my women strip you stark."

Again the silence fell, and for a little while I looked about me. I looked at the feasters illumined by the strong flares of the essence of bitumen; I looked at the blue heaven above in which the great moon floated royally; I turned and looked at the white statue of the goddess showing faint and pure between the curtains in the darkness of the distant shrine beyond. Then I lifted my head and prayed aloud, saying,

"O Thou, that from thy moon-throne watchest all things passing on the earth, O Thou, great Spirit of the world whom men name Isis, Thou that canst spare; Thou that canst avenge; Thou that knowest both life and death; Thou that rulest hearts and destinies; Thou to whose equal sight the king is as the slave, since both kings and slaves are but dust beneath thine immortal feet, hear me, thy priestess and thine Oracle. Thou knowest my strait and that of these thy servants over whom I rule beneath thee. Protect me and them, if thou wilt, or if thou wilt not, then take us to thyself. I ask nothing of thee; I seek not to turn the chariot wheels of Fate; judge thou of my cause who with thy judgment am content. In thine hands hang the scales of doom and the great worlds are thy weights. Who then am I that I should seek to press upon thy balances? Judge now between me, O Mother Isis, and this death-attired king who mocks thee, the Queen of Heaven, in mocking me, thy servitor on earth."

"Have done, woman!" mocked Ochus. "Cease your whimperings to a goddess sitting in the moon, for she is far away from you—and unveil. Bagoas, give me the Marriage Cup, that I may drink to this new wife of mine, who thinks herself divine."

Bagoas beckoned and a dark-faced, black-bearded man whom I knew for the king's physician came forward with a golden goblet on which were vile carvings of the loves of satyrs. This he tasted, or affected to taste, with much ceremony, and as he did so, though save I none noted it, let fall the poison into the wine. Then with humble steps, lifting the cup thrice, lowering it again thrice, doubtless to mix the venom with the wine, he came to the Presence and kneeling, presented the goblet to his master, the King of kings, the King of the world.

"Now," said the drink-besotted Ochus as he grasped the goblet, "now, Priestess, will you unveil or must I call the women?"

"It is not needful," I answered. "Yet, O most glorious monarch, yet, O conqueror of all things first I would add one word. Even a king so great that he dares to clothe himself in the raiment of the Lord of Death perchance may err from time to time. Thus, Mighty One, do you err when you say that Isis is far from me, for Isis is here and *I am Isis*."

Then at a word two priestesses sprang to my side and loosed me of my veil. It fell to the ground and there I stood before them clad in all the splendid pomp of Isis, beautiful as Isis, with the terrible eyes of Isis, and holding in my hands the emblems of Isis and the sceptre with which Isis ruled the world.

They saw, and from that crowded hall there went up a sigh of wonder—or was it of fear? Ochus saw also; his eyes started, his mouth opened.

"By the holy Fire!" he muttered, "here is one worth wedding, be she goddess or woman."

"Then drink the cup, O Ochus-Osiris, and take her, be she goddess or woman," I answered, pointing at him with the Cross of Life.

He drank, he drank deep, and forgetting to offer the wine to me, loosed the goblet from his hand so that it fell upon the little altar where burned the holy Fire, extinguishing it, and thence rolled from the platform to the ground. I glanced at Bagoas and read in his eyes such a look as I had never seen upon the face of man. Oh! it was cruel, that look—cruel yet triumphant, this cold stare of the victim who had become a conqueror. All hell was in that look.

The feasters murmured at the omen of the death of the Fire, but that draught seemed to sober Ochus, who took no heed of it. The wildness left his eyes; they grew cunning as those of a merchant. Merchant-like he appraised my loveliness seen through the gauzy wrappings such as are used to deck the painted effigy of the goddess.

"I look before I take," he said. " 'Twas good to win Egypt; it will be better to win you, O Divine in flesh if not in spirit. Now I understand why in the past you would not suffer me to draw your veil."

Thus he spoke slowly, savouring the words upon his tongue as his greedy eyes savoured my beauty. Then he rose to pass the small altar and advance upon me.

In that fierce moment of time I considered all. It came into my mind that Bagoas had tricked me; that his cup lacked poison, or at least that the plan had failed, and that if I was to be saved it must be by myself. Yet I paused ere I did that which would cause the death of hundreds.

"Stay!" I said to him. "Lay no finger on me lest you shall call the curse of Isis upon your head."

"Nay," he answered, "it is the blessing of Isis that I am about to call upon my lips, O most Beautiful, O Loveliness incarnate!"

He came on. He was past the marble altar. His fierce, bestial face glared into mine and he gripped me; his hot arm was about me, he dragged me to his embrace, while all the beasts of his company shouted in vile joy.

I let fall the *sistrum* that I held. The moment of mercy had gone by. That shout had sealed the doom of all those dogs and satyrs. It was the signal!

By the arts known to us instantly the command was passed on to her who waited below. Instantly this fierce-souled destroyer was at her work with lamp and torch. Never did lover run so swiftly to her lover's side as she did from pile to pile, firing the oil, firing the reeds.

Now that brute-king had me! He pressed his hot kisses upon my breast, upon my lips. I stood still. I struggled not. I stood like the statue of the goddess. This cold calm of mine seemed to frighten him.

"Are you woman?" he asked, hesitating.

"Nay," I hissed back, "I am Isis. Woe to them who lay hands upon Isis!"

He unloosed. He stood staring at me, and as he stared I saw his face change.

"What is in your eyes?" he asked. "All the devils in Egypt are looking out of your eyes."

"Nay," I answered, "all the devils of hell look out of my eyes. Isis commands the devils of hell and unchains them, O death-clothed king."

"What do you mean? What do you mean?" he asked.

"That you will learn presently—in hell. Therefore bid farewell to the world, O Corpse of a king!"

He glowered at me. He swayed to and fro. Then suddenly down he went like one pierced through the heart with an arrow. There he lay upon his back across the altar staring up at the moon.

"Isis is in the moon!" he cried. "She threatens me from the moon. Persians, be afraid of Isis the Moondweller. Bagoas! Physician! Physician! Bagoas! protect me from Isis. She is wringing my heart with her hands. Witch! Witch! loose my heart from your hands."

Thus he wailed in a horrible voice and these were his last words, for having spoken them he lifted his head, glaring about him with a twisted mouth, then let it fall heavily, rolled to the platform, and was still.

Bagoas and the physcician ran to him.

"The Curse of Isis has fallen upon the King of kings," cried Bagoas.

"He who bestrode the world is dead, smitten by Isis of the Egyptians!" cried the physician.

From the royal women and all that company there went up a wail of:

"Ochus is dead! Artaxerxes is dead! The King of kings is dead!"

Bagoas and the physician, helped by the waiting women of Ochus, lifted the body. They carried it from the platform, they bore it down the hall, they vanished with it into the darkness, and presently in the utter silence I heard the gates of the courts and the outer gates of the pylon clang behind them and the clashing of the bolts as they were shot by the guards of the gates.

Still for awhile the silence held, for all were like dead men with terror. Then a voice cried,

"The witch has killed the king with her kiss! Slay her. Tear her to pieces. Slay her and her company!"

The spell-bound mob began to stir; I heard swords rattling in their scabbards. They rose like waves on a quiet sea, and like a wave began to flow toward the platform on which I now stood alone. I stooped down, lifted the *sistrum* from the platform, and held it toward them.

"Be warned!" I cried. "Stay still lest the Curse of Isis fall on you also."

"Witch! Witch! Witch!" they screamed, hesitating awhile, and again swayed forward.

I waved my arm, and as though in answer to it from the grating of stone beyond the platform suddenly arose dense smoke followed by bursts of flame. I waved it a second time, and from the gratings at the end of the hall arose smoke followed by bursts of flame. They looked, they saw, they understood.

"The Curse of Isis!" they screamed. "The Curse of Isis is upon us! Fire rises from hell."

"Nay," I answered, "fire falls from Heaven sent by the outraged gods!"

Now between me and them flared a fence of flame which the boldest dared not face. They paused, one hurled a sword at me which passed above my head: Then they turned, flying for the gateways of the hall, and there were met by another fence of flame. Some of the boldest leapt through it only to find that the gates were shut and that the terror-stricken guards had fled. They rushed back, burning, yea, their silken robes and their oil-anointed hair turned them, yet living, into torches. Now they took another counsel. They dragged the tables together, piling them each on each and striving thus to climb the walls of the hall. This, perhaps, they might have done, some of them, had not every man pulled down his neighbour, so that they fell in tumbled heaps upon the stone flooring where the life was trampled out of them.

I turned and behind the veil of smoke fled from the platform, none seeing me, back behind the hangings that hid the outer sanctuary, where all the company of Isis was gathered, save only that fierce old priestess who yet with lamp and torch lit fire upon fire in the vaults beneath and, at last, doubtless, passed to Heaven on the chariot wheels of flame.

Here my servants stripped off my scared trappings, wrapping me in dark garments and a hooded cloak. While they did so I looked back. The hall was filled with spouts of fire. The platform upon which Ochus had feasted was burning and the royal dead beneath blazed merrily. Only the stone gods by whom it was upborne still stared silent and dreadful through the vesture of smoke and fire, emblems of vengeance and eternal doom.

I could see no more but above the roaring flames I heard the mad screams of those trapped feasters who had come to see their king make a mock of Isis and her priestess, and these were terrible to hear. Then the floor gave way and down they went into the furnace pit beneath. Yes, they who worshipped fire were devoured of their own god.

Thus did I, Ayesha, Child-of-Wisdom, daughter of Yarab according to the flesh, work the vengeance of Heaven upon the Persians and their King of kings. By fire I wrought it, I whose path ever was and ever shall be marked by fire; I, Ayesha, who grew undying in the breath of fire and who, in the caverns of Kôr, clasped it to my breast and was wedded to its secret Soul.

CHAPTER XVII

The Flight and the Summons

WE GAINED the hidden passage, bearing with us the treasures and the holy books of the Sanctuary that to this day lie buried in the caves of Kôr. We came safely to the ruined temple of Osiris that the Persians had destroyed, and through it to the watergate where the boats waited. None noting us, we embarked upon the boats and glided away down Nile. If any saw us pass, they thought us countryfolk, or perchance Egyptians who fled from the Persians in Memphis. But I think that none did see us, since all eyes were bent upon the flaming temple of Isis and all ears were filled with the rumours that flew from mouth to mouth, telling that the goddess had descended in fire and made an end of the tyrant Ochus, his generals, his councillors, and his court.

Thus did I bid farewell to white-walled Memphis which never again my eyes should see, though often my spirit shows it to me in visions of the night, and often I seem to hear the last wild agony of those upon whom I executed the decree of Heaven.

What happened afterward? Of that I know little, though rumours which Philo brought in the later years told me that Bagoas and the physician let fall or flung away the corpse of Ochus. These rumours said that it was found devoured by cats and jackals, so that had it not been for the rent Osiris wrappings, none would have known that here lay all that was left of the King of kings who desolated Egypt and made her as a widow. They told also that Bagoas set Arses, the son of Ochus, upon the throne of Persia, and later poisoned him and all his children save one. Then it seems that he made Darius king, and this Darius Codomannus, knowing that Bagoas would poison him also, smote the first, forcing him to drink of the drugged cup that he had given to so many.

Such, it appears, was the end of Bagoas whom I used as the artist uses a tool, harnessing him to the chariot of my wrath and, like the *Erinnyes* of the Greeks, making of him a sword wherewith I, or Heaven working through me, stabbed Persia to the heart, as through Tenes I had stabbed Sidon and through Sidon, Egypt. For such were the dooms that I was commanded to bring about. Thus Bagoas walked the road down which, aforetime, he drove his victims, and save for an evil name that echoes through the ages, this was the end of him and all his crimes.

Ere dawn our company came to the great reedbed and through it by channels known only to our pilots, reached the secret shrine named *Isis-among-the-Reeds,* where all had been made ready for our coming by the priests who watched there. Worn out, as well I might be, I laid me down and slept in a tiny cell, fearing no harm, since I knew surely that none would come to me or to those with me. Why I knew it I cannot say, but it was so. I knew further that I had done with Egypt; my work there was finished; henceforth we were divorced.

All that day I slept and through most of the night which followed, lulled by the whispering of the tall, surrounding reeds. I suppose that it must have been during those night hours that I dreamed a strange dream. In it I stood upon the desert, a vast waste of sand bordered in the distance by the Nile. I was alone in this desert save for the sun that sank in the west and the moon that rose in the east, and between them, shone upon by sun and moon, by Ra and by Isis, crouched a mighty Sphinx of stone with a woman's breasts and head, which Sphinx I knew was Egypt. There she sat, immemorial, unchanging, stern, beautiful, and stared with brooding eyes toward the east whence morn by morn arose the sun.

Appeared before her, one by one, each adorned with its own sacred emblems, all the gods of Egypt, a grim, fantastic crowd such as a brain distraught might fashion in its madness. Beast-headed and human-shaped, human-headed and beast-shaped; dogs and hawks, crocodiles and owls; swamp-birds, bulls, rams, and swollen-bellied dwarfs, came this rout of gods and bowed before the stern and beauteous Sphinx that wore a woman's head.

The Sphinx opened its mouth and spoke.

"What would ye of me who have sheltered you for long?" it asked.

One shaped like a man but from whose shoulders rose the beaked head of an ibis crowned with a cresceent moon on which stood a feather, and holding in his hand the palette of a scribe; he whom the Egyptians named Thoth the Measurer, the Recorder, stood forward and made answer.

"We would bid thee farewell, Mother Egypt, our shelterer for thousands upon thousands of years. Out of thy mud we were created, into thy mud we return again."

"Is it so?" answered the Sphinx. "Well, what of it? Your short day is done. Yet tell me, who gave you these monstrous shapes and who named you gods?"

"The priests gave them to us and the priests named us gods," answered the ibis-headed man. "Now the priests are slain and we perish with the priests, because we are but gods made of thy mud, O Egypt."

"Then get you gone back into the mud, ye gods of mud. But first tell me, where is my Spirit that in the beginning, when the world was young, I sent forth that it might be a Soul divine to rule Egypt and the world?"

"We know not," answered Thoth the Recorder. "Ask it of the priests who made us. Perchance they have hidden it away. Farewell, O Egypt, farewell, O Sphinx, farewell, farewell!"

"Farewell!" echoed all that monstrous throng and then faded miserably away.

There was silence and with it solitude; the Sphinx stared at Nothingness and Nothingness stared at the Sphinx, and I, the watcher, watched. At length out of the nothingness arose something, and its shape was the shape of woman. It stood before the Sphinx and said,

"Behold me! I am thy lost spirit, but thou, O Egypt, didst not create me, for I created thee by a divine command. I am she whom men know as Isis here upon the Nile, but whom all the world, and all the worlds beyond the world know as Nature, the visible garment of the Almighty God. Gone are those phantasies, man-nurtured and priest-conceived. Yet I remain and thou remainest, aye, and though we be called by many names in the infinite days to come as we have been called in the infinite days that are gone, ever shall we remain until this little floating globe of earth ceases from its journeyings and melts back into that from which it came, the infinite arms of the infinite God."

Then the human-headed Sphinx rose from the rock whereon it had lain from the beginning. It reared its giant bulk, it went upon its knees and bowed to the woman-shape, the tiny woman-shape that was Isis, that was Nature, that was the Executrix of God. Thrice it bowed—and vanished.

The Spirit was left and I, Ayesha, was left. The Spirit turned and looked on me and lo! to my sight it was shaped as I am shaped. Sadly it looked, with grieving eyes, but never a word it spoke.

"Mother. My mother," I called, "speak to me, my mother!"

But never a word it answered, only it pointed to the skies and suddenly was gone. Then I, Ayesha, I stood alone in the immeasurable desert looking at the setting sun, looking at the rising moon, looking at the evening star that shone between, and wept and wept and wept because of my loneliness. For what company is there for a human soul in sun and moon and evening star when the spirit that formed it and them has departed, leaving them to gaze one upon the other, voiceless in the void?

Such was my dream upon which I have pondered from year to year, asking an answer to its riddle from sun and moon and evening star, and finding none. Only the spirit can interpret its own problems, and to me, because of my sins, because, like the gods of Egypt I am fashioned of mud that veils my soul's dim lamp within, as yet that spirit is choked and dumb. Still, one day the Nile of death that I have dammed from me for so long will burst its barriers and wash away the mud. Then the lamp will shine out again; then the spirit will come and refresh it with its holy oil and breathe upon it with its breath, and in that breath perchance I shall understand my dream and learn the answer to its riddle.

Indeed already Time lays its foundations bare, for does not Holly tell me that for nigh upon two thousand years her gods have been dead in Egypt? For awhile they lingered on beneath the Greeks and Romans, changed masks of what once they were; for awhile their effigies were still painted upon the coffins of her people. Then the star of a new Faith rose, a bright and holy star, and in its beams they withered and crumbled into dust. Only the old Sphinx remains staring at the Nile and mayhap in the silence of the night holds commune with Isis the Mother, telling of dead kings and wars forgot, for being Nature's self, Isis alone can never die although from age to age her vestments change.

Yea, when I, Ayesha, fired the hall and burned those

foul Persian feasters, with them I slew the gods of Egypt, and their sad and solemn statues stared a farewell to me through that wavering wall of flame. Nay, it was not I who did it, nor was it I who brought its doom on Sidon and his death on Ochus, but Destiny that used me as its sword, as I used Bagoas, me, Fate's doom-driven daughter.

When I awoke it was still dark save for the light of the sinking moon, and in the night-wind, with a faint continual voice, the tall reeds whispered their prayer to Heaven. For though we know it not, all that has life must pray or die. From the great star rushing through space on its eternal journey to the humblest flower nestling beneath a stone, everything must pray, for prayer is the blood of the spirit that is in them and if that blood freezes, then they are resolved to matter that cannot grow and, knowing neither hope nor fear, is lost in the blind gulf of darkness.

I hearkened to those whispering reeds telling of the mysteries below to the mysteries above, and on the wings of their sweet petitions, sent up my own to Heaven.

For in truth I was troubled and knew not what to do. Here I could not bide for long, since surely, soon or late the Persians would seek me out and surely Bagoas, to cover his own crimes, would slay me as the destroyer of his king. This did not affright me who was weary of the world with all its horrors and in a mood to walk the gate of death, hoping that beyond it I might find a better. But there were those with me, my fellow servants to whom I had sworn safety and who put their faith in me, as though in truth I were the goddess herself, and if I died, certainly they would die also.

Therefore I must save them if I could. Yet how? I had no ship in which to flee from Egypt, and if it were to hand, whither should I fly now that all the earth was Persian? Oh! that Noot were here to counsel me. That he lived somewhere I was sure, since had not his voice spoken in the shrine and this by no priestly trick, for when I put up that prayer for guidance, I knew not how it would be answered or by whom, or if indeed it would but fall upon the deaf ears of the winds, and like a dead leaf, in their breath be blown away and lost.

Yes, he still lived, yet how could I know that it was here he lived? Mayhap he spoke from far beyond this stormy air of earth. Even so he who had counselled me once might counsel me again.

"O whispering reeds," I cried in my heart, "with all your million tongues, pray east and west and north and south, that Ayesha in her need may be helped of the wisdom of the holy Noot."

Yes, thus I prayed like a little, bewildered child who sees God in a cloud and thinks that flowers open for her joy and that the great Pleiades look down from the sky and love her. Yes, toil and grief and terror had made me like a little child.

Well, it is to such, rather than to the proud and learned, the rulers of the earth and the challengers of Heaven, that answers oftenest come and with them knowledge of the truth. At least to me, emptied of strength and wisdom and in that weak hour, forgetful even of my beauty, my great deeds, and the lore that I had won, swiftly there came an answer.

Of a sudden, at the first blush of dawn upon night's pale cheek, a priestess stood by my pallet,

"Awake, O Isis-come-to-Earth," she said, bowing. "A man stands without who would have speech with you. He came here in a boat and when he was challenged answered with all the signs, aye, and even spoke the secret words known to few, those words that open the sanctuary's door. The priests questioned him of his business. He answered that he could tell it only to her who bore the jewelled *sistrum*, to her who veiled her head with cloud like a mountain-top, to that Prophetess who in all shrines is known as Child-of-Wisdom, but who among men was named Ayesha, Daughter of Yarab."

Doubting me of this man and scenting treachery, I caused that instructed priestess to repeat one by one the mystical words that he had spoken. At last she uttered a certain syllable of which even she did not know the meaning. But I knew it and knew also who had its custody.

Filled with a great hope I rose and wrapped myself in a dark garment.

"Lead me to this man," I said, "but first make sure that three priests stand round him with drawn swords."

She went and presently returned again, saying that the man awaited me in the fore-court of the little temple, guarded as I had bidden. To this court I followed her. It was but a small place, like to a large room. I entered it from the sanctuary to the west. Through the eastern door poured the first rays of the rising sun, that struck upon a man who stood waiting in the centre of the court, guarded by three priests with lifted swords.

I could not see his face, though perhaps even beneath my cowl he could see mine upon which those rays also struck. At least I saw him start, then fall to his knees, raising his hand in salute with a quick and curious motion. It was enough. I knew him at once. This man was Philo and no other. With a word I bade the armed priests leave us and the priestess who had accompanied me bide in the shadow. Then I went forward, saying,

"Rise, Philo, for whom I have looked so long that I began to think you were no more to be found beneath the sun. Whence come you, Philo, and for what purpose?"

"O Prophetess, O adored, O Lady divine," he answered in a voice of joy, "I, your slave in the flesh and your fellow servant in the goddess, greet you whom never I hoped to see again after all that has passed in Egypt. Suffer that I may kiss your hand and thereby learn that you are still a woman and not a ghost."

I stretched out my hand and reverently he touched it with his lips.

"Now tell your tale, friend Philo," I said. "Whence come you, most welcome Philo, and by what magic do you find me here?"

"I come from far to the south, Prophetess, out of an ancient land of which you shall learn afterward. For three moons have I struggled over difficult seas driven by contrary winds, to reach the mouths of Nile and to find you, if still you lived."

"And who sent you, friend Philo?"

"A certain Master who is known to both of us, he sent me."

"Is he perchance named Noot?" I asked in a low voice, "and if so, did you sail hither over mortal seas, or over those through which Ra travels in the Underworld?"

This I said wondering, for it came into my mind that he who knelt before me might perchance be not a man but a shadow sent to summon me to the halls of Osiris."

"Mortal seas I sailed; those of the Under-world still await my prow, O Wisdom's Daughter. Here is the proof of it," and drawing a roll from his bosom, with it he touched his brow in token of reverence, then gave it to me.

I broke the seals, I opened that roll, and by the light of the rising sun I read. It ran thus:

"From Noot, the son of Noot, the high-priest, the guardian of Secrets, to Ayesha, Child of Isis, Wisdom's Daughter, the Instructed, the Oracle: Thus saith Noot.

"I live, I do not sleep in my eternal house. My spirit shows me that which passes upon the Nile. I know that you have obeyed my commands which I gave to you before we parted in the bygone years, O my begotten in the goddess. I know that you have waited patiently in faith through many tribulations. I know also that this writing will find you in an hour of great peril when for the second time you have escaped from fire, leaving behind you the ashes of your foes. Come to me now and at once, Philo the beloved brother and the consecrated *sistrum* that is the sceptre of your office being your guides. Philo shall lead you; through all dangers the *sistrum* shall be your shield. I write no more.

"Obey, Mouth of Isis, bringing with you those that are left to the service of the goddess. Read the seal of Noot, high-priest and prophet, and tarry not."

I read and hid away the roll. Then I asked,

"Upon what wings do we fly to Noot who is so far from us, friend Philo?"

"Upon those of a ship that is known to you, Prophetess, the ship named *Hapi*, upon which already you have passed many perils. She lies yonder fully manned in the outer fringe of this sea of reeds."

"How did you find those reeds, and how did you know that I was hidden among them?" I asked curiously.

"Noot marked them on a chart he gave me and told me that in them, where, as the story runs, Isis discovered the heart of Osiris, there I should find the child of Isis. Prophetess, inquire no more."

I heard and returned thanks in my heart. Truly what I whispered to the whispering reeds had been borne to the ears of Heaven.

The trireme *Hapi*, with her mast struck, lay hidden in shallow water midst beds of tall bulrushes and papyrus plants, into which Philo had worked her by the moonlight. All that day we laboured lading her with the treasures of the temple of Isis and those of the secret shrine, which were many, for during these times of trouble much gold and priceless furnishing of precious metals had been hidden here among the reeds. Also with them were some of the most ancient and hallowed statues of the goddess fashioned in gold and ivory and alabaster stone.

All of these together with my own great wealth of jewels and other gear were borne in boats to the *Hapi* and stored within her hold where they lay hid beneath much merchandise that Philo had purchased at the ports of Nile. Hither he had come disguised as a merchant from the south, having his ship laden with the produce of Punt such as ivory and rare woods. These he sold at the ports where he gathered tidings of all that passed in Egypt, and having purchased other goods in place of them, passed unsuspected up the Nile to the secret Isle of Reeds where Noot had bidden him make inquiry for me at the time of full moon in this very month. It was not difficult for him to find this isle as it seemed that, being an initiate of Isis, once in bygone days he had visited it on the business of the goddess.

While we were at this work we saw boats full of Persian soldiers pass down Nile, as though they searched for someone, and toward the evening saw them return up Nile again, heading for Memphis. I knew for whom they sought and noted that they did so very idly, since all believed that I and my company had perished with the Persians in the burning temple.

At nightfall I gathered the priests and priestesses, in all they were thirty and three in number, and spoke to them, saying,

"Here in Egypt we who are the servants of the goddess can stay no more. The gods of Khem are fallen, their shrines are desolate, and death by sword and fire, or by the torturer's hooks, is the lot of those that worship them. Noot, the high-priest, the Master, the Prophet, summons us from afar, bidding us bear the worship of the goddess to new lands that lie I know not where. Philo, our brother, is his messenger and here is the message written in this roll; read it if you will. I, the Oracle and Prophetess, obey the summons; this very night I sail setting my course for seas unknown, and trusting to the goddess to be my guide, mayhap into the gates of death. Noot the high-priest bids you to accompany me. Yet I give you choice. Bide on here if you will and live out your lives disguised as scribes or peasants, for in the temples you can no longer find a home. Mayhap thus you shall escape the vengeance of the Persians. Or come with me if you will, knowing that I promise you nothing. Let each speak as the Spirit directs the heart within."

They consulted together; then one by one they said that it was their mind to be of my company since they held it better to die with me and pass pure to the arms of the goddess rather than to live on defiled, or perchance to perish miserably beneath the stripes of the executioners, having first been forced to do sacrifice to the Persian god of Fire. So man by man and woman by woman they swore the oath that might not be broken by those who would escape the jaws of the Devourer, and in token kissed the holy *sistrum* that I held to the lips of each. Then for the last time we celebrated the rites of

Isis in a temple of Isis on the Nile and with weeping and with woe sang the psalm of farewell, such as is chanted over the dead of our fellowship.

This done we went to the boats and were rowed on board the *Hapi.*

When the moon was bright the mariners, fierce, foreign men most of them, such as I had never seen before, who wore great earrings of gold and had rings thrust through their noses, poled the vessel out from among the reeds into the deep waters of the Nile. Here they hoisted the mast and set the sails which presently filled before the strong wind blowing from the upper land, and bore us forward swiftly.

Passing out of the Nile by a little-used mouth, as we could do now that the river was in flood, we entered the canal that joins the seas, which canal the old Pharaohs dug and the Persians had caused to be cleared of drifting sand. By it, though not easily, for in places it was both narrow and shallow, at length we came safely into the Red Sea and bade farewell to Egypt. None hindered us on this journey, and, having crossed the lakes, only once did we stay at a little unravaged town at the far mouth of the canal, to buy bread, fresh fish, and meat wherewith to stock our ship.

This town we found to be full of rumours, for the news of the death of Ochus had reached it and many tales were told of the manner of his end. That which these coast-dwellers favoured was that Set the god had appeared in person at a feast, and seizing Ochus, had set him upon a winged Apis, that very Apis bull which he had sacrificed and eaten, and borne him away to hell. At this fable I smiled, though indeed in it there was a seed of truth, since without doubt, if there be a hell, the blood-soaked Ochus was its inhabitant that day.

Now of all that journey I, who grow weary of writing, will omit the story. Most marvellously it prospered, so much so that I think, unseen by us, spirits from the Under-world must have stood upon our prow. From

day to day a strong and steady wind blowing from the
north drove us forward swiftly. No storm smote us nor
did we strike upon any rock, and when we made land
for water, either it was uninhabited, or the folk who
dwelt there, strange barbarous folk, were friendly.

So the time went by creeping from moon to moon
and ever we sailed on southward. Nor was the time unhappy, since there I sat in that same cabin which had
been mine when Pharaoh gave me as a bribe to Tenes
and that therefore was familiar to me, having something
of the aspect of a home. Indeed with a certain taste of
acid pleasure, from time to time I recalled all that had
happened to me upon this ship and in that very cabin.
For instance where I had wrung the writing from the
passion-maddened Tenes; where he had stood and
knelt; where his shadow had struck upon the cedar
walls. There, too, in the wood was an arrow hole, which
arrow should have drunk my life.

Then in the waist of the ship was the place where the
boarders from the *Holy Fire* had won aboard, whence
Kallikrates, the Grecian captain turned heirophant, had
beat them back so gallantly. Aft, also, was the shelter
where I had visited him and dressed his wounds that
were almost to the death. Here I placed upon his finger the
charmed scarab ring of Khæmuas, the Magician, whereon were cut symbols with a secret meaning, though
they seemed to read only as "Son of Ra," that this ring
might raise him from the darkness of death, as Osiris
rose and as Ra rises from the Under-world.

Here, too, it was that I heard him mistake me for
another woman and to that woman give his thanks, thus
opening my eyes to all the folly of my heart. Years ago
these things had chanced to me, and now when they
were dead things, I say that I could dream of them with
that soft grief which is like to the tenderness of eve after
the promise of the morning and the burning noonday
heat have become but memories buried beneath the
dust of time. Yet it is true that now and again those
memories renewed their life, especially within the
shrines of sleep.

Oh! it was all so long ago. Had not Philo's beard,

that I remembered brown and rich, since then grown gray, and were not his curling locks thinned upon his temples? And I who then was young, had I not grown to middle-age, though still I remained more lovely than any other woman in the world, and was not my soul burdened with much learning, and had not the sorrows I had passed pierced it with a thousand spears? Now, too, doubtless Kallikrates was dead, and all the dreams to which he alone among men had given birth within me had gone wherever dreams may go, perchance to be lost in the vast unknown, or perchance after the change called death, there to be found again?

Yet I, I wandered forward on my path, Fate-driven as of old, to what end I knew not and did not greatly care to know. For now it seemed my part was played; the world and its stirrings were left behind me and the last shreds of my web must be spun of poor stuff in petty, unknown places, where I should patter prayers beneath an alien sky till it pleased death to enfold me in its wings and bear me to the depths of its enormous habitations.

Well, so let it be, since, as I have said, I was weary of the world; its toils, its bloody issues, and its perpetual strivings to grasp that which man or woman may not hold—except in dreams.

With Philo I talked much, but always of the past; of those things which we had experienced together, or of other events of his earlier, adventurous life, or of my own. A most pleasant companion was this Philo, of a shrewd wit and some learning also, a brave citizen of the world who had seen much, and yet one who revered the gods, whatever the gods might be, and had thoughts of that which lies beyond the world, whatever this may be. But of the present or of what had happened to him since he sailed away with Noot, my Master, when Ochus invaded Egypt, and least of all of the future and whither we went or why, I did not talk at all.

For when these matters came to my lips, as they did even before we were clear of Nile, Philo made a certain sign to me which being interpreted meant that he was under an oath, a very solemn oath, not to speak of any of them, which oath I respected, as indeed I was bound to do. Therefore I asked no more and sailed on careless as a child that recks not of what is to come and from whom death is still very far away.

CHAPTER XVIII

~

The Tale of Philo

ONCE more it was a night of full moon. As we had done for many days we were sailing before that steady wind along the coast of Libya, having this upon our right hand, and upon our left, at a distance, a line of rocky reef upon which breakers fell continually.

It was a very splendid moon that turned the sea to silver and lit up the palm-grown shore almost as brightly as does the sun. I sat upon the deck near to my cabin and by me stood Philo watching that shore intently.

"For what do you seek, Philo? Are you in fear of sunken rocks?"

"Nay, Child of Isis, yet it is true that I seek a certain rock which by my reckoning should now be in sight. Ah!"

Then suddenly he ran forward and shouted an order. Men leapt up and sprang to the ropes while the rowers began to get out the sweeps. As they did this the *Hapi* came round so that her bow pointed to the shore and the great sail sank to the deck. Then the long oars bit into the water and drove us shoreward.

Philo returned.

"Look, Lady," he said. "Now that the moon has risen higher you can see well," and he pointed to a headland in front of us.

Following his outstretched hand with my eyes I perceived a great rock many cubits in height and carven on the crest of it a head far larger than that of the huge Sphinx of Egypt. Or perchance it was not carved; perchance Nature had fashioned it thus. At least there it stood and will stand, a terrible and hideous thing, having the likeness of an Ethiopian's head gazing eternally across the sea.

"What is it?" I asked.

"Lady, it is the Guardian of the Gate of the land whither we go. Legend tells that it is shaped to the likeness of the first king of that land who lived thousands upon thousands of years before the pyramids were built; also that his bones lie in it, or at least, that it is haunted by his spirit. For this reason none dare to touch and much less to climb yonder monstrous rock."

Then he left me to see to the matters of the ship, because, as he said in going, the entrance to the place was strait and dangerous. But I sat on alone upon the deck watching this strange new sight.

Within an hour, rowing carefully, we entered the mouth of a river, having the rock shaped like to a negro's head upon our right. Then it was that I saw something which put me in mind of Philo's tale about an ancient king. For there, unless I dreamed, upon the very point of the skull of the effigy, of a sudden I perceived a tall form clad in armour which shone silvery bright in the moon's rays. It leaned upon a great spear, and when we were opposite to it, straightened itself and bent forward as though to stare at our ship beneath. Next, thrice it lifted the spear in salutation; thrice it bowed, as I thought in obeisance to me, and having done so, threw its arms wide and was gone.

Afterward I asked Philo if he also had seen this thing.

"Nay," he answered in a doubtful voice as though the matter were one of which he did not wish to talk, adding,

"It is not the custom of mariners to study that head in the moonlight, because the story goes that if they do and chance to see some such ghost as that you tell of, it casts a spear toward them, who then are doomed to die within the year. Yet at you, Child of Isis, he cast no spear, only bowed and gave the salute of kings, or so you tell me. Therefore doubtless neither you nor any of us, your companions, are marked for death."

I smiled and said that I whose soul was in touch with Heaven feared not the wraith of any ancient king, nor did we speak more of this matter. Yet in the after ages it came into my mind that there was truth in the story and that this long-dead king appeared thus to give greeting to her who was destined to rule his land through many generations; also that perchance he was not dead at all, but, having drunk of a certain Cup of Life of which I was to learn, lived eternally there upon the rock.

I laid me down and slept, and when I woke in the bright morning it was to find that we had passed from that river into a canal dug by man which, though deep, was too narrow for the sweeps to work. Therefore the *Hapi* must be pushed along with poles and towed by ropes dragged at by the mariners from a path that ran upon the bank.

For three days we travelled thus making but slow progress, since the toil of dragging so large a ship was great, and at night we tied up to the bank, as boats do upon the Nile. All this while we saw no habitation though certain ruins we did see. Indeed that country was very desolate and full of great swamps that were tenanted by wild beasts, the haunt of owls and bitterns, where lions roared and serpents crept, great serpents such as I had never seen.

At length at noon on the fourth day we came to a lake where the canal ended, which lake once had been a harbour, for we saw stone quays where still were tied some boats that seemed to be little used. Here Philo said that we must disembark and travel on by land. So we left the *Hapi,* sadly enough for my part, because those were happy, quiet days that I had spent on board of her, veritable oases in the storm-swept desert of my life.

Scarcely had we set foot upon the land when appeared, I knew not whence, a company of men, handsome, hook-nosed, sombre men, such as I had seen

among the crew upon the *Hapi*. These men, though so
fierce in appearance, were not barbarians, for they wore
linen garments that gave to them the aspect of priests.
Moreover, their leaders could speak Arabic in its most
ancient form, which, having studied it, as it chanced, I
knew. With this army, who bore bows and spears, came
a multitude of folk of a baser sort that carried litters, or
burdens, also a guard of great fellows that Philo told me
were my especial escort. Now my patience failed so that
I turned upon Philo saying,

"Hitherto, Friend, I have trusted myself to you, because it seemed decreed that I should do so. Now tell
me, I pray you, what means this journey over countless
leagues of sea into a land untrod, and whither go I in
the fellowship of these barbarians? Because you brought
me a certain writing in an acceptable hour, I gave myself into your keeping, nor did I even ask any revelation
from the goddess or seek to solve the mystery by spells.
Yet, now I ask and, as the Prophetess of Isis, demand
the truth of you, her humbler servant."

"Lady divine," answered Philo, bowing himself before me, "what I have withheld is by command, the
command of a very great one, of none less than Noot
the aged and holy. You go to an old land that is yet new
to find Noot, your master and mine."

"In the flesh or in the spirit?" I asked.

"In the flesh, Prophetess, if still he lives, as these
men say, and see, I accompany you, I whom in the past
you have found faithful. If I fail you, let my life pay
forfeit, and for the rest, ask it of the holy Noot."

"It is enough," I said. "Lead on."

We entered the litters; we laded the bearers with the
treasures of Isis and with my own peculiar wealth, and
having placed the ship *Hapi* under guard, marched into
the unknown like to some great caravan of merchants.
For days we marched, following a broad road that was
broken down in places, over plains and through vast
swamps, and at night sleeping in caves or covered by
tents which we brought with us.

This was a strange journey that I made surrounded
by that host of hook-nosed, silent, ghost-like men, who,

as I noted, loved the night better than they did the day. Almost might I have thought that they had been sent from Hades to conduct us to those gates from which for mortals there is no return. My fellowship of the priests and priestesses grew afraid and clustered round me at night, praying to be led back to familiar lands and faces.

I answered them that what I dared they must dare also, and that the goddess was as near to us here as she had been in Egypt, nor could death be closer to us than it was in Egypt. Yea, I bade them have faith, since without faith we could not be at peace one hour who, lacking it, must be overwhelmed with terrors, even within the walls of citadels.

They hearkened, bowing their heads and saying that whatever else they might doubt, they trusted themselves to me.

So we went on, passing through a country where more of these half-savage men that I learned were called *Amahagger* dwelt in villages surrounded by their cattle, or by colonies in caves. At last there arose before us a mighty mountain whose towering cliffs had the appearance of a wall so vast that the eye could not compass it. By a gorge we penetrated that mountain and found within it an enormous, fertile plain, and on the plain a city larger than Memphis or than Thebes, but a city half in ruins.

Passing over a great bridge spanning a wide moat once filled with water that now here and there was dry, we entered the walls of that city and by a street broader than any I had ever seen, bordered by many noble, broken houses, though some of these seemed still to be inhabited, came to a glorious temple like to those of Egypt, only greater, and with taller columns. Across its grass-grown courts, that were set one within another, we were carried to some inner sanctuary. Here we descended from the litters and were led to sculptured chambers that seemed to have been made ready to receive us, where we cleansed ourselves of the dust of travel and ate. Then came Philo, who conducted me to a little lamp-lit hall, for now the night had fallen, where was a chair of state such as high-priests used, in which at his bidding I sat myself.

I think that being weary with travel, I must have slept in that chair, since I dreamed or seemed to dream that I received worship such as is given to a queen, or even to a goddess. Heralds hailed me, voices sang to me, even spirits appeared in troops to talk to me, the spirits of those who thousands of years before had departed from the earth. They told me strange stories of the past and of the future; tales of a fallen people, of a worship and a glory that had gone by and been swallowed in the gulfs of Time. Then gathering in a multitude they seemed to hail me, crying,

"Welcome, appointed Queen! Build thou up that which has fallen. Discover thou that which is lost. Thine is the strength, thine the opportunity, yet beware of the temptations, beware of the flesh, lest the flesh should overcome the spirit and by its fall add ruin unto ruin, the ruin of the soul to the ruin of the body."

I awoke from my vision and saw Philo standing before me.

"Hearken, Philo," I said. "Of these mysteries I can bear no more. The time has come when you must speak, or face my wrath. Why have I been brought hither to this strange and distant land where it seems that I must dwell in a place of ruins?"

"Because the holy Noot so commanded, O Child of Wisdom," he answered. "Was it not set down in the writing I gave you at the Isle of Reeds upon the Nile?"

"Where then is the holy Noot?" I asked. "Here I see him not. Is he dead?"

"I do not think that he is dead, Lady. Yet to the world he is dead. He has become a hermit, one who dwells in a cave in a perilous place not very far from this city. To-morrow I will bring you to him, if that be your will. So only can you see him who now for years has never left that cave, or so I think, save to fetch the food which is prepared for him."

"A strange tale, Philo, though that Noot should become a hermit does not amaze me, since such was ever his desire. Now tell me how he came hither, and you with him?"

"Lady, you will remember that in the bygone years when Nectanebes, he who was Pharaoh, fled up Nile, the holy Noot embarked upon my ship, the *Hapi,* to sail to the northern cities, that there he might treat with the Persians for the ransom of those temples of Egypt that remained unravished."

"I remember, Philo. What chanced to you upon that journey?"

"This, Lady: that we were very nearly slain, every one of us, for whom the Persians had set a trap, thinking to snare Noot and his company and torture him till he revealed where the treasures of the temples of Isis were hid away. Nevertheless, because I am a good sailor and because that warrior priest, Kallikrates, was brave, we escaped into the canal which is called the *Road of Rameses* and so at last out to sea, for to return up Nile was impossible. Then Noot commanded that I should sail on southerly upon a course he seemed to know well enough; or perchance the goddess taught it to him; I cannot say. At least I obeyed, so that in the end we reached that harbour which is guarded by a rock carved to the likeness of an Ethiopian's head, and thence travelled to this place, still guided by the wisdom of Noot who knew the road."

"And Kallikrates? What became of Kallikrates—who it seems was with you?" I asked in an indifferent voice, though my heart burned to hear his answer.

"Lady, so far as it is known to me this is the story of Kallikrates and the Princess Amenartas."

"The Princess Amenartas! By all the gods, what is your meaning, Philo? She went up Nile with Nectanebes her father, he who was Pharaoh."

"Nay, Lady, she went down Nile with Kallikrates, or perhaps with Noot, or perhaps with herself alone. I do not know with whom she hid since I never saw her, nor learned that she was aboard my ship until we were two days' journey out to sea and the coasts of Egypt were far behind us."

"Is it so?" I said coldly, though I was filled with bitter anger. "And what did the holy Noot when he found that this woman was aboard his vessel?"

"Lady, he did nothing except look on her somewhat doubtfully."

"And what did the priest Kallikrates? Did he strive to be rid of her?"

"Nay, Lady, and indeed that would have been impossible, unless he had thrown her overboard. He did nothing except talk with her—that is, so far as I saw."

"Well, then, Philo, where is she now, and where is Kallikrates? I do not see him in this place."

"Lady, I cannot tell you, but I think it probable that they are dead and in the fellowship of Osiris. When we had been some weeks at sea we were driven by storm to an island off the coast under the lee of which we took shelter, a very fertile and beautiful island, peopled by a kindly folk. After we had sailed again from that island it was discovered that the priest Kallikrates and the Royal Princess Amenartas were missing from the ship, nor because of the strong wind that blew us forward was it possible for us to return to seek for them. I made inquiry of the matter and the sailors told me that they had been fishing together and that a shark which took their bait pulled them both into the sea; in which case doubtless they were drowned."

"And did you believe that story, Philo?"

"Nay, Lady. I understood at once that it was one which the sailors had been bribed to tell. Myself I think that they went to the island in one of the boats of the people who dwell there; perhaps because they could no longer bear the cold eyes of Noot fixed upon them, or perhaps to gather fruit, for which those who have been long upon water often conceive a great desire. But," he added simply, "I do not know why they should have done this seeing that the island-dwellers brought us plenty of fruits in their boats."

"Doubtless they preferred to pluck them fresh with their own hands, Philo."

"Perhaps, Lady, or perhaps they wished to stay awhile upon that island. At least I noted that the Princess took her garments and her jewels with her, which she could scarcely have done if the shark had dragged her into the sea."

"Are you so sure, Philo, that she did not leave some of those jewels behind——in *your* keeping, Philo? It is very strange to me that the Princess Amenartas could have come aboard your ship and have left your ship, and you know nothing."

Now Philo looked up innocently and said,

"Surely it is lawful for a captain to receive faring money from his passengers, and that I admit I did. But I do not understand why the Child of Wisdom is so wrath because a Greek and a great lady were by chance left together upon an island where, for aught I know, one or other of them may have had friends."

"Am I not the guardian of the honour of the goddess?" I answered. "And do you not know that under our law Kallikrates was sworn to her alone?"

"If so, Prophetess, doubtless that captain, or that priest, remembers his oaths and deals with this princess as though she were his sister or his mother. At the least the goddess can guard her own honour, so why should you fret your soul concerning it, Prophetess? Lastly, it is probable that by now both of them are dead and have made all things clear to Isis in the heavenly halls."

Thus he prattled on, adding lie to lie as only a Greek can do. I listened until I could bear no more. Then I said but one word. It was "Begone!"

He went humbly, yet as I thought, smiling.

Oh! now I saw it all. Noot had made a plot to remove Kallikrates far from me, so that I might never look upon him again. Philo knew of this plot, and through him Amenartas knew it also. Unknown to Noot she bribed Philo to hide her upon his ship till they were far from land, though whether the plan was known to Kallikrates I could not say, nor did it greatly matter. Then the rest followed. Amenartas appeared upon the ship and cast her net about Kallikrates who had sworn to have done with her, and the end can be guessed. Noot was wrath with them, so wrath that when the chance came they fled away, purposing to stay upon that island until they could find a ship to take them back to Egypt or elsewhere. Thus, I was sure, ran the story, and, as it proved afterward, I was right.

Well, they were gone and as I hoped, dead, since only death could cover up such sin, and for my part I was glad that I had done with Kallikrates and his light-of-love. And yet there, seated on the couch of state, I wept—because of the outrage done to Isis whom I served. Or was it for myself that I wept? I cannot say, I only know that my tears were bitter. Also I was very lonely in this strange and desolate place. Why had I been brought here, I wondered. Because Noot had commanded it, sending for me from afar, and what he commanded, that I must obey. Where, then, was Noot, who, Philo swore, still lived? Why had he not appeared to greet me? I covered my eyes with my hands and threw out my soul to Noot, saying,

"Come to me, O Noot. Come to me, my beloved Master."

Lo! a voice, a well-remembered voice answered,

"Daughter, I am here."

I let fall my hand. I gazed with my tear-stained eyes, and behold! before me, white-robed, gold-filleted, snowy-bearded, grown very ancient and ethereal, stood the prophet and high-priest, my Master. For a moment I thought that it was his spirit which I saw. Then he moved, and I heard his white robes rustle, and knew that there stood Noot himself whom I had travelled so many thousand leagues to find.

I rose; I ran to him; I seized his thin hand and kissed it, while he, murmuring, "My Daughter, at last, at last!" leaned forward and with his lips touched me on the brow.

"Far away your summons reached me in an hour of peril," I said. "Behold! I obeyed, I came. In faith I came, asking no questions, and I am here in safety, for I think the goddess herself was with me on that journey. Tell me all, O Noot. What is this place? How were you brought to it and why have you called me to you?"

"Hearken, Daughter," he said, seating himself beside me on the throne-like couch. "This city is named Kôr. Once she was queen of the world, as after her, Babylon,

Thebes, Tyre, and Athens are, or have been queens. From Kôr thousands of years ago in the black, lost ages Egypt was peopled, as were other lands. In those dim days by another title her citizens worshipped Isis, Queen of Heaven, only they named her *Truth* whom in Egypt you know as Maat. Then apostasy arose and many of this great people, abandoning the pure and gentle worship of Isis wrapped in the veil of Truth, under the name of Rezu, a fierce sun-dæmon, set up another god to whom they made human sacrifices, as the Sidonians did to Moloch. Yea, they sacrificed men, women, and children by thousands, and even learned to eat their flesh, first as a sacred rite, and afterward to satisfy their appetites. Heaven saw and grew wrath; Heaven smote the people with a mighty pestilence, so that they perished and perished till few were left. Thus Kôr fell by the sword of God as, for like cause, fell Sidon."

"Of all this afterward," I answered impatiently. "Tell me first, how came you here? Long years ago you sailed down Nile to treat with the Persians for the ransom of the temples of Egypt, a mission in which it seems you failed, my Father."

"Aye, Ayesha, I failed. It was but a trap, since those false-hearted Fire-worshippers thought to take me captive and hold my life in gage against all the treasures of Isis. By the cunning and seamanship of Philo and the courage of a priest named Kallikrates, whom you may still remember after all these years," here he glanced at me sharply, "I escaped when a gang of them disguised as envoys strove to snare me. But the road up Nile being barred, we were forced to fly south, and down Pharaoh's Great Ditch, till at length, after many wanderings and adventures, we came to this land, as it was fated that I should do. You will remember, Daughter, that I told you I believed that we were parting for a long while, although I believed also that we should meet again in the flesh."

"I remember well," I answered, "also that I swore to come to you at the appointed hour."

"I came to this land," went on Noot, "but Kallikrates, the Greek captain who was a priest of Isis, never reached it. He was lost on the way."

"With another, my Father. But now I have heard that story from Philo."

"With another who caused him to break his vows. Be sure, Daughter, that I knew nothing of her plot or that she was hidden aboard the ship, though perchance Philo knew. The goddess hid it from me, doubtless for her own purposes."

"Are this pair dead, or do they still live, my Father?"

"I cannot say; that also is hidden from me. Better for them if they are dead, since soon or late for such sacrilege vengeance will fall upon the head of one, if not of both of them. Peace be to them. May they be forgiven! At least as I think they loved each other much and, since love is very strong, all who have ever loved where they ought not should have pity on them," and again his questioning eyes played upon my face.

CHAPTER XIX

~

The Hermitage of Noot

"TELL me of what has passed in Egypt since Ochus conquered and Nectanebes fled away. Does Ochus still live, Daughter?" asked Noot after a pause during which both of us had sat staring at the ground.

"Nay, Father, Ochus is dead and by my hand, or through it," and I told him all that story of the burning of the temple of Isis at my command and of the Persians who defiled it.

"A great deed such as you alone could have planned," he muttered, "but terrible, terrible!"

"Then your soul must bear its burden, Prophet, since it was your voice that we heard in the sanctuary, when in our extreme we prayed for guidance, and it told us to go forward. There are those with me who can bear witness that they heard your very voice, as I do."

"Mayhap, Daughter. It is true that on a certain day not so many moons ago, I seemed to hear you calling to heaven in great trouble and danger, also that by direction which came I know not whence, I answered in my spirit that you must 'fulfil and fear not.' What you were to fulfil I did not know, though it came to my mind that the business had something to do with the burning of a temple."

"As it had indeed. Well, I fulfilled, as Ochus Artaxerxes and some hundreds of his Persian ravagers can testify before all the gods until the end of time, for those dogs at least have ceased to pollute the earth and to-day are enriching hell. There let them lie with Tenes and Nectanebes also, if in truth he has joined them, and many another false priest and king. Afterward we will talk of them and all their deeds of shame. But first tell me why I am here. For what end did you summon me from Egypt? Was it to save me from death?"

"Nay, Ayesha, from more than that. Why should I wish to hold you back from the great boon of death in which so soon I must have joined you? I summoned you because I was commanded so to do, that now when Isis has passed from Egypt, you should cause her worship to re-arise at Kôr which was her ancient home. It is willed that here you should abide and once more build up this people and make it great by the help of the Queen of Heaven who then will lead it on to triumph and to glory."

"That is a mighty task, Prophet. Still perchance with your aid it may be done if the gods give me life and wisdom."

He shook his head and answered,

"Look not to my aid, for at length my day is finished. Has not Philo told you that I mix no more with matters of the world, I who for years past have dwelt a hermit in a terrible place, sheltered only by a cave and lost in the contemplation of holy things?"

"No, Father, he has told me little or nothing—by your will, or so he said," I replied, amazed.

"Yet it is so; moreover, presently I must return to that prison whence I came, there to await the change called death. I have played my part, but your work still remains to do; Philo will aid you in it."

"Why do you live in that place, Father, leaving me without the guidance of your wisdom?"

"Because there I guard a great secret, that was revealed to me long ago, it matters not how, the greatest secret in the whole world—that of how men may escape from death and live on eternally upon the earth."

Now I stared at him, thinking that age and abstinence had made him mad. Then, to test the matter, I asked,

"If it be so great a secret, why do you tell it to me, Master?"

"Because I must. Because I know well that if I do not, you would discover it for yourself, and being unwarned, would fall into the trap, and still living beneath the sun, dare to clothe yourself with this garment of immortality. It was for this reason that until twice the command had come to me, I would not summon you to Kôr."

Now a new thought thrilled my soul. If this strange tale were true; if indeed here on earth there could be found such a door leading to the divine, why should I not pass it and become as are the gods? Only I did not believe that it was true.

"Surely you have dreamed in your loneliness, my Father," I said. "But know that if you did not dream, if it were true, I, Ayesha, should be minded to wear that robe of life eternal. Why not, O Prophet?"

"Because, Ayesha, the man or woman who dared to eat of this fruit forbidden to their race here on earth, where death is decreed for all, would be a man or woman who dared to enter into hell."

"I think otherwise, Prophet Noot, I think that this man or woman would enter into glory and become the ruler of the world," I answered, and as I spoke the words my eyes flashed and my breast heaved.

"Not so, Ayesha, since from that fatal peak of pride Heaven will beat back all human feet. Oh, hearken to me and purge your soul of the madness of this desire by which I see already it is possessed. It was laid upon me to reveal this secret to you, which I think was given me for that very purpose, so that you might show your greatness by rejecting it, the deadliest bribe that the god of Ill ever offered to mortal woman."

"Or perchance by accepting it, Master!"

"Nay, nay! Bethink you. Is the world a fit place for the undying! Moreover, this secret that I guard is but the world's spirit, not that of immortality; the hidden force from which our earth draws its strength, but which will perish with the earth, as it must do upon a day still hidden in the deeps of time. The drinker of that cup therefore would become, not eternal, but long-lived only, destined to perish at last with this passing star. For him death would not be destroyed, it would only be delayed, waiting ever to snare him in the end. Meanwhile he must endure desolate and alone, watching the generations pass one by one to their appointed rest; while, filled perchance with fearful appetites which he must know eternally and yet remain unsatisfied, he stands but as a frozen rock upon the plain, wearing a human shape, yet alien to mortality, though still torn by its ambitions, its loves, its hates, its hopes, its fears, and waiting terrified for that predestined moment when this globe shall crumble and death shall devour it and him.

"I am old, I am feeble, my hour is well nigh done, I pass to my repose in Heaven. Ayesha, I have no strength to stay your feet, if you elect to drink this cup my weak hand cannot dash it from your lips. Yet as one who has taught and loved you, as one to whom the gods have given wisdom, I pray you to thrust aside this great temptation. As our faith teaches truly, already your spirit is immortal and has its home prepared above. Desire not, therefore, to perpetuate your flesh, since if you do, Ayesha, I tell you that you will become but as a painted mummy in a tomb, simulating life, yet dead and cold within. Swear to me, Daughter, that you will lock this knowledge in your heart and thrust the poison from your lips."

"You speak wisely," I answered, "aye, as one inspired by the truth, and though I take no oaths, it is my purpose to do your will. Yet, Father, what is this secret? Having told me so much, tell all, lest I should go to discover it for myself."

"Daughter, near to this ancient city, amid the mountain cliffs, deep in the bowels of the rocks burns a travelling fire which is the very soul of the world, the flaming heart that gives it life. Yet this fire is no fire, but rather the essence of existence, and he who bathes in it will be filled with that essence and endure while it endures."

"Perchance such a one might be destroyed by that fire," I answered doubtfully.

"Daughter, I would that I could leave you thinking thus, for then a great fear would pass from me. But we who are the chief servants of Isis dare not hide the truth one from another, since to do so is to break our oaths. Moreover, in this matter I do not speak with my own voice, but with that of a Strength which is greater than I, to whom now I stand so near that almost it and I are one. Therefore to your eyes I must withdraw all veils, showing you what is, as it is, and not as I would have it be. Yonder fire will not destroy the mortal who finds the courage to stand in its raging path; it will give him life, and with it such strength, such beauty, and such wisdom as have never been the lot of man born of woman. Also it will give him such passions, such despairs, such unending woes as hitherto no mortal heart has known.

"There is the truth. Ask me not how it comes into my keeping and what that voice may be which is speaking it through my lips. A minute gone this truth was mine alone, or perchance mine and one other's. Now it is yours also, and being yours, I pray to that Divine from which we come and whither we return again, that it may give you strength and the true wisdom, knowing all, to reject all, and turning aside from this glittering guerdon of enduring life, patiently to walk your human path to the end appointed to our human feet."

"Will you show me this fire, Prophet?"

"Aye, if you will, for so I am commanded," he answered faintly; "yet why look upon that which must excite desire?"

Then weariness overcame him and he sank down swooning, so that had I not caught him, he would have fallen.

Noot abode three days at Kôr and talked with me of many things, but at that time of the wonderful Secret of Life he spoke no more. As though by consent both of us let that matter lie awhile. For the rest there was much to say. I told him everything that had passed in Egypt and the outer world since long years before he had left me to sail down Nile, never to return. I told him how I had obeyed his last commands to the letter, and surrounded though I was by foes, had preserved the worship of Isis in her temple from season to season, celebrating her festivals in their appointed course, though I never dared to leave its walls.

"So, Ayesha," he said when I had done, "while I have been a hermit here at Kôr, you have been a hermit at Memphis. Well, each of us has served the goddess as best might be, so may she reward us both according to our deserts, which doubtless are but small. And now my task is finished, but yours lies before you, seeing that you still have strength, even if your youth has gone."

"Yes," I answered somewhat bitterly, "mid-age has overtaken me, my youth has passed in the service of Heaven, and what has Heaven given to me after all my wars and strivings? Just this—that in a savage, desolate land among ruins and barbarians I must begin anew. I must restore a faith decayed, collect those barbarians into armies and order them, enact laws and cause them to be obeyed, fight battles, till lands, build ships and carry on commerce, collect revenues and spend them wisely, labour without cease day by day, finding but little rest at night because of the troubles that await the morrow. I must be at once a high-priestess, an oracle, a general, a law-giver, a judge, an architect, a landtiller and a queen beneath an alien sky; without counsel, without friends, without love, without children to tend me in my age or to pile the earth upon my bones. Such is the lot that the goddess has given to her priestess Ayesha in payment of all her strivings."

Thus I spoke bitterly enough, but Noot answered with a gentle smile,

"At least, Daughter, it might have been more evil. You have a planning and a thoughtful mind and here you can shape all things afresh to your desire. You love power and here you will be absolute, a very queen, you who cannot brook denial. Here there will be none to say you nay. You hate rivals who would rule alone. Here they will be lacking. You desire to remain celibate who are wed to the spirit. Here no more kings or others will come to trouble you, plotting to win your beauty. It has ever been your wish to commune with Nature and that Divine from which it springs; here in this deserted place is Nature's very home and in solitude the Divine draws near to empty souls.

"Truly you should be thankful, therefore, whose prayers have been fulfilled, who have attained to all you sought, whose ambitions are satisfied and who in the holy calm and the healthful weariness that follows upon long-continued labours, at last when your task is done, will sink gently to the grave to seek their reward elsewhere. Soon, very soon, you will be as I am and when that day comes there will be an empty hermitage yonder where in darkness and in contemplation you can patiently await the end and those new endeavours which, after it, may be appointed to you elsewhere. For be sure of this, Ayesha—all existence is a ladder up which painfully and with many slips we must climb step by step."

"And when we reach the top, what then, Master?"

"I do not know, Daughter, but I do know that if we fall to the bottom, all those steps must be climbed again, only this time the rungs of the ladder will be wreathed with thorns."

"It seems that yonder hermitage of yours is no home of joy, my Father."

"Nay, Daughter. It is a home of grief and of repentance. The joy lies beyond. Such are the philosophy of life and the teachings of all religion. Be sorrowful and afterward you will rejoice. Rejoice and afterward you will be sorrowful."

"A sad philosophy, Prophet, and such lessons as slaves learn beneath the whip."

"Aye, Ayesha, but one that must be endured, as, if they could speak, Tenes and Ochus and Nectanebes would tell you to-day."

So he droned on who grew weak and senile, having become but the dry shell of a man, whence the sap had withered, like to a sterile nut indeed, from which, if it were sown, no shoot would spring. At length wearying of his melancholy talk, I fell to the thought of that Fire of Life raging in its eternal vigour beneath his hermitage, which, as he swore, would give unending beauty, youth, glory, and dominion to him who could find faith and courage to dare its terrors.

On the following day I accompanied Noot back to his hermitage for the quiet of which he seemed to yearn, so much so indeed that even for my sake whom he loved more than anything on earth and in whose fellowship he delighted, he would not be separated from it for another hour.

It was a rough journey that we made borne in litters to the foot of the great precipice which surrounds the plain of Kôr like to a measureless wall chiselled by Titans at the shaping of the world. We climbed up a cleft in that wall and entered a hidden fold of rock, invisible from below. Following this fold we came to the mouth of a cave. Here I noted that food was set in plenty by the dwellers in this land who revered Noot as a prophet and thus supplied him with his sustenance. Here also were torches which were lit by those who accompanied us to give us light upon our journey through the cave that was long and rough. At length we came to its end to find before us a terrible chasm. Thousands of feet above us was a line of blue sky and beneath lay a gulf of darkness. Out into this chasm down which winds raved and howled, ran a giant spur of rock of which the end was lost in darkness. I looked at it doubtfully and said,

"Where then is your habitation, Noot, and by what road is it reached?"

"It lies yonder in the darkness, Daughter," he answered, smiling, "and this is the road that those who would visit me must travel," and he pointed to the spur of rock that trembled in the roaring gale, adding, "To my feet it is familiar; moreover, I know that on it as elsewhere I am protected from harm. But if you fear to walk such a path, turn back while there is still time. Perhaps it would be better that you should turn back."

Now I looked at the trembling rock and then I looked at Noot, my Master.

"What," thought I to myself, "shall I, Ayesha, who dread neither man nor devil, be afraid to follow where this frail old priest can lead? Never will I blench from peril though in it lies my death."

So I stared him in the face and answered,

"To the task, Father, and swiftly, for here the wind blows chill. I go first; Philo, follow me close."

Now Philo, who was my companion upon this adventure, glanced at me with questioning eyes, but being a brave man and one who as a sailor was accustomed to perilous heights, said nothing.

For a moment Noot paused, looking upward, perchance to pray or perchance for other reasons. Then having asked Philo how long it was to the time of sunset and been answered it lacked between the half and the fourth part of an hour before Ra sank behind the western cliff, he started, walking boldly down the spur. I followed next, and last came Philo.

Very terrible was that journey in the uncertain light which as we progressed into the gulf grew ever fainter, till at last we were wrapped about with gloom. Moreover, always the spur of rock narrowed, and the raving gusts of wind which blew about that hideous gorge buffeted us more fiercely.

Still we went on leaning our weight against them, and as we went a kind of exaltation seized me, as it does always in moments of great danger, so that my heart grew bold and feared no more. I would match myself against these elemental strengths as I had matched myself against those of hostile and desiring kings, and conquer them. Or perchance it was the breath from the divine fire that burned below that already had entered into me. I cannot say, but this I remember, that before I had reached the point of that fearful rock I was filled with a wild joy and could laugh at Philo crawling after me with hesitating steps and breathing prayers now to Isis and now to the Grecian gods that he had worshipped as a child.

At length we came to the end of that long needle which thrust itself thus into the dark stuff of space, and as we did so all light went out of the sky above, leaving us plunged in blackness. I seated myself upon the throbbing point of rock, clinging to Philo who had done likewise, and cried into the ear of Noot, kneeling at our side,

"What now? Show us and be swift, lest we should be thrown from this place like stones from a sling."

"Hold fast and wait," answered Noot.

We did so, grasping the roughness of the rock with our hands. Then suddenly a marvel happened, since from somewhere, I know not whence and have never learned, a fierce red ray of light, cast doubtless by the setting sun, struck us through some hole in the opposing cliffs. Aye, it struck like a blazing sword, showing all things that could be seen. They were these: ourselves crouched upon that point of rock; infinite space beneath us, infinite space above reaching up to a single star that shone upon the sky, and we three hemmed in by two black precipices. Moreover, they showed, not four paces from the point, a huge trembling stone that was joined to that fearsome spar by a little bridge of wood laid from the one to the other by the hand of man, which bridge rose and fell and rocked as the great stone trembled on its farther side.

"Follow me swiftly before the light dies," cried Noot as he stepped across this bridge and, reaching the crest of the trembling stone, stood there like a ghost illumined with fire; like also to that figure which I had seen watching from the brow of the Ethiopian's head when we entered the harbour from the sea.

I obeyed and joined him, and after me came Philo.

By the last rays of that fleeting light we descended a rough stairway cut on the farther side of the Trembling Stone and of a sudden found ourselves in shelter. Light sprang up and I saw that it was held in the hand of a dwarf, a curious, solemn dwarf. Whence this creature came and who he was I do not know, but I think that he must have been a spirit, some gnome from the Underworld appointed by the Powers which ruled in that dark place to attend to the wants of the holy Noot, their Master and mine.

This I noted at least, and so did Philo, that we could never see this creature's face. Even when he moved about us, always it seemed to be hidden either by shadows or something that hung in front of it like a veil. Yet man, or gnome, or ghost, he was a good servant, since in that hermit's cave, or rather caves, for there were several of them, joined one to the other, all things were made ready. Thus a fire burned, food was prepared upon a table, and in the inner caves beds were spread, each in a little separate chamber.

The outer cave also was furnished in a fashion and I noted that in a niche stood the small statue of Isis which I remembered well, since wherever Noot my Master went in the past years when we journeyed together, that statue went with him and now still it was his companion. Indeed the tale was that it could speak and gave him counsel in all hours of doubt and trouble, and that from this enchanted thing he gathered his great wisdom. Whether or no this tale were true, I do not know, since I never heard it utter words, nor would Noot tell me when I asked him. Yet it is true that it was his custom to pray to it; also that it was very ancient and valued by him more than all the gold and jewels on the earth. Now it stood here as it had done in my Father's house at Ozal, as it had done at Philæ in his chamber, at Memphis, on the ship *Hapi* and elsewhere when we journeyed together throughout the world, and it was strange to me to behold its familiar face again in this dreadful habitation.

"Eat," said Noot, "then sleep, for you are weary."

Philo and I did as he commanded. We ate, we laid ourselves down upon the beds in the inner caves, and slept. The last thing that my eyes saw before slumber closed them was Noot my Master, now become more of a spirit than a man, kneeling in solemn prayer before the hallowed effigy of Isis.

I know not for how long we slept, but it must have been many hours, for when we woke it was to see that dwarf whose face was always hidden, setting another meal upon the table in the outer cave. There, too, by the lamplight, I perceived Noot still praying to the statue of Isis as though he had never risen from his knees, which perchance he had not done who no longer was as are other men. It was a strange sight in that dread place and one that affrighted Philo, as he told me, and left me not unmoved, who felt that here we stood upon the edge of mortal things.

I went to him, and seeing me come, he rose from his knees to greet me, asking me whether I had rested well.

"Neither well nor ill," I answered. "I slept, yet my sleep was full of dreams, very strange dreams that boded I know not what. They told me both of the past and of the future, and the burden of them was that I seemed to see myself living alone from generation to generation in caves as you do to-day."

"May the gods defend you from such a fate, Daughter," he answered as though the thought disturbed him.

"They have not defended you, Father. Oh! how can you bear to dwell in the darkness of this dreadful place round which the winds howl eternally, companioned only by your thoughts and a dwarf who never speaks? How did you find it, how came you here, and what put into your mind the thought of choosing this burrow for a hermitage? Tell me truly, who as yet, I think, have hidden half the truth even from me, for I am devoured with wonder and would understand."

"Hearken, Ayesha. When first we met in Arabia I was already very old, was I not, I who now long have passed the tale of man's allotted days? Before that time for many years I had been a head-priest and prophet of Isis in Egypt, also the chief Magician of that land. Yet I was not born an Egyptian nor did my eyes so much as look upon the Nile until I had counted over sixty summers."

"Where then were you born, Father?"

"Here in Kôr. I am the last descendant of the king-priests who ruled in Kôr before the great apostasy and the falling of the Sword of God. To the holy men who were my fathers had descended their knowledge of that secret of secrets whereof I have spoken to you, and ever it was their custom when age took a hold of them to withdraw into this living sepulchre and there as guardians of the Fire, to await the end. Also under many oaths each of them passed on to his descendants the knowledge of the secret.

"Thus, Daughter, it came into my keeping, for my grandsire told my father, and my father whispered it to me. Then, while my grandsire still lived, the goddess for her own ends of which now I think I see the purpose, called me from this desolate land away to Egypt, there to serve her as I have done. Again she called me to Arabia that there you might be given into my keeping, as you were for certain years. A third time she called me back to Kôr, whither I came with Philo. Here I found my grandsire dead and his son, my father, dead after him, leaving the hermitage of the Watcher of the Fire untenanted. Therefore setting Philo to command the savage tribes who dwell around the ruins of haunted Kôr, hither I came, as for generations my forbears have done, to fill the office that they filled, and—to die."

"Forgetting me upon whose head you left a heavy burden, my Father in Isis," I said bitterly.

"Nay, Ayesha, I forgot you not, who knew well that at the appointed time we should meet once more, as met we have. Always in my prayers I have watched over you and many of your troubles and dangers have been made known to me in dreams. It was in a dream that I heard you calling for guidance, and sent the answer that was commanded. Aye, and before that already I had despatched Philo to Egypt to bring you to me, as also I was commanded. And now you stand here before me in my hermitage and I tell you all these things because last night I learned, while I prayed and you were lost in sleep, that we shall speak no more together. My hour is at hand and since I have to child of my body, to you, my child in the Spirit, I pass on the great secret as to you already I have passed on my high office and wisdom. When the breath has left me, Ayesha, then to you will descend the guardianship of the Fire, and here, doubtless, when age has overtaken you, you also will end your days."

"Is it so?" I asked, dismayed, staring around me at the rocky walls and listening to the tempest that raged eternally without.

"Aye, Ayesha, it is so, since that is the high duty laid upon your soul, whereby it shall find wings to fly to Heaven. Know that no Guardian of the Fire enters into the Fire. He watches it—no more—and if it is threatened he seals it for ever from the sight of man. Listen, I will tell you how," and leaning forward he whispered certain words into my ear and showed me certain hidden things.

I heard, I saw, I bowed my head. Then I asked,

"And if the Guardian of the Fire entered into the Fire, what then, Watcher of the Fire?"

"Daughter, I know not," he answered, horror-struck. "But then I think the Fire would become *his* guardian, a terrible guardian that at the last would also be the destroyer of its false servant. More I cannot tell, because though some have breathed its essence, none of them has dared this deed."

"Two nights ago you told me, O Noot, that this fire gives youth and beauty and uncounted days to those who bathe therein. If none has ever entered it, how know you this?"

"Because it is so, Ayesha. Moreover, I did not say that none had ever entered it. Perchance there are beings now known to the world as gods or dæmons, who, by accident rather than design, have tasted of this cup. Perchance that shape you saw standing on the Ethiopian's head, in some bygone age stood for an instant in its path. At least I repeat that it is so. Believe or disbelieve

as you will, but ask me no more, and above all do not
venture to solve the mystery in your mortal flesh."

"At least, Prophet, let me look upon that which I
must guard," I said.

"Aye, you shall look," he answered. "It is for that
reason that I have brought you here, Priestess and
Daughter of Wisdom, for having looked, I do not think
that you will desire to bathe in that red flame. Eat now
and make ready."

CHAPTER XX

The Coming of Kallikrates

AWHILE later we left the cave, Noot, Philo, and I, each
of us bearing a lighted lamp. Clad in a dark cloak Noot
led the way, his lamp in one hand and in the other a
long staff such as herdsmen use upon the mountain side.
Strange enough he seemed thus arrayed, with his thin,
transparent face, his eyes grown large and luminous
from staring at the darkness, and his long white beard
showing like snow against the black texture of the
cloak; more of a spirit than a man indeed, or like
Charon leading shadows of the dead to that boat in
which all—aye, even I, Ayesha—must embark at last.
Never shall I forget his aspect as he searched for and
found the stair that led to the rock-strewn slope which
stretched downward for a furlong or more to the narrow
passage at its end, through which presently we travelled
into the infernal halls beyond.

Great were those halls or caverns; so great that we
light-bearers were but as ants creeping through their
vastness, so great that we could see neither their walls
nor roof.

We passed through two of them, our footfalls echoing
in their fearful silence, and came to a passage.

"Bide here," said Noot to Philo, "and await us, since it is not lawful for you to look upon that which lies beyond. If perchance we should not return within three hours so nearly as you can measure them, which may happen since we go to where there is danger for mankind, win your way back to the world and say that the gods have taken Noot the Prophet and Ayesha the High-Priestess to be of their company."

So Philo, out of whose eyes all the Grecian joyousness had fled, sat himself down upon a rock to wait, as I could see unwillingly enough, for he loved this adventure little and was troubled for the safety of me whom he loved much.

"Fear not," I whispered to him, "the hour is still far in which Ayesha must fall a ripe fruit from the Tree of Life."

"I pray so, Child of Isis," he answered, "since surely we have entered into Hades where I would not be left without so much as a fellow shade to comfort me. Yet beware! for I know not whither that old ghost is leading you," and he glanced at the tall shape of Noot striding into the tunnel in which this cave ended, the lamp held above his head.

I followed after him, also holding my lamp aloft, though presently it became needless since now the darkness of that hole grew alive with rosy light. On like a swift shadow glided Noot, and I followed him into the heart of the light, into a place, too, where thunder was imprisoned, like winds in the bag of Aeolus, aye, a place filled with glories and with roarings, though whence these came I could not guess.

We entered yet another cavern, not so very large in size and carpeted with fine white sand.

It was empty save for one thing. On the sand lay a withered shape, a hideous little shape that once had been man or woman. Whose it was and how it came there I never learned, since in the marvel of all that followed and afterward I forgot to ask it of Noot, if indeed he could have told me. Perchance some seeker of the Fire who lived a thousand or ten thousand years before had perished of terror at the sight of it, or perchance for his or her impiety that seeker had been sacrificed by gods or men. Yet even then I thought it dreadful and ominous that the first sight my eyes beheld in this terrible place should be this shrivelled, long-haired lump of death lying there in eternal solitude, while in front of and around it played the fierce essences of Life eternal.

This cavern was filled with a light like to that of some tempestuous Libyan dawn. Also it was filled with a muttering, thunderous sound, such sound as is caused by the iron wheels of a thousand chariots rushing to battle adown a rocky way. The light multiplied and was stabbed through as though by many coloured levins flashing hither and thither; the thunders gathered to an awful roar; those unearthly chariots were rolling down upon us.

"To your knees," cried Noot in my ear. "The Fire comes, the god is passing by!"

I knelt; my hand rested by chance upon that little shrivelled form, and lo! at my touch it crumbled into dust. It had been, it was not; the grinning twisted face was gone; nothing of it remained save a lock or two of curling hair—surely it must have been a woman's hair. Then the marvel happened. Before me appeared a turning column of glorious, many-coloured brightness, that roared and bellowed like a million maddened bulls. To my eyes it seemed to take the shape of a mighty man, and in its glowing crest I saw green eyes of emerald like to those of tigers, which eyes fixed themselves upon me. Arms it had also, blood-red, splendid arms that stretched themselves toward me as though to clasp me to that burning breast. It was terrible and yet it was most beauteous. Never until I saw it had I known beauty, no not even in the dawn or in the sunset, or in the sight of the wild shock of battle.

This mighty god of Life seemed to call to the life within me, like a king to his subject, like a master to his slave; I longed to lose myself in that embrace of fire. Half I rose from my knees. Noot caught me by the arm.

"Enter not!" he cried sternly, and again I sank down and hid my face upon the sand.

How long I lay there I do not know, for exaltation seized me and made my senses drunk, so that I could take no count of time. It may have been for a minute or an hour; I say I do not know. When I looked up again, the Fire had gone by, the god was hidden in his secret sanctuary, though still the cavern glowed with rosy light.

Noot drew me from that place. Without we found Philo pale-lipped and trembling, and together, slowly and with labour, we climbed our upward course back to the hermitage beneath the swaying stone. Here we rested in silence until at last Noot drew me aside and spoke.

"Ayesha," he said, "you have seen as it was decreed that you must see. In that burning presence temptation took hold of you, so sharp a hold that had I not been there, perchance you would have yielded, forgetting my warnings and my prayers. Now I beseech you, guard the Fire in the days to come, but look on it no more for ever, since although in other matters you are so strong, in this I feel you frail. While I live indeed never again shall you behold it with your eyes, since first I will call upon the goddess to cut your thread of life and take you to herself."

I bowed my head but made no answer, nor did he ask for any.

What happened then? Oh! I remember that we ate of food that was made ready doubtless by the gnome-like dwarf whom I saw no more. After this Noot looked from the door of his hermitage and called to us to come swiftly, since the moment of sunset that brought with it the falling ray was at hand and the bridge must be crossed and the narrowest of the stone spur travelled ere it departed. Holding lighted lanterns in our hands, he led us to the crest of the Trembling Stone whereon the timbers of the bridge creaked and swayed. Here he clasped me in his arms, blessing me and bidding me farewell, and though he said it not, I was certain that in his mind, as at the moment I did in mine, he believed that our spirits parted for ever upon this earth; yes, believed it so surely that tears coursed down his pale cheeks.

Then suddenly the sword-like ray of fire stabbed the darkness and by it I and Philo crossed the bridge and while it endured clambered swiftly along the spur of which, I know not why, all fear had left me.

As that ray began to fade I turned my head to look my last on Noot. There in the heart of it he stood, clothed as it were with fire, as our faith tells are the messengers of Isis, Queen of Heaven. Yes, there he stood with clasped hands and uplifted eyes like to one lost in prayer. Then the ray went out like a blown lamp and the darkness fell and swallowed him.

We gained the plain in safety and through the night were borne back to Kôr. The litter swayed; the slaves whose shoulders bent beneath the pole sang their low, weird chant inviting to sleep, but its messengers would not touch my eyelids with their rod of slumber. I could not sleep whose soul burned with a fierce wakefulness. Oh! what was this wonder that I had seen? The very fount of Life that, hidden from mankind, burns in the womb of the world! But if it were this, why did Noot speak of it as though it were a fount of Death? Why did he forbid me to taste its cup? Perhaps because not Life but Death inhabited that flame, as the little withered thing which had crumbled at my touch, that once had been man or woman—woman, as I think—hinted to the mind.

I knew not, but what I did know was that henceforth I was plighted to this god of Fire and that in some day to come I must feel his burning marriage kiss upon my brow.

When we came to Kôr at the sunrise I beckoned Philo to me and made to him the sign of silence, which being initiated, he knew well, so that neither then nor at any other time should any word concerning these mysteries pass his lips. Nor indeed could it do so as he had not looked upon the greatest of them and only from afar had listened to the thunder of the wheeling flame.

Then with a new energy, as though inspired by the

breath of that fiery god, I got me to my common daily task of rebuilding a perished faith and people. Let that business be. Why should I speak of it, since Destiny decreed that I must shape my work of water or of drifting sand, not of rock or fired clay. Oh! Fate, why didst thou fool me thus? Oh, Love the Destroyer, why didst thou make of me thy tool, and with me thus bring Isis and her worship to the dust?

How long afterward was it that Kallikrates came? But a little while, I think, though to one who has lived over two thousand years Time loses its measure and significance.

I had sent Philo to the coast, purposing to prepare for the opening up of trade and converse with the outer world. For in this rich place, when its wild people were brought beneath my yoke, who already looked upon me as one half divine, as the spirit of their ancient goddess indeed, sent back to them from Heaven, I knew that we could produce much that the teeming tribes of Libya would seek and buy. One night he returned and was at once admitted to my presence. He told me of all that he had done, or failed to do, and I praised him, then made the signal of dismissal. He hesitated a while, then said,

"Child of Isis, be pleased to learn that I have not returned alone."

"That I know already, Philo, since there were many in your company."

"Be it understood, Child of Isis, that I have brought back with me some with whom I did not set forth."

"Doubtless envoys from the peoples of the coast," I answered indifferently.

"Nay," he replied, "travellers who have wandered long among those peoples and whom I found shipwrecked and in a desperate state. Travellers from Egypt."

"From Egypt! How many, Philo?"

"Nine in all, Prophetess, though the most of them are servants."

"Good, Philo. It will please me who must dwell so much alone to talk with strangers from Egypt. They may have news of what passes on the Nile. Give them hospitality such as we can command, and all they need, and to-morrow, after the morning ceremonies, bring them to me. To-night it is too late and doubtless they are weary."

Again he hesiated, then bowed, and went, leaving me wondering, for there was that in his manner which I thought strange. Still, having spoken my commands, I would not alter them. Yet as I laid me down to sleep terror took hold of me; yes, a terror of I knew not what. I felt that evil overshadowed me with its black wings; that I was about to look upon something or someone I did not desire to see; that a doom unknown had meshed me so that I lay helpless like a gladiator over whom the net-thrower has cast his web and who lies struggling vainly, the trident at his throat. Thus often does advancing peril cast its cold shadow upon our mortal hearts which shiver at the touch of that they feel but cannot discern.

I thought that perchance I was about to die, that already Death gripped me with his clasp of ice; that in the dark recesses of the chamber where I lay already some murderer fingered the dagger which should pierce my breast, as well might happen in this wild land among man-eating savages upon whose necks I had set my heel. Again I thought that the spirits of the ancient dead whose place I occupied, were hunting me, demanding that I should give them back their own, the rule I had usurped.

Next I remembered Tenes transfixed by the sword of vengeance and knowing now that mine was the hand that drove it, and Ochus Artaxerxes when the poison began to burn his vitals as presently the fire would burn his company, guessing at the last that I, the outraged priestess, had brewed the cup and lit the fire. Yea, all these memories gathered round me, rising like black clouds upon my sky of life and threatening its eclipse, I who was terrified of I knew not what.

Lastly there came into my mind this tale of Philo's of shipwrecked strangers whom he had rescued and led hither to be comforted. Who were these strangers, I wondered? Assassins perchance, hid under a disguise of want and desolation, men who sought to kill me and free my spirit with their dagger-points, that it might no longer watch them here on earth. Yet, and this was marvellous, showing how blind are the eyes of our mortal flesh, never did the thought come to me that those strangers might be Kallikrates the Greek and Amenartas, aforetime Royal Princess of Egypt, she whom her desire and hate had made my foe.

I slept at last, though feverishly, only to wake when the high sun was flooding the temple court with its fierce summer rays. I rose, and since the day was one of ceremony and festival, was arrayed by my women in the queenly garments of the high priestess of Isis and hung about with the sacred jewels and emblems of my rank.

Thus splendidly attired, I was led to my seat of state that I had caused to be placed in the inmost pillared court before a wondrous veiled statue of Truth standing on the world, which some god-gifted artist of old Kôr had fashioned in the forgotten days. Here we celebrated our service with pomp and ritual, as once we were wont to do in Egypt, though alas! the heirophants and the singers were few in number. So was the outer congregation of half-converted worshippers creeping back from the blackness of their barbarous rites to the holy fellowship of the goddess.

The office was ended, the ringing of the *sistrum* had ceased, the blessing was given and with it the absolution of offences.

The worshippers had dispersed, save here and there one who remained to pray. I too was about to depart when Philo came, saying, humbly and hastily like one who desires to be done with an unwelcome task, that those wanderers of whom he had spoken waited upon my pleasure.

"Admit them," I answered, wondering within myself upon whom I was about to look. Malefactors perchance, I thought, who had fled from justice into far lands, or merchants driven southward by the gales, or humble seamen escaped from some sunk ship.

They came, a little knot of them, winding in and out

between the great columns of the ruined temple, advancing through the shadows. Idly I noted, as they passed an open space where fell a stronger light, that the two who walked first had a noble air, different from that of those who followed after them. Then once more the shadows veiled them, whence presently they emerged before me, seated beneath the statue, and stood there, the sun's rays pouring down upon them.

I glanced at them and saw that they were man and woman, perfect man and very beauteous woman. Then I lifted my head and looked them fully in the face, only to sink back terrified, amazed, overwhelmed! Did I dream! Had some mocking spirit tricked my eyes, or were these that stood before me Kallikrates, the Grecian warrior-priest, and Amenartas, the Royal Princess of Egypt?

Lifting my hand to hide my face, I studied them beneath its shade. Oh! who could be mistaken? There before me, splendid in beauty as of old, stood the god-like Kallikrates and at his side, dark, magnificent and as yet untouched by time, or perchance protected from its ravages by arts she learned from her sire, Nectanebes the sorcerer, was the imperial Amenartas. For a moment I kept silence, gathering up my strength, ordering my spirit. Then still holding my hand before my face, I spoke coldly as though without concern, saying,

"Whence come you, noble strangers? What are your names and why do you seek the hospitality of the Queen of this ruined land of Kôr?"

Bold as ever, it was Amenartas who answered me, not Kallikrates, who stood staring about him as men do when they are uneasy in their minds or wearied with ceremonies.

"We are wanderers, Priestess, in station neither mean nor great; traders, to tell the truth, from the far north, who having suffered shipwreck and many other things at length were rescued of this servant of yours who led us here," and she pointed to Philo standing near by with a stupid smile upon his face.

"By race we are Phœnicians called——" and she gave some name that I forget. "As to the rest, being in

extremity, for those over whom we ruled rebelled
against us and cast us out, we ask shelter from you until
Fortune smiles upon us again, who of late has dealt us
naught but frowns."

"It is granted, Lady. But tell me, what are you to
each other? Brother and sister, perchance?"

"Aye, Priestess, brother and sister, as you have
rightly guessed, seeing that our names are one name."

"That is strange, Lady; indeed I think that you throw
mud upon your father or your mother, or both, since
how could these have begotten one dark, a high-born
daughter of the Nile, and another fair as Apollo and
having Grecian Apollo's face and mien? Again, how
comes it that the sister of a Phœnician merchant binds
up her locks with the circlet of Egyptian royalty?" And I
pointed to the uræus-twisted band of gold upon her
brow.

"Blood plays strange tricks, Priestess, searching out
now the likeness of one ancestor, and now of another,
so that ofttimes one child is born dark and the other
fair. As for the ornament, I bought it in trade from an
Arab merchant, not knowing whence it came or its significance," she began to answer unabashed, when of a
sudden Kallikrates checked her, muttering,

"Have done!" Then addressing me, he said,

"O Queen and Priestess, take no heed of this lady's
words, since of late, because of our misfortunes, we
have been forced to tell many strange tales according to
the conditions of the hour. We are not Phœnicians born
of one House; we are by blood Greek and Egyptian,
and by relation not brother and sister, but man and
wife."

Now when I heard these words my heart stood still
who hoped that Isis and their oaths might have held this
pair apart. Yet I answered calmly,

"Is it so, Wanderer? Tell me then, of what faith are
you twain and by whom were you wed? Did some minister of Zeus join your hands, or did you stand together
before Hathor's altars?"

Then while he searched for some answer that he
could not find, I went on, laughing a little,

"Perchance, O noble pair, you were not wed at all. Perchance you are not husband and wife but only lover and lover mated after Nature's fashion!"

He hung his head, confused, and even the bold eyes of Amenartas were troubled.

Now I could bear no more.

"O Grecian Kallikrates," I said, "aforetime captain of Pharaoh's guard, aforetime priest of Isis, and O Amenartas, daughter of Nectanebes, by birth Royal Princess of Egypt, why do you waste words, hoping to fool one who cannot be deceived? Doubtless you have bribed yonder Philo to hide the truth, as once you bribed him to hide a certain lady upon his ship and to set the two of you ashore upon a certain island."

"If so, he has betrayed us," stammered Kallikrates, the red blood rising to his brow.

"Nay, he has not betrayed you, being one who ever keeps faith with those who pay him well. Is it not so, Philo my servant?"

I waited for an answer, but none came, for Philo had gone. Then I continued,

"Nay, Philo did not betray you, nor was it needed. Royal Amenartas, whence had you that scarab ring upon your hand?"

"It was my lord's gift to me," she answered.

"Then tell me, Kallikrates, whence had you the ring, also if there be graven on its bezel in the Egyptian writing, signs that mean 'Royal Son of the Sun'?"

"Those signs are cut upon the ring, O Queen, which in bygone years was given to me as a talisman by a certain divine priestess whom I saved in battle, that its virtues might recover me of wounds which I received in the battle. This, as I was told afterward, it had the power to do because that ring was blessed, having been fashioned like to one which Isis the Mother set as her love gift upon the hand of dead Osiris ere she breathed his soul into him again. Or perchance it was the very same that Osiris left upon the earth when he passed to Heaven; I know not."

Thus he spoke, stumbling at the words like an ill-bred mule upon a stony path till, wearying of the tale, I broke in,

"Therefore, O Kallikrates, you in your turn gave the enchanted ancient amulet to a woman you desired, or who desired you, hoping that its virtues might consecrate your unhallowed union. O priest forsworn, how did you dare this sacrilege—to set upon your lover's hand the ring, the very ring of Isis that once great Khaemuas wore, given to you by the Prophetess of Isis to lift you from the gates of death."

Then bending forward so that the shadow of the statue behind no longer hid me, I uncovered my face and looked him in the eyes.

"I thought it!" he said, "though who could have dreamed that here in this ruin——? It is the Oracle and the Prophetess. It is the Child of Isis, the Daughter of Wisdom herself whose voice I knew again through all her feigning," and he fell to the ground so that his brow was pressed upon its stones, muttering,

"Slay me, Queen, and have done, but spare this lady and send her back to her own land, since the sin is mine, not hers, who was no priestess."

Now Amenartas stared at me with her bold eyes, then cried with a hard laugh,

"Be not so sure, my Lord, for this is scarcely possible. Well do I remember looking upon her who was called *Isis-come-to-Earth* in the bygone days, especially at a certain feast that Pharaoh gave when she unveiled to show herself to Tenes, King of Sidon, who afterward took her as his slave. But that seeress was a very fair woman, although perchance even then somewhat faded, or so I who but a little while before had bade farewell to childhood, judged of her. Therefore this ruler of ruins can scarcely be the same, seeing that none could name her fair. Look, she is old and withered, her neck has fallen in, her shape is flattened.

"The seeress I remember had a lovely mouth of coral, but this lady's lips are thin and pale; also she had large and beauteous eyes, but those of this lady are small and almost colourless. Moreover, they are ringed beneath with lines of black, such as are common to

aged virgin priestesses who have never known the love
of man, though of it, perchance, their holy souls still
dream even in the midst of their customary, bead-
checked prayers, while, like those of slaves, their knees
harden upon the stones.

"Nay, my Lord, although time works strange changes
in those who have passed the meridian of their days,
this priestess who hides her gray hairs beneath the vulture cap of her persuasion can scarcely be the same as
that glowing pythoness upon whom once we looked in
Pharaoh's halls and who, as I recall, then looked much
on you."

Now I listened to this vulgar venom, the common
outpouring of a small-natured, jealous heart, and
smiled. Yet it is true, for in these lines I write nothing
which is not the truth, that some of those poisoned
shafts went home. I knew well that all the beauty that
once I had was no longer mine; that the passing of the
years, that care and abstinence and the turning of my
heart from things mortal to those divine, added to the
weight of rule and wisdom and avengement which Destiny had laid upon my brow, had robbed me of my
bloom and that imperial loveliness which once en-
thralled the world. Also it was true that Amenartas was
still a child when I was a woman grown and therefore
had Nature's vantage of me, which indeed must increase
from moon to moon.

Still I smiled, and as I smiled a great thought smote
me, sowing a seed of daring in the kind soil of my
breast where thenceforth it was doomed to grow, to
blossom, and in an unborn hour of fulfilment to bear its
fearful fruit. Oh! if I have sinned against high Heaven
and the commands of its minister, my guide, the holy
Noot, let the recording gods remember that it was the
whip of this woman's bitter tongue which drove me to
the deed.

Now very gently I spoke, saying,

"Rise, Kallikrates, such words as you have heard
spoken of one who once was set above you in her office
can scarcely be pleasing to your ears, nor will I answer
them. I know well that in them there is something of the

truth and I am proud that it has been granted to me to make sacrifice to the Queen of Heaven whom I adore of such small gifts of the flesh and comeliness as once were mine. It is but another offering which I heap upon her altar, one of many.

"Yet, Kallikrates, though as I think you can no longer bow the knee before that Majesty as once you did, I pray you, if you can, to hold this lady's lips from pouring scorn upon her, as she does upon me, her priestess. I pray you to bring it to her memory that once, clad in her veil of Isis, she also worshipped at that shrine, aye, that in a time of peril, often there, she and you and I have sent up our pure petitions, though not in the 'customary bead-checked prayers' of which she speaks. Yes, bring it to her memory that though the temple of Memphis has been given to the flames, Mother Isis hears and watches not in Egypt, but in Heaven, and that though she be slow to wrath, yet she still can smite. Now, Kallikrates, go rest you, taking your love with you, and afterward we will talk alone since, although I can forgive, I am not minded to be stoned with such words as angry women of the people throw at their rivals in the marketplace."

CHAPTER XXI

~

The Truth and the Temptations

NOT that day but on the morrow Kallikrates asked audience of me. Learning that he was alone, I received him in my private chamber and bade him be seated. He obeyed, and for awhile I watched him, the light from the window-place falling upon his golden head and upon his shining armour, battered with storm and war. For now he was clad in his soldier's garb, perchance the very same that years ago he had worn on board the *Hapi*, and thus attired looked like a king of men.

"The lady Amenartas is somewhat sick after all our journeyings," he said, "I think that the disorder which is common on the coast lands has fallen upon her, since her face is flushed and her hands are hot. Therefore she cannot wait upon you, Prophetess. Yet she bids me thank you for your hospitality, and say that she asks your pardon for any bitter words she may have spoken yesterday, since these sprang, not from her heart, but from a fever burning in her blood."

"It is granted. I know this sickness though myself I have been protected from it, and will send her medicine and with it a skilled woman to wait upon her. Bid her not to fear; it is seldom dangerous. Now, my guest Kallikrates, if it pleases you, let me hear your story; you must have much to tell since we parted in the sanctuary at Memphis. Then, you will remember, your purpose was to accompany the holy Noot upon his mission, because you thought it best for reasons of your own to depart from Memphis for awhile. Yet I think it was in your mind to go alone, not accompanied by that royal lady who is your companion."

"This is true, Prophetess," he answered heavily, "nor did I know that the lady of whom you speak was aboard the *Hapi* until, to escape capture at the hands of the Persians, we had fled from the Nile out toward the open sea."

"I understand, Kallikrates, nor can it be denied that Fate dealt hardly, or perchance I should say kindly, with you when it caused the lady Amenartas to embark in error upon the ship *Hapi*, which sailed down Nile, instead of that of her father, Nectanebes, which set its course for Thebes and Ethiopia."

"Mock me not, Child of Wisdom. As the lady Amenartas would tell you to your face, she knew well enough upon what ship she sailed, though I knew nothing who believed that I had said farewell to her for ever. Aye, abandoning her hope of royalty and all else, and taking every risk, she embarked upon the *Hapi*, setting some other woman tricked out to her likeness to fill her place awhile among the company of Nectanebes."

"That at least was bold, and I love courage, Kallikrates. Yet—what was her purpose?"

"Is that a question that you should ask me, Lady, who know well that great-hearted women will dare much for love?"

"Whether I should ask or not, at least I have the answer to my question, Kallikrates. Of a truth, you should love and honour one who for your sake abandoned all to win what she thought more than all, even at the cost of her own shame and the ruin of your soul."

"I do love and honour her," he answered hoarsely. "When she was still a child I loved her and because of that love I slew my brother, believing that on reaching womanhood she had come to favour him, which, it seems, she did only to draw me closer to her."

"It would appear, Kallikrates, that this lady brings no good fortune to your race, since first she works the death of one of you, making a murderer of his own brother, and then of that brother fashions an apostate to his faith, yea, a traitor accursed of God and man."

"It is so," he said humbly. "Yet she loves me much, so much that whether I will it or not, I must love her, since if the woman loves enough what can the man do but follow on the path she leads? Tell me, Prophetess, you who are wise, had you been a man and sat in my place there upon the ship *Hapi*, which is a narrow prison, what would you have done, being a man I say— as I am?"

"Perhaps just what you did, Kallikrates, and therefore have become accursed, as you are, Kallikrates, seeing that the lady was sweet and loving, and that man must remain man however great the oaths he has sworn to goddesses who do not throw their arms about him or kiss him on the lips."

"Once I thought that a goddess did kiss me on the lips, Oracle of Isis, and the memory of that kiss is sweet and holy."

"Is it so?" I answered. "Well, since you are no more of our communion, I may tell you now that in the shrine at Philæ *I* played the part of the goddess and gave that ceremonial kiss."

Now he stared at me, reddening, then muttered,

"Always I guessed it who could not quite believe that a goddess would kiss so sweetly," and again he started like one who would ask a question that his lips do not dare to frame.

I remained silent, watching him, till presently he broke out,

"You tell me that I am accursed, Priestess. Tell me also why Isis is so wrath with me?"

"Did you not swear yourself to her alone and break your oath, Kallikrates? Do you not know that if women can be jealous, goddesses who are set far above them can be more greatly so of those who are bound to them in the mystic marriage? Have you not heard that to turn from them to a daughter of man is to offer them the most terrible of insults?"

"Isis herself was wed to Osiris, Prophetess, and I have heard of priests and priestesses who served her who were also wed."

"Perchance, Kallikrates, after absolution given by one upon whom authority is conferred to strain vows for some high end. But who gave you authority to marry, you, who indeed are not married but only a woman's lover? Did you mayhap seek it from the holy Noot upon the ship *Hapi?*"

"Nay," he answered, "that thought never came to me. Or if it came I believed that he would but heap curses upon me, or mayhap call down the vengeance of Isis upon another. You have heard, Prophetess, of what fate sometimes awaits those who tempt the feet of priests or priestesses from the strait path of their vows."

"Aye, Kallikrates, they die by fire, or they starve, or they perish shut up in some narrow, airless hole; each worship works its own vengeance for that unmeasured crime. Yet you were foolish not to make your prayer of Noot, by whom alone it could be granted, since who knows what he would have answered."

"Is it too late?" he asked eagerly. "For every sin there is forgiveness, why not for mine? Only who could grant it; since now I know not where to look for Noot, if indeed he lives."

"For every sin there is forgiveness, Kallikrates, but only at a price. First the sin itself must be laid upon the altar as a sacrifice. For dead sins there may be forgiveness; for those that live and are continued there is none, but only stripe added to stripe and remorse piled upon remorse. As for Noot it chances that he does live and not so far away. Would you lay your case before him and hear his judgment?"

"I do not know," he answered slowly. "Hearken, Child of Wisdom. I am in a strange strait. I love this lady with my body and am bound to her, but it is not so with my spirit. Our souls, I think, are far apart. Oh! bear me witness that my heart is set on higher things; it would sail into far seas unvisited of man, but always there is this anchor of the flesh chaining it to its native shore. Amenartas does not think thus, she loves to lie bound in life's pleasant harbour, or to wander to its green banks, wafted thither by the fitful breath of common things, there to deck her brow with the wreaths of passion.

" 'Let Heaven be!' she says, 'here is the happy earth beneath our feet, and round us murmur the waters of delight and I am very beautiful and I love you well. If there be gods and they are vengeful, at least their hour is not yet. This moment is ours to enjoy and to our lips it holds a glorious cup. If all the wine be drunk and the cup is shattered, at least there will remain with us their memories. What are these gods whom you seek so madly? What do they give to man save many curses— deaths and separations, sicknesses and sorrows, adding to these promises of woe to follow when they have worked their worst on earth? Are there any gods save those that man fashions from his own terrors? man who will not be content with Nature's food, but needs must sour it with an alien poison, and even when the sun shines round him, shivers in some cold shadow that superstition casts upon his heart.'

"Thus she reasons, and such ever were her arguments."

"Tell me, Kallikrates, has any child been born to you?"

"Aye, one, a very lovely child; he died of hardships that caused his mother's milk to fail."

"And when the royal Amenartas looked upon him dead, did she still reason in this fashion, saying that there are no gods and for man there is no hope beyond the grave?"

"Not altogether, since she cursed the gods, and who curse that in which they do not believe? Also I remember that she wept and prayed those gods to give him back to her while his little heart still beat, and like a moth new-crept from its chrysalis, he yet hung to the edge of the world, drying his soul's crinkled wings in the dawning lights of Heaven. But afterward she forgot and made sacrifice to her familiar Spirit, asking it to send her another child, which prayer she tells me is in the way of fulfilment."

"So Amenartas practices magic like her father Nectanebes?"

"Aye, Lady, and it would seem not without avail, though of this matter of dealing with dæmons I neither know nor want to know anything. I think it comes to her with her Egyptian blood, also that the Pharaoh taught her these arts in her childhood, and what is learnt then is never quite forgotten. At least I know that when we have been in trouble or in danger during our long wanderings, with secret rites upon which I do not pry, she calls upon some Familiar and that thereafter, in this way or in that, our pathway has been straightened. Indeed she did this just before Philo found us starving."

"As the path of your babe was straightened from this world to the next, Kallikrates; as the devious path of Pharaoh Nectanebes was straightened to a road which led from the throne of Egypt—but pray the lady Amenartas to ask of her dæmon whither it led, since here my wisdom fails me and I am not sure. Well, we have spoken long and so stands the case, one that might puzzle Thoth himself. Is it your pleasure, Kallikrates, to visit the divine Noot and take his counsel upon all these matters? I think that he alone upon the earth can give you guidance in them. Yet do as you will."

Kallikrates thought a while brooding, then he answered,

"Yes, it is my pleasure. When Amenartas is recovered of her sickness, we will go."

"The holy Noot is very ancient and the royal Amenartas may be sick for a long while. Therefore might it be wise to go at once, Kallikrates."

"Nay, Prophetess, I cannot. Amenartas has strange fancies and will not be left alone; she thinks that she may be poisoned; indeed that already she has tasted poison."

"Then let her make richer sacrifices to her dæmon and pray him to protect her. Certainly they will not be without avail since I can swear that here in Kôr no poison shall pass her lips, nor any harm come to her—save perchance from those gods whom she denies. Farewell, Kallikrates."

He bowed to me humbly and turned to go, then after a step or two came back and said,

"The gods! The gods! who for you and me in their sum are one god, Isis, Queen of Heaven. Tell me now, I pray you that are named Wisdom's Daughter, who and what is Isis?"

I thought a while since the question was a great one, a problem that as yet I had never tried to solve in words. Then I answered,

"By my soul I do not know. East and west and north and south, men in their millions worship this god or that. Yet is there one among them who save in dreams or ecstasies has ever seen his god, or if he tries to fashion him out before his mortal eyes, can do more than carve some effigy of wood or stone?"

Then I pointed to the veiled statue of Truth behind me, saying,

"Lo! there is Isis, a beauteous thing with a hidden face ruling o'er the world. She is one of Divinity's thousand forms. Aye, she is its essence, frozen to the shape we know in this world's icy air, and having a countenance chiselled differently from age to age by the

changeful thought of man. She lives in every soul, yet in
no two souls is she the same. She is not, yet eternally
she is. Invisible, intangible; ever pursued and ever
fleeing; never seen and never handled, yet she answers
prayer and her throne is not in the high heavens but in
the heart of every creature that draws the breath of life.
One day we shall behold her and not know her. Yet she
will know us. Such is Isis: formless, yet in every form;
dead, yet living in all that breathes; a priest-bred phantasy, yet the one great truth."

"If Isis be thus, what of the world's other gods?"

"They all are Isis and Isis is them all. The thousand
gods men worship are but one god wearing many faces.
Or rather they are two gods, the god of good and the
god of evil; Horus and Typhon who war continually for
the souls of things created by that Divine, unseen, unknown yet eternally existent, who reigns beyond the
stars alone in fearful glory and from his nameless habitation looks down both on gods and men, the puppets of
his hands; on the rolling worlds that bear them, on the
seas of space between and on the infusing spirit whose
operation is the breath of life. So it was in the beginning, is now and shall be eternally. At least, Kallikrates,
thus I have been taught by the wisdom of Noot my
Master, and following his path, thus my searching soul
has learned. Again farewell."

He looked at me muttering,

"Child of Isis, oh! well-named Child of Isis, and
Wisdom's Daughter!" and there was awe in his eyes
and voice.

Now as ever he is afraid of me, I thought to myself,
and how can a man come to love that of which he is
afraid, since love and fear are opposites and there is no
bridge between them. Oh! why did I speak to him of
these high things which as yet his spirit can scarce weigh
or understand? Perhaps because I am so lonely and
having naught into which I can pour my mind, no vase
of gold and alabaster, my deep o'erflowing thought
must fill the first coarse cup of clay that chance offers
to my hand, like to the storing of priceless wine in some
tarry bottle which it will burst.

Surely I should learn a lesson from yonder Amenartas who knows well how to deal with such a one as he; one who still stands at thought's beginnings, looking dismayed at the steep upward path studded with sharp stones, wreathed in cruel thorns, strewn with quicksands and with pitfalls, and bordered by precipices from whose gulfs there is no return, that path which his feet long to tread yet dare not, lacking any guide.

She leads him by a different road, the road of mortal passion, bidding him to cease from staring at the stars; bidding him weave crowns of its heavy-scented flowers to set upon her brow and his. She prattles to him of daily doings, of the joy of yesterday and the promise of to-morrow, aye, even of the food he eats. And all the time she twists the spells her father taught her to strong ropes of charm, purposing by these to tie him to her everlastingly. Aye, like a gilded spider, that black-browed, bounteous-breasted witch meshes him in her magic web, binding him fast and yet more fast, till at length he lies there staring at her stirless as a mummy in its wrappings.

Thus I mused, clothing my musings finely yet knowing in my heart that what prompted them was the vilest of all causes and the most common, naught indeed but the jealousy of one woman of another. For now I knew the truth, it could no more be hidden, no longer could I blind my eyes, for it had come home to me while he told me his sad story. I loved this man; yes, and had always loved him since first I looked upon him far away at Philæ, or certainly since, veiled in the wrappings of the goddess, I had yielded to Nature's promptings and kissed him upon the lips.

Oh! I had beaten down that truth, I had buried it deep, but now it arose like a ghost from the grave and frightened me with its stern, immortal eyes. I loved this man and must always love him and no other, and he— he feared yet adored me, as some high spirit is adored at its appearing—but love me he did not who was set so far above him.

Yes, I was jealous, if the great can be truly jealous of that which is small, for though we were wide apart as continent from continent, yet we both were women desirous of one man. With my spirit I was not jealous, for that I knew must conquer in the end, being so strong, so armoured against all the shafts of mortal change. Yet with my flesh I was jealous. He told me Amenartas had borne a son to him; that she hoped to bear another son, and—I too yearned to be the mother of his son. For is it not true that by a fixed unchanging law, whereas the man loves the woman for herself, the woman loves the man most of all because he may become the father of her child, and thus by the marvel of creation, even in the dust preserve her from perpetual death?

So, so, let me think. I loved this man and would take him for myself and would lift him up and would make him my equal, if that could ever be, and would teach him glorious things, and would show him the secret light that burned within my heart, and would guide him onward by the rays of my own peculiar star. How could it be brought about? Yonder woman, wrapped round with the twice-dipped Tyrian purple of kings, which purple, be it admitted, she wore well although now she lacked a throne whereon to drape it, thought in her folly that I had poisoned or would poison her. Yes, she knew Ayesha so little that she believed that like a Persian eunuch she would stoop to call deadly venom to her aid and thereby rid her of a rival. Never! If I could not win by my own strength in a fair fight for favour, then let me fail, who deserved defeat. Were her life so utterly in my hands that I could destroy it with a wish, that wish would never form itself within my mind, and certainly never shape itself to deeds.

What then could be done? She was right. I began to grow old; Time's acid was gnawing at me so that my beauty was no more what it had been. Aye, I grew spare and old, while on her still shone the full glory of her womanhood. *If I would conquer I must cease from growing old!*

The Fire of Life! Ah! that Fire of Life which gave, it was said, the gift of undying days and of perfect youth and loveliness such as Aphrodite herself might envy. Who said so? Noot the Master who knew all things. Yet

Noot had never entered into that fire, therefore how did he know, unless it were by revelation? At least he had forbidden me to taste its cup, perhaps because he was sure that it would slay me whom he desired to be his successor and to establish here a great kingdom whereof the people should accept Isis as their god.

Still the story might be true, for otherwise why did Noot sit in that melancholy hermitage watching he pathway to the Fire? There had been other tales of the same sort told in the world. Thus the old Chaldean legend spoke of a Tree of Life that grew in a certain garden whence the parents of mankind were driven lest they should eat of it and become immortal, which legend was expounded to me more fully by the Jewish rabbis in Jerusalem, and afterward by Holly the learned man. Therefore it seemed that there was a Tree of Life, or a Fire of Life, jealously guarded of the gods lest the children of men should become their equals. And I, I knew where that Tree grew, or rather where that Fire burned. Yet Noot forbade it to me, and could I disobey Noot my Master, Noot the half divine? Well, Noot was very old and near his end, and when he died, I, by his own appointment, should be the guardian of the Fire, and may not a guardian taste of that he guards?

The gods decreed otherwise, he said. Mayhap, but what if in this matter where I had so much to gain, I chose to match myself against the gods? If the gods give knowledge, can they be wrath with those who use it? Yet if they are wrath—well, let them be wrath and set their worst against my best. Sometimes I grew weary of the gods and all the fantastical decrees which they—or their priests—heaped upon the heads of the sufferers of this earth. Were not life's curse and death's doom enough to satisfy their appetites, that they must load the toilful days between with so much of the lead of misery, denying this, denying that; strowing the path of men with spikes and crowning their heads with thorns?

If Noot's tale were true, what then? I should enter the Fire, I should emerge ever-glorious, beauteous beyond imagining, and ever young, having left death far behind

me. I should need but to wait a while until Amenartas
died, and when she was dead, or having grown weary of
dull life in an ancient place, had departed to seek some
other. Nay, for then in the first case Kallikrates also
would be dead or ancient, and in the second, certainly
she would take him with her.

Ah! now I had it; if I entered the Fire and came
forth unharmed, Kallikrates must enter it after me, for
then we should be fitly mated, even if we must wait
until a little pinch of the sand of time had run out from
between our fingers. Yet supposing that Amenartas
chose to enter it also, as being so fond of magic and so
determined to cling to that which she had won, perchance she might do, would my case be bettered? The
play would be set upon a larger stage, that is all. Well,
should I not be the Guardian of the Fire and would it
not be in my hand to determine who should taste or
who should be denied its glories? Let that matter decide
itself when the hour came, since the decision would be
such as I and not as Amenartas willed.

Here then was my plan. And yet—one thought more.
What if the Fire slew? If so, had I found life so sweet
that I should be afraid to die, as in any case within
some few years die I must? Let me take my chance of
death who was ready to fade away into a land where
Kallikrates and Amenartas and all earthly miseries and
all baulked desires and ambitions, and all hopes and
fears and sufferings must be forgot. Only would they be
forgot? Perchance there they might be remembered and
pierce the soul eternally with an even keener edge. Noot
believed that we were made of an immortal stuff, and so
at heart did I. It must be risked. What is life but a long
risk, and why should we fear to add to its tremendous
count? I at least did not fear.

So all was summed up and balanced. Yet from my
reckoning I left out the largest charge, that which Fate
makes against those who play at dice with the Unknown. The gods may smile at courage and pass a venture by, but who can tell how blind Fate will avenge the

forcing of his rule decreed and the rape of knowledge from his secret store?

This problem I forgot, I who was doomed to learn its answer.

CHAPTER XXII

❧

Beware!

THE days went by and it was not long before Amenartas recovered from her sickness, long at least before she would appear out of the lodging, the best at our command, which had been given to her. It was an ancient, ruined house near to the temple, that doubtless once had been a splendid place inhabited by forgotten nobles of old Kôr. There were gardens round it, or rather what had been gardens, for now these were much overgrown, and in their shelter Amenartas hid herself and wandered, never leaving them to visit me.

Yet Kallikrates came often, though being unshriven and thrust out of our community by his own act, he did not share in the worship of the goddess. Often I would see him as our procession wound in and out of the columns of the great unroofed temple hall, standing afar off and gazing at it wistfully. Aye, and once when it passed near to him, I saw too, that there were tears upon his face, noting which my heart sorrowed for him who was outcast for a woman's sake.

When these ceremonies were ended he would visit me in my chambers where we talked long and of many things. I asked him why the Princess Amenartas, who it seemed was recovered of her fever since now she could wander in her garden ground, laid no offering on the altar of the goddess. He answered,

"Because she will have naught to do with the gods of Egypt who, she says, if they are at all, have ever been the enemies of her House and have dragged her father, the Pharaoh Nectanebes, from his throne and hurled him forth, a discrowned fugitive, to perish amidst strangers."

"Upon those who follow after spells and affront the gods, the gods will be avenged, Kallikrates. For every sin there is forgiveness, save for that of the denial of Divinity, and of the setting of Evil in its place to be propitated by the arts of sorcerers. Moreover, did not this Nectanebes offer deadly insult to the Queen of Heaven when he gave me, her servant and seeress, to be a slave to Tenes, the worshipper of her worst of foes, Baal and Ashtoreth and Moloch, that Tenes from whose grip you helped to save me, Kallikrates?"

"It is so," he answered sadly.

"And now," I went on, "the daughter follows in the father's steps. Oh! I am sure that yonder she spells out her charms, aiming her enchantments at my heart, whence they fall back harmless, as the bone-tipped arrows of wild men fall from a shield of Syrian bronze."

He hung his head who knew well that my words were true, and muttered,

"Alas! she loves you not, Lady, who from the first hour that she set her eyes upon you, as often she has told me, feared and hated you, because, she says, her spirit warns and has ever warned her that you will bring disaster upon her head and call up Death to keep her company."

"At least he would be a better guest, Kallikrates, than the dæmon that, like her father, she harbours in her breast. Oh! unhappy man, my heart bleeds for you, who are linked to this poisoned loveliness that divorces you from hope and charity; to this royal infidel who in the end will bind your spirit's wings and drag you down into her own darkness. For your soul's sake I pray you, Kallikrates, seek out the holy Noot, confess your sins and hear his counsel, since this matter is beyond my strength and I have none to give. Seek him soon, nay, at once, ere perchance it be too late, for I learn that he grows feeble."

"That is my great desire, Priestess, yet how can I, who know not where to find him?"

"I will be your guide, Kallikrates. When the sun rises on the second day from now we will march to visit Noot in his secret dwelling."

"I will be ready," he answered and left me.

On the morrow he came again and we spoke together of the state of Kôr and of my plans for bettering it; also of certain savages who threatened us from without, man-eating tribes that it seemed were descended from the apostates who rejecting the worship of Truth or Lulala, as Isis was named by them in those times, had adopted that of a devil that, as they declared, inhabited the sun or some ill-omened star.

Kallikrates listened, he who at bottom was ever a soldier, for the tale awoke all his general's craft and courage. As a great captain does, he balanced the reasons for or against defence, for or against attack. He questioned me as to the numbers of my people and of their foes, as to their arms, and many other matters that have to do with war. Then having learned all that I could tell him, he set out the plan which he judged to be the best in our conditions, talking of it long and eagerly, he who for a while had forgot his woes. I listened to him, watching his bright and splendid face which seemed as that of the Sun-god of the Greeks. Speaking a word here and a word there, I listened, thinking to myself the while that if only he and I, he with his skill and courage and I with my wisdom, could guide the destinies of Kôr, before our day was done we would drive them like the chariots of a conquering king from Egypt's borders to these of the uttermost southern seas, setting nation after nation beneath our feet, and building up such an empire as Libya had never known.

What had I dreamed? To Egypt's borders? Why should we stop at her borders? Why should we not hurl forth the foul Persian swarms and be crowned monarchs of the world at Susa and at Thebes? Yet it would take time, and life is short, and yonder, not so far away, burned the Fire of Immortality, and I, I held the key to its prison house, or soon should hold it when Noot had sought his rest. Almost these burning thoughts, these high ambitions, in whose fulfilment lay the seeds of peace attained through war and the promise of the welfare of the earth, burst from my lips in a torrent of hot words which I knew well would set his soul aflame. But I, Ayesha, refrained myself from myself, I wrapped myself in silence, I said to myself, "Wait, wait, the ripe hour has not dawned."

He rose to depart, then turned and said,

"At the sunrise I will be here, or rather," he added doubtfully, "we will be here, since Amenartas desires to accompany us upon this journey to visit the holy Noot."

"By whom I trust she will be well received, seeing the manner in which she parted from him upon the ship *Hapi*. Well, so be it; I rejoice to learn that the royal Amenartas again finds herslf prepared to travel. Yet remind her, Kallikrates, that the road we go is rough and dangerous."

"She shall be told, yet it will serve little, since who can turn Amenartas from her ends? Not I, be sure; nor could her father before me, nor any living man."

"Nay, nor any god, Kallikrates, since the ends she follows are those of neither man nor god, but of something that stands beyond them both, as was the case of Pharaoh Nectanebes who begot her. Each of us shoots at his chosen mark, Kallikrates, you at yours, I at mine, and Amenartas at her own; therefore what right have we to judge of one another's archery? Let her come to visit Noot and I pray that she may return the happier."

Next morning ere the dawn I stood at the temple porch awaiting Philo and the litters. Came Amenartas cloaked heavily, for the air was cold, yet splendid even in those wrappings.

"Greeting, Wisdom's Child," she said, bowing in her courtlike fashion. "I learn that you and my husband would make some strange journey, and therefore, as a wife should, I accompany him."

"That is so, royal Lady, though I knew not that you were wed to the lord Kallikrates."

"What is marriage?" she asked. "Is it certain words

mumbled before an altar and a priest, a thing of witnessed ceremony, or is it the union of the heart and flesh according to Nature's custom and decree? But let that pass. Where my lord goes, there I accompany him."

"None forbids you, O Lady of Egypt."

"True, Prophetess. Yet my own heart forbids me. Know that but last night I was haunted by a very evil dream. It seemed to me that my father Nectanebes stood before me in a sable robe that was shot through with threads of fire. He spoke to me saying: 'Daughter, beware of that witch who goes on a dreadful quest, taking with her one who is dear to you. At the end of that quest lies Doom for her, for him, for you, though each of these dooms be different!'"

"It may be so, Princess," I answered coldly. "Then accompany me not and keep Kallikrates at your side."

"That I cannot do," she said in a sullen voice, "since now for the first time he will not listen to my pleading and crosses my will. You have laid your charm upon him as on others in the past, and where you lead, he follows."

"Mayhap as a slave follows one who can show him where he may loose his chains! But let us not bandy words, royal Amenartas. I depart. Follow if you will, or bide behind, one or both of you. See, here comes Kallikrates; agree together as it pleases you."

She turned and met him in the ruins of the ancient pylon, where they debated together in words I could not hear. Once she seemed to conquer, for both of them walked a little way toward their own home. Then Kallikrates swung round upon his heel and came back to me who stood by the litters. She hesitated awhile, ah! what mighty issues hung upon this trembling of the balance of her mind, but in the end she followed him.

After this, without more speech we entered the litters and began our journey.

As we went across the misty plain it came home to me, as many a time it has done during the long centuries that followed, how often the great depends upon the little. Another bitter word from Amenartas, a trifle less of courage in Kallikrates, and how differently would Fate have fashioned the destinies of every one of us. For be it remembered that the choice lay with these two; I did naught save wait upon their wills. Had they so desired, never need they have entered those litters. Alone I should have departed; alone I should have looked upon the Fire and drunk of that Cup of Life, or perchance, as is probable, I should have left it untasted and gone down my way to death after the common fashion of mankind. But it was not so decreed; of their own desire they took the path to doom, though perchance that desire was shaped by some Strength above their own.

We reached the precipice and climbed it, Amenartas, Kallikrates, Philo, and I. We passed the cave by the light of lanterns, and we came to the trembling spur of rock that reaches out like a great needle thrust through the robe of darkness. When they looked upon it, Kallikrates and Amenartas shivered and drew back, seeing which I rejoiced, for it is true that at the moment I found no more heart for this adventure.

"Stay where you are," I cried, "and wait. I go to visit the holy Noot. I will return again, and if I return not within a round of the sun, then make your way back to Kôr and there abide. Or if it pleases you, seek the coast-land and the harbour of the Ethiopian's Head and depart with the help of Philo, if still he lives, or if not, otherwise. Farewell! I go."

"Nay," cried Kallikrates, "whither you lead, Prophet-ess, thither I follow."

"If so," said Amenartas, laughing in her royal fash-ion, "you will not follow alone. What! Shall I not dare that which my lord can dare? Is this the first peril in which we twain have stood side by side? If it be the last, what of it?"

So we started down the spur, Philo coming at the end of our line, and though with many hazards, for once the brain of Amenartas swam so that almost she fell, reached its point in safety. Here we waited crouched upon the rough rock and clinging to it with our hands, lest its quick throbbing should hurl us into the gulf, or the fierce gusts should sweep us away like autumn leaves.

At length at the appointed moment the sword-like sunset ray appeared, striking full upon us and showing that the frail bridge of boards was still in the place, for it swayed and moved like the deck of a ship at sea.

"Be bold and follow," I cried, "since he who hesitates is doomed," and instantly I stepped across that perilous plank and took my stand upon the swaying stone beyond.

For a moment Kallikrates stood doubtful, as well he might, but Amenartas pushed past him and with a laugh crossed it as though she would teach me that I was not the only one to whom the gods had given courage. I caught her by the hand. Then Kallikrates followed because he must, and she caught him by the hand and after him Philo, the seaman, calmly enough, so that now all four of us stood together on the stone.

"Glad enough am I to be here, Prophetess," cried Kallikrates, though in that wailing wind his voice reached me only as a whisper. "Yet, I know not why, it comes into my mind that I go upon my last journey."

I made no answer because his fateful words chilled my heart and choked my voice; only I looked at his face and noted that it was white as ice even in the red light of the ray and that his large eyes shone as though with the fires of fever.

Taking Kallikrates by the hand and motioning to Philo to do likewise with Amenartas, I led him to the little rough-hewn stair. By this stair we descended into the sheltered place that was in front of the hermitage of Noot and rejoiced was I to find myself and the others out of the reach of those raging winds and to see that lights burned within the cave beyond.

"Bide here, all of you," I said. "I will enter the cave and prepare the holy Noot for your coming."

I entered the place thinking to find that strange dwarf who was Noot's servant, but nowhere could he be seen. Yet I was sure that he must be near, since on the rough rock table were set food and wooden platters, four platters as though awaiting four guests. I thought to myself that doubtless the Master had seen us creeping down the spur, or perchance his spirit had warned him of our coming—who could say?

I gazed about me to find Noot, and at length in the deep shadow, out of reach of the lamp's rays, I perceived him kneeling before that image of Isis whereof I have told, and wrapt in earnest prayer. I drew near and waited a while who did not dare to break in upon his orisons. Still he did not stir or look up. So quiet was he that he might have been carved in ivory. I bent forward, examining his face. Lo! his eyes were fixed and open and his jaw had fallen.

Noot was *dead!*

"My Master, my most beloved Master! Too late, too late!" I moaned, and bending down kissed him on his brow of ice.

Then I began to think and swiftly. Had he not warned me when I bade him farewell a while before that we spoke together for the last time? Where was my faith who had forgotten that the prophecies of Noot were always true? So he had gone to his rest in the bosom of Osiris, and on me had fallen his mantle. I, Ayesha, was the guardian of the Fire of Life whereof alone I knew the secrets and held the key! The knowledge struck me like a blow; I trembled and sank to the ground. I think that for a little while I swooned and in that swoon strange dreams took hold of me, half-remembered dreams, dreams not to be written.

Presently I rose and going to the doorway summoned the others, who stood there huddled together like sheep before a storm.

"Enter," I said, and they obeyed. "Now be seated and eat," I went on, pointing to the table on which the food was ready.

"Where is the master of the feast, Prophetess? Where is the holy Noot whom we have walked this fearful road to see?" asked Kallikrates, staring about him.

"Yonder," I answered, pointing to the depths of the shadow, "yonder—dead and cold. You tarried too long

at Kôr, Kallikrates. Now you must seek his counsel and
his absolution at another table—that of Osiris."

Thus I spoke, for something inspired the words, yet
ere they had left my lips I could have bitten out the
tongue that shaped them. Was *this* the place to talk of
the Table of Osiris to the man I loved?

They went to that dark nook where the little sacred
statue looked down upon its quiet worshipper. They
stared in silence; they returned, Philo muttering prayers,
Kallikrates wringing his hands, for he had loved and
honoured Noot above any man that lived. Also—I read
the question in his mind—to whom now should he confess his sins? Who now could loose their burden?

Only Amenartas pondered a space; then she spoke
with a slow and meaning smile, saying,

"Perchance, my lord, it is as well that this old high-
priest has gone to discover whether he dreamed true
dreams for so many years upon the earth. I know not
what you would have said to him, yet I can guess that it
boded but little good to me, your wife, for so I am,
whatever yonder priestess may tell you, who also bodes
little good either to me or to you, my lord Kallikrates.
Well, he is dead and even Wisdom's Daughter there
cannot bring him back to life. So let us rest a while and
eat, and then return by that dread road which we have
trodden, ere our strength and spirit fail us."

"That you may not do, Princess Amenartas, until the
sunset comes again and once more the red ray shows us
where to set our feet, for to attempt it sooner is to die,"
I answered, and went on:

"Hearken. By the death of this holy man, or half-
god, I have become the keeper of a certain treasure
over which he watched. It is hidden deep in the bowels
of the earth beneath us. I must go to visit it and see that
it is safe. This I shall do presently. Bide you here, if you
will, till I return, and if I return not, wait till the ray
strikes upon the point of rock, cross the bridge, climb
the spur, and flee whither ye will. Philo can guide you."

"Not so, Child of Isis," said Philo. "My oath and
duty are to you, not to this pair. Whither you go, I follow to the end."

"I follow also," said Kallikrates, "who would not be left in this darksome place companied by death."

"Yet it might be wiser, Kallikrates," I answered, "since who can escape that company of death of which you speak?" for again dreadful and ominous words rushed unbidden from my heart.

"I care not. I go," he said almost sullenly.

"Then I go also," broke in Amenartas. "This Prophetess doubtless is wise and holy, yet I may be pardoned if I choose to share her fellowship with you upon a road unknown. Perchance it has another gate elsewhere that I might never find," she added in bitter jest.

Oh! had this fool but known that her coarse stabs at me did but harden the heart which she sought to pierce, and drive it whither she did not desire.

"As you will," I answered. "Now eat and rest till the hour of departure comes and I summon you."

So they ate, if not much, though for my part I touched no food, and laid them down in the inner cave as best they might, and there slept, or did not sleep. But I, I watched the hours away by the dead shell of the holy Noot, striving to commune with his spirit which I knew to be near to me. Yet it gave no answer to all my questions. Or at least there came one only which again and again seemed to shape itself to a single word,

"Beware!"

Strange, thought I to myself, that the prophet Noot my Master, who loved me better than any other living upon the earth, and knew the most of my lonely, wayward heart, now that he was justified and made perfect, as doubtless he must be, if such a lot can be attained by man, should find no more to say to me than this one word, which indeed while in the flesh often he had said before. Therefore it seemed that in the flesh and out of it his counsel was the same; one certainly that I should take.

What did it mean? That I should look no more upon the Fire; that I should rise up and get me back to Kôr and there play such parts as I could compass, and wither and grow old and die, nurturing perchance the children of Kallikrates and Amenartas, should they seek the Shades before me; or, growing weary of barbarians and ruins, flee away from Kôr to find the fellowship of instructed men.

That is what this counsel meant. Well, what did that of my own heart promise me? Perhaps a swift death and after it punishment in some dim land beyond, because I had disobeyed the shadowy cautionings of the holy Noot and dared to make trial of a new Strength, against which as yet no man had matched himself. Or perhaps a glory greater than any man had ever dreamed, and a power far above that of emperors and a life longer than that of mountains. Also more—more, the love that I desired, to me a greater guerdon than all these boons added together and multiplied by the snowflakes upon Lebanon or the sands of the seashore. Surely, come what might of it, I would take my own counsel and let the other be.

The hour came; although I saw it not, I knew that it was that of dawn in the world without. I arose, I summoned the others; we departed down that darksome path of which I have written, climbing from rock to rock in the bowels of the earth by the dim light of the lanterns which we bore.

We came to the outer cavern; we passed the passage and reached the second cavern, halting at the mouth of another passage through which at intervals shot flickerings of light, and from time to time sounds as of muttering thunder reached our ears.

"The treasure on which I would look lies yonder. Bide ye here," I said.

"Nay," answered Kallikrates, "now as before I follow."

"Where my lord goes there go I also," said Amenartas.

Only Philo, the cautious Greek, bowed his head and answered,

"I obey. I bide here. If I am needed, summon me, O Child of Isis.

"Good," I cried, who at that moment thought little of

Philo and his fate, though it is true that, cunning as he might be, I loved him well.

Then I went on and with me went Kallikrates and Amenartas.

CHAPTER XXIII

~

The Doom of the Fire

WE stood in the third cave that was carpeted with white sand and alive with rosy light. Making a dark stain upon that snowy sand was a black patch of dust. I knew it again; when last I had seen it, it bore the withered shape of one long dead. The rolling many-coloured fire approached from afar; its muttering grew to a roar, its roar grew to such a thunder as shakes the mountain peaks and splits the walls of citadels. It appeared, blazing with a thousand lights; for a while it hovered, twisting like a spun top. Then it departed upon its eternal round in the unknown entrails of the earth, and the tumult sank to silence.

Kallikrates, terrified, flung himself upon his face; even the proud Amenartas fell to her knees, covering her eyes with her hands: only I stood erect and laughed, I who knew that I was betrothed to that fire and that it ill became the bride-to-be to shrink from her promised lord.

Kallikrates rose, asking,

"Where is the treasure which you seek, Prophetess? If it be hidden here, in this awful house of a living god, look on it swiftly, and let us begone. I, a mortal man, am terrified."

"As well as you may be," broke in Amenartas, "since such wizardries as these have not been told of in the earth. I say it, who know something of wizardries, and like my father have stood face to face with spirits summoned from the Underworld, giving them word for word of power."

"My treasure lies in the red heart of yonder raging flame, and presently I go to pluck it thence," I answered in a quiet voice. "Whether I shall return I do not know. Perchance I shall abide in the fire and be borne away upon its wings. Stay if you will, or if you will, while there is yet time, depart, but trouble me no more with words, who must steel my soul to its last trial."

They stared at me, both of them, and remained silent.

For a space I stood still pondering. It seemed to me that I was the plaything of two great Strengths that dragged me forward, that dragged me back. The spirit of the Fire cried,

"Come, O Divine! Come, be made perfect, and queen it in this red heart of mine. Come, drink of that full cup of mysteries which no mortal lips have drained. Come, see those things that are hidden from mortal eyes. Come, taste of joys wherewith no mortal heart has ever throbbed. Haste, haste to the fiery bridal and in the glory of my kiss learn what delight can be. Oh! doubt no more but take Faith by the hand and let her lead thee home. Doubt no more! Be brave, lay down mortality: put on the spirit and as a spirit sit enthroned beyond the touch of time and with immortal eyes, robed in eternal majesty, watch the generations pass, marching with sad feet from darkness into darkness. Behold there he stands who is appointed to thee, who was thine from the beginning, who shall be thine until the end of ends. Thy new-born loveliness shall chain him fast and he shall grow drunken in the breath of thy perfumed sighs who for ever and for ever and for ever shall be thy very own, turning the winter of thy widowed heart to summer of perpetual joy."

Thus spake the spirit of the Flame, but to it there answered another spirit that wore the shape of Noot, yea, of Noot grown stern and terrible.

"Turn back, O Wisdom's Daughter, ere thou art wrapped in the robe of madness and repentance comes too late," it seemed to say. "Always the tempter tempts and when bribe after bribe is scorned, at last he pours his richest jewels at the feet of her whom he would win. Woe, woe to her who, charmed of their false glitter, clasps them upon brow and breast, for there they shall change to scorpions and through the living flesh gnaw to the brain and heart within. Departing, have I not set thee to watch the ire and wilt thou steal the Fire, therewith to make thyself a god? Do so and this I swear to thee: that the godhead which thou shalt put on will be that of hell. Thy love shall be snatched away; undying, through all the earth, through all the stars, thou shalt follow after him and never find, or, if thou findest, it will be but to lose again. Dost thou dare to wrest thy destiny out of the hand of Fate and fashion it to thy desire with the instrument of thy blind and petty will? Do so, and dæmons shall possess it that from age to age shall drive thee on, torn by the furies of remorse, choked with bitter, unavailing tears, frozen by the icy blasts of sorrow; desolate, alone, unfriended, till at last thou standest before the Judgment-seat hearkening with bowed head to a doom that can never be undone. Daughter of Wisdom, art thou sunk so low that thou wilt forget thine oaths and break thy trust to rob another woman of her lover?"

Those visions passed and I grasped denial's robes. I would not do this thing. I would live out my life upon the earth, I would die—oh! might it be soon—to pass to whatever place had been prepared for me, or to sink into the deep abysm of that rich and boundless sleep which no dreams haunt.

Aye! renouncing joy and renounced of hope, already I turned to go and climb my upward path back to the bitter world.

Then, from far, far away came the faint music of the chant of the advancing god of Fire. Low and sweet it sang at first, soft as a mother's lullaby, and lo! I dreamed of happy childhood's day. It swelled and grew and now I had entered into womanhood and strange, uncomprehended longings companioned me. It took a fiercer note and I bethought me of the beating of the hoofs of horses as, mounted on my crested stallion, I rushed across the desert like the wind. Louder yet, and behold! once more I was in the battle at my father's side; behind me the wild tribesmen surged and shouted; in front of me my foes were beaten down to death. Ah! bright flashed my javelin, ah! free flowed my hair among the flapping pennons. "The Daughter of Yarab! Follow the daughter of Yarab!" cried the thousands of my kind, and on we went, like sun-loosed snows down mountains, on upon the marshalled host beneath. We broke them, for who could stand before the Daughter of Yarab and her kin? We trampled them, Egyptian and Syrian and Mede and the men from Chittim's Isle; down they went before that wild charge, and see! my bright spear was red.

Deeper yet and more solemn grew that mighty music. Now I was alone in the wilderness beneath the stars, and from the stars knowledge and beauty fell upon my heart like dew. Now I was a ruler of men, and kings who would be my lovers bent at my feet and were the puppets of my hands. I cast them down and broke them; I saw Sidon go up in flames and filled my soul with vengeance. Hark! It is the footstep of the goddess, the Queen of Heaven sets her kiss upon my brow; she names me Daughter, her Appointed. Knowledge is mine, out of my lips flow prophecies, a spirit guides my feet. I, I hold my own against the Persian, when all else have fled I cast him from his throne. I give his pomp to the tongues of Fire. Oh! how they cry, those mockers of Egypt's gods, as I watch them scorch and perish.

I am lonely. Where is my love? I wend toward the grave and none are born of me. I seek my love. "There stands thy love—not far away, but at thy side. Take him, take him, take him!" Thus said the Fire.

Now its voice is the voice of trumpets that blare and echo around the hills. They call, those trumpets call: "Where is the captain of our hosts? Where is our Queen? Come forth, O Queen, crowned with wisdom, diademed with power, holding in thine hand the gift of days. No longer would we be left leaderless, we who would march to victory and hold the world in thrall."

The King of Fire is at hand. He opens the gateways of the dark. Behind him march the legions: he comes with splendour, he comes with glory, he comes to take his bride. "Unrobe, unrobe! Prepare thyself, O Bride! The King of Fire calls!"

I unloosed my garments, I unbound my hair that covered me like a sable robe.

"Art mad?" cried the Greek, Kallikrates, wringing his hands.

"Art mad?" echoed the royal Amenartas with a slow smile as she waited to see mine end.

"Nay, I am wise," I answered back, "I who weary of tame days and common things, I who seek death or triumph."

I ran. I stood in the pathway of the Fire. It saw; it stretched out its arms to me. Lo! it wrapped me round and in my ears I heard the shoutings of the stars.

Oh! what was this? I did not burn. The blood of the gods flowed through my veins. The soul within me became as a lighted torch. The Fire possessed me, I was the Fire's and in a dread communion the Fire was mine. By that lit torch of my heart I saw many visions; veils rolled up before my eyes revealing glory after glory, glories that cannot be told. Death shrank away from before my feet; pale and ashamed he shrank away. Pain departed, weakness was done. I stood the Queen of all things human.

Lo! mirrored in that Fire as in water I saw myself, a shape of loveliness celestial. Could this form be the form of woman? Could those orbs divine be a woman's eyes?

Then a great silence and in the silence a silvery tinkling sound that I knew well—the sound of the laughter of Aphrodite!

The pillar of flame had rolled away, its thousand blinding lights had ceased to shine, and there I stood triumphant, conquering, never to be conquered. I came forth speaking with a voice of music, knowing that I had inherited another soul. What now to me was Isis or any other goddess, to me who stood victorious, the equal of them all? Oh! I saw now that Isis was but Nature and henceforth Nature was my slave. I thought no more of sin or of repentance, I who from this day forth would fashion my own laws and be to myself a judge. That which I desired, that I would take. That which was hateful to me that would I cast away. Yea! I was Nature's very self. I felt all her springs stirring in my blood; it glowed with the heats of all her summers. I was kind with the kindness of her fruitful autumns; I was terrible with her winter wrath.

Look! There stood the man whom I desired. Somewhat coarse and poor he seemed to me; I smelt death upon him. To be my mate he must be my equal; he too must taste of the Fire; then we would talk of love. As he was, my love was not for him, nay, it would destroy him as the lightning blasts.

"Look on me, Kallikrates," I cried, "and tell me, in all your days have you seen aught so fair?"

"Fair, yes, fair!" he gasped, "but terrible in beauty. No woman, no woman! A very spirit. Oh! let me shut mine eyes. Let me flee!"

"Be still and wait," I answered, "for soon I shall show you how they may be opened. Look on me, Daughter of Pharaoh, and tell me, has that stamp of age of which you spoke to me not long ago departed from my face and form, or is it yet apparent?"

"I look," she answered, still bold, "and I see before me no child of man, but a very witch. Away from us, accursed witch! Clothe yourself, shameless one, and begone, or let us begone, leaving you to commune with your witch's fire."

I cast my robes around me and oh! they hung royally. Then once more I turned to Kallikrates, considering him. As I looked I became aware that a great change had fallen upon me. I was no longer the Ayesha of old days. That Ayesha had been spirit-driven; her soul had aspired to the heavens; it glistened with the dews of purity. True, I had loved this man, little at the first, and more a hundred times after Noot had suffered me to look upon the Fire, since with the sight and the sound and the odours of it the great change began.

That Ayesha was one who dreamed of heavenly

things; one with whom prayer was a constant habit of the mind; yes, all her thoughts were mixed with the leaven of prayer, so that the humblest deed and the most common of imaginings were by it sanctified! She knew that here was not her home, but that far away and out of sight, beyond the seas and mountains of the world, her everlasting house rose white and stately and that with her earthly toil and sufferings she built it stone by stone, filling its halls and porticoes with ivory statues of the gods, making it pure with clouds of incense that their perfected souls brooding on her soul drew from it, as at dawn the sun draws mist from rivers.

With grief and toil, with bleeding feet; buffeted by the winds of circumstance, wet with the rain of tears, washed by the waters of repentance, she climbed the stony upward path that led to the Peak of Peace. She believed in she knew not what, for always to her those gods were man-shaped symbols. Still day and night she struggled on, lit by the rays of the lamp of faith, sure that in the end the veils would be withdrawn and that she would look upon the Face Divine and hear its voice of welcome. She was obedient to the Law; she knew that time was not her own and that of every moment she must give account. Aye, she was in the way of holiness and before her shone the golden guerdons of redemption.

But now. What was Ayesha now when she had known the embrace of the Spirit of Fire, when she had dared the deed and wrung the secret from his burning heart? Aye, when on the earth she had attained to immortality, since even then a voice cried in her ears:

"Behold! thou shalt not die. Behold while the world lives, with it thou shalt live also, because thou has drunk of the wine of Earth's primeval Soul that cannot be spilled until its mighty fabric is dissolved into the nothingness whence it sprang!"

What was she now? She was that very Earth. She was that Soul poured into the white vase of a woman's form; aye, she was its essence. Its lightnings and its hurricanes lay chained within her, ready to leap out when she was wrath, and who could abide before their strength? She knew all Earth's glory as alone is swung through space, kissed of the light of the Sun its father, or dreaming in the arms of darkness. The planets were her sisters, the bright, blazing stars acknowledged her as kin. Aye; with this mother-world she symbolled she was numbered among the multitude of that hierarchy of heaven.

Nor was this all, for in her reigned and glowed every power and passion of the Earth. Thenceforth all things were at her command, but, like that Earth, *she was alone and could no more speak with Heaven!*

In a flash, in a twinkling, all this mighty truth came home to me, and with it other truths. I did not doubt, I did not dream, I knew, I knew, I *knew!*

There stood the man and I would take him. He was wed according to Nature's law, and now I owned no other. But what of that? The wine that I desired I would drink. I would mate me as the wild things mated, by strength and capture, since I was very strong and who could stand against my might? I, the reborn Ayesha, had commanded. It should be done.

"Kallikrates," I said in my new voice of honeyed sweetness, "behold your spouse, one of whom you need not be ashamed. Make ready, Kallikrates. Go stand in the path of the Fire when it returns, and then let us hence to reign eternally."

"What, Witch," cried Amenartas, "would you rob me of my lord? It shall not be. If you are mighty, so am I, although I remain a woman. Kallikrates, look on me, your wife, she who has borne your child, that lost child who binds us yet with bonds that may not be broken. Have done with this fair dæmon ere she enchant you. Away! Away from this haunted, mocking hell."

"I come. Surely I come," said Kallikrates, glancing at me fearfully. "I am afraid of her, and of that fire I will have none. Surely it is Set himself wrapped about with flames."

"Nay, you go not, Kallikrates. Let Amenartas go if she desires. Here you abide with me until all is accomplished. I command, and when I command, you must obey."

He wheeled about; he flung himself into the arms of Amenartas. They closed around him and held him fast. Then I threw out my will. Saying nothing I laid my strength upon him, so that he was dragged from out those arms and with slow steps drew near to me, as the bird draws near to the snake that charms it with its baleful eyes. Amenartas leapt between us and from her lips flowed words in torrents.

All she said I do not know; it is forgot; but very sore she pleaded and very bitterly she wept. Yet my heart, new steeled in yonder fire, felt no pity for her. An hour past I should have bade him go his way and to look upon my face no more, but now it was otherwise. I was cruel, cruel as Death, King of the world. The wild beast does not spare its rival, neither would I.

Still I drew him with my strength; still Amenartas clung and pleaded, till at last madness took hold of that tormented man. He raved, he cursed us both, he cursed himself who had left the quiet halls of Isis, who had spurned the love divine to seek the arms of woman. He prayed to Isis to be pitiful, to forgive, to receive his soul and shrive it.

Then suddenly from his belt he snatched his short Grecian sword and stabbed at his own heart.

Swift as a snake that strikes, or a falcon stooping at its prey, I sprang. I seized his arm, I dragged it back, and such might was there in my grasp, aye, the might of Hercules himself, that the sword flew far, and the strong man who held it reeled round and round and fell.

We stood aghast, thinking that he was sped. Yet he rose, the red blood running from his breast, and in a quiet voice, a little laugh upon his lips, said to Amenartas, not to me,

"Fear nothing, Wife. Alas! it is but a cut—skin deep, no more."

"Then let the fire heal it, O Kallikrates. Make ready to enter the fire that must soon retravel its circling path," I answered.

"Nay, nay, Husband," cried Amenartas. "By that blood of yours, the blood that flowed in our dead son and flows in that of the child to be, I adjure you turn from this witch and temptress and break her enchanted bonds."

"By our dead son," he repeated after her in a strange and heavy voice. "With what holier words could you conjure, O my wife? With that name of power I am new-armoured. Daughter of Wisdom, I reject your proffered gifts, nor will I enter your charmed fire though it should give to me eternal strength and gloriousness, and with these your shining beauty and your love. Child of the gods, farewell! I go to seek peace and pardon if it may be found. Yes, pardon for you and me, and for Amenartas, the mother of my child. Daughter of Wisdom, fare you well for ever!"

I heard, and it seemed to me that I stood alone in the midst of a great silence while those cruel words, divorcing me from hope, fell one by one upon me like icedrops from the sky, cutting to brain and heart and freezing me to stone. Then of a sudden rage possessed me, such rage as Nature knows in her fiercest moods, and I spoke as it gave me words, saying.

"I call down death upon thee, Kallikrates the Greek. Death be thy portion and the grave thy home. Because thou hast rejected me, because thou hast offered me insult to my face, it is my will that thou mayest die; it is my desire that thy name be blotted out from the roll of Life. Die, then, Kallikrates, that thine eyes may torment me no more and that I may learn to mock thy memory."

Thus I spoke those words of doom in my madness, though what conceived them in my heart I do not know. There they sprang up suddenly at the touch of the wand of Evil, such evil as until now I had never dreamed. Lo! in a moment they fulfilled themselves. There before my eyes the man *died,* smitten of the dominion over Death that was the Fire's fatal gift to me, as now, all unprepared, instantly I learned. Yes, the first service that I made of my dread majesty was to hurl that awful doom at the heart of the man I loved.

He died! Kallikrates died there before our eyes. Yet being dead, still he stood upon his feet and spoke, though even then I knew that it was not he who spoke, but some spirit possessing his perished flesh. His lips did not move, his eyes were glassed, his voice was not the voice of Kallikrates, nay, nor the voice of mortal man. Yet he spoke, or seemed to speak, and these were the words he said,

"Woman, known on earth as Ayesha, daughter of Yarab, but in the Under-world by many another name, hearken to thy fate. Here, where thou hast betrayed thy trust, here where thou didst slay the man of thy desire, here through long ages shalt thou abide undying, until in the fulness of time he returns to thee, O Ayesha, in lonely bitterness shalt thou abide; tears shall be thy drink and remorse thy bread. The power that thou didst crave shall be but a blunted, unused sword within thine hand. Thy kingdom shall be a desolation, thy subjects barbarians, and from century to century thy companions shall be the dead."

The voice ceased and I answered it, asking,

"And when the returning tide of Time bears this man back to me, what then, O Spirit? Is all hope passed from me, O Spirit?"

No answer came, but that which had been Kallikrates sank in a huddled heap upon the sand.

CHAPTER XXIV

~

The Counsel of Philo

ROARING like a whirlwind, shouting triumphantly, once more the wheel of fire rolled on its tremendous course. I watched it come, I watched it go, while in it I thought I saw grinning, elf-like faces that gibbered at me and thrust out tongues of derision. It departed on its secret journey through the bowels of the world. Its thunder sank to mutterings, its mutterings to silence, while I said to my heart that could I be sure that it would slay, I would cast myself beneath its chariot wheels.

To what purpose? Since then, as I believed in those days, in the flames I should find but added life—I who could not die.

It was gone. Naught remained save the cave carpeted with white sand and the rosy light playing on the body of the dead Kallikrates. Nay, Amenartas remained also, and I became aware that she was cursing me by all her gods, or rather by those who had been her gods before she turned her face from them, seeking the counsel of familiar spirits.

Bravely she cursed and long, calling down upon my head every evil that can be found in heaven above or earth beneath; she who did not know that this was needless, for already the winged Furies had made it their resting-place and before they could be uttered all her imprecations were fulfilled.

"Have done!" I said when at length she grew weak and weary, "and let us summon Philo to help us bear this noble clay to some fitting sepulchre."

"Nay, Witch," she answered, "use your magic on me also, if you can. Slay the wife as you have slain the husband, and here let us rest eternally. What tomb can be better for both of us than that which saw our murder."

"Have done!" I repeated. "You know well that I have no desire to kill you and that it was my madness, not my will, that brought doom on Kallikrates, whom we loved; I who had not learned that henceforth my spirit is a bow winged with deadly shafts."

I went down the cave and through the passage that lay beyond and from its mouth called to Philo to follow me.

He came, and perceiving my new loveliness as I stood awaiting him in the rosy light, fell to the ground, kissing my feet and the hem of my robe, and muttering,

"O Isis-come-to-Earth! O Queen divine!"

"Rise up and follow me," I said, and led him to where lay Kallikrates, by whom knelt the widowed Amenartas weeping bitterly.

"Overwhelmed with the sight of glory, alas! this lord

has slain himself," I said, and pointed to the wound in the dead man's breast whence still the blood oozed drop by drop.

"Nay, this witch slew him," moaned Amenartas, but if Philo heard her words, he took no heed of them.

Then at my command the three of us lifted Kallikrates and bore him thence up the difficult ways, which never could we have done had I not discovered that now in my woman's shape that seemed so frail and weak was hid unmeasured strength.

So through the caves and up the winding slopes and stairs we bore the dead Kallikrates, bringing him back to the hermitage of Noot but a little before the hour of sunset. Here I commanded Amenartas and Philo to eat and drink, though myself I needed neither food nor wine. While they did so, aided of this new strength of mine, I lifted the body of Noot from where it knelt and laid it down, crossing the hands upon the breast, and having covered it with a robe, left him to his last sleep.

These things finished, we carried Kallikrates to the crest of the Swaying Stone, and waited the coming of the ray. Suddenly it shone out, and in its fierce light we dared the shifting bridge. Beneath a weight which it was ill designed to bear, the frail thing broke just as Amenartas and Philo, bearing the feet of the dead man, had found footing upon the point of the spur beyond. It seemed that I should have fallen, yet I fell not, who, I know not how, found myself at their side still supporting Kallikrates in my arms.

Then it was that first I learned that as I was protected from the gnawings of the tooth of Time so also I was armoured against all the strokes of chance. This indeed became very clear to me in the after days. Thus once when the roof of a cave fell upon me and others they were slain but I remained unbruised, and again, when a deadly snake bit me, its poison harmed me not at all. But what of these things which are not worthy to be chronicled, seeing that if I could die, in the passing of two thousand years and more, what men call mishap must long since have brought me to my end.

We bore Kallikrates down the spur and through the

cavern whence it springs, till at length we found the litters waiting for us, and in one of these we laid his quiet
form.

Thus at length we came back to Kôr at the hour of
the dawn.

Again we lifted up the corpse of Kallikrates and carried it to the chamber where I slept. A thought came to
me.

"Philo," I said, "did you not tell me that among those
who serve us, in this temple are certain aged medicine-
men who declare that knowledge of the arts whereby
the people of old Kôr preserved their dead from corruption has come down to them, which arts they still practise from time to time?"

"It is so, O Queen," for so he named me now.
"There are three of them."

"Good. Summon them, Philo, and bid them bring
with them their instruments and spices."

Awhile later the three appeared, very aged, cunning-
looking men who had upon their hook-nosed faces the
stamp of high and ancient blood. I pointed to the body
of Kallikrates and asked,

"Are ye able to hold back this holy flesh from the
foul fingers of decay?"

"If he be not more than forty hours dead," answered
one of them, "we can do so in such fashion that when
five thousand years have passed it will seem as it does
at this hour, O Queen."

"Then to your office, Slaves, and know that if ye do
as ye have promised ye shall receive great reward. But
if ye lie to me, ye die."

"We do not lie, O Queen," he said.

Forthwith they lit a fire outside the chamber and
thereon set a large earthen pot. In this pot, mixed with
water, they placed dried leaves of a certain shrub, in
shape long and narrow, and boiled them to a broth,
whereof the pungent odour seemed to fill all the air
about. While the pot was boiling they took the corpse of
Kallikrates, and, having washed it, brushed it everywhere with some secret stuff that gave to it the aspect of
white and shining marble. Then they brought a funnel

of clay with a curved point, and having opened the great artery of the throat, inserted the point into the artery.

This done, they stood the stiff corpse on its feet and while two of them held it thus, the third brought the pot into which they poured stuff that looked like glass when it is molten, mixing all together with a rod of stone. Then he set a ladder, perhaps four paces in length, against the wall, and carrying the pot, climbed to the top of it, whence slowly he poured the brew into the funnel beneath so that its weight forced it through all the dead man's veins. When the most of it was gone he descended and the three of them finished their work in some way that I did not stay to watch, for the sight of this grim preparation for the tomb and the scent of these spicy drugs overcame me.

At length they summoned me and showed me Kallikrates lying like to one in a deep sleep, calm and beautiful as he had been in life.

"O Queen," said their spokesman, "by to-morrow at the sunrise the flesh of this man will be as marble, and so everlastingly remain. Then bear him where you will, but till then let him rest untouched."

I bade that they should be rewarded, and they went their ways. But first I asked them where the inhabitants of old Kôr were wont to lay their royal dead. They answered that it was in the great caves at a little distance across the plain, and I commanded that on the morrow they should guide me thither, bearing the body of Kallikrates.

Philo came and said that the priests and priestesses of Isis would have speech with me and that they were gathered in the inmost court of the great temple before the veiled statue of the goddess Truth. I bade him lead on, but he wavered a little and said,

"O Queen, there is trouble. The royal lady, Amenartas, has told a tale in the ears of those priests and priestesses. She has sworn to them that you are not a woman but a dæmon; aye, a witch risen from the Under-world, and that you murdered the lord Kallikrates because he would not give himself to you. Also she swore that you strove to murder her who, being protected by the magic which her father Nectanebes, the great wizard, taught her, was too strong for you and therefore escaped alive."

"As to the last, she lies," I answered carelessly.

We came to the inmost court. It was the hour of sunset and the place was filled with glowing light. I took my seat upon the throne-like chair beneath the statue and the light beat full upon me, a glory on a glory.

The priests and priestesses who were standing still with folded arms and bowed heads looked up and saw me. A murmur of astonishment rose from them and I heard one say to the other,

"The Princess has told us truth."

At first I did not understand; then I remembered that I was no longer as mortal women are, but rather, as my mirror told me, an incarnate splendour, a very goddess to the sight.

"Speak," I said, and they shook at the new rich note of power in my voice, as leaves vibrate at the sudden swell of music.

The first of the priests, a large man of middle age, Rames by name, stood forward and fixing his round eyes upon my face, said,

O Prophetess, O Daughter of Wisdom, O Isis-come-to-Earth, we know not what to say, since we have heard that you have changed your shape, now as is evident to us. Prophetess, you are not the same high-priestess who ruled over us in the temple at Memphis and whom we followed to this desolate land. Some magic has been at work with you."

"If so," I answered, "is it an evil magic? Tell me, Rames, am I changed for better or for worse?"

"You are beautiful," he answered, "so beautiful that madness must take all men who look on you. But, Prophetess, your loveliness is not such as mortal woman wears. Nay, it is such as Typhon might give to one who had sold her soul to him. Also, there is more. We learn that you murdered that Grecian, Kallikrates, who once was of our fellowship, because he refused his love to you; yes, that you, the high-priestess of Isis, murdered a man because he turned from your arms to those of his wife, the royal Amenartas, and that if you could, you would have murdered her also."

"Who tells this tale?" I asked slowly.

"The Princess herself," Rames answered. "See she is here. Let her speak."

Amenartas appeared from among the throng, and cried,

"It is true, it is most true. Here before the statue of Truth herself, I swear it in the face of Heaven and to all the listening earth. There is a wound on the breast of my dear lord, Kallikrates. Ask yonder witch how that wound came there. Clothed only in her hair, she entered into a fire, a fire of hell. She came forth beautiful with a beauty that is not human. She called my lord to embrace her. Yes, this shameless one, she named herself his spouse. This she did before the eyes of his own wife and in the hearing of her ears. She bade him enter the Fire of Hell, and when he would not, when he turned to seek refuge in my arms, she sent him down the path of death by her words of power. She said:

" 'I call down death upon thee, Kallikrates. Death by thy portion and the grave thine home. Die, Kallikrates, that thy face may torment me no more and that I may learn to mock thy memory.'

"These were her very words. Let her deny them if she can. I say, moreover, that always she has desired to lead astray the lord Kallikrates, and that when she could not do so of her woman's strength, then she made a pact with Typhon and strove to mesh him in her magic, but strove in vain. Therefore she slew him in her rage."

When the priests and priestesses heard these words they turned pale and trembled. Then they called to me to answer. But I said,

"I answer not. Who are you that I should render account to you of what I have or have not done? Think what you will and do what you will. I answer not, save this, that what has chanced, has chanced by the decree of Fate who sits above all gods and goddesses, throned beyond heaven's remotest star."

They drew apart, they talked together. Then Rames came forward and, still staring at me, said:

"Whether you yet serve Isis, O Ayesha, daughter of Yarab, we do not know. But we who are her children, sworn to her obedience for which we have suffered many things, reject you from your place of rule in which you were set above us by the holy Noot, whom we learn has passed to the keeping of Osiris. No more are you our high-priestess, Ayesha, or Evil Spirit, and no longer shall you stand with us before the altars of the Queen of Heaven."

"Be it as you will," I answered. "Go and leave me to make mine own peace with Isis, who now and henceforward am her equal, I who have learned what Isis is, and been clothed with that same majesty. I see that you believe me to blaspheme; the horror upon your faces tells me so. Yet I do not; here in the shadow of Truth—if it were but known, the only goddess—I speak with the voice of Truth. Farewell. I wish you good fortune, and in all things will aid you if I can. Tell me, Philo, do you desert me like these others?"

"Nay, O Queen," he answered, "we are old comrades, you and I, who have gone through too much together to separate at last. I am a Greek who entered into the company of Isis chiefly after I met you, fair Daughter of Wisdom, and noted the deeds you did upon the ship *Hapi,* and to be short—whatever road you take is a good road for me. I know not whether you slew this Kallikrates, or whether he slew himself with his own sword, of which I noted the mark upon him, but if you offered him your love and he refused it then I hold that he deserved to die.

"For the rest, I am a merchant who take my gain where I can find it, and I know that you pay well. Therefore I follow your banner to the end, whether it lead me to the Heaven of Isis or to the Hades of my forefathers, where doubtless I shall meet Achilles and Hector and Odysseus and many another gallant seafaring warrior of whom our Homer sings. That place whither you wend is home enough for me, for in your palace I shall always find a chamber, and on your ship of state I shall always stand upon the poop, however far the voyage."

Thus spoke that gay and cunning Greek, hiding the loyalty of his heart beneath his jesting words, and truly in that hour of deserted loneliness my gratitude went out toward him, as still it does today and will do for evermore. For though Philo would take a bribe where he could find it, as is the way of those who serve Fortune and must earn bread, still he was ever loyal to those he loved, and he loved me in that high fashion which is born of long service and of fellowship. When at length I come into my great inheritance, and rule otherwhere—as rule I shall—my first care shall be to reward Philo as he deserves, although once or more he did fill his pouch with the gold of Amenartas, or so I believe.

Yet at this time I only smiled at him and asked,

"These things being done, what of the Princess of Egypt? Let her speak her desire that I may fulfil it, if I can."

"It is simple," answered Amenartas, "that I may be rid of you, no less and no more. I would go hence to bear my child and to rear him to wreak vengeance on you for his father's blood, O Witch of the Under-world, and until I die, to work and pray that the Furies may be your bedfellows, O murderess and thief of love."

"Let these things befall as they are fated," I answered very quietly. "The stage of doom is set and on it throughout the ages until the play ends at last, we, the puppets of Destiny, must act our appointed parts to a consummation that we cannot forsee. But how will it end, Lady Amenartas? You know not; nor do I, though already some master's hand has writ the last scene upon his roll. Philo, it is my command that you lead Pharoah's child to the coast, or wherever she would go, that thence she may find her way to Greece or Egypt as Fortune may direct her. That done, return and make report to me. Farewell, Amenartas."

"Fare ill, Witch," she cried. "We part, but as I think, to meet again elsewhere, seeing that between you and me there is a score to settle."

"Aye," I answered gently enough. "Yet boast not,

Amenartas, and be not too sure of anything, since when at length that sum is added up, who knows on which side the balance will be struck."

"At least I know that the count will be long and that murder is a heavy weight in any scale," she answered.

Then she went; they all went and left me alone brooding there upon the chair of state, in which I sat for the last time. The darkness closed about me, then came the twilight of the rising moon in whose soft rays I saw the figure of a man creeping toward me as a thief creeps.

"Who comes?" I asked.

"Beauteous Queen," answered a thick voice, "it is I, Rames, the priest."

"Speak on, Rames."

"O most fair among women, if indeed you may be named woman, hear me. Those fools of priests and priestesses have thrown you from your place."

"So you told me but now, Rames, nor can they be blamed."

"So I told you because I must, not of my own will, and that which is done, cannot be undone. You are cast out and here in Kôr the worship of Isis is at an end, since who is there that can fill your throne? Yet, hearken, hearken! I cling to you, I worship you. I desire you to be my wife, O most lovely. Here together we will rule in Kôr and you shall be its Queen and goddess, and I will be its Captain. It is most wise that you should consent, O Lady divine."

"Why is it wise, Rames?"

"Because, Lady, I can protect you. You know the sentence that goes out against those who break the rule of Isis. I say that it is already uttered against you. I say that those bigots seek to murder you. But if you take me as husband, then we will be beforehand with them and kill or drive them away. Yea, now that you are lonely and deserted, I shall be your sure shield."

I heard and laughed aloud, and I think that this madman interpreted that laugh in a strange fashion. At least he threw himself upon me. He seized my hand and lifted it toward his lips, though by those lips it was never touched. For now rage took hold of me, such rage as had possessed my soul in the cave of the Fire of Life; rage and the desire of destruction, that with other evil gifts had come to me in the breath of the Fire.

"Accursed one!" I cried, "vile and insolent thief! Do you dare to touch me with your hand? Away with you to Set! Let the world know you no more!"

As the words passed my lips it seemed to me that from some strength within a withering flame leapt out of me and smote that man as the lightning smites. At the least he lifted his hands to his head; he reeled back, he fell, he groaned—he died.

Looking at him lying there in the moonlight, still and bereft of life, at the last I came to know full surely that henceforward I could slay with a thought, that I was the Lady of Death, and that such wrath as others express in words went forth from me with all the might of Heaven; moreover, that now this wrath rose suddenly and swiftly in me, easy to unchain, hard to hold. Yea, I was both a fury and a terror whom no man might cross or vex if he would continue to look upon the sun.

Philo came. He stared at me and at the dead Rames, then questioned me with his eyes.

"He would have laid hands on me, Philo, and I slew him," I said.

"Then what he has earned, he has been paid," answered Philo. "Yet, Queen, how did you slay him? I see no bruise or wound."

"By a power that has come to me, Philo. I desired him dead and he died. That is all the tale."

"A strange and a terrible power, Queen. Often when we are angry we wish that this one or that were dead— yet that they should forthwith die—! Henceforth you must watch your moods well, Daughter of Wisdom, since otherwise I think that you and I will soon be parted for, as I know, at times you are angry with me, and when next that chances I shall be sped."

"Aye, Philo, so I have learned. I must watch my moods very well. Yet fear nothing, since never could I wish you dead."

"Are you sure, Ayesha? Hearken. What was the crime of this poor wretch? Was it not that he, who hitherto had been a virtuous man, a good and earnest priest who never turned to look at woman, of a sudden went mad for love of you, and in his madness urged his suit—well, as men do when they have lost hold of the reins of reason, whereon you slew him? Now if men must die for such a crime, who is there that would live to grow old? I think that all of them would soon be driven to dwell in such a hermitage as that wherein the holy Noot sleeps to-night. Is it not true? I ask you who know the world."

"It is true," I answered.

"If so, Lady, I would ask another question. What was it that sent this man mad? Was it not the sight of such beauty as has never yet been known upon the earth? Which beauty, Ayesha, if I look upon it much longer, I think will send me mad also, or any other man. Daughter of Wisdom, such loveliness as you wear to-day is the greatest curse that the gods can grant to woman, because being above Nature, all Nature must obey its might. Daughter of Wisdom, henceforward you must veil your face from the eyes of men, or become the murderess of more ill-fated ones."

"It seems that this is so," I answered heavily. "I have desired beauty and beauty has come to me, but however great, all gifts are not good."

"So I have heard philosophers preach in Greece, Lady, yet never did I know one of them to turn his back on any gift. Ayesha, hide those eyes of yours, hide them swiftly. While Rames lies there dead, love is frightened, but once his clay is gone, who knows? But I forgot, I came to warn you that a certain decree has been uttered against you, the same, Queen, that you have uttered against Rames, also to protect you, if I can."

Now I laughed outright.

"Foolish man," I said, "do. you not yet understand that I cannot be killed or even harmed?"

"Ye Gods!" said Philo, holding up his hands in amazement. Then he was silent.

That night I slept by the cold shape of Kallikrates and oh! it was the most fearful of all nights that ever I had passed upon the earth. Evil, very evil were the dreams that came to me, if dreams they were. In them it seemed that Noot spoke with me. Nay, not Noot, but a flickering tongue of fire which I knew to be the spirit of Noot. Naught could I see save that burning tongue, and from it came terrible words.

"Daughter," it said, "you have cast my counsels to the winds, you have betrayed your trust, you have broken my commands that I gave to you out of the wisdom that was given to me. You have entered the Fire that you were set to watch. You have been embraced by the Fire and received its gifts. Behold the first fruits of them. The man whom you would have taken lies dead at your side, and yonder in the temple court another lies dead also, who was good until your hell-granted beauty made him evil. The worship of Isis is destroyed in this land that now nevermore will become a nation great and strong and pure. The heart of Amenartas is broken, yet she will live on to beget avengers, one of whom will overtake you at the appointed time. In loneliness, in remorse, in utter desolation you must endure till the Fire dies that cannot die while the world is; seeking yet never finding, or finding but to lose again. Henceforth you are an alien to the kindly race of men, a beauteous terror that all must desire and yet all fear and hate. Ever that which you seek will flit before you like a wandering star which you may never overtake, and in following it you will bring death to thousands. Daughter, you are accursed."

"Is there then no redemption?" I asked of Noot in my dream.

"Aye, Ayesha, when the world is redeemed, then perchance you may find your part in that great forgiveness. Hearken. There is a vision which throughout your life has haunted you. In that vision Aphrodite and the evil gods, those gods that she had led into Egypt to destroy its higher faith, were summoned before the throne of Isis. In it also a fate and a command were laid upon you—that you should war against those gods and bring its punishment on Egypt that received and welcomed them."

"It is but a fantasy," I answered. "Now I know that there are no evil gods; there lives no Aphrodite; even no Isis."

"Daughter, you err. True, there is no Isis who was shaped only by the faith of earth and in the dreams of men. Yet there is that which they name Isis, as the highest that they know and can fashion in their thought. There is the eternal Good and that Good is God. Throughout the countless ages man, warring against Nature, has lifted up his heart till almost he seems to look upon the face of that almighty, regnant Good. Thus it was with you, Daughter, and now whither have you wended? You have fled down the backward path. You have undone all, you have gone back to Nature. Henceforth you are Nature's self, shining with her false and passing beauty, inspired with her law of death, you who once drew near to the new law of Life that awaited you beyond the grave, which now you may not seek."

"Whate'er I did, I did for Love and Love shall save me," I seemed to answer in my agony.

"Aye, Ayesha, doubtless in the end Love will save you, as it saves all things that without its grace must perish everlastingly. Yet for you that salvation is now far away, and ere it can be found, one by one you must conquer those passions that found you in the Fire. You who sought undying beauty, must see your fair body more hideous and more horrible than the leper of the streets. You who are filled with rage and strength must grow gentle as a dove and weak as a little child. By suffering you must learn to soothe the sufferings of others. By expiation you must atone your crimes, by faith once more you must lift up your soul. By the knowledge you shall win you must come to understand your own blind pettiness through time untold. Ayesha, this is your doom."

Such was the substance of that dream and when I awoke from it, oh! how bitterly I wept. For now I understood. I was fallen—fallen! All that I had gathered through the long years of prayer and abstinence and service had been reft from me, and I who stood near to joy had sunk into a hell of unending sorrow. There was no Isis, so I had dreamed Noot to say, and so my new knowledge told me. Yet there was the eternal Good which in Egypt men knew as Isis, and in other lands by many a different name, and from that Good I was excommunicate.

Now like my savage ancestors of a million years before, I was but a part of Nature as we see her upon the earth and feel her in our blood and—this was the most dreadful of my punishments—my wisdom and my lost faith had become rules by which I could mete out the measure of my fall, for ignorance can smile at that which to knowledge is a hell. All Nature's gifts were mine; all her beauty, all her desires, all her fierceness, all her hates, and one by one, through countless time I must weed her every evil growth from the garden of my poisoned soul. The curse with which she was accursed had smitten me also, and in the end her death would be my death. Such was the doom that I had brought upon my head when I had listened to the calling of that god of Fire.

Oh! looking upon the cold corpse of Kallikrates and feeling the primeval passions surging in my breast, little wonder that I, the rejected of Heaven, wept as still I weep to-day.

For such is the lot of those who trample on all good as they run to seize the glittering gauds that the tempter spreads before their lusting eyes. Perchance Noot never broke his holy rest to speak to me in dreams; perchance it was the strength in my own soul that spoke to my heart, as that strength, of which now I knew the power, in the old days wrought marvels that then I believed to be done by the invisible hand of Isis. At least the lesson taught is true.

CHAPTER XXV

In Undying Loneliness

ERE the dawn, guided by those old embalmers and bearing with me the dead Kallikrates, I departed from that hateful Kôr. As I think, none saw me go, for forgetful of their promised vengeance, the priests and priestesses were gathered trembling about the corpse of Rames in the inmost court of the Temple of Truth, though it is true that I felt the baleful eyes of Amenartas watching me. Or perhaps it was her pursuing hate I felt, and not her eyes.

Veiled so that no man might look upon my deadly beauty, I crossed the plain and came to the vast cave-sepulchres. Here those old embalmers lit lamps and showed me a deep and empty tomb. It had two shelves or niches, on one of which I laid my dead, choosing the other to be my couch. Thus then I took up my abode in the Sepulchres of Kôr that for some two thousand years were to be my home.

At my command Philo led the royal Amenartas from the haunted land of Kôr, and returning three moons later, told me, truly or not, that she had passed the swamps and departed on a wandering ship, sailing north, whither he knew not. I asked him no more who did not desire to learn of her words and curses, though as it chanced this I must do after long ages had gone by. Some of the priests and priestesses went with her. Others remained in Kôr and, if they were young enough, took wives or husbands and ruled there. Indeed, the last of their descendants whom I could trace before their blood was utterly swallowed up in that of the barbarians, died after five hundred years or more had passed away.

Philo, too, lived on at Kôr, making trading journeys to the coast and along it in his ship and grew rich and, after a fashion, great. For Philo would never leave me whom he loved, though no more would he look upon my unveiled face. At length, very old, he died in my arms, he who would have none of the Fire and its gifts. When his breath left him, for the first time since that night at Kôr, I wept. For now I was quite alone.

While he lay dying he prayed me to unveil, saying that now, when no harm could come of it, he would look upon my face once more. I did so and he studied me long and earnestly with his hollow eyes.

"You are wondrous beautiful," he said, "nor during these past forty years or more, since last I beheld you unveiled in the sanctuary of the Temple of Truth, has your loveliness lessened by one wit. Indeed, I think that it has gathered. What is the meaning of this, fair Daughter of Wisdom?"

"It means what I have told you before, Philo, that I do not die until the world dies, although I may change and seem to pass away."

"Yet I die. Do we then part for ever?" he asked.

"Nay, I think not, Philo, for at last Death overtakes everything and in its halls we may meet again. Moreover, the world lives long and to it, ere its end, you may return once, or often, and if so, perchance you will be drawn to me."

"I trust so, O Wisdom's Daughter. They call you witch, and doubtless such you are, who can slay with a glance, whom age does not touch, and whom Death scorns. Yet, witch or woman, or both, there lives none, no, not even wife or child, whom I so desire to meet hereafter."

So Philo died, and since those medicine-men who had embalmed Kallikrates now were dead also, leaving behind them none who had knowledge of their art, I buried him unpreserved in the great sepulchres.

Awhile ago the fancy took me to go to look upon

him, but alas! after the passing of some sixteen hundred years, save for the skull, his naked bones had crumbled into dust.

What more is there to tell? All died and came again in their children: generation after generation of them did I watch arise, flourish in their wild fashion, and go their ways down the path of Death. I ruled those barbarians, if rule it can be called. They were my slaves who feared me as a spirit, and I was kind to them, but if they angered me, then I slew them, for thus only could they be held in a due subjection even to one that they believed to be an ancient goddess whom their forefathers worshipped, Lulala by name, whose throne was in the moon.

For these Amahagger were a terrible people, barbarians who loved the night because their deeds were evil, and who, if strangers wandered among them, slew them by the setting of red-hot pots upon their heads, and afterward ate their flesh. Yet among them were some of a nobler sort, descended, as I think, either from the unmixed blood of the ancients of old Kôr, or perchance from those priests and priestesses of Isis who had been my companions. Such a one was a certain Billali whom my lord Leo and Holly knew. But for the most part they were hook-nosed, treacherous, dark-haunting savages, and as such they must be handled.

In the course of those long ages, to divert myself in my loneliness and for the purposes of study, I reared certain of these savages up to this and that. I stunted them to dwarfs, I bred them to giants. Musicians of a kind I made of some of them, though to do so took ten of their generations. Then I grew weary of the game and all these variants died back into the common stock; that fundamental type to which, if left alone, every species that springs on earth returns in time, and this more quickly than might be thought. The last breed that I created, or caused to create itself, was one of mutes evolved from a faithful strain who had served me well, since I found these mutes more docile and less wearisome than the rest.

But enough of that people with which I have done for ever.

What did I do through all those awful ages? At first, as I found I had the power, I threw my watching eyes across the world, and learned all that happened there. Thus I saw the battles of Alexander, his conquests and his death, and the rise of the Ptolemies in Egypt; also many other things in the countries with which I have had to do. But soon I tired of it all.

Men arose of whom I knew nothing. Peoples changed, and ever the play repeated itself afresh, though with new actors. I had naught in common with them and their petty aims and passions, I who watched as a god might watch those that served him not, or as an idle child watches the labours of colony after colony of ants. Yea, I tired of them and took no more heed of what they did or did not do upon their short journey to that forgetfulness wherewith the dust of Time would bury them. I was dead to the world, and the world was dead to me.

In the ages that followed I sent out my soul to seek kindred souls and found some with whom I communed, though they never knew who it was that talked to them. With wise men throughout the earth I held this converse, and from them gathered knowledge, giving them in return something of my wisdom, which doubtless they presented to the generations as their own. If so, the world was the gainer, and if Truth comes, what matters it whence it comes?

I did more. I sought out the dead in their habitations beyond the stars, aye, and found not a few of them. Always they were eager to learn of the world and in return paid me with the coin of their unearthly lore. They told me of those other worlds and I made acquaintance with their princes and their rulers: I gathered up the broken fragments from the feasts that were spread upon these alien tables and drank of the dregs of their new wine. But, and here was the mystery, here was the grief: never once could I grasp the robe of any whom I had known upon the earth. I found not my father, I found not Noot, I found not Kallikrates, I found not Philo, I found not Beltis or Amenartas. In all that countless multitude I discovered no single soul to whom my mortal lips had spoken in its little day. Of friend or foe I found not one. Perchance all of them were still asleep and resting in their sleep.

I looked into the secrets of Nature and they opened themselves to me like flowers beneath the sun. I inhaled their perfume, I admired their beauty, so that at length little was hid from me. I learned how to turn clay to gold and how to harness the lightning to my service, aye, and many another thing. Yet what was the use of all of it to me, the dweller in a tomb?

Knowledge, the lord, is a barren grant unless it can also be a servant; aye, a slave at command to work good for man.

For the rest, what did I do? Without the caves I sowed the seed of trees. I watched them spring, I watched them grow to saplings and, in the slow progression of the centuries, swell to great timbers with far-stretching arms beneath whose shade I rested. Thus they stood for many a hundred years. Then for many another hundred they decayed, grew hollow, rotted to dust and fell, their long day done at last. And I, I sowed me others.

To mark the passage of those years lest I should lost count of them, in a certain cavern I laid me stones, a stone for every one as from the hand of Time it fell ripe into the bosom of Eternity. As on their rostaries, here and there, priests set larger beads to mark the tale of their completed prayers, so when ten years had gone I set a larger stone, and when a hundred had passed by, one larger yet and white in colour, while the thousandth year I marked with a little pyramid, two of which now stand in the Caves of Kôr. It was a good plan whereby I could reckon easily, only some of the softer stones that lay near to the mouth of that cavern where sun and rain could reach them at length crumbled into sand.

"Why did I stay at Kôr? Why did I not wander forth through the world? Because I could not, because of the curse that had been laid upon me, that here I must wait until Kallikrates came again, as come I knew he would.

Therefore no captive ever was more chained and fettered in his dungeon than I, Ayesha, by that compelling curse in the Sepulchres of Kôr, where night by night I laid me down to rest in the cold company of the dead. From time to time, once in a generation mayhap, I would lift the cloths that covered him and look upon his pale beauty (for those old embalmers did not lie), and kiss his brow of ice and weep and weep. Then once more I laid the shroud, or a new shroud, upon him and went my weary way.

Oh! it is terrible in this world where all is change, where even the stones grow and die to re-form again, to be the one thing that changeth not for ever. Yet, that was my lot, such was the gift of the Fire-lord whom I had wedded and embraced. There I sat in my eternal beauty which I was doomed to hide, lest brute men should be maddened at the sight of it, so that I must slay them with the lightning of my will. There I brooded, gathering to my breast all that wisdom of Mother Nature of whom now I was a part, all the useless wisdom whose weight at length clogged my sense and cramped my soul. There I sat, eaten of desire for one dead and burning with jealous hate of that woman who had borne his child and who, as I knew well, wandered with him, greater than I perhaps and still more fair, in some Elysium that even my spirit could not reach, taking the place that I might fill, if only I could attain to the boon of death which is everlastingly denied to me, until the old world itself shall die. There, I say, I sat while the slow fire of the forturer Time, burning in my breast, ate its path through all my being, till the hot soul within me turned to the bitter ash of hopelessness.

Oh! why did he not come? Why did he not come? Surely the circle must be complete and the time fulfilled. Surely he must weary of those unknown heavenly fields and of the coarse love of Egypt's Lady. Surely he would come and soon. Only then, what if here, as there, she still companioned him?

At length one came, and when I learned of it my heart flamed up with hope as a torch flames in these dark caves. Alas! it was not he. So soon as my eyes fell on him afar, I knew it, yonder in the temple of Kôr whither I had gone upon the matters of some petty savage trouble, such as had arisen thrice since the days of Philo. I saw and grew sick with hope destroyed, so sick that had he but known it, this little, wizened wanderer at that moment stood near to the world's edge. Yet aferward I came to like him well, perchance because he reminded me so much of Philo that once or twice almost I thought—— But let this matter be.

He was a strange man, that wanderer; very shrewd, but one who believed nothing which he could not see or touch or handle. Thus when I told him tales concerning myself and my length of days and why I sat at Kôr in beauty, yet like one who is dead in a desert, openly he mocked at them, which angered me. Not all of these were true, be it admitted, because, being a part of Nature as I am, how can I always speak the truth?

Nature shows many faces to those who court her; Nature has desert-phantasies wherewith the traveller is oft deceived, thinking he sees that which he does not see, though in some shape or form of a surety it exists elsewhere. Nature also keeps her secrets close and ever instructs in parables that yet hold the seed of perfect verity.

So, being a part of Nature's self, did I with that wanderer, as indeed I do to this day with Holly the learned, who followed after him. Yet here the example has its flaw, for this man who was called Watcher-in-the-Night, a name that fitted him well enough, did not court me, as her watchers court Nature the beautiful. Nay, he turned his back upon me saying he was not one who loved, moth-like, to singe his wings in a flame, however bright; I think because often he had singed them already.

Still, I found this so strange that almost I began to wonder whether once more my beauty was on the wane and whether it needed longer to be hidden beneath a veil, or whether perchance men had grown wiser than they used to be. Therefore, once for a little moment I put out my strength and brought him to his knees and having taught him certain lessons, I laughed at him and let him go. Yet be it said that I held and hold him dear, and look onward to the day when we shall meet again, as perchance we had met in those that are long past. So enough of this brave and honest man, gently born also, and instructed in his fashion. Doubtless he died many years ago.

I tire of this long, sad task; let the end of my tale be short.

At last, at last, came Kallikrates reborn, lacking memories, changed in spirit, and yet in face and form the very same. Holly brought him hither, or he brought Holly, because of an ancient, lying screed that Amenartas wrote upon a sherd, which from age to age had passed down in his race, urging some descendant of her blood to find me out and slay me, for this Egyptian fool thought that I could be slain.

He came, and by Heaven! I knew not that he was here until the crabbed Holly led me to the couch whereon he lay fever-stricken and at the very point of death. By my arts I dragged him back from between those doors of doom, that almost once again had closed behind him, and afterward, revealing to him my beauty and my burning love, caused him to worship me. Yet, mark! He came not alone; as I feared would chance, something of Amenartas prisoned in a savage woman's breast came with him, and already he was her lover.

I slew that woman who was obstinate and would not leave him; though the deed grieved me, I slew her because I must. It mattered little, for soon she was forgot, and I held him fast.

Of the rest little need be said, for Holly knows it all and tells me that he has written it in a book. Because I might not wed with mortal man I led Kallikrates, he who now was known as Leo, down the perilous ways to that hid cavern where ever the bright Spirit of Life, clad in flame and thunder, marches on his endless round. Behold! as it had been over two thousand years before, so it was now. Again Kallikrates feared to enter the flames and, putting on majesty, to become undying king of all the world. Aye, even though the prize of my glory lay to his hand, his flesh shrank from the Fire.

Therefore that he might learn courage, once more I gave myself to the embrace of the god, and lo! this time he slew me. Yes, in utter shame and hideousness before my lover's eyes, there I died, or rather seemed to die; an ancient, shrivelled, ape-like thing. Yet dying, my unconquerable spirit gave me strength to mutter in his ear that I should come again and once more be beautiful.

Nay, I did not die. Far away again I became incarnate in this distant Asian land, which after all is my own, since in a part of it first I saw the light. Here in this cavern-monastery where still lingers some shadow of the worship of the moon and of the great Principle that in the old days was named Isis, Queen of Heaven, once more I was clothed with mortal flesh.

The years went by, but two or three of them, and I found the power to search out Kallikrates, or Leo Vincey, still living on the earth, and in a vision showed him the mountains that I inhabit. He was faithful. Yes, like Holly he was faithful, and together they followed that vision. For twice ten years they searched, and then at last they found me. They passed the perils and the tests; Kallikrates, or Leo Vincey, escaped the web spun by the Queen Atene, she in whom Amenartas once more shows herself upon the earth. They endured the appointed trials. Aye, when I unveiled before him on the mountain peak, my Love, my eternal Love, my doom and my desire, found strength and faith to kiss my hideous, withered brow. Then was that faith rewarded. Then before his very eyes I changed into the flower of all beauty, into the glory of all power, and he worshipped, worshipped, worshipped!

Now soon we shall be wed. Now soon the curse shall fall from us, like to a severed chain. Now soon my sin will be forgiven, and side by side we shall tread the endless path of splendour, no longer two but one, that path which leads through perfect joy—oh! whither does it lead? Even to-day I know not.

But this cannot be yet awhile. First he must bathe him in the Fire, since mortal man may not mix with my immortality and live as man. For while this world endures—have I not said it?—I who have drunk of the very Cup of its Spirit, aye, twice drunk deep, must also endure, and I think the world is still far away from the gates of Death. Aye, though I change a thousand times, still I shall be the same in other shapes, and though I seem to vanish, yet I must appear again.

Where I go, also, thither Kallikrates must follow me, or I must follow him, since he and I are one, and on me is laid the burden of the uplifting of the soul of him whose body once I slew.

And yet, and yet—oh! he is still human and death dogs the heels of man. As I write a horror seizes me. Aye, my hand trembles on the scroll and my spirit quakes. What if some chance, some sickness, some fate should strike him down, leaving me once more desolate and divorced, so that elsewhere all this dark tragedy must be played afresh?

Away with that hell-born thought! There are no gods and, Fate, I defy thee who am myself a Fate and thine equal. I will conquer thee, O Fate; thou shalt not conquer me. There is naught but that eternal Good whereof the fiery tongue which was the soul of Noot spoke, or seemed to speak, to me in my haunted sleep at Kôr, and to that Good I, Ayesha, make my prayer.

Lo! I have suffered. Lo! I have paid the count to its last coin. Lo! I have endured. Through the long ages I have sown in tears, and my hour of harvest is at hand; aye, the night of sorrow dies, and already on the peak of heavenly Peace shines the dawn of joy. . . . My lord hunts upon the mountain after the fashion of men, and I brood within the caves after the fashion of women. . . .

". . . Holly, Holly! Awake! Look yonder! What is this? I seem to see my lord struggling on the snow and the spotted beast has him by the throat— . . ."

Here ends Ayesha's manuscript. Its last words are almost illegible and are written by one whose agitation was evidently great; indeed their appearance suggests that they were set down in some half-automatic fashion while the writer's mind was occupied with other matters. With them Ayesha ends her tale of which in outline the rest is to be found elsewhere—in the book that is named after her. Suddenly she appears to have tired of her task. Perhaps, heralded and induced by the incident of the snow-leopard that went near to ending the life of Leo Vincey, the presage of terrible woes to come, to which she alludes and not obscurely, paralyzed Ayesha's mind or filled it with forebodings that rendered her incapable of further effort of the kind, or at least unwilling to endure its labour, of which, it is clear, already she was wearying.

EDITOR.

ANNE McCAFFREY